# SECRET STORY

by Ramsey Campbell
from Tom Doherty Associates

*Alone with the Horrors*
*Ancient Images*
*Cold Print*
*The Count of Eleven*
*Dark Companions*
*The Darkest Part of the Woods*
*The Doll Who Ate His Mother*
*The Face That Must Die*
*Fine Frights* (editor)
*Gathering the Bones*
*The Hungry Moon*
*Incarnate*
*The Influence*
*The Last Voice They Hear*
*The Long Lost*
*Midnight Sun*
*The Nameless*
*Nazareth Hill*
*Obsession*
*The Overnight*
*The One Safe Place*
*Pact of the Fathers*
*The Parasite*
*Scared Stiff*
*Secret Story*
*Silent Children*
*Waking Nightmares*

SECRET

A Tom Doherty Associates Book · New York

# STORY

Ramsey Campbell

SECRET STORY

Copyright © 2006 by Ramsey Campbell

This book is printed on acid-free paper.

A Tor Book
Published by Tom Doherty Associates, LLC
175 Fifth Avenue
New York, NY 10010

www.tor.com

Tor® is a registered trademark of Tom Doherty Associates, LLC.

Library of Congress Cataloging-in-Publication Data

Campbell, Ramsey, 1946–
    Secret story / Ramsey Campbell.—1st ed.
        p. cm.
    "A Tom Doherty Associates book."
    ISBN-13: 978-0-765-31616-5
    ISBN-10: 0-765-31616-1
    1. Novelists—Fiction. 2. Serial murderers—Fiction. I. Title.
PR6053.A4855S43 2006
823'.914—dc22

                                          2005033821

First Edition: June 2006

Printed in the United States of America

0  9  8  7  6  5  4  3  2  1

for Mat and Sharika
with love and spices

# ACKNOWLEDGEMENTS

As always, Jenny was my first reader and editor.

Since I've had some fun with Liverpool restaurants in the course of this novel, I think that in fairness I should recommend some of our favourites. These include the Sultan's Palace (Indian), the Maharaja (South Indian), the Jumbo City (Chinese), La Tasca and Don Pepe's (Spanish), the Alma de Cuba (South American), the Olive Press (Mediterranean), the Istanbul (Turkish) and Zorba's (you guess). On our side of the river we're fond of—among others—the Mezze (Turkish), the Magic Spices (Indian), the Ming Vase (Malaysian and Cantonese) and the Thai Rooms (Thai and Chinese).

I've a special, if somewhat bemused, thank you to my friend Margaret Murphy, the crime writer. At the launch of a booklet of Liverpool short stories in the summer of 2004, she read her contribution while I did my best to amuse the audience with the Gollum chapter of this novel. Imagine my surprise when her tale proved to have virtually the same narrative as chapter two of *Secret Story*! I emailed that to her the next day, and we marvelled at the coincidence.

SECRET STORY

ONE "Dudley, there's something I haven't been telling you," she said, and at once he was terrified that she knew.

TWO    Her first mistake was thinking he was mad.

As the train left the station he started to talk in a low passionate voice. They were alone in the carriage farthest from the driver, except for two beer bottles rolling about in their own stains and bumping together as if they were trying to mate on the unswept floor. Greta pretended she was moving away from them and not from the young man crouched low on his seat. She sat close to the doors into the next carriage and was taking the latest prize-winning bestseller by Dudley Smith out of her handbag when she saw he was talking to a mobile phone. "I don't know what you want," she could just hear. "I thought you said I gave you what you asked for. If that's not love I don't know what is."

She moved to sit with her back to him in case she embarrassed him. When the train pulled into Birkenhead Park she glanced over her shoulder—she could have been looking for someone on the platform. He'd slipped the phone into his discreetly elegant suit jacket and was staring straight ahead. Even at that distance she saw the unused intelligence in eyes blue as a summer sky; he looked mature beyond his years. His hair was neatly cropped, his nose straight, lips firm, chin square. She turned away before he caught her watching. Then four men in track suits stampeded over the pedestrian bridge.

They made for the front carriage. She let out a breath of relief and wished she'd taken the opportunity to make some remark to the young man. As the train gathered speed she opened her book. She was anxious to find out what happened next, but she hadn't finished a paragraph when she heard a door slam. The men were coming up the train.

She felt trapped by the overgrown embankments that were tarred with dark. Then an underground tunnel chased those away and closed with a roar around the train. The first man flung the door between the carriages wide, and the four of them strutted down the aisle. There was room for one of them next to her, and three on the facing seat. Before she could move closer to the young man with the phone, they boxed her in.

The man beside her put his feet up, blocking her escape. He smelled of sweat and tobacco smoke and too much aftershave—perhaps he'd slapped it on his bald grey scalp. The man opposite her gave her a loose wet grin with yellow teeth and a bloody gap in them under his broken nose. "On your own, love?"

"Must be," said the man in the middle and spat across the aisle. "She's got to read a book."

The man he'd spat past rolled up his purple sleeve and scratched a hairy tattoo of a skull inside a heart. "What's it about?"

Greta never liked to be rude. "Someone everybody thinks is ordinary," she said, "but really he's a master criminal."

"Sounds great," bloody-mouth seemed to think. "Give us a read of it."

He opened the paperback so wide she winced, and stuck his finger in. She would have asked him to be gentle, but the tattooed man took out a packet of cigarettes. "You can't smoke on the train," she said.

"We can do what we like, love," said the man with his legs up. "Plenty's said we can't and learned different."

"And plenty can't say much any more," the tattooed man said.

Gap-teeth crumpled a page out of his way. "This twat in your book's useless. Hasn't got a car and doesn't even nick one."

The train had stopped at Conway Park, where the lines were open to the sky. Greta always imagined the station was raising its roof to her. "May I have it back now, please?" she said.

"I've not had a read yet," said the man who'd spat.

"Me neither," said the tattooed man.

She didn't want to leave it with them—but as the train moved off, the reader threw the book to the man with his feet up, who bent it in half and ripped the spine apart. "Here, you have that bit and I'll have this."

Greta felt as if they'd torn her open. She could buy another copy—they were everywhere—but it was like having some precious part of herself damaged beyond repair. She restrained her tears and faced the tattooed man, who'd stuck a cigarette between his sneering lips. "The sign says no smoking," she said loud enough to be heard down the carriage. "It's dangerous."

"So are we," said spitter. "Who're you shouting for? Your friend's hiding. He'd better stay hid."

Greta twisted her head around to look. The young man must be crouching out of sight for fear of the gang, unless he'd left the train. The clunk of a lighter reclaimed her attention. The tattooed man lit his cigarette with a page of her book, then sailed it at her legs. "Don't do that," she said, trying to steady her voice as she brushed the paper to the floor and stamped on it. "That's just stupid."

"We say what's stupid," gap-teeth said, wiping a red trickle from the corner of his mouth. "You are for saying that."

"Shouldn't have," the tattooed man told her, setting fire to another page and poking it at her face.

"You can scream if you want," said the man with his legs up.

"We like it when they scream," spitter said.

Greta's eyes and nose stung with smoke. She knocked the burning page aside, showering the man next to her with sparks. "Watch what you're doing, love," he sniggered at saying.

The train was slowing. Had the driver seen her plight? Perhaps he was only getting ready for the station—Hamilton Square. "Excuse me, please," Greta said loudly. "This is my stop."

"Show us your ticket," the tattooed man said.

"It's not our stop, so it can't be yours," said the man with ash on his legs.

Greta was about to stand up when gap-teeth shoved a knee between hers and pulled out a knife. He flicked the blade free and rested it against the inside of her thigh. "Don't shout or you'll be no good to your boyfriend."

She had none just now. She could have sat with the young man behind her, too far away. As the train reached the platform, cold sharp metal inched up her thigh. The doors of the carriage opened as if they were gaping on her behalf. There was nobody to board the train, but she heard a shout. "Anybody here?"

"It's your friend," said the man with the knife. "He wants reinforcements."

Greta's heart leapt and sank. Nobody was coming to help. Why didn't the young man call the driver or go to him? Her forehead grew clammy with wondering as the doors shut tight. The train jerked forward and the knife nicked her thigh, and she thought she would do anything to make the man put it away. Then a voice behind her said, "Do you all know one another?"

"We don't know you," the man with his feet up said.

"Don't want to neither," said the tattooed man around his cigarette.

The young man sat across the aisle, planting his feet on either side of the sputum on the floor. "How about her?"

"She's with us," said the man with the knife.

Greta couldn't speak. She felt the blade advance another inch, and backed against the seat, but there was nowhere she could go. She almost didn't hear the young man say, "I'm surprised."

"Think we aren't good enough for her?"

"The other way round. I'd say you're lowering yourselves."

"She'll do for now," said the man with the knife, stroking her thigh with it under her skirt.

"I wouldn't want to be seen with her."

Greta thought his contempt was the worst of all. "Why not?" said the tattooed man, clanking and unclanking his lighter.

"I expect she's a virgin for a start."

"We'd like that."

"Or maybe she isn't. Did you see that look?" The young man peered at her. "Well, are you?"

"That's my business and nobody else's."

"Sounds like she isn't or she'd be boasting. Sounds as if she hasn't got a boyfriend either. You can see why, can't you?"

The four men were growing visibly uncomfortable. "We don't want to be her boyfriends," said the man next to her, closing a hand over her breast.

"On your way to meet some friends, are you?" the young man asked her. "I bet you work with them."

How could he know about her? Hearing him tell the gang felt like being raped. "If you had more friends," he said, "you wouldn't be reading a book."

"Can't you see what they did? They tore it up and he's been burning it."

"About all books are good for, do we think, gents? So can I join in the fun?"

"He's something, this character," the tattooed man said with an incredulous admiring laugh.

"Here's James Street," the man with the knife announced. "Time you fucked off, pal."

"How are you going to get me to do that?"

"With this," Greta's captor said, snatching out the knife.

She thought he'd cut her on the way to slashing the hem of her skirt, but the cold that ran down her thigh was only metal. The blade gleamed in the light from the station. "Off or I'll do her with it," he said. "And don't call anyone or she gets it."

"I keep telling you she's not worth it. You should listen," said the young man, but stood up.

At least he'd kept them talking and distracted them from doing worse to Greta. He stepped onto the deserted platform and hurried alongside the window. Greta's captor brandished the knife in front of her to remind him. The young man hesitated, and she felt as if her nose and mouth were stuffed with charred paper. Then he pointed at the gang, stubbing both forefingers on the glass.

"Bastard!" the man with the knife screamed. The young man sprinted into the carriage, and all the gang jumped up. Greta was afraid for him till two railway policemen strode past the window to board the train. The tattooed man threw the door between the carriages open. As the gang fled, the young man caught the spitter by the scruff of the neck and threw him face down in his own leavings. "That's it, wipe it up," he said.

When the police chased the gang off the train and up an escalator he sat at the far end of the seat opposite Greta. He didn't speak till the train moved off. "All right?" he said.

"Why, I shouldn't think I've ever felt better in my life."

"He didn't cut you, I meant."

Greta swept the pages that had been thrown into her lap onto the seat. "Oh no, I'm not hurt at all. Can't you see?"

"I'm sorry I didn't stop them ruining your book. It's all over the place though, isn't it?"

"It is now." She pressed her legs together so that they wouldn't shake when she stood up. "Here's my stop," she said.

"And mine."

She stepped down on the platform at Moorfields and hurried to the escalator that was taller than a house. The young man walked up the escalator beside hers. Though it was stopped, he easily kept pace with her. Halfway up he said, "I called the police, you know."

"Oh, did you?" Greta said as if he was a lying child. "How did you manage that on a mobile when we were in a tunnel?"

"I called before we went in."

"There wasn't anything to call about then," she felt clever for saying.

"I saw them get on smoking and come along the train. I could see they were heading for you and what they were like. I tried to call again when we were underground to make sure the police were waiting, but as you say, the phone wouldn't work. That's why I stayed low when I did."

"Well, if you really did all that, thank you."

She was being polite—more than she felt he deserved. They were at the top of the escalators now. A broad low corridor as white as cowardice stretched ahead. It was empty except for the echoes of her footsteps and the young man's alongside her. "Excuse me now," she panted. "I'm late."

"I don't mind hurrying. I wouldn't like to think you might end up in any more danger."

Even to Greta her voice and its echoes sounded shrill. "I'm perfectly capable of looking after myself now, thank you."

"Suppose you run into someone else like them?"

"At least they mightn't insult me in every single way they could think of."

"Is that meant to be me?"

"There's nobody else here."

"I thought the best idea was to pretend I was worse than them."

"Why did you have to pretend?"

"To take their minds off you. It seemed to work."

The passage ended at a bank of escalators half the height of the first one. The middle escalator was switched off. He climbed it as the stairs carried Greta upwards. "I just wanted to say—" he said.

Greta didn't care. She clattered up the rising metal steps, but he took his two at a time and was less breathless than Greta at the top. On either side a short tiled passage led to the Northern Line. She dashed up the stairs between them, which led to the exit to the street at the far end of a broad white corridor the length of a football pitch. "Are you sure you're all right?" the young man said.

She had to catch her breath. "I told you once."

"I was saying I expect everything I said about you was wrong."

"Most of it. Far too much."

"I was trying to shock them. Except . . ."

She was walking as fast as she had breaths for, but she used one to ask, "What?"

"I'm guessing you haven't got a boyfriend at the moment or you'd have threatened them with him."

"Maybe."

"Are you looking for one?"

"I don't need to look."

"I mean, do you think you might like one who's shown he can take care of you?"

"I can take care of myself."

"Don't you think two can do it twice as well?"

They were at the corner of the passage. Beyond it was yet another deserted bank of escalators. "This isn't the way," she said. "I've gone wrong."

As she turned back, he did. "What do you think?" he said.

Her question seemed to scratch the walls. "What's the matter with you?"

"I don't think we should just part, do you? Not when we went through that together. Let me give you my number."

"No thank you."

"Or you can give me yours if you'd rather."

"Thanks even less."

She was hurrying, but he was faster. "Let me just escort you," he said, "till you get to wherever you're going."

Greta turned with her hand on the banister of the stairs that led down to the Northern Line. "Look, I was pretending I was lost before. I'm going the wrong way now."

"Seems like you don't know where you're going."

"Anywhere you aren't."

"No need to talk like that."

"What do you expect?"

"Respect for a start. When a gentleman used to defend a lady's honour he'd be sure of that, and a lot more."

"You really don't understand at all, do you?" Greta said and started down.

"I thought you weren't going that way."

"I am if it gets rid of you."

She was at the bottom of the stairs when he followed her. "I'll forget you said that. I honestly think it's my duty to stay with you even if it isn't appreciated. You never know what kind of maniac you might run into down here."

"I've got a pretty good idea."

"I'll come with you just the same."

"No. I can't think of any shorter way to put it. No."

"Why not?"

"If you don't know by now you never will. I've been as polite as I'm going to be. If you don't leave me alone I'll be the one who calls the police."

"Shall I lend you my mobile? You know it won't work."

"If you don't go away I won't need a phone to make myself heard."

"Are you going to hurt my ears again? As you said, there's nobody else here. I think you're playing."

"No, I'm not playing."

She spat the last word in his face. As he wiped it off, his eyes grew so wide they seemed to flatten too. "You'd really call the police? You think I'm as bad as those criminals on the train."

"I think maybe you got your wish. You wanted to be worse."

She felt a sudden wind in her hair and heard underground thunder. "Here's a train. There'll be someone on it," she said and ran into the passage.

The platform was empty. All at once it put her in mind of the life she was running towards, and she wondered what she was running away from. He knew so much about her—what might he know that she didn't herself? It was too late for her to stop running. The fists that rammed her shoulders made sure of that. They flung her out of the passage, and she ran helplessly over the edge of the platform.

The train rumbled out of the tunnel no more than the length of a carriage away. That seemed enormously far to Greta in the moment it gave her to think. She'd heard that people saw their entire lives in such an instant, but there was so little of hers. She saw the front of the train tilt as if the driver was putting his head to one side in surprise. She had time to regret having run away from a life she would never know. Then the train knocked that out of her, and she felt nothing at all.

THREE   Walt rested his upturned hands on their blurred impressions at the head of the long polished table, and the reflections moistened at once. "So who's our winner?" he said.

Valerie tried to fan the June heat away with her notepad. "I thought 'Beating the Beatles' was the best written."

"Frig the pretty writing. It's nearly all in Manchester," Shell objected, adding a line to the grid with which she was blackening a quarter of her notepad. "We're meant to be the Mersey magazine."

"I was only thinking we could mention stories we liked that didn't fit the rules."

"I know where I'd fit it. If he wants to write about how great the Manks are he should go and live with them."

Vincent finished writing BEATLES and followed it with a question mark almost too tentative to stand up. "I liked 'A Child Composed of Celluloid'."

"You'd like anything about going to the pictures, you. I couldn't be doing with that title. If he'd sat by anybody with a ciggy he'd have gone up in smoke."

"I just enjoyed reading about how there were dozens of what you'd call movie theatres, Walt, all over Liverpool and everyone saw every new film."

"I'm sure a lot of people will see yours, Vincent," Valerie said. "That essay wasn't fiction, though. Against the rules."

"What did anyone think of 'The Cavern Mystery'?" Walt said.

"Country house stuff stuck where it shouldn't go," said Shell. "Like one of them old murder books. My aunt in Scottie Road used to get four out of the library every week."

"So which story are you rooting for?"

"I'd have 'Foghorns on the Mersey' if it was up to me."

"It's up to all of us," said Valerie, "but it wasn't written by a Merseysider."

"It was like the stories my grandad used to tell about all the ships on the river. If I can't vote for that I'll shut up."

"No need to be defensive, Shell."

"I've no call to be, Vincent. Not like some that don't want to sound Scouse."

"How we sound is part of what we are," Walt intervened. "That's a New Yorker on location talking."

"We've not heard from the editor's daughter yet," said Shell.

"She does have a name like the rest of us," Valerie murmured. "What was your favourite, Patricia?"

Patricia was gazing across the Mersey rather than argue with Shell. Beyond the fourth-floor window of the converted warehouse a ferry swung its ample rear towards the landing-stage at Birkenhead. Above the ferry terminal the town ruddy with sunlit brick stretched along the riverbank and sprouted architecture—

the town hall spire crowned with a green dome and a spike, the red tower of Hamilton Square Station, the riverside ziggurat containing a giant fan for the road tunnel. Behind all this an observatory squatted on Bidston Hill in front of a pastel horizon of Welsh mountains. The bare brick wall to the right of the window hid towns closer to the bay, not to mention those around the end of the peninsula, where Patricia lived. She suspected that Shell regarded her and her mother as no less foreign than Walt, but she wasn't going to let this intimidate her. " 'Night Trains Don't Take You Home' stayed in my mind most," she said.

"Better pull the chain then, girl."

"It's the one that got me thinking."

"What's there to think about? If you want women being terrorised I can introduce you to plenty. We don't want to read about it, specially not by a man."

"Gender isn't in the rules," Valerie pointed out.

"It doesn't matter who wrote it if it works, does it?" Patricia said. "It did for me."

"You're joking or you've been at university too long. Spend some time in the real world and see if you still like that kind of porn. See if you like men reading it if you ever have a daughter."

Patricia almost blurted a retort that would have roused a memory she had successfully kept from her parents. She closed her fists to rub away a clammy prickling with her fingertips as she told Shell "I wasn't joking. You're our comedian."

"Vincent?" Walt said. "Any thoughts?"

"It's pretty lean and pacy. I wanted to find out what happened."

"I wanted to find out she chopped off his meat and two sprouts," Shell said. "But she ends up wanting him. It's like saying we want to be raped."

"I read the ending as ironic," said Patricia. "Either Greta's in shock or it's the killer's fantasy of what he'd like her to think."

"I mustn't be clever enough. I just read what's there, me."

"Can I table my opinion?" Walt said.

"It's your magazine," said Shell.

"Hey, I'm just the money man. I'm looking at my fellow judges."

"Tell us your judgement," Valerie said.

"I'd publish the story. It got everyone talking. We can use the word of mouth. Bring readers in with a bit of controversy and they'll stay to read whatever else we're offering. But that's only one man's vote."

"It gets mine," said Patricia.

"I'll support that," Valerie said.

"No point us drawing breath, Vincent," said Shell.

Patricia thought he was distancing himself from Shell by saying "I didn't like him putting his name in. What was it, the prize-winning bestseller by Dudley Smith."

"There are a few amateur details I'd edit," Valerie admitted. "I expect he won't be too unhappy when it's his first publication."

"Maybe it isn't," Shell said. "Then he'll be disqualified."

"How'd you like to check that, Patricia," Walt said, "and what else there is to know about him?"

"You're never giving her another job," Shell said with what a newcomer might have assumed was sympathy for Patricia. "She's already got night life and what's on."

"I thought you might like to interview him, Patricia."

"Did you do many interviews at university?" Shell was apparently interested in learning.

"She had to conduct quite a few on her journalism course," Valerie said. "They earned her some of her best marks, not to embarrass you, Patricia."

"I'll do anything I can for the magazine." While she'd nominated the story, her mother would take any editorial blame. Patricia ought to find out what she could about the author. She drew a fat exclamation mark on her pad and inked a smiling face within the dot, only to realise that it looked as though a blade was hanging unsupported over it. "I'd like to meet Dudley Smith," she said.

FOUR    Dudley was sure that she was pouting at him through the glass in the middle of the cubicle that enclosed them. "Just tell me how to sell myself," she said.

He ducked to the form that he was filling in on her behalf: seven O levels, three A levels, a middling degree in philosophy and history . . . "No, look at me," she said.

Though the June sunlight fell short of the counter full of half a dozen cubicles, the heat seemed to flare up around him. He levelled his gaze at her and saw a small pale pretty face rendered whiter by a mane of red hair, clothes that would have cost more than they should for the little they were, especially the sleeveless yellow top exposing inches of a freckled cleft. "What experience have you had?" he cleared his throat to ask.

"Plenty. Just not the sort you can put in a box."

Dudley rested the tip of his ballpoint inside one. "Anything that will help us find you a job?"

"It might. Promise you won't blush."

He felt as if the heat had seized him by the cheeks. All his interview questions had fled into hiding. "Why should I?" he heard himself protest.

"How would you fancy me as a table dancer?"

The fan behind the cubicles creaked towards him, tousling his hair and plastering his damp shirt to his back. The glass showed his hair fluttering erect as the fan lingered on him, and he clenched his fists in order not to slap his scalp. "I don't mean personally," she said, tilting a pink and white smile up to him, "though you'd be welcome if you got me the work."

The heat in his face seemed to swell his lips tight shut. Could all this be a joke? If so, played by whom? He grew aware of Mrs Wimbourne's voice as low as a priest's in a confessional, Trevor's weary baritone intoning every question on the form, Vera turning brisk whenever her client hesitated over an answer, Colette sounding even more sympathetic than Dudley had felt when he was as new to the job. None of them struck him as a likely culprit, and Morris was surely too busy having a breakdown at home, while Lionel seemed preoccupied with talking on a headset to his fellow security personnel in the shopping precinct. "I don't suppose it would be a full-time job," the girl was saying. "I could model as well. Same line of work."

Dudley licked his lips to prise them apart. "I'm sorry," he said on his way to the truth. "We don't deal with that kind of thing."

"What kind?"

"I think you must know."

"I really don't. Your job is finding people jobs, isn't it? Why are you saying you can't touch those?"

"I'm not saying it. The government does."

"You're the one talking to me. You tell me what kind."

"The s—" His hiss glistened on the window as he lowered his voice. "The sex trade," he mumbled.

"That's what the girls do on the dock road. Are you calling me a prostitute?"

Sometimes the cubicles reminded him of the kind prison visitors in films used, and never more so than now. "I didn't say that," he protested.

"You looked it. I wouldn't feel superior to anyone if I were you, not with your job."

"I'm sorry, I must ask you to keep your voice down."

"Why must you?" she said louder still. "So nobody knows what you've been calling me?"

"Trouble, Dudley?"

He didn't need to hear Mrs Wimbourne's question to know she had arrived behind him. He was trapped between her reflection, which looked flattened even broader than she was, and her cloying perfume that didn't quite disguise the smell of the cigarettes she smoked outside during her breaks. "I came for a perfectly legal job," the girl said, "and he's making me feel like a whore."

Dudley's face blazed afresh. "I didn't use any such word."

"We both know what you meant. And you spat at me."

"That's an absolute lie. I was trying to find this young lady a job she was qualified for."

"My friends from uni had to settle for nothing jobs," the girl told Mrs Wimbourne, and shoved her chair away. "I want to make some real money while I'm young enough," she said and lowered her gaze to Dudley. "I won't be doing anything bad except in your grubby little mind. Maybe you need one of those to work in this grubby little place. You can do better."

The last remark was aimed only at Colette, who emitted the

beginnings of a timid giggle. As the girl stalked past the rows of pale green bucket seats and out of the job centre, Mrs Wimbourne said "Nothing wrong with my office that I can see."

She'd left just enough room for Dudley to swivel his chair. "The public spend all day playing on the computers where my mother works," he said. "I wouldn't want to work where you can't be private."

The fan fluttered Mrs Wimbourne's dress and swept her perfume at him before he could hold his breath. When she frowned he thought she didn't want to be reminded that her centre hadn't been converted to the open plan, but she said "I didn't care for your client's attitude. I hope none of it rubbed off on you, Colette."

Colette giggled a nervous denial as Dudley turned to the form on the counter. "Mark it terminated by the client," Mrs Wimbourne said and watched Lionel lock the door. "That's another day dusted. Fetch your belongings and we can hop off to our burrows."

As they converged on the dull yellow three-seater staffroom that smelled of stagnant tea, Vera said "Dudley, were you making up to that rude woman? You've a nice girl right here, or am I being an interfering old bag, Colette?"

Colette bit her plump lower lip and shook her head vaguely and made a joke of hiding her round chubby suntanned face behind her long black hair as she stooped to grab the white rabbit that was her rucksack. Trevor bowed and passed it to her, then smoothed the remnant of his greyish hair over his glistening scalp. "I think as long as we're saying what we think you can both do better."

Vera rubbed her forehead under her short dyed auburn hair as if to erase all the wrinkles and rounded her mouth until it tugged her thin cheeks against the bones. "I think they make a lovely young couple," she objected.

"Not better than each other, better than this treadmill. When I was your age, Colette, or even Dudley's I wanted adventure. Don't get stuck here or you'll end up like me and Vera with nothing to look forward to but dying on a pension."

He ambled to the door to bow out Vera and Colette, and Dudley felt as if he might never escape the room that looked steeped in weak tea. The outer office had already grown stuffy now that the fan was still, but the instant he left the office behind he felt as if someone had thrown a pailful of sweat over him. A plastic bag from Woolworth's up the sloping pedestrianised street lay exhausted outside Virgin, having failed to crawl to a pavement artist's chalked seascape. Along the middle of the uneven pavement, the topmost branches of caged saplings fingered a breeze that stayed well out of Dudley's reach, but he no longer felt trapped behind hot glass. Away from the job centre, he was himself.

The world might have been a show staged for him. Beyond Blockbuster and the other shops on the ground floor of Mecca Bingo, boys in swimming trunks were too intent on fleeing from some mischief at Europa Pools to notice him. Inside Conway Park Station, which was tiled pale as an ice cream, a lift opened at both ends to him. Between two underground tunnels a train for New Brighton shed commuters to make room for him.

The train snaked up into the sunlight at Birkenhead Park, stoking the interior and filling his nostrils with the hot dusty smell of the upholstered seats but leaving behind the harsh hollow roar of the tunnel. At Birkenhead North the nearest doors halted exactly opposite a passage too short to contain more than the ticket office. His mind seemed to own everything around him now: the two-storey terrace, hardly more than a wall with windows and doors in, that faced the station; the clash of a football against the wire mesh of a sports compound opposite a rudimentary supermarket; the frustrated smell of petrol fumes from cars backed up by roadworks at a five-way junction with a church in the middle; the overalled men and women hosing down soapy vehicles in a car wash or wiping them like beggars at traffic lights. Everything assured him how much more there was to him.

Five minutes' easy climb of a street smug with fat pairs of houses opposite the car wash brought him in sight of the disused observatory, its grey dome squatting like a torpid introverted turtle on the ridge of Bidston Hill. It sank away from his progress, and by the time he arrived at the road that almost followed a contour line, the bulk of the hill had been foreshortened into a slope crowded with foliage and tattered with butterflies. His house was one of a long row that stood together in pairs to challenge the vegetation across the road. He tramped past his mother's rockery, where weeds flourished leaves above the flowers they were overcoming, and let himself in. "Kathy," he called as the door lumbered inwards, "are you home?"

More than the silence, the absence of any aroma of dinner told him that his mother wasn't back from work. He marched along the hall, flinging doors wide. They irritated him by never quite fitting their frames since she'd had them stripped to tone in with the naked banisters and the pale pine hallstand. He kicked off his shoes on the way upstairs and collected them in one hand while he tugged off his socks with the other. He abandoned these on the stairs, but couldn't remove his shirt until he'd dispensed with the jacket of his office suit. He dropped it on the desk chair that faced his bedroom window and the hillside beyond his computer, and dumped his trousers and the lasso of his quietly striped tie on top. He shied a wad composed of the shirt and his equally sodden underpants at the washing basket outside the bathroom and only just missed. He shut the door with one foot, and once his bare sole unstuck itself from the wood he hauled the sash of the window as high as it would strain, then fell on his back on the bed.

He gazed across his naked body at the room. The toy revolver his father had bought despite Kathy's protests lay on the dressing-table, dwarfing plastic soldiers years older. Then came books he'd won at school, and sets of encyclopaedias from his parents, followed by true crime books he'd bought himself. The wall between the dressing-table and the bookshelves was still decorated with posters his friend Eamonn had given him. Kathy wrinkled her nose at all these images from horror films and at the gun whenever he let her glimpse his room. How would she react if she knew what else was there? He was smiling and grimacing and otherwise greeting his thoughts when he heard her arrive home.

"Oh, Dudley," she complained over a muted slam of the front door. He guessed she'd found his socks, since her footsteps made an issue of how wearily she was ascending the stairs. She was almost on the landing when she called "Are you up here?"

"I was going to have a shower."

"Go on then, and then we can talk."

He could hear her nervousness even through the door. "What about?"

"Dudley, there's something I haven't been telling you. Let me go downstairs so you can have your shower and then we'll talk about it."

She knew, he thought, and all the heat deserted him. His hands jerked out to drag the quilt around him. He heard his mother hurry down the stairs, and willed her to carry on out of the house, beyond any possibility of the confrontation she was afraid of. What had he said or done to alert her? He couldn't think of anything—couldn't think. Perhaps if he stayed cocooned by the quilt the encounter would never take place, since she wouldn't dare to venture into his room. If that made no sense, what did? Only that she was his mother and would have to keep his secret: hadn't that been in her voice? He was suddenly anxious to put the confrontation behind him. He threw the quilt away and sprinted, penis wagging like an admonitory finger, to the bathroom.

Kathy had tidied his clothes into the basket, surely a promising sign. He bolted the door and climbed into the bath. It was as large as she liked it, and for the first time it made him feel stunted to childishness. As the water that had been lying in wait in the shower found him, he began to shiver. Hot water followed it, and he could have imagined that the June heat had been transformed into a mass of needles to prick him. He did his best to rake the sweat off his body with it before challenging his own gaze in the mirror while he dried himself. Once he'd knotted the cord of his towelling robe he padded downstairs. He was ready for a fight, he tried to think, since he was robed like a boxer.

Kathy was washing breakfast dishes in the kitchen sink. She must have released her greying hair from whatever style she'd worn to work—however she'd looked when she'd waved him off that morning—because it was halfway down her back. She was in her civil service clothes, not the faded russet kaftan she so often wore at home. As she turned to him the sunlight caught the hint of a dark moustache that he sometimes thought was the badge of her ambition to contain all Dudley needed of a father. Her broad large-boned wide-eyed face, which was rather let down by a small flat knob of a chin, looked determined to be reasonable, as always. She rested a fingertip in the groove above her mouth as though holding the expression still before releasing her lips to ask "Which room shall we sit in? Would you like a drink?"

"I don't want anything." This sounded defensive, and he tried to rescind his mistake. "You wanted to talk," he said close to accusingly, and pulled out a chair with a screech of pine on linoleum.

"I just don't want you to be . . ." She recaptured her voice as she sat across the table from him, but only to say "Do you know when you really upset me?"

Until now, was she implying? The obliqueness of her approach turned his thoughts into hard spiky lumps that scraped the inside of his skull. "No idea," he mumbled.

"Try and think. There's a reason."

"The first day I went to school."

"And you kept running back to me in tears. You're not still angry with me over that, are you? Remember I told you I felt the same on my first day. That wasn't the time, though it was bad. I knew you had to get used to school. We couldn't afford to have you taught at home even if you were ahead of the other children."

He found her wistfulness even more suffocating than usual. As heat swarmed over him he realised she was still awaiting the answer to her question. "The first day I wanted to walk to school by myself."

"You were too young, Dudley. Do you remember the tantrum you threw? I was fond of that vase. I never told you it was my mother's, did I? But no, not then either. Part of me admired you for wanting to be independent when you were only eleven."

"When I went for my job interview and wouldn't let you come."

"What makes you think I was unhappy then? I was so proud of you."

That wasn't how he remembered it. He'd heard her sobbing as soon as she closed the front door after waving him off. "When I went to look for my dad," he suggested impatiently.

"I was afraid for you till the police found you. You were just thirteen, you know. But I didn't mean that kind of upset. I'm sure I realised Monty leaving was something you had to work through."

At the time and for years Dudley's impression had been that

she'd felt betrayed by her son. "Then I don't know," he complained. "Tell me."

"When you tore up that story I said you should try and get published."

"You shouldn't even have read it."

"You know I thought you'd left it on your bed for me. If I wasn't meant to read it, why didn't you shut the door?"

"I did." Surely this argument had been buried a decade ago. "That's why it's always shut now," he said.

"I'm sure I'd have liked whatever you wrote. You didn't even let me finish it." Her eyes continued glistening with a threat of tears as she said "You ought to have known I was on your side when I'd been to the school about the other one you wrote."

"We've been through all this. Where's it leading?"

Kathy reached towards him. When he left her hands stranded on their backs she said "Have you heard about the new magazine that's out next month? The *Mersey Mouth*. How would you like to be in it?"

"Get a job there, you mean? I thought your idea was I should have a secure one just like yours."

"They ran a competition for the best short story set on Merseyside by someone from Merseyside who'd never been published before."

Dudley's twinge of frustration was immediately succeeded by relief. "Won't they have chosen it by now?"

"They have, Dudley."

This revived his frustration, though mostly with her. "What are you telling me about it for, then?"

"You've won."

"I've . . ." She must think he was gaping with no worse than disbelief or shock, but the heat wasn't just all over him, it was rendering his mouth as dry as his fists were clammy. "What've you done?" he spluttered.

"I don't pray much, but I used to pray every night you wouldn't stop writing because you didn't like me reading the story you tore up. I was sure you hadn't really, but don't hate me, I couldn't help looking for new ones. I only wanted to see I hadn't destroyed your talent."

Dudley's voice felt harsh as a mouthful of sand. "You've been reading my stories."

"I did, and when I heard about the competition I wanted to tell you to send one. I was afraid you might tear them up instead if you knew I'd seen them."

"So you . . ." The rest of his words seemed incapable of crossing the desert of his mouth. "You . . ."

"I sent one in. Under your name, of course, since you hadn't put it on."

She seemed actually to be waiting for gratitude. "Which story?" he forced himself to ask.

"The one that had me on the edge of my seat and scared I mightn't finish it before you came back from seeing your girlfriend. About the man with the phone on the train."

If he hadn't pretended to have a date he would have been at home. The irony made him stagger as he lurched to his feet. "You're not going to harm anything," she cried.

"Stay out of my room or I will," he shouted as he slammed his door behind him.

He dragged handfuls of encyclopaedias off the shelf and dumped them on the bed. For the first time he saw that the length of plywood against which they had been resting wasn't quite the same colour as the wall. It was always in shadow, and nobody who hadn't been searching his room would have noticed. As he lifted the last volumes down, the strip of wood fell flat on the shelf, releasing the typescripts it hid. He saved them from sprawling on the floor and separated them on the bed.

They were all there, including "Night Trains Don't Take You Home".

He took a breath that smelled of hot stale paper, and gave the door a slam that he hoped would make Kathy's head throb as badly as his own was throbbing. "You only said you'd sent it," he yelled from the stairs. "You were trying to make me think it'd have to be published, weren't you? Did you honestly think I'd agree—"

His mother was pushing an envelope across the table at him. The top left-hand corner bore a bright blue masthead. Upside down it resembled an unequal pair of sharp blades preceded by two bits of gibberish. He righted it to see a large M lending its support to both ersey and outh. "Open it," his mother urged.

He ripped it open so savagely that she recoiled. Inside were two copies of a contract to publish "Night Trains Don't Take You Home". Perhaps she was afraid he would tear them up; she began speaking as if to distract him. "I photocopied your story at work. The magazine phoned to say you'd won. I wanted to tell you, but I thought I'd be better waiting till they wrote."

"Then they can't publish my story if I don't sign, and I don't want it published."

"I'm sorry, Dudley, but they can."

She sounded by no means sorry enough. "Who says?" he demanded.

"If you send something to a competition you're agreeing to the rules. Even if you don't sign that they can publish so long as they pay you. It'll be five hundred pounds, look."

"I didn't send it."

"You wouldn't say I did against your wishes, would you? You're making me feel I shouldn't have tried to help your writing. I thought you'd be pleased someone besides me knows you're as good as I've always known."

Long before she finished speaking Dudley's brain felt clogged with words. "Will you sign so we're in time for the post?" she said. "Here's a pen."

She snapped her canvas handbag open and extracted a ballpoint, which she pushed towards him. It looked shrivelled by the sunlight or by his trapped panic, and made a small protracted scraping sound that lingered on his nerves. He closed his prickly fist around it and considered snapping it in two, but what would that achieve? He imagined her passing him an endless succession of pens until he collapsed beneath her pleading. He felt his lips bare his teeth in a smile or a grimace as he scribbled his signature on both contracts. "There," he said so harshly that his throat grew raw. "Happy now?"

"So long as you will be, and I know you will. Let me have one of those and keep the other."

When he only capped the ballpoint she leaned across the table and slid the topmost contract out of his reach. From her handbag she produced an envelope she'd addressed to the *Mersey Mouth* and already stamped. She inserted the contract and sealed the envelope as she stood up. "I'll just run to the post," she said, and did.

He dragged his nails over the contract she'd left him. He thought of crumpling it up and shying it into the bin, but that would be pointless while Kathy wasn't there to see. Instead he tramped upstairs to drop the contract among the typescripts, then sat on the bed to gaze at the story that had been taken out of his control. "Her first mistake was thinking he was mad . . ." He must have read it dozens of times, but it had never felt capable of betraying him until now. "Come and get me," he said under his breath.

The sunlight seemed to blaze at him like a floodlight as he became aware what he was inviting. He sprang to his feet and almost heaved the tall wardrobe on top of himself in his haste to find clothes that would let him chase after his mother. He was clawing at the knot of the cord at his waist and only managing to part his fingernails from the quick when Kathy reappeared at the junction of the roads. She waved at him, displaying her empty hand. "All done," she called.

FIVE "They aren't coming. I'm going out."

"Give them a few more minutes, Dudley. I know they'll be here."

"I've given them plenty. I've given them more than I should. See, they don't think as much of me as you said."

"Of course they do. They'll just be delayed. Why don't you ring the magazine?"

"I don't want to talk to them."

Was this one of his random attacks of suppressed panic? Kathy didn't like to draw attention to them, even if she always felt she was to blame, because he would only lose his temper and deny them. Nobody except her would sense them, and she supposed that as his mother she would never stop worrying about him. He pushed himself to his feet with a creak of the upholstered wicker sofa and scowled through the window. "There's nobody. I'm going."

"Promise you won't go far. Take your mobile so I can call you when they turn up. Don't get dirty when you're going to be photographed."

His disdainful grimace made him seem younger to Kathy. "I just want you to look your best for everyone who'll see you," she said as he tramped out of the room.

She followed as far as the front door. He turned to frown at her from the end of the short cracked path, but she was seeing how much he resembled her except for his hair that she trimmed every month: the face even broader than the bones required until it trailed off at the comedown of a chin, the pale blue eyes that were wider still with whatever emotions they fronted. Once Monty had written a poem called "Four Eyes" that pretended to be about spectacles until the eyes proved to be hers and their son's. "I'll bet the press arrive the moment you're out of sight," she said.

He hunched his shoulders towards his large protruding ears, the sole feature she could hold Monty responsible for, and hurried up the track across the road. In seconds he was hidden like a beast in a jungle, though not before the unyielding sunlight clamped itself to Kathy's scalp. She ought to have suggested he wear a hat. There was no sign of anybody in the one-sided street, and so she retreated into the house.

Dudley had spent the last half-hour in leafing through his old true crime magazines, but they'd inspired him only to critical sniggers. She retrieved the magazines from the sofa and the floor and dropped them in the pine rack by the television. Since the contract for his story had arrived he'd been untidier than ever. She would rather this was deliberate than unconscious; she didn't like to think he might be less than fully in control of his mind. At least she was as sure as she could be that he'd never taken drugs—not like her and Monty years before their son was born. If he sometimes stayed in his room for hours without even switching on his computer, no doubt he was reading. If he wanted to keep his girlfriend Trina to himself, perhaps that would change. Only his secret panics reminded her of her LSD experience, of the night that she'd been convinced would never end as she became aware how infinite the dark was, how the passage of time would simply put more stars out, not least the sun. Monty had been scribbling poems that the daylight would show to be incomprehensible; he'd been as distant and preoccupied with his writing, she thought, as he'd grown later in their marriage. Surely their single night of indulgence hadn't affected Dudley, but her fear that it might have was never far away. It took her to the kitchen to splash cold water on her face and drink a glassful to clear her mouth of a reminiscent metallic taste. She was resting her hands against the relatively cool interior of the steel sink to rid them of prickling when the doorbell rang.

She hoped Dudley had forgotten his key. She had to produce a less reproachful smile at the sight of two people on the path, an oval-bodied balding red-faced man as middle-aged as her with a thin fawn cardigan draped over the camera bag that dangled from his stubby neck, and a small slim woman Dudley's age or younger. She had cropped gently spiky bright red hair, a compact delicate instantly friendly face, and wore a pale grey lightweight suit down to almost her knees and a white blouse with a silver brooch at the throat. "I'm awfully sorry we're late," she said. "We got off at the wrong station. We thought you'd be Bidston. I'm Patricia. This is Tom."

"Kathy. My son thought you'd let him down." Kathy gave this a moment to make its point before adding "Come in and I'll get him back."

She indicated the front room as she lifted the phone from the little high pine table. Six pairs of rings brought her his voice, but all it said was "Dudley Smith. I can't talk now. Leave me a message."

"Dudley, they're here. Hurry up and pick this up and come back."

The journalist and the photographer sat forward on the sofa with interrogative wicker creaks. "I'm sure he won't be long," Kathy said. "Would anyone like a drink?"

"Love one," said Tom.

"That would be wonderful, thanks," Patricia said.

Was she a shade too professionally friendly and eager to please? Kathy led them along the hall, only to feel clumsy and big-boned by comparison with Patricia. Tom lingered to poke his face at the framed photographs of sixties Liverpool. "Where'd you buy these? I hope you didn't pay much."

"I took them. I used to think I was creative," Kathy said. "What will anyone have to drink?"

"Coldest you've got."

"I'll second that," Patricia said. "And thanks."

Kathy planted a bottle of lemonade and three glasses on the table. "So while we're waiting, tell me about your magazine."

"I'm freelance," Tom said. "Go anywhere I'm told."

"Walt who owns it likes giving people a break. That's why we had the competition." As Kathy poured a spitting glassful Patricia said "Did your son send that story anywhere else before us, do you know?"

"He never sent it anywhere."

"Except for us, obviously."

"Not to you either." It was bound to come out, Kathy thought, and wasn't she entitled to a little credit? "He can be shy of pushing himself," she said. "I sent it for him."

"Sounds like your mummy getting you the job, Patricia."

Having sipped her drink, Patricia said to Kathy "Your son knew though, did he?"

"He didn't. I don't think he's convinced how good he is."

"We'll use what you're telling me if that's all right with you. Is there anything else he mightn't say that you think I should know?"

Kathy thought the question rather too cunning, but said "That's just one of his stories. There's more than a dozen upstairs."

"Have you read them all? Did you decide that was the best one?"

"One of the best, but I'm just his mother. Maybe somebody more qualified ought to look at them."

"I'd be happy to."

"If you'd like to stay here I'll see if I can find them."

"Do you write yourself?"

"I used to a bit. It wasn't worth keeping. Well, I did keep one story I wrote about Dudley."

"I'd love to see that if it's handy."

"I expect it may be," Kathy said and ran upstairs with an eagerness more straightforward than she had been experiencing. Beyond her unnecessarily double bed she slid aside one hot sallow door of the Nordic wardrobe to grope among her dresses. She retrieved the exercise book with a jangle of hangers and a rustle of fabric, to find that the dull red cover bore the corpse of a moth. She crumbled the insect between finger and thumb and rubbed the silky dust to nothingness as she made for Dudley's room.

If possible it was even untidier than the last time she had seen it, as though to challenge her to admit she'd ventured in. Typescripts were piled next to the computer on the desk, and it took her only moments to confirm that they were Dudley's stories. Since he was no longer bothering to hide them, mustn't he intend them to be read? She closed his door tight and almost tripped on the edge of a stair in her haste to rejoin the journalist. "Don't read mine now," she said. "Save it for when you've time."

"You'd rather I read his first. I understand."

Perhaps in fact she realised Kathy would prefer not to watch her story being read. Dudley had liked her to read it to him when he was little, but had taken refuge in his bedroom to avoid hearing the expanded version with which she'd tried to celebrate his teens. Monty had condemned as far too motherly even the section their son used to like. Once Patricia slipped the exercise book into her scaly silver handbag and began to leaf through the typescripts, Kathy turned to the photographer. "Have you read the story he won with?"

"I don't read fiction. It's just another word for lying. Photography magazines do me."

"Will you have read it, Patricia?"

"I voted for it." As Kathy started to like her, Patricia said "Are all these set on Merseyside?"

"I believe they are."

"I think someone may be pleased," Patricia said, but her next question came with the faintest frown. "Are they all about the same killer?"

"That's how I took them. I like the way he gets inside the girls."

She meant the writing. The photographer grunted with surprise if not with disapproval, as if he'd heard another meaning. She was about to revise her comment when he and Patricia lost interest in her and gazed along the hall, at the sound of a key in a lock. Kathy's weight pinned the chair down, and she was struggling to turn it when she heard the front door open. "Dudley Smith?" Patricia said and stood up. "I hope you don't mind, but your mother has been letting us into your secrets."

SIX   As Dudley climbed the slope he heard creatures fleeing through the undergrowth. Perhaps they sensed his baffled
rage. They made him think of a question the interviewer could
have asked him if she had bothered to turn up. "Mr Smith, what
was the first thing you ever killed?" She had to have a face, and
so he gave her Colette's chubby suntanned one, and the job centre as the setting for the interview. She looked as impressed as
Mrs Wimbourne and the others that he was about to be published; Lionel had removed his headset to listen, and even Morris
had taken time off from his breakdown to be present. "How do
you expect your career to develop?" the interviewer ought to
ask, and the answer was that Dudley felt capable of writing a
bestseller. The girl from the magazine could have scooped his first
interview, instead of which she'd let him down.

The trees that cramped the winding path and poked low

branches at his face gave way to shoulder-high ferns and gorse parched dull gold. A twig snapped like a finger beneath his tread, and he yielded to a reminiscent grin before snarling at a thorny bramble tendril he was elbowing aside. Unshaded sunlight fastened on him with an electric buzz of insects, and he felt as if a spotlight had been turned on him. It was about time. If "Night Trains Don't Take You Home" was going to cause any problems, someone at the magazine would have noticed by now.

The path widened into an open space where brown turf exposed slabs of sandstone patched another shade of grey by lichen. A hypodermic needle glinted in the shadow of a charred bush he could smell. Gnats whined like a chorus of dentists' drills, and a huge voice blurred by distance bellowed at him. "What's ailing you this time, Smith? Still too sickly to join in, or do you think you're better than your classmates?"

"I had asthma. I haven't got it any more," Dudley was provoked to retort even as he grasped that he'd heard the voice but not its words. There must be a sports day at his old school down in Birkenhead; the amplified voice belonged to Mr Brink, the sports master. "Mr Brink and his awful stink," Dudley shouted, remembering the stench of sweat and rubber soles that had filled the gymnasium, and seemed to hear the giant voice respond in his head. "Still scribbling, are you, Smith? Still think it's healthier to sit and make up stories when you should be in the gym or on the field?"

"Mr Fender said I could write. Maybe you turned him against me. Maybe you told him to say what I could write about," Dudley said, and controlled himself. "Anyway, I'm not here to talk to you. The first thing I killed, that must have been the caterpillar I ate."

Nearly twenty years later the memory was as immediate as the sunlight: tilting his head back to drop the squirming wasp-striped object in his mouth; the tickle of its many feet inside his throat; his efforts not to cough even when he felt it try to twist around and clamber upwards until he gulped it down; its dying struggles in his stomach, where he was sure he'd felt it growing softer before the sensations faded and a faint bitter taste reached his mouth. Colette the interviewer gazed at him in shock and admiration. "Why did you do that?" she breathed.

"My cousin Bert was meant to as well, only he was sick instead. We used to set each other challenges and that was one of mine. He killed as many things as I did by the time we finished. When he got a bit older he helped them chase the hares into the field for the hounds at Altcar."

"Did you ever help?"

"My parents wouldn't let me go." A residue of discontent took Dudley by surprise as he recalled how he'd never seen the hare-coursing—had never witnessed two hounds catch the same hare and, as Bert had delighted in telling him, pull it apart like a squealing bag full of meat and blood. "I killed lots of frogs, though," he said. "Dozens and dozens."

"How did you manage to catch them?"

"They were stuck together like people." He remembered the disgust that had turned his mouth sour as he'd realised. He'd peered in repelled fascination at the couples jerking as if they were too feeble to hop, and then he'd trampled some before running for a stick. By the time he'd selected the biggest and heaviest he could wield, he'd been afraid that the frogs might have escaped into the pond, but the grass around it had swarmed with them. Their legs had continued to jerk once he'd smashed their slimy bodies, yet it had taken him years to comprehend that the males might have been unable to stop pumping their slime into the crevices that had trapped them. How could anything so slimy exert such a grip? Even when he'd heard his mother calling him he had pursued his mission around the pond until he could see nothing moving except him, and then he'd tossed the stick into the water and run back to his parents and the picnic. "They didn't seem to notice they were being killed. They might as well have been toys you wind up. I don't believe things feel," he said and wished he were speaking to a real journalist. His mobile couldn't interrupt him; he felt as if that was why he hadn't switched it on. If the interviewer and the photographer had bothered to show up, they would have to wait—and then he wondered if they might ask his mother to show them where he wrote. They might see the stories on his desk. They might read them.

He hissed through his teeth as he ran home. Flies like black lumps of mindlessness bumbled into his face while a sour burned taste gathered in his mouth. No car was parked outside the house. He drew several ragged breaths that felt almost too hot to inhale as he stumped across the road. By the time he reached the front door, all he could think of was a glass of water. He flung the door open as a preamble to reminding his mother that he'd been right about the people from the magazine, only to see a bulky man and a young woman half the size watching him along the hall. "Dudley Smith?" the young woman said. "I hope you don't mind, but your mother has been letting us into your secrets."

Kathy was making an issue of trying to turn to him. The young woman stood up as if to demonstrate how much more petite and in control she was. "Which—" Dudley began to demand and caught sight of a heap of printouts on the table. His words distorted themselves into another shape, and he thought his face did. "Where'd you get those?"

"Your mother brought them," the man declared. "She said Patricia could look at them."

"I'm sorry we were late," Patricia said. "We went too far on the train."

All that his panicky anger would let Dudley say was "I want a drink."

"Better fetch a glass, then," the photographer took it on himself to tell him.

"I can get it, Tom," Kathy said and did.

"Maybe you can, but you shouldn't. Just my opinion, of course."

Dudley ignored him and watched Kathy pour the lemonade. He leaned against the refrigerator while he swallowed a mouthful and another, and felt sufficiently cooled down to talk. "How much did you read?"

"Less than I'd have liked," Patricia said. "I didn't have time to read any all the way through. Enough to think we might want to use more of them."

"Patricia voted for your story," Kathy said and gave him a surreptitiously pleading look.

Dudley turned the printouts face down on the table as he sat opposite the journalist. "All right, I don't mind being interviewed now."

Tom released a wordless noise, which Patricia made it clear she was disregarding. "Do you mind if I tape this?" she asked Dudley.

"I wouldn't have minded," Kathy said.

The remark with which Patricia had greeted his arrival flared up in his head. "What have you been saying?"

"That you don't believe in your achievement," Patricia told him.

He kept his stare on his mother. "That's all you said."

"It's your interview, Dudley. You should be the one to talk."

"Go on then, Patricia. Ask about me."

She depressed two buttons on the dinky tape recorder with a single fingertip. "What made you start writing?"

"My father." He thought that was the safest answer. "He wrote poems," he said. "Used to read them like a lot of local poets do. Still does. I saw a poster he was on the other week."

"You could have gone to hear him if you wanted," Kathy said. "I wouldn't have minded."

"What's his name?" Patricia waited to ask.

"Monty Smith," Kathy said at once.

"He used to read to me a lot. That must be what made me want to write."

"Just your father?"

"Her as well."

"That isn't what you call your mother," Tom objected, "her."

"No, I call her Kathy when I call her."

"She's helped you too, I expect," Patricia intervened.

"She kept saying I should keep on writing. And a master at school did."

"Maybe I could talk to him."

"No."

"He turned against Dudley in the end, you see," Kathy said. "One of Dudley's stories shocked him because it was so real. It shocked me too, but that's not bad, is it? Not bad for a fifteen-year-old. It showed how imaginative he was even then. All he had to go on were the news reports about a murder."

"I don't want to talk about it."

"Then you shouldn't have brought it up in the first place."

"Now, Tom, let me do the interviewing." To Dudley, Patricia said "Do you remember when you became interested in crime?"

He felt as if everyone in the room was eager to scrutinise his answer. "Lots of people are," he protested. "It's normal."

"Maybe, but if you write without trying to be published you have to find it satisfying all by itself."

He didn't have to respond, but then he saw how he could deal with it. "I know when I started being interested," he said to Kathy. "When you let me watch Eamonn's videos."

His mother risked a smile. "They weren't supposed to watch them at their age, but I knew he could tell the difference between fiction and real life. His friend's parents owned a video library."

"Eamonn watched the films as well, and he ended up work-ing for the government like us. Eamonn Moore. He's in the tax office. His parents ran Moore and Moore Video."

"So where do you find your inspiration?" Patricia said.

"You started with real murders, didn't you?" Kathy said.

Dudley struggled to produce an expression that felt like a grin. "Did I?"

"I'm sorry to keep bringing it up, but the story Mr Fender didn't like was about a real murderer and the things he did. Mr Fender said it was too real, as if a story could be."

"Do you still have it?" Patricia said.

"Why would I? It was only a school thing."

"You could have given it to me," Kathy said wistfully. "So you didn't just destroy the story I wanted you to send somewhere."

"What was that about?" Patricia asked them both.

"Nothing but me being a teenager. It was awful."

"I was never sure if it was meant to be you," Kathy said. "Were you really so lonely? Did you honestly think girls couldn't see how much there was to you? There wasn't actually a girl who laughed at you when you went to kiss her, was there?"

"It was a story like all my stories." That didn't quite rid him of it, and so he demanded "When are we doing the photograph?"

"We can now if you'd like a break from being questioned."

The photographer unzipped his bag and cocked his head at Kathy. "Can I borrow a knife? The biggest you've got," he said and passed Dudley the carving knife she gave him. "Come at me with this. Try and look dangerous."

Dudley was resisting temptation when Kathy said "Is that necessary? He's a writer, not a murderer."

As Dudley dropped the knife on the table Patricia said "How about where you write?"

"Let me just run and tidy up a bit," Kathy intervened. "I shouldn't be long."

"You've messed about in my room enough. You can't go in there any more."

As the photographer narrowed his eyes Patricia said "Maybe I've got a solution."

"I do hope so," Dudley's mother said in more words than he would have used.

Patricia took a phone from her handbag and thumbed a stored number. "Walt? Patricia . . . Fine so far, but I was wondering about the photo . . . I thought we could wait till he meets Vincent, if Tom doesn't mind."

"Tom won't have to," the photographer said, zipping his bag shut.

"He is. I'll put him on."

Dudley was eager to see Tom being reprimanded for his comment, and was thrown when Patricia handed him the mobile. It carried the warmth of her cheek and the faintest scent of soap. He held it away from his face to say "Hello?" and more forcefully "This is Dudley Smith."

"How's the star?" an unexpectedly American voice enquired. "We're all anxious to meet you, one of us in particular."

"You, you mean."

"Nobody more so but no, not me right now. A young moviemaker called Vincent Davis. He's made a bunch of short movies around Liverpool that we're giving away with our first issue. He's fired up to make a feature, which is why you need to get together pronto."

"Why do I, do we?"

"For the movie of your story. He wants more ideas from you."

In an instant Dudley's brain was empty of ideas and even of words he could risk uttering. He was gazing at the display that appeared to be built of fragments of charred matchsticks, as if it could somehow help him think, when the mobile said "Let's plan for the world to know your name and Vincent's by the time we're through. He's away this weekend, but I'll track him down. See you very soon. Let me have Patricia."

"It's fixed, then?" she asked the phone. "Good enough," she said and dropped the mobile in her handbag. "Shall we continue?"

"I don't want to answer any more questions," Dudley blurted. "I've got one. Suppose I don't want my story filmed?"

"I think you've given us the right, if you remember what you signed."

Dudley would have shouted that he didn't, but Patricia was swifter. "Thanks for looking after us, Kathy. It was good to meet you both."

Dudley watched his mother let her and Tom out of the house, and then he used the carving-knife to flick typescripts aside. "Do be careful," Kathy said as she rejoined him. "You don't want to hurt anyone with that."

He felt the blade nick the margin of a story and imagined it cutting into flesh. The contract with the magazine was almost at the bottom of the pile. *All subsidiary rights, including reprint, translation, cartoon, merchandising, electronic, motion picture, television, dramatic—* his gaze fled across the text until several phrases arrested it—*will be negotiated by the Publisher and/or their Agents on behalf of the Author, all proceeds to be shared equally between the Publisher and the Author after deduction of any Agent's fees.* He jabbed at the clause with the knife, almost pinning the page to the table. "You made me sign it. You didn't even give me time to see what it said."

"You could have taken the time, Dudley. You're a grown man, after all." She ventured to stand next to him and used a fingertip to slant the contract towards her. "I suppose you can't expect too much when you're just starting out," she said. "Once you're established they'll have to give you the terms you deserve."

The division of his income hadn't been the issue, but now it aggravated his trapped rage. "Do put the knife down," his mother said. "You're making me nervous."

Was she leaving her hand beside it to coax him? Stabbing her might be a substitute for teaching his own hand not to obey anyone except him. He imagined driving the point between the tendons and twisting the blade, but there would be no pain for him to feel. He dropped the knife, which spun like a compass blade and ended up indicating him as he gathered the contract and typescripts. He was in the hall when Kathy said "You aren't worrying what the film will be like, are you? I'm sure they won't spoil your story if they're asking you to be involved."

He told himself that she wasn't deliberately taunting him, and retreated to his bedroom, where he stared hot-eyed out of the window. He had to be even more careful now that so much was out of his hands—and then a smile crept over his face. Kathy had meant to reassure him, and perhaps she had inadvertently succeeded. Hardly any films stayed true to the stories they were based on, but that was no reason to assume this one would stray closer to reality. Indeed, he would be able to ensure that it went nowhere near.

SEVEN  As Dudley's client—a fat pallid twenty-year-old in baggy purple shorts and sandals with a shirt tied around his waist—set forth from the counter to take up stacking shelves in Frugo, a woman seated on the front row of bucket chairs stood up. She was dressed in a white sleeveless blouse with pearl or at any rate pearly buttons and a loose yellow ankle-length skirt of little shape. Though she wasn't holding the next ticket, she hurried to Dudley's booth, fanning herself with a wide-brimmed straw hat. "You're the one, aren't you?" she said. "You're the man I'm looking for."

She was well past forty, and he'd been hoping someone else would have to tell her how few jobs she was eligible for, but now he saw that she wasn't a client. "If it's to do with my story I am," he said.

"Your story."

"The one that's going to be published. Or the story of my life if that's what you want."

"My daughter and I know quite enough about you, thank you."

"Are you the editor? She can ask me more things if she wants, or you can."

"What are you—" The woman sat forward so sharply that the hat in her lap creaked like an overloaded basket. "Yes, I'll ask you something," she said, raising her voice. "Why did you call her a prostitute when she came looking for work?"

His expectations gave way, dumping him back into the banality of the office and worse. He was barely interested in protesting "I didn't."

"She says you did. Just you tell me why she'd lie, which she never does. You'd better take more care what you say if you want to keep your job."

"Maybe I don't. Maybe I won't need it." As he tried to keep his lips still while he muttered this, the stagnant heat grew perfumed. "Trouble, Dudley?" Mrs Wimbourne said as if echoing herself.

"My daughter came looking for work I won't pretend I approve of. But it isn't up to anyone behind your counter to approve or disapprove of it, and your junior called her a prostitute."

"I'm nobody's junior."

"All right, Dudley, I'm dealing with this." To the woman Mrs Wimbourne said "I remember the incident. I believe there was a misunderstanding."

"All I told her was there are jobs we aren't allowed to offer."

"I'm afraid that's the case, madam."

"What is? That you set yourselves up in judgement on how people make a living or my daughter is a liar?"

"I wouldn't say either, and I'm sure Mr Smith—"

"If you want my opinion or for that matter if you don't, you're surer of him than he deserves. I'd advise keeping an eye on him." The woman demonstrated this before thrusting back her chair as if recoiling from him. "I expect you can get away with anything if you're working for the state," she said and immediately made for the door.

As Lionel stood aside to let her out, Mrs Wimbourne said "What's this about being published? Come and enlighten me."

Why did she want to talk in private? His colleagues were eager to hear. As he followed her into the staffroom he pretended to close the door but left it an inch ajar. Mrs Wimbourne reached into her handbag on the table before apparently realising that even she wasn't allowed to smoke on the premises. Perhaps that was why her voice sharpened. "What's it about, then?"

"I've got a story in a magazine and it's going to be filmed as well."

"How definite is that? You're not just trying to impress Colette."

"I'm certainly not," he said, indifferent whether Colette heard. "It's very definite."

"The story's not based on reality, is it?"

Though they were shut away from the sun, the light seemed to flare up around him. "Why should it be? It's a story."

"It isn't based on what you do."

He cleared his throat, which helped him more to speak than think. "What? What do I do?"

"Once you leave this office that's no concern of mine. I mean your work here. You haven't written about that."

He couldn't quite suppress a splutter. "I wouldn't. What's there to write about?"

"I didn't know you thought so little of your job. You ought to have asked permission to be published."

"What's that to do with anybody here?"

"You may well ask, and a bit late too. You seemed to want everyone to hear about it before. Perhaps you've forgotten your conditions of service. You're supposed to apply to us in writing before you accept any competing employment. Where are you going?"

"The door isn't shut."

"Leave it open, then. What have you to say for yourself?"

"How can writing be competing? Except I won a competition." When she received this with no esteem of his wit he complained "It doesn't make sense."

"I'll decide that. Let me have full details. I want to be told, and right now."

"It's about someone who gets herself murdered because she doesn't appreciate someone and thinks she knows all about him." Having given Mrs Wimbourne time to interpret that how she liked, he said "It'll be in the first issue of *Mersey Mouth*."

"I'll need to have a word with someone at the top. Meanwhile you'd better warn your magazine that there may be a problem. I certainly remember civil servants being forbidden to have all kinds of other jobs when I was your age. Are you going to give your magazine a quick call?"

"Not yet."

Her lips parted with a curt dry sound. "Then you'd best get back to work."

How dare she talk about his age and act like a headmistress? As he took his hot stiff face out of the staffroom he glared at the backs of his colleagues' heads and at the scattered hopefuls, challenging any of them to betray that they'd overheard. "Thirty-seven," he shouted, summoning a young mother and her baby, which commenced screaming at the sight of him. While she rocked it in its push-chair and then in her arms and attempted to placate it with a bottle that aggravated its distress, he yelled questions and eventually managed to select a job with a playgroup from the descriptions twitching up the computer screen. At last that rid him of the cries that made the screen appear to throb as if his headache had been rendered visible. He didn't know if any aspect of his performance brought Mrs Wimbourne to stoop over him as Lionel opened the door for the strident push-chair. "Better take your lunch now," Mrs Wimbourne said.

Someone else would have to deal with the young man who strode into the office as if searching for a fight, his thin pale face mottled with more than the freckles that resembled faded samples of the red of his hair. Dudley was giving him a wide berth on the way to the door when his mobile rang. "Dudley Smith," he said.

"It's Patricia from the *Mouth*."

"I'll step outside," he said and emerged into the crowded sunlight. "I'm here."

"Vincent's back in town. Would tomorrow work? Walt suggests we all meet in Ringo's Kit in Penny Lane."

"Tonight if you like."

"Don't worry, meeting isn't quite that urgent. Eight o'clock tomorrow, then? Vincent wants you to bring all your stories. I've been talking them up."

"Which?" he said so fiercely that his spit glistened on a woman's back.

"Just generally. None in particular."

"Then don't tell him any more."

He only had to think up new ideas to offer the director. Dudley did away with Patricia and dropped the phone in his breast pocket. He was heading for the sandwich shop beyond the discount markets and charity stores when a man shouted "Dudley Smith."

He was unable to identify the speaker until the fellow took another step towards him. "Are you called Dudley Smith?"

His thin pale face was blotchier than ever; even the freckles looked angry now. "I'm sorry," Dudley felt bound to say. "Were you after me before?"

"Still am."

"Where are you from?"

"Where does it sound like? Round here. What's it to you?"

This was more combative than Dudley thought reasonable. "Who sent you, I mean."

"Nobody sent me." Pallor was turning the freckles virtually incandescent. "I came by myself."

"You're freelance, you mean. Nothing wrong with that. You're like me."

"I'm bloody not. Don't you make out I am."

"Look, what exactly do you want? I'm supposed to be having my lunch."

"So you can get your strength up to hurt some more women?"

All the heat and light seemed to converge on Dudley as if the sky had been transformed into a magnifying glass. He had to work his tongue inside his mouth and lick his lips to say "I've no idea what you're talking about. Where did you get my name?"

"Where do you think? You were shouting it all over the place before."

"Why shouldn't I? I'm a writer."

"So that's why you think you can sneer at anyone that comes to you for help."

"Who says I do?"

"My sister and my mother. Go on, call her a liar as well."

His face blazed white and red as if ensuring Dudley recognised the similarity to the freckled would-be table dancer. "I didn't say that about anyone," Dudley said. "You'll have to excuse me. I want my lunch."

As Dudley turned towards the sandwich shop the man stepped in front of him. "I won't excuse you, no."

"Then you'll be making a fool of yourself in public," Dudley said loud enough to be heard by everyone near. "I'll leave you to get on with it."

He sidestepped only for the man to mirror him. "I want to hear how you're going to apologise when I bring them in."

"I've nothing to apologise for. Go and ask the woman in charge if you don't believe me."

"You're hiding behind a woman now, are you?" the man said, mimicking Dudley's sidestep again. "What a completely pathetic little creep you are."

He thrust his face so close that Dudley saw how every inflamed freckle was embedded in the skin, an oppressive proximity that drove him past caution. "Get out of my way," he bellowed, "or—"

"Or what, you sad snobby little sadist?"

Dudley had hoped that his outburst would attract at least one of the security guards, but they seemed as idly amused by the confrontation as the passing audience. "Words don't hurt," he said and planted his hands on the thin shoulders, and pushed.

His persecutor stumbled backwards until the edge of a metal bench caught him behind the knees. He rebounded with a grimace. "See if this hurts," he snarled, jamming a hand between Dudley's legs. "You've not got much, have you? No wonder all you can do to women is hurt them."

The ache that blazed in Dudley's crotch seared away his ability to think. The man twisted his grip, widening his eyes in triumph or a challenge. Dudley imagined how they might swell if he dug his nails into them, but he was afraid of yielding to the impulse in public. "Help, someone," he managed to shout more than scream. "Look what he's doing. Stop him."

A woman laughed, but that was all. Beyond his tormentor he could see a litter of plastic dogs bumping mechanically against the sides of a carton on the pavement and staggering back to renew their mindless assault. The pain rose to impale his stomach. "Let go or I'll kill you," he said through his clamped teeth.

"Go ahead if you aren't going to apologise," the man said and pressed against him.

The back of the hand with which he was gripping Dudley shielded his own crotch. Dudley could choke him by his wiry mottled neck, but suppose he was unable to desist once the man was released? As he emitted a moan, which he wanted to be only of frustration, the man said "What was that? Sorry, was it?"

"I'm sorry they thought I said something I didn't."

"Not good enough," the man said and twisted harder.

Dudley's next ruse came out nearer to a scream. "I'm sorry they heard me insult your sister."

Two passing women booed this, and the man considered it for several seconds before relinquishing his grip. "I'll tell them," he said. "Maybe you won't be seeing us again. Just don't even dream of getting your own back."

As the man turned away, Dudley thought of flying after him and seizing him from behind by the eyes. He imagined how the mob would cry a warning, not in time. Instead he tried not to move while the man reverted to one of the crowd, which gradually became composed of people who hadn't witnessed the incident. Once he was sure that nobody was observing him, he set about transporting the ache somewhere he could keep it still.

Each of his paces threatened to sharpen it, and more than a few of them did. He was almost desperate enough to sit on a metal bench, but succeeded in waddling back to the job centre. He walked stiff with rage and pain to the door that admitted him behind the counter. He hadn't reached the staffroom when Colette swung her chair around. As he managed not to scream at her to stop looking at him she said "Are you really going to have a story published and made into a film?"

"Maybe," he snarled and retreated into the staffroom.

He was lowering himself gingerly onto the softest of the three chairs when Mrs Wimbourne plodded into the room. "Your attitude to your workmates needs improving in a hurry, Dudley. I suggest you give some thought to exactly what you want to do with your life," she said and went out, leaving him crouched over an ache that felt as if it mightn't be assuaged until he transferred it to someone else. The trouble was that he couldn't remember ever having believed that anybody experienced pain but him.

EIGHT "At least it isn't us that's late this time," Tom said and took a mouthful of his second pint of McCartney's Marvel. "Did you get much out of your interview? There's questions I'd have asked him."

Patricia almost executed an impatient paradiddle on the table with her fingertips. After all, the crown of the table took the form of a drum. So did the seats of all the chairs in Ringo's Kit, while their backs were skeletal metal guitars. Photographs of the Beatles in a selection of coiffures, images that Tom had already declared he could top, adorned the walls of the wine bar. Plastic notes lay cradled on foursomes of strings under the black ceiling of the long low room. None of this could distract her from realising that the photographer was only voicing the dissatisfaction she'd been levelling at herself ever since her pathetically feeble interview. She took a sip of Starr's Sauvignon, though she had expected it to be white rather than a cabernet, on the way to saying "Don't be shy if Walt's agreeable."

"I'll leave you your job." As if the thought had arrested his pint on its way to his mouth Tom said "Have you followed up those names he dropped yet?"

Walt touched his smooth forehead with a dewy bottle of Lennon's Lager, depositing a bead under his elevated hairline before lowering the glass stem past his long well-nigh rectangular suntanned face. "Which were those?"

"He didn't seem to want to talk about one of them if you remember, Tom."

"All the more reason to check up on it. If he really didn't want you knowing he wouldn't have mentioned it."

Vincent deposited his tankard of Best's Best on a stained Sergeant Pepper beer-mat and wrinkled his small nose to hitch his large spectacles higher on his round widemouthed face. "You've got me interested," he said.

"There was a teacher who tried to stop him writing what he writes," Patricia had to say. "All right, maybe I should have probed more. I've still got time."

"It starts now," said Tom. "Here's your murder man."

She stood up to welcome him. He was approaching at a pace that looked positively uncomfortable. He wore a grey suit and white shirt and discreetly silver tie, and her instincts told her that Kathy had chosen the outfit. "Walt, Vincent," she said, "this is Dudley Smith."

"And you'll remember me," said Tom.

"Name your poison," Walt said, having grasped Dudley's hand. "Let me ask you, have you poisoned anybody yet?"

Dudley muttered something like a no as he ducked to the drinks list as if the weight of his broad face was too much for his chin. "If you want an adventure nobody's had yet," Vincent said, "there's Harrison's Hock."

"I'd better, then."

"What's everyone having to eat?" Walt said.

A mop-haired waitress in a Beatles uniform came to take their order. Tom plumped for George's Grill, and Vincent for Pete's Pizza. Patricia decided on John's Jambalaya and Walt, having waited in vain for Dudley to make up his mind, opted for Paul's Prawns. "Looks like you're for Ringo's Ratatouille," Vincent said.

"I'll have that," Dudley told the waitress.

"You know it's vegetarian," Patricia felt impelled to murmur, only to be met by an unfriendly glance that inhibited her from pointing out how many other items named after members of bands the menu offered. She suspected that he was unused to this kind of social gathering, especially when he didn't wait for the Beatles to leave before he remarked to Vincent "So you want to film my story."

"I'll record this if you two don't mind," Patricia said.

"You want to film my story."

Vincent seemed no more certain than Patricia whether Dudley was repeating himself for the benefit of the tape. "I think it could be a good starting point."

"It'll be the opening, you mean."

"Or maybe just the back story. We'd have to make it more real if I was going to stage it."

Dudley shifted on his chair. "What's not real about it?"

"How did he get away with not being caught? There are security cameras on all the underground stations."

The way Dudley's face stiffened and grew blank showed how close he was to his fiction, Patricia thought, and so did his grin of relief. "They couldn't have been working."

"Pretty lucky for him."

"You can call him lucky if you want. Nobody's ever caught him."

"Could the cameras have been vandalised?" Patricia suggested.

"That's right, of course they were."

"Let's start with the basics," Vincent said. "What's his name?"

"Nobody ever finds out who he is or anything about him."

"The public needs something to remember him by. They're going to want to know more, and I am."

"He's never had a name," Dudley said with a frown that Tom's camera trapped.

"That doesn't work for me. Let's think of one that'll stick in people's minds. It could be so ordinary nobody would think he was a killer."

"Like Dudley Smith," Tom commented, and captured several expressions in fewer seconds.

"I don't want to think about names just now."

"I should have asked you in advance," Vincent said. "Maybe you'll have an idea when you aren't trying to. Let's work on something else, then. How does he get caught?"

Patricia had a notion that the camera was driving its subject deeper into himself. After a pause that a party of Japanese tourists filled with laughter he said "He never is."

"Even the greatest can make mistakes," Patricia said, though she felt that was to overrate his character. "Sherlock Holmes caught Professor Moriarty, didn't he?"

"That was just," Dudley said and gulped a mouthful of hock, "that was just a film."

"It was a story first."

"Right, an old story. Some people have got cleverer since then."

"You think a lot of yourself," Tom said.

As Dudley gave him a look that appeared to contain more than simple hostility, Vincent said "There has to be something he's overlooked. That's how real killers are caught."

"He wouldn't. I know. He never would have."

"I'm going to tell you this is fascinating," Walt said. "I've never met a writer who was closer to his creation. But listen, I guess you weren't expecting to be asked to rethink your ideas. We could give you a day, why not a couple of days before the next session. What's easiest for you?"

"I know what Patricia said you were ace at," Vincent said.

"What?" Dudley demanded, and she felt as if he was doing so on her behalf.

"Finding places for killing people."

"He means I said you were good with locations," Patricia felt bound to translate.

"So tell us a few our character can use. Tell us some he's used."

"They won't be any good for filming. I'll need to find some new ones."

Was it possible for an author to be too proprietary about his material? Patricia was wondering if a thought along these lines was behind Tom's grin when he spoke. "Here's someone that knows her way around."

Patricia turned to see Shell tramping over, an inch or two in combat boots above her own five feet tall. She wore a combat outfit as well, complete with a peaked cap tugged low as if to give her permanently flushed face somewhere it could huddle even smaller and observe the world. "Hey, Shell," Walt cried. "This is a surprise."

Shell jerked her knuckly chin up, almost raising the shadow of the cap past her eyes. "I thought we'd got to eat at places with ads in the *Mouth*."

"I guess I said it'd do no harm to support our advertisers. If you're on your own I'm sure you're welcome to join us, am I right?" When Patricia and quite possibly Dudley kept their reservations to themselves, Walt said "This is Shell Garridge, Dudley. She's a comedian and she's writing a column for us."

Dudley gave her half a grin. "If I called someone in a story that, nobody would believe me."

"It's Shell all right. I made the rest up. It's a joke." She watched his grin fail to expand before she said "You're the one that gets your kicks out of killing women."

Patricia wasn't sure how much of the twitching of his face was produced by the flashes of Tom's camera. "Gee, you're as sharp as a razor," Walt said, "but go easy on our competition winner."

"I never voted for him." Shell's stare at Dudley hadn't relented. "If you didn't enjoy thinking about it you wouldn't write it," she said.

"The last I heard we were still allowed to like creating what we create," Vincent said. "Don't you like making up your jokes?"

"I don't make them up, I observe them. How about you, Dud?"

Dudley's lips made such an issue of what he was going to say that Patricia didn't expect it to be "My father used to call me that."

"Wonder what he was thinking?" Shell looked away from him at last to tell a larger female Beatle "I'll have Elvis's Enchiladas and a Jagger's Jigger," and then said "Don't let me stop you geniuses working on your masterpiece."

"So where are we going to kill people?" Vincent said.

"Someone could wake up and she's tied up with something in her mouth on the edge of the roof of, I don't know, where's the highest building? And then she falls."

"She'd wake up a long time before you got her there," Shell said and downed half her Jagger's Jigger, "if she had the sense any woman's got."

"It's kind of close to an old serial, is it?" said Walt. "Not so much if she's not rescued."

"All right, they're laying concrete somewhere and he could tread her face in it, and she wouldn't be able to make a noise. And if she wasn't dead when it got hard she'd be stuck."

"You boys love things getting hard, don't you," Shell said. "What's making you sit like that, Dud? Like tying women up and gagging us?"

As Dudley finished squirming Vincent said "Nobody could shut you up, Shell. Any more ideas, Dudley?"

"He could get into wherever she lives while she's drying her hair. You know how hot those dryers get, and he could tie her up and—"

"Are you maybe forcing it too much, Dudley?" said Walt. "I have to say you aren't convincing me this is how a real killer would think."

"God, that's a look," Shell said. "You want to snap that, Tom."

As Tom photographed the scowl that appeared to have sent Dudley into a crouch, Vincent said "Do you think you need to see things more from your character's viewpoint?"

"There's nobody else's in that story," Shell objected. "If that's a woman's view of anything I've just sprouted a knob."

"Try telling us about him," Walt urged Dudley. "What's his background? What's his tale?"

Patricia wondered if Dudley was in some kind of pain to be huddling so low. "I'll have to think," he muttered.

"What's anybody need to think about?" said Shell. "They're all the same, his kind of thug. There's so many these days they must be breeding."

"How would this work?" Walt said. "Tell Dudley how you see his character and maybe that'll help him figure what he's like."

"Nothing like you think," Dudley said.

"Hey, that sounds like a challenge. Let's hear from you, Shell."

"I told you, he'll be like they all are. Tortured animals when he was a kid. Scared of women. Hasn't got a girlfriend. Likely brought up by a single mum. I'm not dissing them, but she'd have kept telling him how he was better than everyone else, treating him like every time he farted somebody should bottle it and sell it. Only deep down he'll know he's nothing and hate her for not stopping him knowing. That'll be another reason he's got it in for women even more than most men have. So whenever he's feeling more than usually knobless, because I don't reckon he'll have much to play with and anyway he won't be able to get it to salute, he goes creeping after women on their own so he can pretend he's worth knowing about. Most of the time he can't catch them, because women aren't as stupid as him. Just now and then one of them's unlucky, thinks he's so pathetic he has to be harmless. Any chance of another drink without me having to screw anyone?"

As Walt signalled at the empty glass she was brandishing, Vincent ventured to deal with the silence. "I wouldn't mind him not managing to catch someone. We could see it from his point of view."

"He's nothing like that, none of it," Dudley said and scraped his chair backwards.

"Looks like it went home if you're off home," Shell remarked.

"I'm going to the toilet."

Patricia thought it might be time to suggest that Shell finish harassing him, but the buxom Beatle was wheeling dinner to their table. As Dudley emerged from the door marked Roadies next to Groupies, Shell called "What have you been doing to yourself in there? I hope you're just trying to walk like John Wayne."

"I've no choice at the moment," Dudley said through a fixed grin as he sank with some caution onto his chair.

"Everyone's got them. I expect you'd say your character's got none and it's all our fault, the rest of us."

"He's got plenty and he makes them. He loves what he does."

Shell dismissed his vehemence with more laughter than humour. "You haven't told us why you've got no choice."

"I was attacked at work."

"Why, for having a big head?"

"A girl wanted me to find her a sex job."

"Don't tell us you got close enough to catch something."

"I said I was attacked," Dudley protested, wriggling gingerly on the chair. "Just because we aren't allowed to offer table dancing and the rest of it."

Shell chewed a forkful of enchilada while she built up a smirk. "What'd she do, twist your equipment to make you deliver?"

Dudley poked at his ratatouille with his knife, apparently in search of any element that might appeal to him. "She told her mother and she came in as well."

"You never got yourself attacked by two women at once. How much would you pay for that if you had to?" Shell's mouth turned wryer as she enquired "What did you say to make them bend your banana?"

"They kept saying I made out she was a prostitute."

"And you weren't thinking anything like that."

"I may have thought it, but—"

"What gives you the right to think about women that way? No wonder you tell nasty little stories. Women ought to cover themselves up or they're whores and they deserve whatever men dream up to get their own back 'cos they feel threatened, is that what it's about? And women that can see through men as well. Good on the girl and her mother. I hope they made you realise we aren't things you can fantasise about however you like."

"They didn't touch me. They wouldn't have dared," Dudley said, waving his knife. "They had to send her brother. He attacked me in the middle of a crowd of people. I called for help and nobody did anything."

"Pity it wasn't the women instead of just another man putting on his hormones in the street. Funny all the same," Shell spluttered and lifted a song-sheet napkin to wipe her mouth.

Tom contented himself with a grunt that could have expressed amusement. Once the unresponsiveness of the rest of the party had made itself felt, Walt said "I hope you're not in too much pain, Dudley, and I guess I'm speaking for just about everyone. Did you want to bounce off what Shell said before?"

"I've said all I've got to say for now."

"Don't say you're sulking because I told you all about your character," Shell cried. "That's too sad."

"Give the guy a break," Patricia thought Walt could have said rather earlier. "We aren't here to stop him working."

Shell shovelled a large forkful of enchilada into her mouth and helped it down with the last of her second jigger. "Thanks for the nosh, Walt. If I'm not allowed to talk, no point me being here."

"Now who's sulking?" Dudley said.

Shell marched halfway to the door and swung around. "If anyone wants to hear what I've got to say," she announced loud enough to hush the Japanese, "I'll be at the Egremont Ferry on Dud's side of the river on Friday. Hang on, though, it's a girls' night. You'll just have to imagine what I may be saying about you, Dud."

As the door shut behind her, wafting in more of the heat that appeared to be condensing on Dudley's brow, Walt said "Is it easier for you to think now?"

"Not yet," Dudley said and dragged his wrist across his forehead.

"If Shell's got you thinking how to kill someone nobody would blame you," Vincent said. "Use it if you can. It's all material."

"I'll try," Dudley said before risking a forkful of ratatouille that did away with whatever expression might otherwise have gained his face.

"That's it, eat hearty," Walt urged. "Maybe when we're through dining you'll find it's fed your brain."

Patricia saw that Dudley hadn't much time for the notion, or perhaps only for revealing any more of his ideas. At least she needn't blame herself. She shut off the tape recorder in case it was helping to inhibit him, but he seemed committed to clearing his plate. When a flash paled his face, she started as he did. It felt as if the tension Shell had left behind had exploded into lightning. Tom hadn't sneaked a shot; the Japanese were photographing the interior. "Don't worry, nobody's spying on you," she told Dudley, and caught sight of an answering glint in his eyes.

# NINE

As Dudley took another pace up the concrete slipway, it began to rain. Across the river any lights in the warehouses appeared to have been put out by the nine o'clock darkness, while beside them the illuminated Liverpool waterfront glowed with a rainy aura. Beyond the top of the ramp he could see the low roof of the Egremont Ferry, but nobody would see him. Nevertheless when another wave of the rising tide sent him father up the slipway he crouched low as if he'd been seized by his bruised crotch. Before he could straighten up, the downpour that was visible across the river found him.

He hadn't waited for hours below the promenade to be driven away now. At least the rain wasn't as cold as the waves that had taken him unawares just once. In a very few moments it soaked his hair and was streaming down his face as it plastered his shirt and trousers to him. It enraged him, and so did a wave that took advantage of his distraction to slop over his ankle and spill into his shoe. None of this made him show his teeth in an expression he shared with the dark, however. It was the woman's amplified voice that blundered out of the Egremont Ferry. "Here's the treat you've been waiting for, girls. Shell Garridge and her world of wankers."

As all the women he'd heard arriving at the pub began to cheer and clap and stamp, he trudged up the slipway until his eyes were above the edge of the promenade. A cyclist without lights was pedalling desperately towards Seacombe, where there was still a ferry, but otherwise the road overlooked by the town hall and large lit houses on top of grassy slopes was deserted. Across a wide space occupied by benches and a few dripping streetlamps, the windows of the pub reminded him of glass cases in an aquarium. In the case that contained the bar he saw Shell leap to her feet and throw her peaked cap down like a challenge in front of the beer-pumps, exposing a scalp that looked raw and bald through the distortions of water. She wrapped the cord of a microphone around her wrist and began to strut back and forth, putting Dudley in mind of an outsize bath toy bobbing on a string. "Men," she said.

This brought a chorus of derision that sounded by no means entirely humorous. Dudley saw a figure behind the bar throw up his hands and use them to protect his head. No doubt the insecure blob of his face was amusingly defensive too. "No worries, no boos for your booze," Shell told him. "Carry on pulling us pints and you're safe. You won't be pulling anyone tonight, though, so don't go pulling anything else. Which reminds me, girls, I heard about a feller who got pulled in the street this week. A bit more than pulled, more like yanked and tied in a knot, that's if he'd got enough to tie a knot in."

Dudley needn't lurk beneath the promenade as if he had something to be ashamed of. Beyond the ramp an area the size of his bedroom was unlit, and in any case the rain would make him unrecognisable if not invisible from the pub. He stepped boldly onto the promenade, baring wet teeth at the additional downpour, as Shell finished waiting for the hoots of gleeful mirth to subside. "Pity it wasn't us girls that gave him what he was asking for," she said.

Dudley glared at her prancing fluid shape and clenched his fists as he folded his arms, a gesture that seemed to squeeze a juice of rain out of him. "It was on our behalf, though," Shell was saying. "What's he like? He's a civil servant, you know the breed. About as civil as a teenager having a row with her mam about staying out all night, and thinks everyone's his servant, like we ought to touch our forelock and call him sir. Face like a rat sniffing in a bin. Dressed up in a suit and tie so nobody'll notice him skulking off to a sex show to have it off with his fist. Wouldn't you know he works in the jobs office."

The derisive uproar this provoked coincided with an especially sodden gust of rain in Dudley's face. They were only jeering at his job, he thought, and it mightn't be his much longer. He shook water off his face and blinked it out of his eyes, and was close to laughing aloud at how little Shell knew about him when she said "They think we're a lower species 'cos we've got to crawl to them for jobs, don't they? Here's the worst. One girl went to him and when she'd finished telling him all the stuff they make us tell them so they can look at us like we shouldn't have bothered getting out of bed, he treated her like she was a whore."

The pub erupted with hissing louder than the storm. The women were behaving as if they'd seen a villain. Dudley grinned until his mouth dripped, because they couldn't see him. "I'm not saying I approve of the job she went for, like," Shell said, "but it's her choice how to use her body, right? The joke is it's men like him that see women's pay is so crap they're better off selling themselves, and men like him that pay for them, and now it's men like him are trying to make them ashamed of doing it as well. We all know why, don't we? He's scared of real women in case they mess up his fantasies about us. That's the kind of joke that doesn't make me laugh."

"Tell us about what happened to him," a woman's hoarse shout urged.

"Seems her brother caught up with this dud in the street. Maybe he thought if the feller was going to think up sexy stuff about her it should hurt him to. The way I heard it, he twisted his tap till it needed a plumber. What's funnier, the street was full of people and none of them did anything when the dud started squealing for help. Must have known he deserved it, or they thought he was busking. He'd have sounded like a lot of different singers. Here's a what do you call them classical thingies, an alto. Here's the soppy one, a soprano. Here's a choirboy. Here's a eunuch."

As Shell demonstrated by shrieking increasingly high, the ache from which the rain had distracted him renewed its attack on Dudley's groin. "I told him I was here tonight," Shell was saying. "He wouldn't have got in, but he might have hung around outside to listen, only it's pissing down so much that would have chased him off. He'll be making up stories about shutting up women by doing them in."

He didn't move as she pressed her face against the glass. He liked the way the rain on the window made her face look as if bits were being torn off to wriggle for his entertainment. "Here's a bunch of women nobody's going to shut up," she thundered as she turned her back on him. "Women, we're the real wild bunch, and men had better know it. Haul on your pump, lad, if you don't want me ending up with no voice."

Dudley wished she had. He was more aware of the relentless downpour than of anything else she said. Male drivers raging on the roads, single fathers making fools of themselves by trying to raise daughters, solitary men embarrassed by washing their clothes in front of women in the laundrette: none of this involved him. She imagined she had dealt with him; she thought she'd turned him into a joke. He cupped his hands around his ache and kept crouching over it as though the rain was beating him down, when in fact he was adding every gibe she made about men to his fury, a hard cold lump at the centre of him. Even her abandoning the subject of him, and his having to sweep rain out of his ears in case she revived it, enraged him. What right did she and her cronies have to cast him out in the storm? What kind of man would cower behind the bar and reduce himself to acting as their accomplice? Dudley couldn't tell if his eyes were blurred by pain or rage or water by the time she said "Well, girls, are we done with the wankers for another week?"

As the cheers and stamping trailed off she released her wrist from the microphone cord and vanished into the depths of the tank that was the window. Almost at once the doorway to its left illuminated slanting parallels of rain. Neither of the women who ducked as they ran to a car was Shell. The headlamp beams swung towards Dudley but failed to locate him before the car crawled up-hill to the main road. Nobody he didn't want to see him would.

For too soddenly long after that, however, nobody else emerged—just a hubbub that showed no sign of abating. It didn't falter even when the barman hung a towel over the pumps. The gesture reminded Dudley that judges used to don a cap in the days when they were allowed to pronounce a death sentence. Very eventually it began to drive the women forth, and he liked the notion that each of them was bowing her head in deference to him, although they were unaware how close he was to them. He hoped Shell was waiting for the last of them to leave; he could imagine her ensuring that she had the final word. The pub sounded empty now, and all at once he was afraid he'd overlooked her leaving in the midst of a clump of her admirers. The door opened again, and two women he had never previously seen dashed out, screeching at the rain. Both their noise and their uselessness to him knotted his rage tighter and harder, and he almost missed seeing the door reopen before it had quite shut. "Anybody want a lift?" Shell called.

Dudley's mouth gaped in a silent protest that let rain gather on his tongue. As he swallowed so as not to cough, one woman shouted "We're only round the corner, thanks."

Dudley watched them sprint uphill as Shell ran to the farthest car beside the streetlamps. The moment they disappeared around a corner, he followed her beyond the light of the lamps. She was poking at the door of the Viva with a key when he enquired from some yards away "Have I missed it? Is that Shell?"

As she twisted her head towards him she used her free hand to yank the peak of her cap down, perhaps to fend off the rain. "You're joking. You're not, it's Dud. I've been talking about you. I said I would."

"What were you saying?" he asked with his face in the dark.

"What do you reckon? How you're the hottest thing around."

Was the second part a question or a joke? She mumbled it as she shut herself in the car. Could she have said it to her audience once she'd given up the microphone? After all, it was no less than he deserved. He was making to enquire when she lowered the window an inch. "So what are you hanging round here for?" she hardly seemed interested in learning.

"I wanted to hear what you said."

"I told you it was just for girls." She aimed the peak of her cap at his streaming forehead while she peered through the slit at his face. "Don't say you've been out here in this all the time I've been on."

"I couldn't find you in time. I had to walk from home," he needed her to believe. "There's no bus from me to here."

Shell turned the key in the ignition, and the engine emitted a splutter that sounded like mirth. "Well, it doesn't look like you can get any wetter. Maybe your mam will give you a rub with a towel when you get home. What are you waiting for?"

"You were asking if anyone wanted a lift. Don't you want the hottest thing around in your car?"

For some moments she stared up at him, and he hid his eyes by clearing them of rain with a thumb and forefinger. "Christ, you're so pathetic," she said. "I'm going to the tunnel. If that way's any use to you, get in."

As he opened the front passenger door he imagined the tunnel that led under the river to Liverpool, a long deserted passage with protracted stretches of lonely darkness between a very few lights. It was nothing like that and no use to him. He was lowering his renewed ache on the seat next to Shell when she cried "Jesus, don't just sit like that. Put something over the seat. There's some plastic in the back from when they fixed the car."

No doubt she didn't want the upholstery soaked, but she was treating him as if he was diseased. Before he'd finished dragging the plastic sheet between the seats to drape it over his, his back felt naked to the rain. At last he was able to slam the door with a fierceness that earned a scowl from Shell. He risked leaning back, only to recoil from feeling his shirt squelch. He was about to hope aloud that there was nothing wrong with the car, which hadn't moved, when Shell leaned forward to glower through the windscreen. "Here's something else men have done to the world, this weather. I wanted to drive along the prom for a bit to see the lights over the water."

"You can't drive along the promenade. Look, the sign says."

Shell turned her head as if it was hardly worth the effort to observe him. "God, and you want people to think you know about criminals," she said. "I could introduce you to a few but you'd run away crapping your pants. You're nothing but an office worker that's scared of breaking any rules."

Dudley let her see his eyes and teeth glint in the dark. "I was trying to warn you. You wouldn't want to drive along there alone with me."

"You what?" Shell almost choked with mirth or pretended she did. "Are you trying to be like that pathetic sod in your story?"

"He isn't pathetic at all. You're too fond of calling people that."

"Only them that are. Am I supposed to be scared?"

"You aren't doing what I said you shouldn't, anyway." When this failed to provoke her he said "I expect it was a man who put the sign up."

"You won't be sure of that much longer. We're taking over everywhere."

"You're doing what men say you have to now, though. You know we know best really. Women just need to do as they're told."

When she glared at him he was afraid that he'd miscalculated and angered her so much that she would order him out of the car. The staff of the pub might be able to hear whatever happened. As he struggled not to take back anything he'd said, she faced the windscreen. "Watch this," she invited, and sent the car screeching past the lamps towards the pub.

The headlamp beams lit on the empty street that climbed to the main road, and then they swerved to find the promenade that led all the way to the mouth of the river. She jerked them high to show that the promenade was deserted except for swaying sheets of rain, and sped the car past the No Entry sign as if she was entering a race. "Scary enough for you yet, Dud?" she said.

He took time to laugh before saying "About as much as a little girl having a tantrum."

She rammed the accelerator down and gave him a tight smile that widened in triumph. "You're sweating cobs."

He finished wiping his forehead and showed her the back of his hand. "That's rain. Can't you tell the difference? You're no more scary than any other woman driver."

"Aren't I?" she cried with a vehemence that left reason behind. "Try this."

It was happening, he thought—in fact, she was improving on his plan. As the car swerved down the nearest slipway he saw how high the tide had mounted. It must have thrown Shell too, because she tramped on the brake so hard that the wheels on his side of the car skidded almost to the edge of the concrete. The vehicle shuddered to a halt halfway down the ramp. "How's that then, Mr Frightening Writer?" Shell demanded. "Will that do you?"

A wave caught the headlamp beams before flattening itself under the car, and Dudley thought he felt it tug at the front wheels. "You want to back up now while you can," he said.

He was just in time to turn her against putting the car in reverse. "Come ahead, tell me why I shouldn't," she said, hardly bothering to scoff.

"You might be too scared to work it. You don't want to be alone down here with me where nobody can see us."

Her hand darted from the gear lever to the handbrake, on which she hauled with all her strength, adding her right hand to drag it another ratchet higher. "Now you've got what you've been drooling for. Let's find out who scares who."

"You can't scare me. You don't even make me laugh."

"Half of that back at you, Dud."

He stared into her face, which looked squashed into hiding by the cap she had yanked lower. "That doesn't mean anything to me," he said as rain clattered the windscreen wipers against the glass.

"You're never going to scare me. You're even more pathetic when you try. You're a joke, a crap one. You make me laugh 'cos that's all I can do with creeps like you."

He let her wonder what was in his eyes before he spoke. "You've never met anyone like me."

"Christ, is that what your mam tells you? Maybe she thinks it and maybe she doesn't, but it won't fool the rest of us."

"Don't you talk about my mother. She doesn't know all about me." That was far too defensive, and so he added "She'd be scared if she did."

"You've only got one line, have you, Dud? Do you try it on all the girls? No wonder you're on your own. It won't work with me either."

The corners of his mouth began to creep up. "But it does," he said.

"I've got to hear this. You're an act all by yourself, you are. I could get you booked along with me if they mightn't think you're funnier than I am. Are you sure the girls you try it on don't? Go on then, what do they do?"

"Some of them scream. Some of them can't."

Her lips twitched in disgust, putting him in mind of worms turned up from beneath the rock that was her cap. "Jesus, you're really trying to convince yourself of all your garbage. Maybe you even have. You want to see somebody."

"I'm seeing you."

"Not for much longer," Shell said, reaching for the handbrake.

"You're scared at last, then. You're scared to hear about them."

"No, I'm bored of hearing you come out with so much bollocks." Nevertheless she twisted her body, so far as he could distinguish it within its camouflage, towards him as though to issue an additional challenge. "You won't give up till you've told me a bedtime story, will you? Let's see if you can even do that. Your mam sent in the story, maybe she wrote it as well."

That almost goaded him to waste time denying it. "You should have known where it came from. I thought you were supposed to be from Liverpool."

"I'm Scouse and proud of it. I reckon you're the kind that's a Merseysider when it suits them, and I've no idea what you're on about."

"Try and think back. Didn't you ever hear about a girl that fell under a train at Moorfields?"

"That's just that crap story of yours again," Shell said, and then she blinked hardness into her eyes. "Stick around, though. Didn't something like that really happen now you mention it?"

"Angela, her name was. I forget her last one. It was in the paper. On the radio as well." Dudley's thighs had begun to shiver with the rain that encased them. "I called her Greta in my story," he said. "Close but not too close."

Shell thrust a hand into her trousers and snatched out a mobile phone. "Who are you calling?" Dudley said at once.

"You'll find out," Shell assured him, then glowered at the unilluminated phone before shoving it back in her pocket. "Out of action when you need it, just like a man. You're lucky, but you won't be for long. I'll be telling Walt tomorrow."

"What do you think you'll be telling him?"

"Oh, was that supposed to be the bit where the killer owns up because his victim's helpless? Not this girl." Shell left mockery behind to say "I'll be telling him you turned some poor girl's accident into your little piece of porn. I don't think he'll want it any more. Maybe I'll give your mam a ring as well to let her know how sick you really are. What are you laughing at? I'm not joking."

"You mean you don't think you are. You don't realise what you're missing."

"Jesus, are you still in love with yourself? There's nothing to miss because you've got nothing to offer."

"I've got the truth." He hoped his pause robbed her of breath before he said "The real girl didn't just fall either."

For at least a second Shell appeared to be struck dumb, and then she turned away from him. "Why don't you try telling everyone that when we launch the magazine," she said, "except you won't be in it if I am. That's what I'll be saying to Walt. That's a promise."

Dudley's thighs were beginning to annoy him as much as she did. Perhaps he'd talked too much; certainly she had. He didn't bother speaking as he seized the handbrake and used both thumbs to push the button in while he leaned all his weight on the lever. It fell flat like an animal cowering from a blow, and the car rolled down the slope at a speed he was happy to think of as eager. As Shell stamped on the brake pedal a wave drowned the headlamps and flooded across the bonnet, clogging the windscreen wipers with seaweed. "How mad are you?" Shell cried. "Want to kill us both?"

"Not both."

She threw him a look of more contempt than there were words for as she grabbed the gear lever to throw the car into reverse. "You're just a nasty little boy, aren't you. You don't know when to stop playing, but you're going to frigging learn."

Her voice was rising past a snarl. Before she could let out the clutch and accelerate, Dudley had used both hands to drag the handbrake as high as it would strain. "I told you," she said so fiercely that he felt her saliva on his cheek. "Let fucking go."

He managed to grin and to keep both hands on the lever while he reassured himself that the rain still trickling down his cheek would wash away her filthy spit. "No competition, is it?" he couldn't resist declaring as the engine produced a frustrated screech that shook the car. "I'm a man and you're just a machine."

Without easing up on the pedals Shell reached in a pocket. She had barely produced the item when he snatched it from her with his left hand. It was a spray she would have liked to use to blind him. Still hauling on the brake, he lowered the window and shied the weapon into the river, where it sank with an unimpressive plop. "Anything else?" he said, and remembered what he hadn't told her yet. "I was outside all the time. I heard everything you said about me."

At last she seemed fully convinced of his seriousness. "You really are that mad," she said flatly, and dug her nails into the back of his uppermost hand on the brake.

"Scratch away. That won't stop me."

By the time he'd finished saying this, his grin was gritting his teeth. A gust of rain drenched him through the window he'd had no time to shut. When Shell made to claw his face he raised a fist raw with pain to ward her off. "Go on, knock me about," she cried over the juddering shriek of the engine. "I've had some of that in my life."

"Then you should be glad it's nearly over."

All at once the engine fell silent, and Shell cocked her head at him. "That's all the fun I'm being," she said, reaching for her door. "I was going to scrap this old heap anyway. Christ, though, I'm looking forward to you trying to explain this."

She released her seat belt and clutched at the handle to open the door. It had swung less than a foot when a wave closed it again, which delighted him so much that he almost couldn't move. Shell nudged the door wide with her shoulder and glanced back at him, just as he lurched across her for the handle. He flung her at the door as he hauled it shut. He thought—he very much hoped—that he glimpsed realisation in her eyes as the window and the corner of her forehead met with a satisfying crack.

She could only be stunned, but that was enough. As she wobbled and fell towards the door, perhaps to fend it off, he was able to slam the window against her forehead, and again, and once more for luck. At the second impact she made a blurred sound as if she was fighting to awaken from a dream, but after that she was silent. "I'm your nightmare," he told her, although his was that the glass would shatter from the hardness of her skull before he could be sure she was unconscious. When he let go of the handle she lolled half off the seat into a wave that spilled into her side of the car. He crouched above his own seat and his aching groin to retrieve the plastic sheet from behind him. As he used it to wipe his fingerprints from her door handle, a wave made her nuzzle the back of his hand. He was reminded of a beaten dog trying to placate its master. "Good bitch," he muttered to rid himself of his disgust, "down now," and almost forgot to plant her slack fingers on the handle so that her prints would still be there. He wiped his own from the handbrake and closed her other hand around it, then let her fingers slump in the water on the floor. He had to erase his prints from the passenger door in case anyone bothered examining it. He shut the window next to him and removed his prints, and grasped the handle through the plastic sheet to release himself as the driver's door heaved Shell at him. He elbowed her away until the wave subsided, and planted a fist alongside the handle to help shove his door wide. He lowered his foot onto the concrete just in time to meet a surge of water that filled both his shoe and his sock. That wasn't why he gasped "Useless bitch." Her wretched driving had left him virtually no room to stand on the ramp beside the car.

He leaned into the car to grip the steering wheel with both hands through the plastic and wrenched it as far right as it would turn. "Thought I couldn't drive, did you?" he asked the slumped figure. "Wrong as usual. There's nothing I can't do that's worth doing." All the same, he had to perch beside the vehicle while the waves did their best to overbalance him into the river. He braced his legs apart, though that spiked his crotch with pain, and ducked to release the handbrake. He had to grip it two-handed and bruise a thumb on the button in order to move the lever. The moment it lay flat he straightened up, scraping the back of his head on the doorframe. He slammed the door, still keeping hold of the plastic sheet as a wave glued its hem to his ankles, and prepared to stand firm whatever the car might do. He wasn't expecting it not to budge an inch.

He'd assumed the waves would drag it down the ramp. Instead they seemed to be anchoring it in place. He blinked to clear his eyes of the latest bout of rain as he sidled upwards to give the stubborn vehicle a push. He was resting his hands above the rear passenger door when he felt the car shift. It rolled forward, taking his balance with it, and the rear wheel caught the toe of his shoe. He could topple off the ramp or be dragged after the car—and then he snatched his foot back. He wasn't meant to end up in the river, only Shell was. The thought gave him back his control, and he dealt the metal roof a shove that brought him upright as it sent the car down the ramp. In seconds a wave crashed over the roof and carried the vehicle into the river.

He stood at the top of the ramp to watch. For a moment he thought Shell's body was adrift inside the car, but it was her cap that blundered against the rear window. It ranged back and forth like a bloated dead fish in the few moments before the car sank under the black water. The heaving of the waves seemed to render his excitement visible, though that was growing as calm as the depths. When the tide reached his feet again he turned homewards.

The buses had stopped running. He had at least an hour's walk ahead. The rain was as implacable as ever, and stung the scratches on the back of his hand. All the same, he welcomed it. The very few people he encountered in the drenched streets looked almost as wet as he was, and in no mood to make comparisons. He had to remember not to let them see him grin too much. It wasn't just that he had a new secret none of them was worthy to learn, any more than Shell had been until it was too late. The best part of the night's work was that she'd helped him. His session with Vincent had left him feeling unsure of himself, but it needn't have. Shell had proved that he hadn't run out of ideas.

TEN    Patricia was helping herself to coffee from the percolator when her father said "Why, you could have been catching up on your beauty sleep, Trish. We don't all have to get up for work on Saturdays."

"I'd like to see you cooking your own meals if we didn't, Gordon," said her mother. "And don't you think she's beautiful enough?"

He dealt his narrow forehead a glancing slap as if to disarray its parallel ruled lines and wrinkled his small mouth, drawing the halves of his neat moustache together. Next he raised his equally black eyebrows high, economising on the space between the lines under his receding hair while his large blue eyes displayed their honesty, and only his broad blunt nose didn't join in the activity. "Trish knows I do," he said to Patricia.

"No need for that, dad. You know that isn't how I grade myself."

"You'd get honours if you did. You ladies or is it women now must forgive me for waking up feeling old-fashioned. I blame all this misbehaviour of our computers at the bank."

"So long as you don't go away thinking dinner is all we'll be up to," Valerie said. "How are you getting on with Dudley Smith, Trish?"

"Is this someone I should know about?"

"There's nobody like that," Patricia said as she spooned scrambled egg from the russet Cretan platter onto her plate. "Just plenty of friends."

"Wasn't one chap at university rather more than that?"

"Gordon, I hope you show more tact when people come to you for advice."

"It's all right, mummy, I'm perfectly over it now. He wanted to be more, in fact he insisted till I had to turn very nasty with him, and I don't care to risk that kind of unpleasantness again."

"Good God, if you mean what I think . . ."

"I nearly do, daddy, but as I say, it's dealt with. I left enough of an impression that I don't think he'll try it with anyone else. Now if you two don't mind, and don't look so worried, mummy, it isn't something I ever meant to discuss."

To ensure that was the end of it she gazed past her parents and out of the floor-length windows of the dining-room. Beyond the trim privet that boxed in the long garden sparkling with sunlight and last night's rain, an early golfer in a buggy chugged to the top of a knoll and trundled down the far side with all the leisure of a pensioner. Patricia was enjoying the resemblance to a wind-up toy when Valerie said with determined neutrality "Dudley Smith is the young thriller writer, Gordon. You've heard us mention him. Trish has to turn in her copy by Monday for the printer."

"I think I've covered nearly everything we need. Except I tracked down where his old English teacher works, but he was off sick till next week."

"We're supposed to be introducing Dudley Smith to our readers. I wouldn't like to include things he doesn't want us to," Valerie said as the phone rang in the hall.

"Speak of the devil, do you think? Maybe he wants to get together with Trish," Gordon said, throwing Patricia a more than apologetic smile that instantly reversed itself in case it needed to and vanished. A few lanky strides took him down the hall. "Martingale," he said, and then "Well, good morning. Which of the creative partnership would you like to speak to? The senior first. She's on her way."

Patricia watched a golf ball dwindle to a speck of chalk in the bright air towards the sea until her father rejoined her. "That's me proved wrong, then. You journos have to be up and about at least as early as an old bank manager," he said, and looked ready to revive his earlier concern when Valerie called "Trish."

Patricia hurried down the wide pale hall that was decorated with flowers she'd collected on childhood picnics and pressed under glass. She couldn't tell how much of Valerie's troubled expression related to the phone call. "It's Walt," Valerie said.

"Walt," Patricia said as her mother left her alone with him. "Patricia."

"Hey." After a pause she could have done without he said "I'm sorry to have to tell you we've lost Shell Garridge."

"You mean we'll have that space to fill."

"Not lost that way. She was killed last night or early this morning."

"Oh gosh." Patricia was shocked but tried to sound upset as well. "How?"

"They aren't saying much on your local news station yet. A guy walking his dog found her in her car on the beach. All I can get from the police so far is she must have driven into the river somehow. I guess we did see how she liked to drink."

"That's awful. What a waste." Patricia lingered over a silence she hoped would imply sadness before she said "So you want me to . . ."

"How soon do you think you can deliver a tribute to her?"

Patricia felt a little guilty for not having anticipated the request, but disconcerted by it too. "How long?" she said.

"Much more than two thousand words could be a problem."

"Would less?"

"I should think you might have trouble keeping it that short. That'll give us four pages with some photos and subheads. The printer needs it first thing Monday morning. You can email it direct, right? Valerie can edit it before you send it if she has to, and you could let me have a preview too."

Patricia might have admitted that she didn't know much about Shell, but that would reflect on her mother's choice of a journalist. "Get all the quotes you can from people who knew her," Walt was saying. "Maybe you can find a tape of her to listen to. Okay, don't let me keep you from it, but before you pass me back to Valerie—"

"Phone, mum," Patricia called and felt absurdly as though she was appealing for help.

"Before you do, has your Dudley Smith piece gone to the printer yet?"

"I was going to give it a bit of a polish this morning."

"So long as it gets there first thing Monday also. Now I'd better speak to Valerie."

"What will we have to drop?" Valerie asked him, then told Patricia "We'll have four extra pages, I see, of course" as if it solved more than that problem.

Patricia made for the comfortably uncluttered discreetly antique dining-room, only to find her father awaiting her with a murmur. "Are you quite certain this swine you mentioned has been sufficiently dealt with?"

"More than quite, daddy. It really wasn't as bad as I expect you're imagining, and it wasn't entirely his fault. I could have been more definite sooner."

"Just remind me of his name again."

"It was Simon, wasn't it, Trish?" Valerie said on her way into the room. "As in pure, I don't think."

"This is why I never talked about it." They were making her feel that just because she was smaller than average she couldn't look after herself—the mistake Simon had made, she suspected. "I didn't want you two upset when there's completely no need," she said.

"You shouldn't keep bad things inside you," Valerie insisted. "That isn't how a writer deals with them. I knew there was something wrong when there was. I asked, if you remember."

"I'd better make a start," Patricia said, feeding herself a last mouthful of breakfast before carrying her items to the kitchen sink. In her bedroom she straightened the quilt that was printed with a night sky and transferred the Margaret Atwood novel she'd finished last night from the floor to the bookshelves in the corner flanked by pages of the student newspaper bearing her byline. By this time the computer had produced its opening screen. An online search brought her several references to Shell, starting with her web site. She clicked on the address, and Shell's face commenced spreading down the screen.

It appeared beneath a banner that proclaimed **SHELL GAR-RIDGE STANDUP** in red. It came in strips, beginning with one that contained her eyes, which offered less a welcome than a challenge. Her small blunt nose had little to add to that, but as it was produced Patricia had an unnecessary impression of watching grey water drain away to reveal Shell's head. Now here was the mouth, its right corner awry on the way to a grin or a smile, what sort wasn't clear. Shell's image stopped at the chin to leave room for a banner reading **DO I MAKE YOU LAUGH?** Patricia thought that could as easily be taken for a dare as for an invitation. The page contained nothing else apart from Shell's email address and phone number. Other pages were promised—press quotes, photographs, Shell interviewing herself, links to sites for people she admired—but they were still under construction. "You're another one who isn't giving much away," Patricia murmured, having thought of Dudley Smith, but he had no relevance to Shell. She fetched her mobile from the bedside table and dialled the number on the screen. At least she would have followed the solitary lead, if it was one, that the page provided.

The phone rang five times, and then she seemed to hear someone pick it up. "Shell Garridge," Shell said. "If you're not a stalker there's nothing to be scared of. Say who you are and what you want and where I can call you back."

Patricia had hoped the message might be humorous. The reference to a stalker suggested paranoia, which would scarcely fit into a tribute. She was wondering if she ought to leave a token response in case anyone played the tape when a not entirely steady voice said "Hello?"

It could have been Shell's or an attempt to mimic hers. Patricia had to overcome both notions so as to say "Hello."

"Who's that? What do you want?"

"I'm a reporter. Patricia Martingale. Could I ask who you are?"

"One of them, are you. I expect they'll be all over her now." Almost as bitterly the woman added "I'm her mother."

"I'm sorry, Mrs . . ."

"Don't you even know that? Garrett," Shell's mother said with either pride or resentment.

"I'm very sorry for your loss. I worked with Shell for a little while."

"You don't sound like anyone she'd know. Worked on what, like?"

"The *Mersey Mouth*. The new magazine. She was writing a column for us."

"She told me. She used to say you named the magazine after her."

"Did she?" Patricia tried to sound amused but not too much. "I'll put that in. We're publishing a tribute to her."

"What else are you going to be putting?"

"I'm just starting my research. I only heard about the tragedy a few minutes ago. Please don't talk if you'd rather not, but is there anything you think I should include?"

"I can talk. I'm not surprised she went the way she did. It'd have been the drink one way or another if she didn't get herself done in by some man to shut her up. I reckon you won't be writing that, though."

"Perhaps not," Patricia admitted.

"Don't you lot like the truth? Shouldn't have had her working for you, then. You won't want to hear why she was like she was neither."

"I'm certain I would, Mrs Garrett, if you don't mind telling me."

"Being made to have a man when she didn't think she could say no."

"I wish I'd known that. We could have talked."

"You've had some as well, have you?"

"Not as bad, but I'd certainly have been sympathetic."

"Not as bad is right, I reckon. She was twelve and he was her dad."

"Gosh, I'm sorry," Patricia said and realised she already had been twice. "That's dreadful. What became of him? Did Shell—"

"She only told me after he was dead. Got in a fight when he was drunk and six of them stamped on his head."

"Well, I suppose that's . . ." Patricia had no idea what she was entitled to say, and felt she had presumed too much. "Do many people know about him and Shell?"

"She used to say stuff about it in her act sometimes when she was feeling down. She never said it was her."

"Are there any recordings of her act, do you know?"

"I've got none. Not heard of any either." Mrs Garrett stayed discontented as she said "You'd rather have them than what I told you. Thought as much."

"Ideally I'd like to use both and anything else you think I should know."

"That was her secret, the only one she had. If it's not enough for you, no use asking me."

"I assure you I wasn't implying—"

"Never mind the fancy language. You're just doing your job and I'm being a sour old bitch. Let me listen to the news now. See if any of her friends have something good to say about my Shell."

"I'm sure I will have," Patricia felt bound to undertake, but before she finished, nobody else was listening. She left the computer screen saving itself to the sound of waves and ran down to the kitchen, where Valerie was chopping garlic not quite in time with a Mozart march. "Shall we find out if Merseyside is saying anything about her?" Patricia suggested.

At first it seemed there might be no room for Shell among the robberies and police raids, but then the newsreader announced that "tributes have been pouring in to Shell Garridge, the controversial stand-up comic who died earlier today." "She was one of a kind. She did comedy like nobody else," said Sharika Kapoor, and Tulip Bandela described her as the most fearless comedian she'd ever worked with—"she wasn't afraid not to be funny." As for Ken Dodd, he said "She'd have gone far. She'd have got Liverpool even more of a reputation."

"I was just speaking to her mother," Patricia said. "She was raped by her father when she was twelve."

Valerie turned the radio down as the newsreader forecast even hotter weather. "If we've got anyone who can give that some insight it's you."

"I know you believe in me, but honestly you don't need—"

"Believe in yourself, Trish. That's a lot more important." Valerie watched her as far as the door and said "Perhaps writing about her will let you feel things you haven't wanted to admit you're feeling."

Rather than wonder aloud how that would help her meet the deadline, Patricia retreated upstairs. The computer screen had turned as blank as her mind; only the watery sound reassured her the system hadn't crashed. She revived the image and backtracked to her search for Shell to call up the next reference, the Scouselebrities site.

It was considerably more informative than Shell's. Michelle Garrett had been born in 1978 in Toxteth. She'd first made a name for herself at Paddington Comprehensive, where she had edited and mostly written a single issue of an alternative school magazine called *Tamp,* and was proud how many parents and male pupils had complained to the headmaster. In 1997 she and her fellow polytechnic students Tulip Bandela and Sharika Kapoor had formed Cuntry Folk, a feminist song and comedy trio. In 1999, when her colleagues insisted on renaming the group Sisterhood of Wit, she had changed her name to Shell Garridge and left for a solo career. She'd played Debbie the Docker in the pilot episode of an unshown television series, *Don't Call Us Ladies,* and Buttonless in a Christmas musical, *Panto without Pants.*

Dudley Smith could have talked to Shell about causing controversy at school, Patricia thought. Perhaps finding common ground would have helped them overcome their differences. She felt as if Dudley was loitering in her head. She moved him on by scrolling up to Tulip Bandela's entry, and was starting to email her when her mobile rang.

"Is that the reporter? I forget your name."

"Patricia Martingale. It is."

"Mary Garrett," Shell's mother said. "I got your number off the phone. I was short with you before."

"Please don't worry about it, Mrs Garrett. Anyone would understand why you were. If that's all you're ringing about—"

"It's not. You got me thinking and I rang the pub where Shell was last night. Just spoke to them."

Patricia felt eager without knowing why. "Yes?"

"I've got you something." Perhaps she wasn't hesitating for effect, but that was how it seemed to Patricia. "I'll tell you what I reckon you should do with it," Mrs Garrett said.

ELEVEN "Why are you looking like that, Dudley? Have you been killing off somebody else?"

At first all he could see was the light that was shining into his eyes. He knew Vera by her voice but couldn't tell how many of the crowd had halted to watch him. Then the edge of the roof of a block of shops took the sun out of his eyes, and he saw her outside the locked door of the job centre a coffin's length away. Nobody but she appeared to be concerned with him. "What do you mean?" he demanded just loud enough for it to reach her.

Her thin wrinkled face put on a smile that flirted with apology. "Trust a woman to see you've been up to something at the weekend. You haven't found yourself a girlfriend, have you?"

Amusement tugged at his lips, and he saw no reason not to let it. "You're right, I was out with a girl."

"Were you really? You're not just making up one of your stories."

He didn't understand her disappointment, which seemed insultingly close to disbelief, until he noticed that Colette was joining them. "That's not the kind I write," he said.

"We hope it will be, don't we, Colette? We'd like to see our Dudley write a nice romantic sloppy smoochy love story."

"Don't listen to them." Trevor had arrived too and was rubbing his hairline as if to polish it brighter or drive it even further back on his skull. "You write whatever you need to write if it gets you a better job," he said.

Colette shook her face clear of her long black hair. "I didn't say he shouldn't."

"And this old busybody didn't either." Having vainly waited for someone to contradict her description of herself, Vera said "We don't want to change you, Dudley. All I was saying to begin with was you looked pleased with yourself."

He had reason enough, not least that none of them could suspect why. He was happily aware of the poster on a newspaper seller's stand: **LOCAL COMEDIAN DEAD IN RIVER**. Several of his fellow commuters had been reading the paper on the train, so that he was able to observe that she was said to have been drinking before her accident. No doubt her condition had not only made her take the wrong route in the storm but also rendered her incapable of escaping from the vehicle before the waves had caused the door to knock her unconscious. Dudley was grinning at all this, since Vera had given him an excuse, when she said "I hope you'll be bringing in your story for us all to read."

"Everyone can see it when it's published."

"Aren't even your friends going to get a free look?"

"Don't be doing him out of his royalties," said Trevor.

Dudley managed not to admit that he wasn't expecting any. Until that moment it hadn't occurred to him that his mother had rushed him past this detail of the contract too. He was struggling to conceal his rage when Colette said "I'll buy it if you tell me what to buy."

"There you are, Dudley," Vera said. "Now say she isn't your friend."

"I never have," he retorted as he turned entirely to Colette. "It's out this week. The *Mersey Mouth*."

"Isn't that—"

Had she recognised someone behind him? He swung fiercely around to discover that the interruption was Mrs Wimbourne. "Haven't you dealt with that yet?" she said with the start of a frown.

His movement had roused the ache in his crotch. "What?" he mumbled through his teeth.

"Please do not grimace at me." Not until his lips were entirely shut did she add "You were meant to be contacting your publishers."

Did she intend to embarrass him in front of his colleagues? He was trying desperately to think how to silence her when he realised they would witness how unreasonable she was being. "What was I supposed to say again?"

"I'm quite certain you know." Presumably her pause was designed to force him to confess. "You had to tell them they may need to get along without you," she eventually said.

"That's a bit mean, isn't it?" Trevor protested.

"I wasn't opening a debate, Trevor. Nobody's one hundred per cent safe in their jobs these days, not even me. If I were you I wouldn't do anything that could make it less secure."

It wasn't clear to Dudley how much of this was aimed at him. As she produced keys from her grey metallic bag and unlocked the door Trevor mouthed "A bit mean" behind her back. He attempted to bow her in after Vera and Colette, but she flapped her fingers to urge him through the doorway. He was heading past the rows of bucket chairs when she said "We haven't heard your answer yet, Dudley."

"I thought you had to get in touch with someone."

"I shall be today. He was on holiday last week." She shut the door with a vigour that jangled the window, then snapped the bag shut, apparently as aids to sharpening her voice. "Are you telling me you've made no attempt to inform these people how things stand?"

"There's no point. I've sold them my story. I can't stop them bringing it out."

"Dear me, are you really so helpless?" Before he could warn her that he was anything but, she said "I'm surprised you want to give that impression to Colette."

"I don't want to give her anything."

Vera sent him a quick reproachful pout over the booths as Colette retreated fast into the staffroom. "Just keep your mind on what you're being told," Mrs Wimbourne said. "I'm sure whoever you have to deal with will listen to reason if you say it's jeopardising your job."

"You don't know if it will be yet. I don't believe it can."

"Shall I tell you what certainly can? An attitude like that."

He felt as if she was determined to rob him of all his achievements—and then he saw how he might transfer some of the powerlessness she was trying to impose on him. "Will you take the responsibility, then?" he said.

"I rather think that ought to be yours. For what, may I ask?"

"All the money they'll want. They've printed my story. It'll cost them a lot to take it out now."

"You aren't saying they'd propose to claim it back from you."

"It's in the contract if I stop them publishing my story." Since the lie seemed to be reaching her, he added to it. "I'd have to pay them back a lot more than they're paying me."

"It sounds as if you ought to have taken some advice before you signed anything. How much have you received?"

"It isn't till I'm published," Dudley said, reverting to the truth. "Five hundred."

"That's the competition prize, I take it." She wasn't nearly as impressed as he would have expected anyone who heard to be. "And how much so far for the film you say they're proposing to make?"

"Nothing till it's made. One per cent of all the profits."

"I should think I know as little about such matters as you do, but I wouldn't be surprised if they're taking advantage of your inexperience."

Dudley felt as if the heat was massing inside his skin. He had to hold his rage in like an aching breath until he knew how her presumption would make her act towards him. He released it silently as she said with visible displeasure "Let me explain the bind you've got yourself into and hope the powers that be will see it your way. Now you'd better be getting ready for work."

She waited for him to raise the flap in the counter for her. As she waddled into the Ladies' Vera emerged, followed by Colette. "You weren't being very nice before, were you?" Vera murmured at him. "Watch out you don't get scratched again."

"What do you mean, again?" he objected, though he knew.

"We can see he's been in a bit of a fight since the last time we saw him, can't we, Colette?" Vera said, only to have to indicate the scratches on the back of Dudley's hand. "Was it something you said, Dudley, or did you try and push yourself too far?"

"She was being a bitch, that's all."

"We don't like that, do we? Us girls have to stick together." As Colette tried on expressions to convey agreement Vera said "Are you teasing us, Dudley? I thought you must have been in an argument with a cat or a bush on the hill where you live."

He felt as if he'd strayed into a trap he couldn't even identify. "You don't think I could have been out with a girl, then."

"Not one that'd do that to you. I wouldn't have thought you're the kind to do anything to make her, either. Still, it's the quiet ones you have to watch out for, isn't it, Colette?"

Colette appeared to take this and much else as an invitation to be one. With more frustration than she could conceal Vera said "What were you wanting to ask Dudley outside when our leader interrupted?"

"You know your magazine, that's if you're still going to be in it—"

"I am. Nobody can stop me."

"Wasn't that the magazine Shell Garridge was meant to be writing for?"

"Still is as far as I know, or has she annoyed someone so much they've got rid of her?" With a show of panic he had to be careful not to smile through Dudley gasped "You don't mean something's happened to the magazine."

"Not the magazine. She's dead. She drowned in the river."

He'd wanted to enjoy keeping his secret from the office staff, but he'd neglected to prepare a reaction to the news. The best he could improvise was "How'd she do that?"

"They don't know yet. She's supposed to have driven off the promenade. I don't see how she could have even in all that rain, someone like her." This sounded too close to an accusation for his taste, and so did "You don't seem very upset. Didn't you ever meet her?"

"No." At once he regretted his caution, which made him appear far too insignificant. "Of course I did," he said. "She wanted to meet me after she read my story."

"Was she as great in person as she was on the stage?"

This threw him sufficiently that he retorted "I didn't think she was much either way."

"Some men wouldn't like what she was telling them," Vera reassured Colette. "You ought to have tried to understand her viewpoint, Dudley. It might make you more of a writer."

"She gave me some ideas all right."

"I hope you'll thank her when you write them. Thank her in print, I mean." As he struggled to contain his response Colette added "So where did you see her?"

"I told you."

"You didn't, you know, and Colette means where did you see her perform."

He could think of only one answer that seemed safe. "On television."

"What was she doing on there?" Colette said. "She used to say she was against it because it didn't really let women have a voice, only what men wanted to hear."

"I don't know," Dudley said and grinned at more of the truth. "I switched her off."

"I don't think there's much to laugh at when she's just died," Vera said.

"There wasn't while she was alive," said Trevor.

"That's only your opinion," Colette told him.

"Then let's hear yours, sweetheart. What was so great about her? That she made chaps like Dudley uncomfortable? Look at him. I'd say she still was."

As Dudley wondered desperately how to fend off Trevor's assistance that had turned into anything but, Colette said "Are you remembering when you met her?"

"What did she do to you, Dudley?" Vera was eager everyone should hear.

"Nothing. She couldn't."

He didn't know what else he might have said to end the nagging that was picking at his brain if Mrs Wimbourne hadn't marched out of the Ladies' in the wake of her perfume. "Are we all ready for today's adventures?"

At least she was drawing attention away from him—unwelcome attention, not the sort he deserved. He had almost reached his booth when his mobile set about performing the theme from *Halloween*. "Cut whoever that is short if it isn't an emergency," Mrs Wimbourne warned him. "We're open in less than five minutes."

"Dudley Smith," he said as if he was speaking from his private office.

"How are you this sunny morning?" Walt must feel that the question had answered itself, because he immediately added "Did your weekend bring any ideas?"

"It could have."

"Anything you'd like to share?"

"I don't know yet," Dudley said and at once meant no.

"Okay, I realise it's nearly time for your day job. Did you know you were one of the last people that ever met Shell Garridge?"

For moments that felt dangerously prolonged Dudley couldn't speak. "How do you know that?" he eventually managed.

"You won't have caught the news, then. Friday night her car ran into the Mersey and she drowned."

Dudley had to reassure himself that nobody in the office would understand he was lying when he said "I didn't know."

"I can hear it's a shock. It was to all of us. You've just seen someone as alive as that, you can't believe she's gone, am I right?"

"Something like that."

"Now I don't need to tell you we want to give her the best send-off we possibly can. I'm going to ask you a favour."

"I don't think I've got much to say about her." The request was so unexpected that Dudley gave it more of a response than it deserved. "I don't think I've got anything," he amended.

"I wasn't asking you to talk about her, though I'm sure if you find you've a couple of thoughts they'll be welcome in the next few hours. No, the situation is we have the only column she wrote, and Patricia put together a solid piece about her. So we were going with all that when Patricia, well, I guess you know how thorough she is. She turned up a real scoop."

Dudley supposed he couldn't very well avoid enquiring "What?"

"A complete recording of one of her performances. Apparently some lady taped it for her daughter who couldn't be there. Ideally we'd have liked to release it with our first issue, only the quality's too amateur and we haven't time to get it enhanced. We want to run a transcript in this issue and maybe give the tape away with number two."

"I still don't know what you want me to do," Dudley complained as Mrs Wimbourne gave him a sharp glance on her way to unlock the door.

"All this extra material has thrown the makeup of the issue out of whack. Would you mind very much if we held your story over till the next one? It's the only item that gives us the right space. We'll run an extract that'll make everyone eager to read it, and we'll put your name on the cover next time and give you the lead spot."

Mrs Wimbourne let Lionel in and frowned at Dudley. "So do you think you could make way for her?" Walt prompted in his ear.

Dudley might have found it easier to agree if Walt hadn't phrased it like that. He had to clench a fist on the counter before he was able to say "If it'll help you."

"It does more than that, it saves us. I won't forget what you've done for us today. I should tell you one more thing."

Dudley saw Mrs Wimbourne bearing down on him with the guard behind her, a sight far too suggestive of an imminent arrest. "What else?" he blurted.

"The tape Patricia has is Shell's very last performance. Which is perfect except I think she may include some stuff about you in there. Don't worry, we'll make certain nobody can tell it's you."

Mrs Wimbourne leaned over the glass of the booth. "Are you just about finished, Dudley?" she barely asked.

"Sounds like everyone's after you today," said Walt. "Okay, see you Friday at the launch. I'll get the media to you there for sure. Stay well and creative."

The next moment the phone was as dead as Shell. Dudley thrust it into his pocket as if it was a secret too shameful for him to acknowledge, and raised his eyes to the expanse of suited flesh that was cutting off his view and invading his nostrils with femaleness. "Everything under control now?" Mrs Wimbourne said.

He didn't leap up. Even though she'd added to the pressures that had driven him to accede to Walt's proposal, he didn't grab her by the hair and lean all his weight on her head while he sawed her throat back and forth on the edge of the glass—not with so many witnesses. He took a breath, although it stank of perfume, and met her gaze. "Yes," he said.

TWELVE   As she followed Dudley through the stout brick colonnade Kathy saw him cast more than one sidelong glance into the opaque waters of the Albert Dock. She knew instinctively that he was thinking of the girl who'd drowned. His sensitivity was yet another aspect of him she was proud of, even if it meant he would be embarrassed for anyone to learn he'd surrendered his appearance in the first issue of the magazine to make way for a tribute. Outside the Tate Gallery she pretended to be struck by a poster for an exhibition of images of violence—a face so outraged it appeared to have screamed away its gender— so that she could watch him walk ahead. In the pale grey summer suit she had insisted on buying him he looked at least as elegant as she imagined anyone would look. Nevertheless she winced at noticing that he hadn't entirely unhobbled himself of a limp. She'd persuaded him to confirm that it was the result of the first fight he'd had with the girlfriend whom she was glad she'd never met and who had left him a parting gift of scratches on the back of his hand. Perhaps now that he was free of Trina he would meet a girl more worthy of him, particularly since he was mixing with people nearly as creative as himself.

She caught up with him outside Only Yoko's. As he showed his ticket at the door of the Japanese bistro she couldn't help saying "Here's Dudley Smith."

"Don't care if he's Jack the Ripper, love," the guard said, "so long as he's got an invite."

When she stepped over the threshold she was engulfed by laughter. As long as it wasn't about Dudley it didn't matter. The elongated unexpectedly deep room was stuffed with conversation and crowded with people eating sushi from minimal tables or drinking beer from bottles or pouring one another sake from china decanters, all of which distracted her from immediately noticing that the place was savagely air-conditioned. As the chill settled on her unprotected back above the ankle-length black silk dress, the uproar and confusion produced Patricia Martingale in jeans and a T-shirt that bore a jovial mouth with a river for a tongue. "Dudley, I'm looking forward to hearing you read," she had almost to shout. "Kathy, I'm sure you are too, or does he read to you at home?"

"I wish he would. Perhaps he will in future. It was my idea for him to read tonight so he won't be overlooked."

"I'm glad you thought of it," Patricia said as a large suntanned man in expensive slacks and a T-shirt like hers dodged fast through the crowd. "Here's the guy we were looking for," he declared.

"And this is Kathy, Dudley's mother."

"Walt Davenport. Dudley, see where Vincent is? The media are there for you as well. Get yourself a drink on the way, and let me get one for the lady who set you off on your career."

Kathy accepted a small china bowl as she watched Dudley sidle through the throng to join a young round-faced bespectacled man in the midst of a group of reporters with notebooks. "Will you excuse me if I try and hear?" she said and followed him.

The bespectacled man appeared to be doing most of the talking. As the crowd forced her to meander with frustrating sluggishness across the stone floor, the artificial chill and the heat of so much flesh played a game with her that neither won. She hadn't reached the group when one reporter shouted "Shall we save it for the press conference? I'm not getting half of this with all the row."

"Make sure you speak up for yourself then, Dudley."

Kathy wouldn't have called that for everyone to hear, but she might have taken him aside to encourage him if a man in an orange shirt and blue trousers hadn't dashed at him like a footballer intent on a tackle. "Who's living up to his name at last?" he bellowed. "I'm chuffed for you, son."

Even when he swung to face the audience, displaying how his ears competed with Dudley's for prominence, Kathy didn't immediately believe what she was seeing, or perhaps she only wanted not to. Despite the sudden lull, he hardly moderated his voice to proclaim "He's my boy, everyone. I'm Dud's dad."

Kathy stared at his piebald reddish face crowned with grey skin, at the small eyes that didn't bother to acknowledge her and that made his nose and mouth look squashed too wide by contrast, and wondered how she could ever have fallen in love with him. The question wasn't solved by the way he veered towards their son, shouting "Give us a hug." Instead of delivering one he pretended to punch him and then to be punched. "He got me," he yelled, staggering backwards.

Dudley was visibly bemused, uncertain even of how to move. Kathy took a step towards him, which decoyed his father's attention from him. "Is that Kath?" Monty seemed to be asking the entire gathering. "You're looking spruce. I've not seen you in that rig before, have I?"

"You wouldn't have. It's less than fifteen years old."

"Ooh, that was a low one. Call a copper. I've been assaulted." Dudley's father doubled over while he said this, then sprang up. "His mam wants you all to know I haven't been around as much as I could have been, but I wouldn't have missed this any more than she would."

"Just most of his growing up," Kathy said almost to herself.

"I wasn't that out of the way, was I, Dud? I used to take you places till I went off touring. Anyway, I'm back where I belong now. I'm discovering me Scouseness."

Kathy found the way his Liverpool accent thickened intermittently almost as unbearable as the sight of him beside their son, especially since Dudley seemed frozen by awkwardness. "Where are you telling everyone you belong?" she couldn't resist enquiring.

"That's up to him to say, isn't it, Dud? Reckon I've got anything to do with where you are now?"

Dudley cleared his throat and mumbled in it, and tried again. "I expect you started me off writing."

"That's telling them. I'm part of you, so I never really went away," his father said and turned wholly to his audience. "If anybody's wondering who's the bald sod that's making all the racket, I'm Monty Smith the poet. Proud to be Scouse in verse," he added in an increased accent and pounded his heart with a fist. "Pomes ought to be about how real people feel, not ponces prancing through the flowers and wetting themselves in lakes."

In the midst of her resentment Kathy was dismayed to hear how he'd coarsened since they'd parted. She hoped some of the laughter and applause he'd provoked was ironic, as well as Walt's shout across the bistro. "Maybe you ought to be writing for us. Do you have any of your poems with you?"

"Got some in me head. Here's one to a credit card company." Monty adopted a loosely pugilistic stance and recited

"Please debit me account
Wid de 'ole of de amount.
An' why don't all youse at de bank
Piss off an' 'ave a wank."

Kathy might have imagined that she'd failed to hear what was surrounding her with mirth if Dudley hadn't hesitated before politeness made him join in. She was most disconcerted to observe Walt laughing with his head thrown back. She hadn't thought how to win Dudley the general attention when a woman's voice said "Shell used to love that one."

"I'd rather hear that than be the cowboy poet. You know the one, the Poet Lariat," Monty said, and once the response he'd waited for tailed off "Did you know Shell well, then?"

"As well as anybody did," the dumpy grey-haired woman said from her corner. "I was her mother."

"You still are, love. So long as anyone remembers her you are, and nobody here's going to forget her. Saddest news I heard all year, that. A great Scouser cut off so very early in her career. She told the truth and made us laugh, and if that isn't being what Scouse means I'm an Arab and I've just set off a bomb." He dabbed his right eye hard enough to redden his cheek further and tug it out of shape, then appeared to control himself. "It was me privilege to work with Shell, and now it's me privilege to be in the same room with her mam that gave her to us. It's everyone's privilege here tonight. I reckon you know how to let her know it is."

Even when his father clapped to demonstrate, Dudley seemed uncertain about joining in. Didn't he care for the way the interest of the audience had abandoned him? When bespectacled Vincent started to applaud, Dudley made it rather too plain that he was copying the gesture. "I should mention we've dedicated this issue to Shell," Walt called.

"Don't let me take over your show. It came from de 'eart, dough, everyt'ing I said. Just couldn't stop meself."

"I'm sure nobody would have wanted you to. I'd say that was a very excellent story," Walt told the reporters, "our magazine bringing a father and son back together. And now here's what we've all been waiting for."

That was the kind of announcement Dudley warranted. Was he so modest that he didn't understand it referred to him? Kathy was mutely exhorting either him or Walt to speak up when she heard a thud as if someone had fallen senseless, and then another thump. She whirled around to see two large parcels of magazines that a delivery-man had dropped just inside the bistro. "Don't anyone leave without a free copy," Walt urged and used a knife a waitress in a kimono handed him to cut the tape on both.

Dudley hurried over as Walt split the cellophane wrapping. He barely hesitated before placing a copy of the magazine in Dudley's outstretched hand. "Where's my part?" Dudley said at once.

"At the back. Next time you have the front, and that's a promise."

As Kathy joined them she just had time to glimpse the cover photograph, which depicted Liverpool at dawn with one metal Liver bird silhouetted against a gigantic sun, before Dudley flicked to the last page. It was indeed occupied by an extract from his story, headed by the legend **COMING NEXT MONTH: GREAT SUSPENSE FICTION FROM COMPETITION WINNER DUDLEY SMITH**. She would have enjoyed lingering over the accolade, but he was leafing backwards through the magazine. He stopped at a photograph.

It showed the bullet head and shoulders of the girl who had taken up the middle six pages—taken some of them away from Dudley, Kathy was a little ashamed to think. Nor was she happy that the headline—**SOUNDING SHELL**—was in print twice the size of the letters in Dudley's caption. She had the impression that Shell was thrusting her face at the camera to challenge the audience not to share whatever joke had brought the implication of a smile to her lips. Did this explain why Dudley appeared to be confronting the photograph? Before Kathy knew if he was, he turned to the pages that reproduced a performance of Shell's. His head shook rapidly as if to deny the lines he was scanning, and then it steadied and ducked towards the magazine. Whatever he was reading, it preoccupied him so much that the typescript of his story began to slither out of the manila envelope under his arm until Kathy rescued both. "You didn't change it all," he blurted.

"They better hadn't have."

That was Shell's mother. Kathy understood neither remark, nor why he sent Mrs Garrett a look beyond dislike, nor Walt's response to him. "We didn't think anyone could figure out who it was."

"May I have one?" Kathy asked.

"Sure," said Walt, though after a hesitation she couldn't mistake.

She had scarcely begun skimming the text of Shell's final performance when the chill and the blur of conversations seemed to mass around her like soft but jagged ice. Half a page was filled with gibes at a civil servant who had been assaulted by the brother of one of his clients. Some of the comments were so outrageous she refused to admit them to her mind, but one word let too many others in: this dud, the dud. "Is this supposed to be you?" she wished she could delay saying.

Dudley glanced at the page and then at her with not much less dislike. "Maybe."

As Monty accepted a copy of the magazine, she turned on him. "This is what being a Scouser's about, is it?" she hissed. "This is what you call the truth."

"Eh up, you're spraying me." He dabbed at his eyes, meaning to be comical. "I'm calling what the what again?"

She beckoned him fiercely to read it outside. She was tapping one foot in frustrated nervous rage by the time he said "You reckon this is about Dud?"

"Stop calling him that. You've left him so unsure of himself he can't even tell his own mother when he's been involved in violence."

"That's never violence, two young fellers having an argy in the street. No wonder if he thought it wasn't worth the breath." Nevertheless Monty thrust his head into the bistro. "Come here a mo, son," he shouted.

Dudley crushed the magazine in his hand with such fierceness that Kathy held her copy all the more protectively. She could understand his reluctance to ask "What?"

"Your mam says I'm not to call you Dud. It's not really been buggering you up, has it?"

Dudley suppressed some emotion. "I don't want to be called it any more."

"Fair enough if that means we'll be keeping in touch. Anything I can do to spread your rep, you know it's done. And listen, don't let what Shell said crawl up your nose. She was only taking off on an idea like she always did. You could be proud to be part of her act. Maybe you won't need to be a slave of the state now you're getting published."

Kathy took this as an attack on her as well, but there were more important issues to confront. "Dudley, this incident she talked about, that's why you've been having trouble walking."

"Ouch," Monty said with a sincere wince as their son mumbled "I'm fine."

"If you say so. Only why did you tell me you'd had a fight with your girlfriend?"

"Because you kept on at me," Dudley said with a look at his father she tried not to feel was disloyal.

"I thought you were trying to hide what she'd done because you didn't want me to think badly of her. I don't think you can say I kept on. I didn't even mention it at first." She was angriest to be taking time to impress this on his father before saying "It really was her that you had the fight with last weekend, though, wasn't it?"

As he covered the scratches with his free hand he threw Mrs Garrett a glance not far short of loathing. Kathy had spoken too loud, of course, and he was embarrassed. Most of his reply stayed behind his clenched teeth. "I said."

"Sodding hell, son, sounds like you've had even less luck with the judies than me."

"You said other things as well, Dudley." She was so busy ignoring his father that for a moment the sight of a couple on their way out of the bistro signified too little to her. "Anyway, let's not argue now," she said and held up a palm to detain the two young women. "You aren't leaving yet, are you? Dudley Smith's about to read."

"Good luck to him, whoever he is," one said as they escaped on either side of Kathy. "We were expecting Shell Garridge."

"She wasn't as much news as she'd have thought," Dudley commented.

Kathy hoped Mrs Garrett hadn't overheard him through the doorway. "Shall we tell them you're ready to read before anyone else leaves?"

"I've stopped feeling like reading."

"See, that's how you've left him," she almost cried at Monty, but that would be as unhelpful as blaming herself. "Don't do yourself down," she appealed to Dudley. "The magazine wanted you here. I know you wouldn't like to disappoint anyone."

"I'll fix it," Monty said and darted into the bistro. "Walt, shall I tell them he's reading or will you?"

"Why don't you. Keep it in the family."

This goaded Kathy into the bistro as fast as she could shoo Dudley in front of her. "Shurrup, youse lot," Monty was shouting. "Shurrup for Dudley Smith."

"Who?" asked someone Kathy would have been glad to locate.

"Only a chip off the old block, that's who. One chip and no fish. What're you going to read, son?"

Kathy held her breath until Dudley said "My story that would have been in except for Shell."

"Next issue for sure," Walt called.

"Means you're all getting a sneak. What's it called again?"

" 'Night Trains Don't Take You Home'," Kathy mouthed as Dudley said.

"Because the railway companies put profits before people. Should be their slogan, Profits Before People, shouldn't it? About time the workers and the passengers took over public transport if you ask me. Anyway, we've had enough of me for now. Here's Dudley."

Kathy heard him nearly fail to pronounce the final syllable. She thought this was one reason why Dudley hesitated not far from the exit until Patricia took pity on him. "Shall we have you over here?" she said, indicating the corner farthest from the door. "Then you can sit if you like."

A few people did so as he made his way to the stool. He seemed either eager or determined now. The audience was largely silent by the time he slid the typescript out of the envelope. All the same, Kathy wouldn't have been able to distinguish his first words if she hadn't already read them. "Hang on," Monty interrupted. "Shout up, son."

"Night trains don't take you home by Dudley Smith. Her first mistake was thinking he was mad. As the train left the station he started to talk—"

"Can't hear a word," Mrs Garrett announced, though it sounded less like a complaint than triumph.

"Don't rush it quite so much, Dudley," Kathy took the chance to say. "And even a little louder, do you think? You don't want anybody missing anything."

He gave her a scowl she thought he could have saved for Mrs Garrett and ducked again to his task. "Night trains don't take you home by Dudley Smith. Her first mistake was thinking he was mad. As the train left the station he started to talk in a low passionate voice . . ."

He might have been trying to convey its lowness, but certainly not its passion. From gabbling the text he'd halved his speed, and his utter monotone was threatening to drag it slower. Even worse, he was still reading as though he'd never seen the words before. He raised his voice a little at ". . . taking the latest prize-winning bestseller by Dudley Smith out of her handbag", but this only provoked a stir of embarrassment and a few titters. His forehead had begun to glisten, though Kathy was having to restrain her shivers. "I thought you said what you asked for, sorry," he blundered onwards, "I thought you said I gave you asked for. I thought you said I gave you what you asked for," and his gaze left the page at last. Three people were murmuring goodbyes to Walt as they collected their magazines on the way to the door.

Dudley looked trapped by the sight of them and incapable of speaking. "Go on, son," his father urged. "I've had worse down south."

"She moved with her back to him, she moved to sit with her back to him . . ." Dudley stammered and droned to the end of the page, which he slipped under the envelope. Perhaps this demonstrated how much he had yet to read, because five people headed for the exit as he retrieved the page to remind himself which sentence he was halfway through. Everyone would be gripped once he reached the scene with Greta and the gang, Kathy vowed on his behalf, except that as he read the dialogue his delivery became yet more monotonous. "On your own love must be said the man in the middle and spat across the aisle she's got to read a book . . ."

Walt coughed, and after half a page of this, coughed more sharply. "Well, I think maybe—"

Kathy was on the point of crying out that they should give her son another chance, since even his father seemed tired of his performance, when Patricia spoke. "Could it need a female voice, Dudley, if it's supposed to be told by a girl?"

He stopped glaring at the typescript long enough to scrutinise her face across the room. "You want to read the things she says, you mean?"

"Or the whole story might be easier if you like. They used to say I wasn't bad at drama."

Dudley frowned, and then his eyes widened to let acceptance in. "All right, you should be able to. You've already read it."

Kathy sensed more relief around her than she thought was fair. He handed Patricia the typescript and retreated into the audience. "Shall I start at the beginning again?" she said.

"Just pick up where Dudley left off," her mother suggested.

She and several groans meant everyone was anxious to learn what happened next, Kathy assured herself. Patricia read in a strong clear voice, altering it subtly when Greta or the young man spoke and characterising all the members of the gang with a dull Liverpudlian sameness. When Kathy made her unobtrusive way to her son, she found he looked enraptured by Patricia, so intent on her that he scowled impatiently at Kathy for touching his arm. Occasionally a listener stirred, but she thought it was from unease. There were satisfying gasps when Greta was pushed under the train, and silence after the last paragraph, followed by applause. Kathy might have proposed a second round of it for Patricia if Mrs Garrett hadn't spoken over it. "That's what they thought Shell was more important than, is it? Good on them. Shame they have to publish it at all."

"Don't mind her, son. She has to be missing her kid." Dudley's father gave him a look more meaningful than Kathy felt it had any right to seem, especially once he added "Fair bit of writing, but it's not the only sort of stuff you do, is it? You want to try and find your roots like me."

Kathy was addressing him as well, and anybody else who needed it, as she raised her voice. "Thanks, Patricia. Thanks for doing Dudley justice."

Bespectacled Vincent strolled over through the dissipating crowd. "That was inspiring," he told Dudley. "Best part of the do. It gave me a great idea for the film."

"What one's that?"

"I thought what he has to be, the killer."

"What are you thinking he does?" Dudley asked with, Kathy thought, undue wariness.

"I hope you like it. We can get moving on the screenplay then. You might even have come up with it yourself." Vincent let a smile fiddle with his lips before he said "Tell us how this grabs you, Patricia. What do you think the killer poses as? Maybe you're too close to it to see it, Dudley. A crime writer just like you. That's why nobody suspects him."

THIRTEEN As Patricia stepped out of the lunchtime sunlight into Les Internationales, a waitress in a blouse based on the Italian flag bustled to meet her. "Have you booked, love?"

"I'm meeting Mr Moore."

The phrase sounded like a title in any number of genres, and brought a man to his feet halfway down the broad room full of executives at tables draped with various flags. "Miss Martingale?" he called. "Or I expect I should say Ms."

"So long as it isn't Mrs I don't mind."

By now she had joined him and was receiving a loose pudgy handshake. His large pale somewhat more than well-fed face hiked up a smile. His padded chin bore stubble, perhaps celebrating his day off from work as well as toning with his reddish curls, but he wore a white shirt and a dark suit so discreetly patterned that the stripes looked surreptitious. Only a tie swarming with pink cartoon pigs belied the civil servant's uniform. "I'm having the set lunch," Eamonn Moore said, "but you have whatever you fancy."

A card held between bottles of soy sauce and olive oil in the middle of the table spread with a Greek standard listed the set courses: gazpacho, dim sum, gumbo, baklava. "Well, thanks," Patricia said and felt bound to add "I'll have that too."

His crooked finger summoned a waiter emblematic of France. As the waiter made for the bar decked with pennants to fetch her a fino, Eamonn remarked "You're not much for marriage, then."

"Did I say that? I'm just not married."

"You shouldn't till you find the right person. Is Dudley yet?"

"He isn't married, no."

"He's not still living with his mother, is he?"

"I'm afraid he is. Well, not afraid, I don't know why I should be that. We wouldn't be publishing him except for Kathy. Have you rather lost touch?"

"Rather. That's why I was surprised you wanted to interview me."

"He says you influenced the kind of thing he writes."

"I don't know what that is."

"You ought to have come to our launch last week. You'd have heard me read his story," Patricia said, although doing so had left her less sure how it worked: the only way she'd found to perform it had been straight, in the hope that her listeners would take it as ironic. "It's a murder story seen through the eyes of the girl who's going to be the victim."

"I should have known that'd be his thing."

"Because of the films you used to watch together, you mean?"

Eamonn didn't answer until the waiter moved away from delivering Patricia's sherry. "What did he say we did?"

"Watched lots of thrillers was my impression. I wasn't clear how old you were."

"We were at primary school. He sat next to me in class one year. I must have told him my parents ran a video library. He asked to see some of the films."

"Any in particular?"

"Horrors when he saw we'd got them. My parents didn't know what the worst of them were like then. Someone in a van used to drive round the video shops and sell them cheap."

"You're saying those were the ones you watched."

"They were the ones he liked best. Anything with people being tortured in. I couldn't watch them now."

"Do any titles come to mind?"

"Lord, I don't know. *Cut Her Up* and *Pull Her Guts Out*. That's what you could have called any of his favourites."

"Were you this unhappy about them when you were watching them?" Patricia felt she was asking on Dudley's behalf.

"I was young. Didn't know any better." Eamonn fell silent while a waitress sporting Portuguese insignia served them chilly soup. "Are we having wine?" he suggested with a good deal more enthusiasm.

"If it's dry and white."

"A Chilean sauvignon should do us." Having displayed his expertise, he lowered his voice as the waitress headed for the bar. "Anyway, yes, I didn't like the ones he kept rewinding even back then," he said. "I ought to say we never watched them at my house. I'm not blaming his mother, mind. He always managed to keep her out of the way during any of the bad bits. He'd ask her to bring us a drink or make us something else to eat. And his father was pretty well always out or upstairs writing and couldn't be disturbed."

"Do you think there's much to blame anyone for? It doesn't seem to have done you or Dudley any harm."

"I had nightmares." As if this was more than he'd wanted to reveal he said "Are you planning to put all this in your magazine?"

"I'm not sure yet. Is there anything you wouldn't want me to?"

"Anything about my parents. They'd hate to be reminded. They never really got over having the shop raided by the police when they'd never been in trouble with them before or since. They were in the papers and had to pay a fine, and twenty years later the law says those films are all right for people to see after all." His face seemed to absorb his anger so as to let him say "And don't tell anyone how old we were in case that reflects on them."

"Perhaps I could just mention you were at school."

"Will you have to? I wouldn't be talking about it at all if he hadn't told you. I only wanted you to hear my side of it."

This struck Patricia as an odd way to refer to watching films, but at least it let her ask "Is there anything else you'd like me to hear?"

Once he'd swallowed a spoonful of gazpacho more dramatically than she thought was called for, he said "One of the nightmares was about him."

"Gosh, I don't think he could have that effect on me. I suppose it was because you were so young, was it? What was the nightmare?"

"About something he told me. I shouldn't think you'd want to hear about it just now."

"I certainly would. Don't keep me in suspense, or are you trying to compete with him?"

"I wouldn't want to," Eamonn said and dropped his voice until she had to lean across the table to listen. "He'd been to the library, I think it was, and he came across a stray dog in the park. The way he told the story, he just started throwing sticks for it."

"He might have, mightn't he?"

"You or I might. According to him he didn't realise one was a bit of old fence with a point on the end. That's till he threw it and it went in the dog's eye."

"Oh, poor thing," Patricia cried and had to remind herself that they were talking about perhaps twenty years ago. "What did he do? Was anybody there to help?"

"Nobody about, he said. So he just stood and watched the dog try to shake the stick out of its eye, and at last it did."

"He was afraid to touch it, you mean."

"He touched it all right. When it lay down, or he said it fell. I'm only telling you what he told me." Eamonn gazed at her, possibly in case she wanted him to stop. "He pushed the stick back in and the dog ran off, and he never saw it again."

Patricia took a spoonful of soup and kept it down until that required no effort. "How much of his story did you believe?"

"All of it. I told you, I had nightmares."

"How much do you believe now?"

"I've no reason not to I can think of. Why would anyone that age make up something like that, or any other age for that matter?"

"Little boys can be pretty nasty sometimes in my experience." Rather than suggest that Eamonn had recounted the anecdote with more relish and hesitation for effect than he was admitting, Patricia said "Might it have been his first story, do you think? Maybe he was trying to compete with the films you were both watching."

"Are you going to put it in your magazine, then?"

"I don't know yet," Patricia said, although she thought it quite unlikely. "Depends what else you tell me."

"Nothing much else to tell." When she raised her eyebrows and an encouraging smile he said brusquely "Nothing at all."

She didn't speak while a waiter garbed as Germany served them dim sum, and then she said "Who else do you think I should talk to?"

"Juicy," Eamonn enthused over a prawn dumpling, and licked his lips and rubbed them over each other. When he'd finished he said "If he hasn't told you anybody, I don't know."

"Even if you aren't in touch with them, could you give me the names of a few friends?"

"There was just me if he says I was."

She had to wonder if he was claiming this for the sake of fame. "He must have played with other children, surely."

"Nobody wanted to. They got tired of him telling stories all the time."

"Do you remember any of those?"

"I mean he told lies," Eamonn said with a fatigued look.

"I'd still be interested in hearing any that come to mind."

"There were so many I ended up not listening. How his father had published lots of books instead of just a couple and sold millions of copies, that was one. And his mother was supposed to be publishing a book too that people told her was the best they'd ever read. You can see why he started being bullied. I'm not saying it's right."

"I'm not sure I can see. How long did it go on?"

"The last couple of years he was at that school. I don't believe his mother knew."

"If he told so many lies I don't understand why this story about the dog couldn't have been one."

"Maybe it was. It's too far back to tell." He devoured a pork bun and admitted "He did send me an invitation to your show. Sent it to my place of work."

"You sound as if you wish he hadn't."

"No reason for my boss to know what we used to get up to when we were out of control. Watching films we shouldn't have, I mean." Eamonn raised his face as if to slough off any guilt. "I mostly didn't come because I had a prior family commitment," he said. "They take precedence."

"I understand."

He seemed to feel that she didn't sufficiently. He spent the rest of the meal in acquainting her with his domestic life, not least by showing her several folders of photographs he had apparently collected from the developers on his way to the restaurant. By the time he called for the bill and left an impressive tip she felt as if she'd attended the most recent birthdays of both his young daughters; she had certainly had to exclaim at dozens of pictures of them in party hats. She was feeling full of lunch but empty of information she could publish as she thanked him for the meal. "My treat in every sense," he said, patting his stomach and then her arm.

Outside the restaurant the sunlight smelled of all three lanes of traffic jammed into one-way Dale Street. Had she been too anxious to compensate for Dudley's setbacks at the launch while she was interviewing Eamonn Moore? At least Valerie had edited out Shell's comments that might have identified him; there were no references to his writing. Was Patricia his publicist or a reporter? Perhaps soon she would know.

She turned off Dale Street up Moorfields and climbed an escalator to the ticket barrier so as to descend to the trains. As the passages and sluggish stairs led her deeper she realised that she was retracing Greta's route in the tale. She looked behind her only once while she waited for a train that carried her around the loop under Liverpool to Birkenhead. Beyond Hamilton Square the newest station, Conway Park, was open to the sunlight for the length of its platforms, after which the tunnel closed down again all the way to Birkenhead Park.

She ran up stairs that boxed in her clatter, she hurried along the narrow street packed with small cheap shops. As she reached the intersection with the road that linked Bidston with downtown Birkenhead, she saw children already at the bus stop outside the school that backed onto the extensive Victorian park. Before the lights allowed her to cross she had time to observe that the children were stoning the traffic. "Stop that," she shouted as she set foot on the pavement within a stone's throw of them, and they jerked up fingers to acknowledge her in advance of running off.

Many more children were swarming out of both ends of Park Comprehensive. Patricia couldn't see a single adult in the concrete schoolyard. She tried addressing three teenage girls who had halted to stare at her inside the gates. "Could you tell me where the office is?"

"Are you police?" said a girl with a heart tattooed on her forearm.

"Is it 'cos Denzil stabbed someone again?" a pregnant girl with yellowed fingers said.

"I'm here for a chat with one of your teachers. Mr Fender, if you know where he is."

"Wouldn't want to. Boring English," the third girl said and spat. "It's through them doors, the office."

Patricia made for the stout oak double doors in the middle of the elongated two-storey red brick building. Beyond the doors a wide hallway led almost at once to a window in the left-hand wall. A plump secretary with her linen jacket drooping on the back of her chair directed her to the second of the imposing doors in the opposite wall. Patricia tapped on the muntin under a plaque that said STAFF. Having waited several seconds, she was about to knock once more when a thin sharp male voice called "Come."

He sounded bent on instilling nervousness in the listener. When she opened the door, that was how he looked too: eyes as fierce as the red moustache that bristled wider than his bony balding head, arms folded so tightly across his chest that the leather elbows of his tweed sports jacket pointed straight at her. He was alone in the barely decorated room full of unmatched chairs surrounding two low tables strewn with newspapers. "You are?" he said.

"I am." Since this earned her no more than a single impatient blink and a thinning of his pale lips, she was quick to add "Mr Fender? Patricia Martingale from the *Mersey Mouth*. We spoke at the beginning of the week. You wanted me to give you time to think."

"I've had precious little of that. Thinking isn't required in this job these days, just filling in forms while you try to hold back the flood of illiteracy. Half these nitwits believe their computers will do all their spelling for them and whatever their wretched toys tell them is right," Mr Fender said and twitched his disappointed face at her. "Can you spell 'It's unacceptable'?"

"I should imagine so," Patricia said, and demonstrated.

"You're one of a shrinking minority. Perhaps you'd like to interview me about the state of affairs that has been allowed to develop."

"Maybe we can talk about it later if there's time. You must be pleased that one of your old pupils is keeping literacy alive."

"I won't ask you to sit down." The beginnings of interest had drained back into the teacher's face. "I've plenty of marking before I can call the day my own. I know the kind of marks I'd like to award most of them," he said, and almost as severely "What were you saying Smith is doing now?"

"At the moment, working in a job centre."

"And having to read out the information to half the wastrels, no doubt. At least he'll be putting his skills to some use," Mr Fender said and leaned his elbows on the back of a lumpily upholstered chair. "But that isn't why you requested this meeting."

"As I said, he's written a series of stories and we're about to publish one."

"You also said it was going to be filmed, did you not? That won't help anybody read. More likely the reverse."

"It won't make his story go away, though, will it?"

"Perhaps you ought to be wishing it could. Is he still up to his old tricks?"

"I don't think I know which those are." When Mr Fender let his eyelids slump with ostentatious weariness, Patricia said "He seems to feel you encouraged him to write."

"He already had a good idea what he was doing by the time his year came up to me."

"Doing in the sense of . . ."

"Grammar. Punctuation. Syntax. Spelling. All the particulars we aren't supposed to think worth taking care of any more. He was a rarity even then."

"I think he meant you gave him a reason to write his stories."

"I was asked to set him work when he was excused gym. There was no point in testing skills I knew he had, so I had him write essays. I was hoping they might help him develop." The teacher's lips pressed each other bloodless and parted a slit before he said "He offered me stories instead, and I was lax enough to accept them. I've wondered since if his real skill wasn't manipulation, if he exaggerated his nervous complaint so as to dodge any physical education."

"Why do you think he would have done that?"

"Shyness is often the motive if it isn't sloth. In my view and that of my colleague who took his year for gym, that kind of over-sensitivity means the boy bears watching closely."

"You're saying that's what you both did."

"In Smith's case I suspect it may not have been closely enough."

"Is there something you feel responsible for?"

"I think no one can accuse me of shirking any responsibility we in the profession are still allowed to observe." Once his eyes had finished daring her to contradict him, the teacher said "In retrospect I think I might have taken Smith to task about his stories sooner than I did."

"What didn't you like?"

"There was never anything to like. Monsters, violence, all the rot teenagers think they have the right to watch these days. Well written, which is why I let it pass for far too long. What is he writing now?"

"Stories about murders around Merseyside."

"I was all too correct, then. He's up to his tricks again and you're paying him to do it."

"You haven't told me which those are yet."

Mr Fender straightened up behind the chair, and she was afraid he was about to terminate the interview until he said "I take it Smith hasn't told you why I eventually objected to one of his effusions."

"His mother did. You thought it was too real, didn't you? I'd say that was a compliment, not a criticism."

"I fear she didn't understand, or perhaps she prefers not to. Of course she's a modern parent. They can't bear any criticism of their offspring, let alone the slightest attempt to correct them." By now he was gripping the back of the chair like a lectern. "It was real because it was based on fact," he said. "The entire case had been in the papers. All Smith did was to change the names and the places and work out details the press had the good taste in those days not to print. The man is still in jail. I wish I'd sent him the story. He might have contacted Smith to give him a taste of what real killers are like."

Patricia thought this improbable but said only "He's writing fiction now."

"If I were your editor I would take care what I published."

Patricia felt protective of her mother. "Why do you say that?" she less asked than objected.

"I should want to ascertain how fictitious the stories are." Mr Fender seized a briefcase from the chair, and it was clear that he was ending the interview. "I said his work was correctly written, and so it was," he told her. "That's all that one could say for it. I'm of the very strong belief, and you may quote me if you have the stomach for it, that Smith was wholly devoid of imagination."

"Thank you for your time," Patricia said as he turned his back and stooped to gather a heap of red exercise books. She didn't feel inclined to thank him for anything else. As she left the staffroom and then the school she had the unwelcome impression that he'd left her sense of Dudley Smith more incomplete than it had been before she'd visited the school. She was crossing the empty schoolyard when her phone rang.

She hoped the call wasn't urgent. She had to attend a Weegee exhibition at the Walker Art Gallery and then the first night of *Playing at Murder* at the Playhouse. She disentangled the mobile from the keys in her handbag and halted on the baked concrete that smelled of dust. "Patricia Martingale."

"Patricia, it's Kathy Smith. I wanted to thank you for reading Dudley's story to the audience last week."

"Think nothing of it, Kathy. Part of the job."

"I'm sure it was a great deal more than that. I could hear it in your voice." Dudley's mother cleared her throat hard enough to twinge Patricia's ear and said "I meant I really wanted to thank you. We'd very much like it if you'd come to dinner."

FOURTEEN As his latest client left the window Dudley saw two men staring at him from the front row of bucket seats. "That's not himself, is it?" said the thinner of the pair.

"I think it is, you know," said his squat and even sweatier friend.

Dudley's crotch gave a reminiscent twinge until he realised they were members of his audience. When the lanky man approached, blinking rapidly and jerking his long angular head higher as if it had been tugged back by the corners of his grin, Dudley was sorry that he had nothing to autograph. "You're the writer, right?" the man said. "The one that's in the paper."

"The only one," Dudley said while he considered standing up to shake hands across the glass. "This is what I do as well for now."

"Can you get us a job writing books?"

Dudley wasn't sure how appreciated he should feel. "Both of you, do you mean?"

"May as well," the squat man called, "if there's enough to go round."

"There's meant to be a book in everybody, isn't there," the man at the window informed Dudley. "You just write about your life."

"No I don't. Nothing like it," Dudley said and then grasped that the comment hadn't been about him.

"All right, keep the top of your head on. What makes you write your stuff if it's not real?"

"I didn't say it wasn't. Things like that happen, just not the ones I write."

"Give us some tips, then. Do you think what you're going to write first or just sit down and do it?"

Dudley wished Patricia could be there to record him. "It's not that simple," he said.

"We aren't either," the squat man retorted, "so teach us."

"Research for a start."

"How do you do that?" the lanky customer said. "Creep after people and think how you can kill them?"

"They're stories. I write stories," Dudley said, perhaps louder than was necessary. "Anyway, it doesn't matter what I do. You wanted me to tell you what you should."

"That's it then, is it? We've got the job."

"There's more to it than that. You need to have the talent, which most people don't, even some that are published. And then you have to work at it to get it right. It can take years."

"I thought this was meant to be where we get jobs," the man at the window said with another outburst of blinking.

"We never have any writing books."

"What are you scared of?" the squat man raised his voice to ask.

"Nothing," Dudley shouted, though he felt as though his interrogators had wished their sweat on him.

"Competition, it sounds like."

"You're wrong and you know it," Dudley said, managing to laugh. "If you read the paper you should know I won one."

"Still sounds like you want to keep all the writing for yourself," the lanky man said. "It can't take much doing or you wouldn't have this job as well."

"Greedy if you ask me," the squat man called. "There's not that many jobs to go round. You should do one and let somebody else have the other. Watch your back, Reg, the heavy's on his way."

"Don't bother. We're going," Reg told Lionel, who had left the doorway. He blinked faster as he stood up and then leaned towards Dudley's window. "Better remember lots of people know about you now," he warned.

Dudley was struggling not to take this as more of a threat than it had any right to be while the pair sauntered out, followed to the door by Lionel, when heat and perfume seemed to blotch the glass in front of him. "What was it about this time?" Mrs Wimbourne enquired.

"Dudley can't be blamed for being in the paper," Vera said.

"Can't he?" With no more of the respect he deserved Mrs Wimbourne said "Does it mention this office?"

"It's about his story and his film. I can show you if you like."

"I think you'd better," Mrs Wimbourne said.

At the mention of the film Dudley hid his grin behind his hand. Vincent's idea would help conceal him. The last person anybody would suspect was a crime writer who'd invented one who was a killer. The character was his, and it had been presumptuous of Vincent to change it, but didn't his doing so in that way prove Dudley was perfectly camouflaged? He drew his finger across his lips to erase some of the grin as he swivelled his chair. "I haven't seen it either yet," he said.

Mrs Wimbourne parted her lips with a sound like a truncated tut at the copy of the local weekly and lowered her frown towards the page Vera had folded open. With very little delay she said "I thought you weren't supposed to have mentioned where you worked."

Dudley jumped up to stand by her. **MURDER'S MY MEAT, SAYS COMPETITION WINNER**. He wasn't sure the headline was entirely adequate, but at least they had printed the photograph of him fingering the keyboard at his desk, despite his mother's protests about the tidiness of his room. The report said that he worked in a local employment agency, but why should Mrs Wimbourne complain about that? He was enjoying how she was continuing to hold the paper as if she was his servant when a line of print was suddenly all he could see. "I never said that," he blurted.

"Don't worry, anybody looking at your picture can see you aren't thirty-eight," Vera assured him. "They'll know the paper's put ten years on you."

"Unless it's working here," Trevor said to nobody in particular.

Dudley felt as if their voices were crowding into his skull. "I didn't say my stories were based on reality," he said loud enough, he hoped, to bring the senseless chatter to an end.

"What did you say?" Mrs Wimbourne accused more than asked.

"I write about real places."

"I can't imagine what else anyone would think that read the paper. I don't understand what you're so worried about," Mrs Wimbourne said and stared at him.

"Nothing. I'm not worried. I never said I was. The paper ought to tell the truth, that's all."

"At least they didn't put that you were in the first issue of the magazine," Colette said.

"Pardon?" Mrs Wimbourne said. "Please explain."

"It doesn't matter," Dudley had to lie as he resumed his seat. "It isn't worth talking about."

"It looks as if it is to me. Colette?"

"Dudley's story won't be in till the next one. I expect that's because Shell Garridge died and they did a special section about her. I still bought it, Dudley, because it had part of your story to get people interested. I was."

"There you are, Colette's interested," Vera apparently believed he needed to be told.

Mrs Wimbourne took a heavy pace towards him. "I think you owe me an explanation."

For the first time ever he could have wished that the office were busier, but there wasn't a single client to distract her. "Why?" he pretended not to know.

"You went to a good deal of trouble to convince me it would be prohibitive for the magazine to drop your story, and that's what I told London. Now it's obvious these people weren't bothered about losing it."

"They haven't lost it, they've just delayed it."

"Don't be so sure of that. We've had a taste of the kind of attention you're bringing us. I don't know what that noise is meant to mean, Trevor, but I'd advise you to keep it to yourself. I'll be having another word with London, Dudley, and when they hear what I have to tell them I doubt they'll be so accommodating."

He mustn't leave the chair, Dudley thought with an effort that made his skull feel brittle and shrunken. He was at the office. There were witnesses. He was reduced to mutely urging them to intervene on his behalf. He'd begun to hate them almost as much as he hated Mrs Wimbourne's gaze, which she appeared to be resting on him in the belief that it would force him to capitulate in some way, when the mobile in his jacket went off like a tuneful alarm. As he laid the mobile on the counter he recognised the displayed number. "It's my magazine."

"In that case start your break now and speak to them." Once he was facing her again Mrs Wimbourne said "And make sure you let them know we may not be giving permission for your story to be published."

"You won't want me talking in front of the public," he said as two young mothers wheeled toddlers into the office, but answered the phone on the way to the door for fear the caller might ring off. "Dudley Smith the author."

"Hey, Dudley. Up to much?"

"Nothing that can't wait for our magazine, Walt," he said and closed his eyes as he turned his face up to the sunlight. "What do you need me for now?"

"Let's see. There's some good news and—well, I know we're going to be able to work out the rest."

As Dudley opened his eyes he thought the crowd was surging towards him, but they were avoiding a magazine seller and her invitation to help the homeless. "What is it?" he demanded.

"The good news is your father's agreed to take over from Shell."

For a sunless instant Dudley saw her face bobbing up at him from inky water. "How can he?" Dudley said, as much to fend off the glimpse as to know. "What's he taking?"

"He'll be writing a column for us. Poetry, humour, comment, whatever fires him up. It won't be Shell, but I'm betting it may be just as good along her lines. You know how much he admired her."

Dudley couldn't grasp how the prospect of working alongside his father made him feel. Monty's reappearance still struck him as far less significant than his own inept reading at the launch, a distraction from it if not a cause. "What's the rest?" he was more anxious to discover.

"The rest, sure." Walt sounded disappointed by Dudley's reaction. "It may be turning out for the best that we had to put off publishing your story," he said.

"Why should it?"

"I need to ask you if it was based on anything in particular."

"My imagination. Why?"

"You didn't know a girl was killed in the subway where you set your story. Not just down there, on that station on that line."

Dudley raised his voice to fend off the crowd and the details with which Walt seemed to be fishing for him, but the only riposte he could think of was "When?"

"Coming up to seven years ago."

"It won't matter, will it, when it's been that long?"

"I'm afraid it will, Dudley, especially when it's the anniversary in a few weeks."

Was that true? Dudley couldn't remember. "Who says so?"

"Her family. Seems they were never convinced her death was an accident. It was put down to her running too fast for the train, so you can imagine how they must feel."

Dudley almost said he couldn't and had no interest in trying, but instead protested "Then they ought to think my story's on their side."

"It doesn't work that way, sadly. They're very angry and upset because it looks as if you were writing about her. If you say it's a coincidence I believe you, or do you think you may have had the real thing at the back of your mind and not realised?"

Too late Dudley grasped that he could have used this as an excuse. By then he'd said "My story came first."

"Fine, I'll tell her family. Now forgive me for asking you this, but there's no way we could run into the same kind of problem with your other stories, obviously, is there?"

"That's right," Dudley said, which wasn't nearly vehement enough. "There isn't, no. Of course there isn't."

"As far as you know, but then you didn't know about this one, did you? Well, I guess we'd need to have worse than bad luck to be hit by another coincidence like that. Do you have a favourite among your other stories?"

"I like all of them. They're all as good as that one."

"Maybe the best solution is you call Vincent and tell them all to him. We don't want to keep creativity waiting."

Dudley lowered his voice and his head as though he meant to butt the crowd away from overhearing. "Solution to what?"

"To which of your stories he'll have to use now. He'll be staying clear of the subway, and you'll realise the magazine has to as well."

Dudley's surroundings seemed to grow as flat and garish as floodlit painted cardboard. "Aren't you going to publish my story?" he pleaded for nobody except Walt to hear.

"You can understand our position. Controversy could help our sales, but not that kind. We don't want to get ourselves disliked by our public."

"It isn't fair. I won." Dudley saw passers-by gazing at him with amusement or glancing away in embarrassment, all of which left him vulnerable to a sudden belated panic. "Anyway," he objected as if this could make the situation cease to be, "how do the family know about it when you haven't published it yet?"

"Somebody at the launch called them about it. Either they didn't know who or the girl's father wasn't telling me. I wish I knew who it was as much as you."

Dudley doubted it. He tried to recall the faces of his audience, but all that he could bring to mind was how they'd looked uncomfortable in entirely the wrong way, and once Patricia had taken over the reading he'd devoted his attention to her. If she hadn't read the story, it would have been published before the girl's family could interfere. Patricia had interfered by reading it, and his guts were beginning to tighten when Walt said "Would you rather have Valerie choose? We'd still like to try and publish you when you've been so understanding. Why don't you email us all the stories when you get home. Valerie needs to select one as soon as she can."

Panic was closing around Dudley again. He should never have let himself be driven to claim he'd made the other stories up. He felt as if people he couldn't locate in the crowd were watching him say desperately "I want to look at them first. I haven't read them for a while."

"Do that tonight, then, and send as many as you like. Okay, let me leave you to call Vincent."

The babble of the crowd seemed to flood the earpiece as the heat fastened on Dudley with its claws. He was so distracted that he almost keyed Vincent's number, but he had worse than nothing to say to him. He thrust the disloyal mobile into his pocket and forced himself to turn back to the office. He'd taken the phone outside so that Mrs Wimbourne couldn't listen to him in the staffroom, but now he felt as if he was being dragged back to a prison she'd built for him. He strode behind the counter to her booth as her head swung towards him like the cow's that she was. "You've got what you wanted," he said with an expression that made his lips ache. "They aren't publishing my story after all."

FIFTEEN "Oh, thank you, Patricia. They're lovely. Quite beautiful. Thank you so much."

"My pleasure, and I'm on time this time as well."

"If anything I think you're a little bit early, are you? No, actually you aren't. He mustn't be watching the clock. Dudley? Our guest is here."

Patricia used both hands to shut the uncooperative front door while Kathy carried the bouquet to the stairs and took hold of the blond banister as if it might help convey her voice to her son. "Dudley?" she called again, and told Patricia "He was writing, he said."

"Do we want to interrupt that?"

"Even authors ought to be polite." Kathy knocked not too hard on the banister. "It's your friend from the magazine," she called. "Patricia."

This earned a mumble from above, too curt to include a welcome. Patricia saw that Kathy wanted to pretend it did, and so she tried to leave the subject behind as she followed Dudley's mother along the hall. "I do like your photographs," she said.

"Still, we're not experts, are we? Your photographer spotted I was just an amateur. Do you mind if we eat in the kitchen? Dudley likes to be close to the fridge so his drinks are as cold as can be."

"It'll be cosy," Patricia said, though that wasn't the word that occurred to her. Everywhere she looked were corners—of the washing machine that steeped the room in a faint soapy smell, the tall refrigerator, the steel sink, the rectangular table. Only the pine chairs were at all rounded, and they were also straight and hard. "It is," she felt bound to add.

"We've always thought so, Dudley and I. What would you like to drink?"

"Is wine a possibility?"

"I can run out and get some by all means."

"I should have brought a bottle. The lemonade we had last time would be fine."

"We've plenty of that. It's his favourite." Kathy stood a bottle of it among the settings on the table and began to clip the stems of the bouquet into the pedal bin. "While he's not here to be embarrassed, did you have time to look at my story about him?"

"I'm hoping I may find a quote."

"Anything and as much as you like." Kathy ducked lower as she said "I shouldn't think you'd want to use all of it. Obviously you wouldn't."

"I don't think we'd have anywhere near enough space, even with the trouble with his story."

Kathy gave a small low cry. The stem of one of the roses in her grasp had snapped. "Which trouble?" she gasped and sucked blood off a finger. "Does he know?"

"Shall I get you a plaster for that?"

"There's no need, really. I can't even feel it." As Kathy thrust her finger under the tap she twisted to face Patricia. "You haven't told me what the trouble is," she said.

"They're scared of my story."

Patricia didn't let the closeness of Dudley's voice unnerve her. She turned her head without haste, only to be confronted by a deserted hall. The next moment he ran down the very few stairs he hadn't descended unheard and flashed her a grin too knowing for her taste. "What on earth could anybody be afraid of about you?" Kathy said with a stab at a laugh.

His lips shifted, apparently in search of an expression rather than an answer, and Patricia turned to her. "Would you remember a girl who was killed on the underground?"

"Too many people are these days, aren't they? They don't seem to take as much care as they should any more. I expect it's drink or drugs or just being too used to things that are dangerous. Sit down, Dudley, and we'll start."

As he took the seat opposite Patricia she said "This one was at Moorfields."

"That's strange," Kathy said once she finished ladling soup into bowls. "It's sad, of course, but don't they say life imitates art? Mushroom soup. Our favourite."

Patricia suspected that meant Dudley's, even if he was loading it with salt and pepper from the cruet in the shape of a new moon and a star. Enough mushrooms had drowned in the greyish liquid to lend it their taste. Having enthused about it twice, Patricia asked Dudley "What made you choose that location for your story?"

"Best place." When she raised her eyebrows he said "Farthest from people. Nobody to hear if she screamed. Nowhere else you could be sure of getting her alone down there."

Did this apply to the story less than it should? Presumably he had the process of conceiving it in mind. Kathy removed the bowls, although his still contained all its mushrooms. Patricia made no comment, but he read her eyes. "Slimy," he informed her. "I only like the taste."

Kathy scraped the mushrooms into the pedal bin and produced from the oven a grill tray full of lamb chops. "I hope you won't miss the bones," she said to Patricia. "His father used to say I was indulging him, but I could never see the point of forcing something on a child."

A decided silence followed except for the slaps of meat and the plumps of boiled potatoes Kathy was transferring to plates. Carrots came with muted thuds, and parsnips with a mushy thump, before she brought the plates to the table. Once Patricia had sprinkled mint sauce from a jug shaped like a fat pink cartoon tulip and been vehemently polite about her sample mouthful of it all, she felt entitled to resume her questioning. "Vincent wanted me to ask you a couple of things," she said. "He's trying to understand your character."

"Isn't he just supposed to film what Dudley wrote? That ought to help him understand anything there is to, though I don't see what there could be."

"Vincent isn't too clear why Mr Anonymous—" When Dudley frowned at that, Patricia said "Did you come up with a name for him?"

"No, because nobody ever knows who he is."

"You're definitely writing about the same killer all the time, then."

"Of course I am. He's what my stories are all about."

Rather than speak up for victims who didn't exist, Patricia said "Do you know more about him than you put in the stories?"

"Maybe." Dudley sawed at a piece of lamb and brandished half in front of his lips until he'd finished saying "Such as what?"

"Excuse me interrupting again, Patricia, but do eat up your vegetables as well, Dudley. I'll bet they have vitamins to keep you creative in them."

He redoubled his stare at Patricia. Much less distinctly, not least because he had to wipe his lips with the back of his hand, he repeated "Such as what?"

"I know I didn't read the stories properly, but I couldn't say why Mr Anonymous kills anyone."

Perhaps the repetition of the name annoyed him. A frown squeezed his gaze narrow as he swallowed. "Because they ask for it," he said.

"You're saying that's what your character thinks."

"Him, yes." As the frown lifted it appeared to tug at his lips. "Mr Killogram," he said, "the opposite of Kissogram."

"Are you calling him that for the film?"

"Why don't you make it the title?" Kathy said.

"We'll see what Vincent thinks, shall we? So Dudley, you're saying he blames his victims somehow."

"He doesn't blame them. He doesn't care that much."

"He has to have a better reason than not caring."

"They don't know he's there, that's all."

"That's more how he does it than why, isn't it?" Kathy said.

"It's both." Perhaps he felt doubly interrogated, since he added with some irritation "It's when everything goes right for him."

"I don't think I understand that," said Kathy.

"It's when there's nobody about except him and whoever it's going to be, and the place helps as well. It's as if it's meant to happen," Dudley declared, then shook his head so violently that a forkful of meat on the way to be eaten smeared his lips. "Not as if. When it is."

However direct an insight into his character this was, it discomforted Patricia. "Maybe you're best talking through some of your stories with Vincent," she felt relieved to have thought of suggesting. "Have you decided which you want him to think about?"

"Let me just—" Kathy leaned backwards to tear off a section of kitchen roll with which she dabbed Dudley's mouth. "You'll still be using the underground one, won't you?"

He snatched his head aside and glared at Patricia until she admitted "Unfortunately not when the real girl's family would be upset."

"But you have to publish it at least."

"We won't be using that one. I'm sure whichever we do use will help Dudley's reputation just as much."

"I thought you signed a contract to publish that story."

Patricia hadn't but felt nearly as accused, since her mother had. "It doesn't actually commit the magazine to publishing it," she said.

"That's a bit unbalanced, wouldn't you say?" When Patricia failed to do so Kathy said "Besides, how do you know the family will mind? It's only the same station, after all."

"They heard about the reading and they weren't at all happy. We don't know how they heard."

"Who'd want to ruin everything for him?" Kathy protested, then released a loud breath. "No, you're right, the family should be considered. I don't want to think what would become of me if I lost my son. Are you sure you've finished, Dudley? There's lots of goodness in front of you still."

"I've had what I like," Dudley said and thrust his knife into the vegetable mush.

Kathy didn't speak again until she'd cleared the table of plates. "Let's have a bit of sweetness," she said.

As Kathy brought out of the oven a pie so collapsed it seemed bent on negating its own shape, Patricia couldn't resist asking Dudley "Is this your favourite too?"

"No, I made it because we had a guest," Kathy said.

Patricia did her best not to wonder what was involved in creating pastry with such a close resemblance to leather while she cut through it with just her spoon. Once she'd managed to establish that the filling consisted almost as much of honey as of apple she was able to rhapsodise about the dessert, not too belatedly, she hoped. She thought she'd failed to be convincing until Kathy said "Which story do you think he should send in instead?"

"I don't think I had time to judge." Patricia couldn't tell how much of the impression that she retained—of the same sly face peering from behind every tale—derived from the stories, how much from Dudley's comments. "Which do you?" she said.

"None of them will be the winner, will it?" Kathy objected before chasing away her bitterness with a smile at her son. "Except they all are. How about the one when he pretends he's going to help her out of the sinking mud on the beach and pulls her on her face instead and stands on her? That gave me the shivers. Or is it a bit too nasty when he'll be the hero of the film?"

"I shouldn't think he'll quite be that," Patricia said.

"The centre of it, then. The person everybody's going to want to come back." Mostly to her son she said "I know the one that frightened me the most—when he meets the girl out walking in the country on a day like this and gives her the water with all the ecstasy in it. How he watches her dance herself to death, that's horrible enough, but someone giving you a drug like that when you don't know, that's worse."

"Could that be what trips him up?" Patricia suggested. "The drugs could be traced back to him."

"No they couldn't. He was out walking like she said and he found them where someone had hidden them, and right then he put them in the water in the bottle. They weren't ever his."

"How about his prints on the bottle?"

"He got it back from her after she drank all the water while she was getting hot from jigging about. He didn't throw it away there, he took it home and put it in the dustbin because he knew nobody would think of looking there."

"That isn't in the story," Kathy said.

"So I didn't write it down. So who cares? I know what happened. I don't have to tell everything."

"No need to take it personally. Don't let it put you off your sweet," Kathy urged, and when he only glowered at his plate "Anyway, which is your favourite story?"

"I don't want any of them published. I'm writing something new."

"Will there be time for that, Patricia?"

"Not very much. I'll find out, but I shouldn't think more than a week."

"How long are you expecting to take, Dudley? Wouldn't you be better letting them have one of the others and then they can use the new one another time?"

He shoved his chair backwards and sprang to his feet. "I'm not doing that. I don't know how long it'll take me to write. Longer if you go on about it," he shouted from the hall and stamped upstairs.

"Excuse him, Patricia. That must be what artists are meant to be like," Kathy said, but didn't look at her until the contents of his untouched dessert plate were binned. "Would you like a coffee?"

"I'm fine, thanks," Patricia said, meaning rather that she felt hot and edgy enough. "Let me help you wash up."

"Why, you're already like one of the family, but you mustn't waste any more of your visit on me. Have you seen our hill?"

"I did as I came along."

"You haven't been up on it." When Patricia had to agree, Kathy called "Dudley, I know you can hear us. You didn't shut your door. Won't you take your guest for a walk on the hill?"

As Patricia turned to face him he descended considerably fewer stairs than he'd made the sound of climbing. "Might help," he muttered.

"Thanks for dinner, Kathy. I enjoyed it."

"I'm sure it can't be what you're used to, but I'm just a simple person in some ways."

Kathy hurried to lug the front door wide for them. The sun had gone to ground behind the ridge, and the mass of greenery across the road was steeped in twilight. As Patricia followed Dudley up a narrow path between trees and tall weeds she heard the door shut with a discreet thud. She ducked under the lowest branches of a tree and felt as if the stealthy gloom was taking hold of her, especially since Dudley had halted, blocking her way. "What's that?" he whispered.

In a moment she heard a rustle vanishing into the undergrowth. Perhaps he wasn't attempting to play on her nerves, but she said "What would you like it to be?"

"I'm asking a question for once."

"Mr Killogram's victims coming back to find him."

Darkness seemed to gather in his eyes. "They don't do that," he said and turned his back as though grinding an object beneath his heel.

"He must think about what he's done sometimes though, mustn't he? He ought to in the film."

"Why must he?"

"Unless he's got absolutely no imagination."

"He's got plenty."

"Then oughtn't he to show it?"

"Oh, he will."

Did he really think a stare like that could frighten her? Identifying with one's character was all very well, but he was starting to look capable of taking it rather too far. "Carry on," she said and walked at him until he couldn't avoid moving.

In less than a minute they emerged into a stony open space hemmed in by trees that fluttered and chattered with magpies under a blue sky turning pale. "I hope you aren't going to mind," Patricia said. "I've been talking to a couple of people about you."

She had to raise her voice to compete with the jagged racket, and so it was hardly surprising that he glanced about to check there was nobody to overhear. "Who?" he said so loud that the magpies clattered into the sky.

"Mr Fender from your old school."

"Why would I mind him? Kathy used to say he was jealous because I knew more about writing than he did." Dudley tramped to the start of a path that led to the disused observatory above them on the ridge and then swung to confront her. "What did you tell him about me?"

"Do let's keep moving if we're going to walk." Once Dudley began to climb towards the squat blind one-eyed tower beside the dome she said "He did most of the talking. Didn't he object to your story because it was based on an actual case?"

"So what if it was? Writers have to start somewhere."

The noise like bones snapping came from a bush against which he had abruptly pressed himself. "You go ahead," he urged, and didn't speak again until he was behind her. "What else did he say about me?"

"That's pretty well it. The interview wasn't terribly productive."

"Then you should have stayed away from him like you knew I wanted." All at once Dudley's voice was lower but felt closer. "Did you tell him about her?"

"You mean the girl at Moorfields."

"Her, yes. The one that's causing all the trouble. Angela whatever her name was. I'll bet he had plenty to say about her."

"Actually, he didn't. Nor did I."

"Do I believe that?"

She wasn't sure if she was meant to hear that or even if it was addressed to her. She didn't acknowledge it until she had stepped onto the deserted ridge, and then she turned to look down at him. "You do if you have any sense," she said without retreating, though his tight grin was only inches from her breasts. "I hadn't heard about her when I went to see him."

"I've got plenty of sense. There's quite a few people who've found out how much. Maybe you ought to meet them."

Patricia was amused by the threatening manner he seemed unable to relinquish, but she stopped short of laughing. "By all means tell me anyone else you want me to interview," she said. "I had lunch with Eamonn Moore."

"How'd you manage to get in touch with him? I invited him to my story reading but he never came."

"He asked me to pass on his apologies. He had a family occasion. He's a walking picture galley of his little daughters."

"I should have found out where he lives and not sent his invitation to the office. I'll bet he told his boss about it and they put him off."

"Why would they do that?"

"They won't like imagination where he works any more than where I do. You know why, don't you? Because it makes them feel inferior. It should."

Though Patricia merely lifted an eyebrow, this was enough to provoke him. "Who are you going to believe, Eamonn or me?"

"Whoever's telling the truth." She wasn't even certain what his question was supposed to refer to, but it enabled her to add "I wouldn't mind knowing which of you did about one thing."

"Me," Dudley said and stared at her as if he'd resolved to force any disagreement too deep into her brain to be grasped. "What?"

"You probably won't even remember it. It was just a nasty anecdote about a dog."

His gaze retreated inwards, apparently in search of an expression. "What did he tell you?"

"That you gave him nightmares with it."

The left side of Dudley's mouth tried on a smirk. "I expect that's true."

"The story wasn't, though, was it?"

"Why shouldn't it be?"

"You don't want me to think you never make up stories."

His mouth worked without settling on which half of its expression it ought to extend. "Why not that one? Too real for you?"

"No, I just think you were being like little boys are. If you'll forgive me, you're doing it now."

"I never was. You could have asked Kathy." He crossed the ridge to a gap in the low wall alongside the observatory. "This is the best bit. Let's go down here," he said.

Patricia ventured close enough to distinguish through the canopy of foliage a series of worn steps descending through the twilit woods. "Actually, I think I should be heading for the train."

"We can go this way."

"I'll stay up here, I think. No need to walk me to the station. Thank Kathy again for me, and thank you for an interesting evening."

Might he suspect her of being ironic? When she glanced back to catch how he looked, he'd advanced several yards but was standing still. "I used to play that game when I was little," she let him know. "Shouldn't you be going home to write?"

"I'm thinking about it right now."

"Then I'll stop interrupting you," Patricia said and turned away from his unblinking gaze. She didn't look behind her until she'd walked at least a hundred yards along the wide uneven ridge. There was no sign of him, nor indeed of anybody all the way to the opposite end, where an obsolete windmill guarded a bridge forty feet above a road. A wiry hound as grey as the name of its breed was tugging a woman across the bridge. "Good evening," she panted at Patricia.

"It is."

Perhaps the woman was dissatisfied with the answer. "Good evening," she said more loudly as she reached the mill.

Patricia peered at her before stepping onto the bridge. Nobody else was visible, but wasn't the woman a little too distant to have been addressing her? The bulk of the windmill, against which the greyhound was lifting an elegant leg, was enough to conceal half a dozen people, but no shadow betrayed that anyone was hiding. Perhaps the twilight was too dim to cast a shadow. For a moment Patricia was tempted to seek company, except that she didn't fancy discovering how else the woman might behave if in fact she had been talking to herself. Instead she crossed the bridge, staying clear of both sets of railings, which struck her as rather too flimsy and low, and hurried downhill.

It was clear that she'd chosen the long way to the station. The weathered path of slippery plates of rock led to a pinewood in which she kept hearing twigs snap and pine cones crunch beneath the tread of an otherwise silent walker somewhere close. When she emerged into a field of rank grass bordered by a dense stretch of pines she was hoping the other might stray into view, but the noises stayed among the trees. Beyond the field a rubbly track brought her to a section of the Smiths' road alongside an abandoned churchyard. This struck her as such a cliché that as she marched past it and down a side road she grew furious with herself for even noticing the clinks of stone or glass or both that seemed to pace her under cover of the high wall.

Behind the graveyard a broad road sloped down towards the station. There was still a main road to be followed to a five-way junction surrounding a church. By the time she took the route that led past a chain-link cage jangling with football to the station she'd had more than enough of the heat that her nerves and the speed they'd urged on her had stoked up. At least her train was almost due. Alone on the platform, she calmed her breath and sighed aloud, and then she had nothing to distract her from the station entrance that yawned at her back. Nobody could have crept so close that she wouldn't have heard them, and yet as the train drew into the station she couldn't help retreating a step. She stalked in a fury to the nearest doors and glared through the windows as she made for a seat with its back to the wall. Of course she hadn't glimpsed anyone dodging out of sight beyond the exit to the street, but what if she had? The doors shut and the train set off, and she deliberately looked away from the platform. "End of story," she said.

SIXTEEN When the dawn made the tips of the highest branches on the hillside flare like matches, Dudley lurched out of bed. The edge of the quilt captured his feet, and as a toenail scraped the slippery fabric he almost fell across the chair in front of his desk. He might have screamed at the hindrance if that wouldn't have been likely to waken his mother. He kicked the quilt away so hard that the nail on his big toe twinged, and then he switched on the computer. He had to write. It was all the more urgent now that he'd found he couldn't produce a new story for the magazine until he had dislodged Shell Garridge from his head.

How much more was going to be her fault? If she hadn't stolen his place in the magazine his story would have been published by now, before anybody could prevent it. She was to blame for the night he'd just had, and so was Patricia Martingale. Not only had she added to the pressure in his brain, she had also made him waste more of the evening by tracking her all the way to the station from the hill. Sometimes simply tracking and imagining what could happen was enough, but this had left him so frustrated that once he'd watched the train bear her out of reach, he had dashed home to try and write, only to be waylaid by his mother. Did he think Patricia had enjoyed herself? Would he like to invite her again? She was a nice intelligent girl, wasn't she? Had they discovered anything in common besides the magazine? At last, having muttered noncommittally in response to these questions and several more, he'd escaped to his room, where he'd found that the interrogation had robbed him of the impulse to write. He'd watched a disc of Vincent's films in the hope that they might revive his genius, whether by making him eager to contribute to the collaboration or merely helping him relax. He'd felt less than revived by the documentary about Lez and the Keks, a mop-headed female Beatles tribute band, and the award-winning short film in which a young black prostitute had dreams or perhaps more than dreams of acting as a costumed vigilante. At least the latter had left him impatient to encourage Vincent to film a more realistic story—one of Dudley's—but that had brought him nothing but a brittle headache. He couldn't think of a single tale that didn't involve Shell.

He'd thrown himself on the bed at last and dragged the quilt over him, only to continue straining his brain. Whenever sleep succeeded in closing over him, his mind clawed its way back to the surface. He didn't know how often he'd returned to an idea before he had accepted that it was the solitary answer: if he couldn't write for publication as long as Shell was wedged in his brain, he would have to write about her first. Nobody could ever read the story if he didn't print it out; perhaps he wouldn't even keep it once it was finished. The computer awoke as sunlight inched like syrup down the trees, and he tried to blink grittiness out of his eyes while he waited to start typing.

"Murdered by the Mersey", "Mumbling by the Mersey", "Mumbling in the Mersey" . . . "Put Down for Good". Each title brought more of a grin to his lips, and his choice of a name for her stretched them so wide that they stung almost as much as his eyes.

"You'd think a pack of men was weeing out there," Mish shouted, peering at the rain that slashed at the pub window. "They can't even do that proper, can they, girls? Have to do it standing up like the dogs they all are. Like they can't bear to sit down for a moment because they're too anxious to get some more lager in them or go and look at some porn or kick a ball about or whatever else is the poor little pathetic best they can do. Weeing's all they'd better use their peepees for when they're anywhere near us. And even that's an insult. Next time any of us find a man weeing on a wall I reckon we should chop their peepees off."

She was still shouting at the window. She hoped anybody outside in the storm could hear her and the women laughing. She had a gulp of her pint of lager, because women were allowed to drink pints now and it wasn't the same as when a man did, and

As Dudley's finger loitered on the final key, the word extended itself to the tune of half a dozen consonants before he snatched his hand away. His mother had come out of her bedroom. Of course she knew not to invade his room without permission, but if she heard him typing she might ask to see, and he could do without the distraction of having to respond. He didn't realise that her very presence upstairs was distracting until he heard the noises she started to make in the bathroom. Perhaps the dialogue he'd put in Mish's mouth had left him unduly sensitive, but he had to bung his ears with his fingers to ward off the sounds and the images they threatened to conjure up. He barely heard Kathy reopen the bathroom door, and then he had to keep uselessly still while she plodded down stair after stair. Once he heard her carpeted footsteps grow flatter on the kitchen linoleum he swept away the proliferating letters and did his best to type more quietly as well as faster.

shouted, "Any men listening? You'd better keep your hands over your peepees if you are. Not you behind the bar, you're safe because you're our slave for tonight. Just do everything we tell you and you'll leave in one piece. Any other men, this is Mish Mash talking to you, specially if you're hiding outside. Come in and face us if you dare. It'll be you that ends up weeing yourself."

Some of the women looked puzzled by now. Maybe they thought she'd had too much to drink, even if she was a woman. "Keep on laughing. It's still funny," she snarled at them and started to shout again. "There's a man you'd all hate even more than the rest of them if you read his stories. Don't worry, I've got them stopped so nobody can ever read them. Only I wouldn't be surprised if he's hanging round outside because I did. If he is I hope he drowns out there. I expect he feels like someone's weeeeee

"Dudley?" his mother called again from further up the stairs. "Are you out of bed yet?"

"Yes for the second time. Yes," Dudley yelled and had to wipe the screen.

"Will you be long? Your breakfast's on its way."

"Trying to write."

"Sorry, pardon? I can't understand you if you mumble."

"I don't. Mish Mash does," Dudley said, and also through his teeth but several times as loud "Trying. To. Write."

"When do you think you may be finished for now?"

She was almost as bad, or perhaps not even almost, as Shell. She'd driven the end of the sentence out of his aching head. All he could see was the way the spellcheck had underlined his last protracted but incomplete word in jagged red like a bloody saw. He almost didn't save the document before he closed the computer down and hurled his chair backwards against the bed. "Now I can't write," he bellowed. "Happy now?"

"Oh, don't say that. You know the last thing I'd want is to stop you. I haven't really, have I?"

"I've stopped. I'm going to the bathroom."

He didn't move until she returned to the kitchen with all the slowness of a mourner at a funeral, and then he sprinted across the landing to bolt himself in. He was hoping he could think now that he was alone, but his body wouldn't let him. A cramp kept tweaking his stomach as he performed the task Kathy used to call sitting on his throne and doing what royalty did. Brushing his teeth only let him see himself grimace and foam at the mouth. When he stepped into the bath, his skin felt so nervously taut with his efforts to recapture Mish's thoughts that he couldn't judge the temperature of the shower. He flinched away from being nearly scalded, but the icy onslaught that followed was no use to him either. He towelled any portions of him that had ended up wet, and sprayed each armpit twice with deodorant before hurrying back to his room, where he glowered at the blank screen as he dressed for the office. His scowl failed to squeeze out any thoughts. He'd meant breakfast to come as a reward for his work, but now its aromas were yet another distraction, and eventually sent him flouncing downstairs. "Are you all right now?" his mother asked at once.

"Don't put my eggs next to my beans or I've told you, I won't eat them." Not until he was satisfied that the items were barred by sausages and bacon from ever touching did he say "I won't be writing any more."

"Before you go to work, you mean. Your other work. I'm sure you'll write when you come home."

"You carry on being sure, then. That's all that matters."

"You know that isn't true. You are. Would you like me to ring and say you're ill?"

"No use. Too late now. I can't write."

"You mustn't keep saying that, Dudley. You wouldn't like it to get stuck in your head, would you?" She waved her fork at him above the small breakfast she'd kept for herself. "You'll be writing your new story for the magazine," she apparently felt he ought to be informed. "Can you tell me anything about it yet?"

Dudley stuffed his mouth with half a sausage in the hope that her question would have atrophied by the time he finished chewing, but the appeal lingered in her eyes. "No," he said as he took another mouthful.

"Are you afraid you mightn't write it if you told someone the story first, even me? You mustn't let that happen, certainly. I don't suppose I could read what you've written so far."

"I don't either."

"I only want to help. I don't want to feel like a hindrance." Having waited in vain for a response, she said "Are you going to be killing off another girl?"

"Mr Killogram will be if that's what you mean."

"You haven't run out of girls, then."

That felt uncomfortably pointed and all the more disconcerting because he couldn't tell why it bothered him. "He never will. There's plenty," he said.

"You think you can still see things from their point of view."

"Obviously I can," Dudley said, but his mind was mocking him with his inability to finish Mish's sentence, repeating "wee wee

wee" like a pig in a childish rhyme. "What's hard about that?" he demanded.

"Nothing if you say not, only if you get stuck I just had an idea. If you find you're having trouble coming up with a new female viewpoint I might be able to do something about it."

All at once he wondered whether his conviction that he had to write about Shell before he could move on was simply an excuse, a way to postpone knowing what he had to do. He had no idea why Kathy was gazing at him. "What?" he cried.

"Maybe I could try and write a bit of it with you if you liked."

"You mean on my computer? My computer in my room?"

"If you'll let me. Whatever's best for you."

"Being left alone is. Being left absolutely one hundred per cent alone."

"I know that's how you can feel when you're writing, but it doesn't mean you have to." For the moments she had to spend on a token mouthful of egg she appeared to have capitulated, but then she said "You're collaborating with your film director, after all."

"You're supposed to be leaving me alone." As he backed his chair away from the table, the screech of pine on linoleum felt like the voice of his nerves. "Now I've got to go to work," he complained.

"You aren't late yet. Have a bit more to eat." When he picked up his knife and fork and dropped them on his plate, their handles sinking into the leguminous morass, she said "Have some of your orange juice at least. Start the day healthy."

He seized the glass and emptied it into his mouth. He hadn't finished swallowing when acid rose to mix with the drink. He rushed to the front door and lurched off the path barely in time to spill the mouthful behind the overgrown rockery. As he straightened up he saw Brenda Staples, one of the elderly sisters who lived in the next house, pinioned in her downstairs window by handfuls of the curtains she was opening. Rage at the contempt she was daring to exhibit sent him down the path. Before he stopped digging his fingernails into the gate, Kathy followed him. "You could try and write in your lunch hour, couldn't you?" she wanted to reassure him or herself or both. "And maybe in your breaks as well."

"No," Dudley said, "no," and repeated it all the way to the street that led downhill. He imagined his colleagues reading his story over his shoulder, even finding an excuse to pursue him into the staffroom. He wished he had let Kathy tell Mrs Wimbourne that something was wrong with him, although there certainly was not. Perhaps he could pretend there was so as to be sent home from work.

"Wee, wee, wee . . ." His mind had rediscovered this theme now. Crossing the road to be out of earshot of early shoppers at the supermarket, he began to chant it in a voice he hoped was sufficiently idiotic to shame it into leaving him. "Weeing on his head," he gasped with sudden inspiration. "She wanted him to feel someone was weeing on his head, the stupid unimaginative vindictive bitch." The trouble was that he felt like that, or at least as though senselessness was falling drop by sluggish drop into his skull, dousing any thoughts he almost had. Surely that was the fault of his lack of sleep. He just needed something to waken him.

He managed to keep quiet as he reached the station. As the train moved off, the rhythm of the wheels set about repeating "His head, his head, his head . . ." The young woman sitting opposite him slanted her knees away from him and stared blankfaced past him. Before he could fit a single thought together, a metallic voice announced Birkenhead Park. The next stop was his, and it was hardly worth struggling to think while he was buried in the midst of a mass of people with no idea who he was. His surroundings were growing flat and unfocused when a phrase caught his eye. **MURDER FILM**, it said.

The newspaper was three seats away. He had to strain his already stinging eyes to be sure of the words. The remainder of the headline was covered by a thumb like a pallid caterpillar with a crimson head. The thumb stirred as if it was about to writhe across the paper, and then it slithered sideways to help the woman turn the page. The artfully tousled mass of straw that was the back of her head almost blocked Dudley's glimpse of the entire headline. **VICTIM'S FAMILY CONDEMNS MURDER FILM**.

He nearly shouted at her not to turn over. Who else was reading that paper? By the time he finished twisting on the seat while he ignored the antics that the girl across from him performed to keep her knees uncontaminated by his, he'd located three copies. The train kept up its chatter on the subject of his head as lights embedded in the tunnel walls plucked at the underside of his vision faster than he could form a thought. He only just managed not to snatch the nearest of the papers as he sidled to the doors. The moment they parted he dug his fingers into their rubbery lips and sprinted across the platform.

He might have dashed up the ninety-nine steps to the street if a lift hadn't been open and waiting. The instant he saw daylight Dudley squeezed between people and then the doors and ran along the parched swaying street. Cars screeched as he darted across the main road. He raced past the Bingo building and down the alley to the newspaper stand by the job centre. **REPORT: TOO FEW NEW MERSEY COPS**, the poster on the stand declared, which had nothing to do with him. He grabbed the topmost paper and forced himself to linger until the unshaven man in shorts gave him change of a pound coin, in case haste somehow betrayed him. He set about clawing the pages apart as he made for the nearest bench.

The lack of applicants to join the police took up the front page, but the item about a film wasn't on the second, nor the third, fourth, fifth . . . Surely the headline couldn't relate to him if it was so far into the paper. He tore the next spread open, and crouched over it and a renewed cramp in his stomach.

### VICTIM'S FAMILY CONDEMNS MURDER FILM

The family of Angela Manning, who was killed by a train at Moorfields Station in August 1997, have attacked plans for a new Merseyside film.

Based on an unpublished novel by local writer Dudley Swift, the film is to include a scene shot on location at Moorfields where a girl is pushed under a train by a serial killer.

Speaking for Poolywood Productions, American entrepreneur Walt Davenport said that the scene may not appear in the finished film. This is unlikely to satisfy Angela's family. "They say it's not about Angela, but leaving out the scene is as good as admitting it is," her father Bob Manning said. "The film will still have a man who kills someone like her. It's not letting us grieve in peace, and it's spreading the idea that Merseyside is full of criminals as well."

If he was saying that the area was full of Mr Killogram, Dudley supposed he might take that as a compliment, except that being branded a criminal angered him, though by no means as intensely as being called by the wrong name. He had difficulty in wielding his fingers to phone the *Mersey Mouth*. A machine responded with Patricia Martingale's voice. "It's Dudley," he protested. "Dudley Smith. Someone ring me as soon as you're in."

He slapped the pages together and made for the nearest bin. Just as he reached it, he heard Mrs Wimbourne call "Dudley, don't throw that away. I'll have it."

"No you won't," he muttered as he dropped it in the concrete barrel. It sprawled open at the story about him. He ducked to the bin so hastily that the edges of his vision blackened like the borders of an old photograph. By the time he flung the paper shut,

Mrs Wimbourne was upon him. "Do you think I would now?" she said.

She must imagine he intended to retrieve it for her. He had a panicky notion that if he left it she would change her mind just because she was a woman and pick up the newspaper. A can of lager was balanced on the concrete rim. It proved to be half full, and he emptied it over the paper. "Where was the sense in that?" Mrs Wimbourne demanded.

"You wouldn't like some child drinking it, would you? Anyway, I thought you didn't want the paper."

She let her gaze bear on him long enough to establish that it was only a sample of her disapproval, and then she spun on her heel. "You've wasted quite enough of my time. Come along at once and make sure you're some use."

She wouldn't like to learn the sort of use he could be. He was mouthing some thought of the kind at her waddling back when he saw that Trevor and Vera and Colette were watching from in front of the job centre. They turned away from him as Mrs Wimbourne jabbed her key into the lock. Having thrown the door wide, she retreated with heavy dignity. "I'll just be a minute," she declared. "All of you go along in."

Nobody spoke until Trevor closed the door behind them, trapping the already oppressive heat, and then he said "What did you do to put her in a mood, Dudley? No need to make it hard for the rest of us."

"I wasn't thinking about you."

"Not even Colette?" Vera rebuked him.

"Why did you throw away that paper?" Colette wanted to know or at least to interrupt.

"Were you thinking people should be reading you instead?" Vera suggested. "When are we going to?"

"The real girl's family asked them not to publish his story, remember," Colette said. "You can understand how they must feel, Dudley."

"Why must they?" He hardly knew what he was saying as he watched Mrs Wimbourne buy a paper at the stand. "Who says they must?"

"What I was getting at," Vera intervened, "why don't you bring in the story for us to judge for ourselves?"

He might have enquired who she thought they were that they could judge him, but he was meeting Mrs Wimbourne's stare as she let herself in. "Thank you, Dudley, for the trouble and expense," she said.

Colette fled to the Ladies' while her colleagues trailed after Mrs Wimbourne to the staffroom. Dudley was the first to follow her in, despite Trevor's murmur of reproof on Vera's behalf. All that mattered was for Dudley to keep an eye on the paper until he thought how to prevent any of them from discovering his latest setback. When Mrs Wimbourne dumped herself in a chair he took the seat opposite and gazed at the blank page of the ceiling. At the raw lower edge of his vision he was aware of her leafing through the paper too swiftly to let him think. She'd turned over once, and now twice, so that at any moment—"I'm sorry you had to pay for it," he blurted. "I'll buy it if you like."

"I think not, thank you. I'd rather keep control of it."

He was growing desperate enough to consider promising to make her a present of it, except that this would solve nothing, when Colette reappeared. Mrs Wimbourne folded the newspaper before dropping it on the table on her way to the Ladies'. That door had barely shut when Trevor leaned across the table for the paper. "Leave it," Dudley cried. "You heard her. It's hers."

"I didn't know you were so scared of her."

"I'm not scared of anyone. They should—" Dudley managed to head the boast off so as to confront Vera. "What's funny?"

"Just thinking there's someone I think you are."

"I'm who?" As her meaning caught up with him Dudley struggled to restrain his voice. "I'm what, scared? Who of?"

"Maybe just a teeny bit of our Colette."

"Her? I don't feel anything about her. No wonder you were laughing. It's a joke."

He stared at the floor in the hope that they would see he needed to be left alone. When Trevor headed for the Gents', however, Vera lingered as if to protect Colette. A taste as stale as the heat in the room had invaded Dudley's mouth by the time the other man returned, at which point Vera made for the Ladies' and Colette followed as far as the counter. Trevor sat at the table and waited for Dudley to meet his eyes. "What's got into you today, lad? Won't you be satisfied till you've upset the lot of us?"

"I'm trying to think of a story," Dudley not much less than screamed. "I need you to shut up and stay away from me."

Trevor gave him a look that laid claim to a lifetime of weary experience. "I don't agree with the boss about a lot of things, but maybe you should leave some of what you think you are at home."

"I know what I am. Don't you go thinking you do."

As Dudley strove not to let fly any more of the truth, Mrs Wimbourne emerged from the Ladies'. "Time we were at the counter," she announced. "That's everybody, even budding novelists."

Trevor stood up with his hands in his pockets and sauntered to the door. "Better shake a leg. Sounds as if at least one woman wants you."

He loitered in the doorway to leave him a doubtful frown that made Dudley feel immobilised by all his nerves. As soon as Trevor moved away, Dudley lunged for the newspaper and dragged the offending page out of hiding, along with its twin. He took a second to tidy the remains of the paper before crumpling his prize into a ball he stuffed in a hip pocket as he hurried to the counter. "Just going to the toilet," he informed Mrs Wimbourne.

"In future please don't leave it till the last minute."

He almost retorted that it was her fault and everybody else's that he had. He didn't bother closing the door of the solitary cubicle as a preamble to shying the lump of newspaper into the toilet. He urinated on it for good measure and hauled on the chain, then strode back to the counter, suppressing a grin. He took his place at the counter as Mrs Wimbourne unlocked the door to admit Lionel and the public, represented by a man who, having drained a bottle of lager, threw it into the concrete bin and stumbled after the guard. Dudley thought there might be some violence to watch until the man brushed past Lionel and scurried to the Gents'.

There was nothing for him to find, and certainly no reason for him to mention anything he found to anyone. Dudley tried to drive away the threat by staring at the blank computer screen, then switched on the computer as the man reappeared. He made straight for the door, to Dudley's stale-tasting relief. He'd almost reached the street when Lionel accosted him. "Aren't you looking for work today? We're not a public loo, you know."

"You're a public building, aren't you? Should be when the public pays your wages." The man set one foot on the pavement outside and tarried to add "Anyway, I left it how I found it. Someone's chucked some newspaper in the lav and it won't go down."

"Not guilty," Trevor informed whoever ought to know.

Mrs Wimbourne rose up in her booth and stared across the partitions. "Dudley?"

He kept his shrunken gaze on the screen as if the icons might offer him an inspiration. "Why would I do that?"

"Precisely what I'd like to know," she said and marched to the staffroom. He heard a flurry of rustling that put him in mind of a poisoned rat seized by convulsions in its nest, and then her heavy tread closed in on him as her reflection walled off the glass of the booth. Her perfume merged with the acid in his throat as she said "What have you been playing at with my paper?"

"I offered to buy it from you."

"Very well, you may."

Her pudgy hand appeared beside his shoulder and came to rest palm upwards on the counter. The fingertips curled, urging him to contribute. How would they wriggle and jerk if he drove a ballpoint into the palm and leaned on it until the metal tip crunched through the flesh all the way to the wood? How might she scream and plead? Far too loudly when there were witnesses; someone or all of them might try to stop him before he was done. He fished out change and counted it onto her hand, but this didn't rid him of her. Instead she brandished her moneyed fist above his booth. "Lionel, could you get me a paper?"

As the guard took the money Dudley crouched lower while a cramp jabbed at his guts. Mrs Wimbourne's reflection looked close to engulfing the sight of Lionel trotting to the newspaper stand and returning with yet another copy of the paper. "Thank you, Lionel. Perhaps now we can establish what all this has been in aid of," Mrs Wimbourne said as pages rustled above Dudley's skull. The noises seemed to be pressing his cranium thin, and so did the silence that followed until Mrs Wimbourne's voice added its weight. "At least your behaviour says it all, Dudley. You know exactly what you have to do."

"I don't know what you're asking."

"I'm afraid if you care about continuing to work here you're going to have to keep your stories to yourself, and that includes your film."

"You can't tell me to do that. You said you had to ask the bosses at the top."

"I need do nothing of the sort. This is my decision and London will support me in it. I presume you have your phone on you as usual."

"I might."

"For once you may use it here. I want to be able to hear what you say to your American."

Dudley seized the edge of the counter to hold his prickly fingers still. "What are you expecting me to?"

"It's immaterial how you achieve the result so long as it's the one that's required." She leaned forward as if to ensure he couldn't escape and moistened the nape of his neck with her breath. "You could explain that you're undermining our reputation. Anything you do is associated with us now people know it's you in the papers."

He had a sense that she actually fancied she was extending him some help. He considered speaking to Walt in her terms and then calling him to take the nonsense back, but the immediate prospect was so demeaning that his entire body recoiled from it. Either she'd retreated or she hadn't been as close as his sweaty neck suggested, because the chair failed to knock her down as he thrust it back and swung to confront her. "What kind of a reputation do you think you've got?" he demanded.

"Perhaps you'd care to tell me."

"Dull. Unimaginative. Not just you, the whole boring lot of you. If you knew half of what I am none of you would dare to talk to me the way you do. You ought to be proud if you're associated with me. People might even think you were interesting."

"Dear me," Vera said with a pitying laugh that drew echoes from Colette and Trevor.

Mrs Wimbourne let her face grow briefly slack to acknowledge their reactions or Dudley's remarks before she told him "I'm giving you your last chance. Make the call I told you to or you can hand in your notice forthwith."

"I won't bother doing either." He strode to the flap in the counter and threw it aside with an impact like the shutting of a clapperboard. If his mouth tasted dry and stale, it was from all the triteness he was escaping at last. As he emerged into the sunlight he turned to see Trevor and Vera and Colette exhibited in their glass cases, figures no livelier than the paralysed fan behind them, while Lionel guarded them and Mrs Wimbourne stood over them, folding the newspaper as if tidying Dudley away. None of them seemed quite to believe they were watching him quit, and perhaps they hadn't all seen the last of him. "Thank you for helping me write," he called with a grin.

SEVENTEEN "No, no, no . . ." As Dudley's voice dwindled Kathy had the impression of watching him shrink, become a little boy again. Either he fell silent when he reached the corner of the downhill street or he'd passed beyond her range. He was rejecting her suggestions, not her. Perhaps in time he would decide that some of them made sense, but he didn't need her to add to the pressure he was suffering. She lingered for a final sight of him on his determined grown-up way to work, and then she turned to find that Brenda Staples had come out of the house next door.

Despite the heat, she was lagged in a padded pink housecoat that covered her down to her matching slippers. Once she pinched the collar shut around her wrinkled neck, nothing but her veinous hand betrayed how her thin fragile face beneath the dyed black curls was carefully made up. "We didn't know Dudley was a problem child," she said.

Presumably she was also speaking for her older sister. "Nor did I," Kathy said with some politeness. "What gave you that idea?"

"Didn't we just see the end of a tiff?"

"We don't expect to agree over everything. Perhaps you and Cynthia do."

"Of course if you don't mind him causing a scene in public we mustn't be expected to complain. Had he been celebrating?"

"Not to my knowledge. I'm not sure what he has to celebrate."

"Well, quite. Is he ill in some way?"

Kathy had a disconcerting sense of being quizzed about the excuse she'd proposed to make to his employer. "Which would that be?"

"Whichever he was being before you came to speak to him. We assumed that was why you had."

All at once Kathy was afraid to learn more. How might her persistence have affected his already tense brain? Could the drugs of her youth have found their way into his genes and lain dormant until his mind was at its most vulnerable? Everything around her seemed to grow flat and bright as a sheet of painted tin. "What was he doing?" she heard herself have to ask.

"Really being quite disgusting," Brenda said and nodded in the direction of the rockery. "You'll forgive me if I don't look."

Kathy craned over the weedy tufted rocks and viewed the evidence. Though it dismayed her, it was so preferable to her fears that she had to conceal a relieved smile before turning to her neighbour. "That must have been a bit much. I'll say sorry for him."

Brenda was eyeing the weeds. "I expect he'll have more time to help you in the garden if he's giving up his hobby."

"I'm afraid he's very little time for those."

"These stories we hear he writes, you wouldn't call them a job."

"I won't yet. I hope I may be able to. People are only just starting to see what he's capable of."

"I should have thought you'd hope it will all come to nothing."

Kathy managed to hold on to her politeness. "What an extraordinary suggestion. Do explain."

"Because of the report in the paper."

"Why, just because they put a few years on him? That's the press for you. Either they're deaf or they can't read their own writing. I was here when he told them his age."

"I was speaking of today's paper."

"I haven't seen it, I'm afraid," Kathy said with a twinge of unease.

"Then I think you should." Brenda padded purposefully into her house, where she became if anything more audible. "May I take the paper for a few minutes, Cynthia? The paper, Cynthia. The newspaper. The one you have there."

"Don't put yourselves to so much trouble," Kathy called while she tried to ignore the mute rebuke of the sisters' trim garden, but Brenda was already marching back to her. She folded the newspaper open before passing it to Kathy across the fence. "I fancy he won't thank me if he's kept this from you," she said.

"We don't have a morning paper. I can imagine plenty of bad things that are happening without one," Kathy said, and then she saw the headline Brenda wanted her to see. As her gaze raced down the uneven steps of the paragraphs, tripping over sentences and the thoughts that lodged against them, she felt as if her mind was toppling into darkness that the sunlit morning had cracked open to reveal. She kept her eyes on the story until the words were reduced to meaninglessness and she'd stowed her emotions out of Brenda's reach. "I think they're making far too much out of a coincidence," she said as she looked up.

"If you believe that's all it is."

Kathy found she was rolling up the newspaper as if she planned to use it as a club. "What else would you like me to believe?"

"Nothing, I'm sure, if Dudley says it's one. Would you mind not doing that to our property?"

"He does," Kathy said and let the club uncurl as she handed it back. "He does say."

"If a mother can't take her own son at his word then nothing can be relied on." Brenda smoothed the newspaper against her flat chest before adding "All the same, being stubborn won't help anybody's reputation."

"Whose do you think needs helping?"

Brenda fixed her with a look she plainly thought should be enough of an answer, but spoke. "I hope this neighbourhood isn't going to acquire one because of all the publicity. I especially hope we aren't going to be overrun by the press. Well, I mustn't keep you. Aren't you usually on your way to work by now?"

"Not today," Kathy said and shut herself into her house. The hall seemed gloomier than her having left the unobstructed sunlight behind could account for. At first she thought it was blackened by her anger, but when she closed her eyes in search of calm, that felt like slipping helplessly into her own depths, into a darkness no amount of daylight could relieve, because it consisted of being alone and fearful. Wasn't she as good as alone if Dudley wouldn't let her into his secrets? She hadn't known until the magazine was launched that he had been attacked at work. She'd had to learn from Patricia that his story wasn't being published and now, unbearably, from Brenda about the film. Surely there was no scope for further revelations, and at least he'd allowed her to glimpse the problem with which he was struggling. That had to be an appeal for help, even if he couldn't admit it. As soon as she was able to make out the digits she phoned the office.

Her voice answered, listing the office hours and inviting a

message. Mr Taylor had persuaded her to record the tape on the basis that hers was the friendliest voice. "It's Kathy," she told her own silence. "I won't be in today. I'm afraid it looks as if I've got a summer bug."

She didn't head straight for Dudley's room. In the kitchen she gazed at the breakfast he'd left. Sometimes he ate heartily for him; sometimes he would even ask for seconds—now that Kathy thought about it, whenever he'd been visiting his girlfriend. Surely he would if Kathy could make life easier for him. She cleared his plate and hers into the bin and drowned them in the sink before hurrying upstairs.

As she switched on his computer she wished with all her might that Dudley would have no password. Apparently he trusted her enough not to sneak into his room that he hadn't bothered with one. She hadn't time to feel ashamed as she searched for the last document he'd opened, "Put Down for Good". The experience of reading a new story of Dudley's before it was even printed made her feel so special that she grinned almost all the way to the end of the first sentence.

What was he trying to do? Didn't he realise the magazine could never publish this? Every sentence Kathy read made her more nervous for him. She couldn't even keep up a wry grin at his naming the woman Mish Mash. Was he so distracted that he thought this would amuse the editor instead of ensuring she rejected the story? But there wasn't a story to publish. Halfway down the second page it simply trailed off, extending itself in a word that seemed unwilling to end.

As she stared at the shrill extra letters and the raw red jagged line the spellcheck had etched beneath the elongated word, she remembered how in the months after she'd given up recreational drugs she had sometimes watched words she was reading begin to crawl about the page. They'd looked as desperate to flee as she had been to escape the sight, and each had seemed to aggravate the other, driving her deeper into the chasm of her panic. Could the mental state that had produced the squealing word have anything in common with the one she'd needed tranquillisers to overcome? Surely the word was only a cry of despair at how the story was wasting his time, or perhaps a protest at her interrupting him at work. The entire story must be intended as a protest at the way his work and his reputation were suffering. He was trying to write a deliberately unpublishable tale out of defiance—a story that pretended he based his fiction on real incidents and that let him retort to Shell's comments about him. Its savagery had startled Kathy, but he must be unable to write a story for the magazine or work on the film until he'd dealt with Shell. Could Kathy help? There was no need for her to change her plan. She reached for the keyboard and deleted the redundant letters from the last word.

It felt like accepting the biggest dare of her life with no turning back. Of course she could erase everything she wrote, and that allowed her to begin. ing all over him she typed, and read the sentence she'd completed. I expect he feels like someone's weeing all over him.

That meant Dudley. It was a gibe he and now Kathy imagined Shell Garridge might have made about him; it was no worse than the remarks with which the magazine had replaced his story. Kathy glared at the rest of the insults Mish Mash had directed at him, and began typing in a fury that only just kept pace with her thoughts.

Why weren't the women laughing any more? Some of them seemed to think Mish had stopped being funny. Maybe they could see she was afraid to stop. Unless she kept on joking, her fears would catch up with her. She wanted them to scream with laughter so there was no chance she would scream. She was carrying on about how soaked the man she was insulting would be getting in the rain because really she was afraid she might wet herself with fear. If he was really listening outside she had already gone too far. The knowledge made her rash. All she could do was say the worst she could imagine about men and him in particular to convince herself he wasn't there.

Kathy didn't know when she had last felt so close to her son. She could fancy she was writing out ideas he would have added if he'd had time. She was certain she was sharing his anger at the character he'd invented to help him clear his mind. It didn't matter how viciously she wrote about someone who didn't exist and events that had never taken place. All she cared about was her son, and he would be the only reader.

"I expect he's got his hand down his trousers if he's out there," Mish Mash scoffed, and lots more. Long before she'd finished ranting, most of her audience found reasons to leave. A last loyal pair were lingering over their drinks when she had to bolt for the Ladies', but when she'd finished getting rid of her ambitious lager intake, only the barman was waiting for her to leave. She wasn't going to ask him to see her to her car. She would never be so desperate that she had to ask a man for assistance. "Better put a pinnie on if you're washing up," she told him as she lowered her head at the rain.

Her car was hundreds of yards away along the dark promenade. She floundered to it through the storm that was blinding her. Was that a man beckoning her into his clutches? Just a bush the rain was jerking about. Were footsteps tiptoeing rapidly behind her? Just the dripping of a broken drainpipe. By now Mish could barely see, and

Kathy was delighted to visualise the woman stumbling soggily onwards, as helpless as any victim who didn't realise she was in a thriller. She might have been halfway to her car when she heard a whisper close to her, so thin and chill that at first she thought she was making it up out of rain. "Mish, you look a mesh" it said, at least until Kathy deleted the line. "What's your mission, Mish?" she preferred it to say instead.

The comedienne twisted around and staggered in a circle as if she was performing slapstick for whoever her audience was. She could see nothing but the rain that filled her eyes. She blinked and rubbed them till she was able to make out the crouching shape of her car. As she fled to it the whisper closed in on her. "You're in my mesh, Mish." She glanced wildly over her shoulder, but the storm seemed to have cleared away everybody except her. Was the whisperer hiding behind the car? He sounded too close, which was worse. "Think you're a fish, Mish? Going for a splash?" All of a sudden a streaming silhouette reared into sight beyond the edge of the promenade as if he had been lying in wait underwater and rushed at Mish. "Have some of thish, Mish," he shouted,

hardly worthy of him but the best Kathy could produce as he flung the liquid in the woman's face.

It wasn't acid or even a chemical—too unlikely, despite the temptation. It was merely a bucketful of rainwater. Nevertheless it swept away her vision and almost overbalanced her, so that she needed only a gentle push to send her blundering down the ramp from which Mr Killogram had ambushed her. Before she could regain control the promenade was towering over her and she was up to her waist in the river. She'd managed to back just one unsteady waterlogged pace up the slippery incline when he trod on her scalp.

The impact or the shock of it cost Mish her footing, and she slithered underwater until a wave broke on her chin and poured into her gasping mouth. The next moment his foot located her cranium again and pushed her all the way under. As he stood on her arms to keep her down he began to sing and eventually, once her hands had abandoned their mimicry of impaled crabs, to dance. "Splish splash, I was taking a bath" he sang until Kathy decided he ought to be singing "Mish mash." Perhaps that was the last sound the woman ever heard, or perhaps she heard the waves and thought they knew her name.

When Kathy was certain that had to be the end, she raised her face. Sunlight had been resting on her forehead for hours, and still felt like inspiration. As she reread the collaboration she was able to believe that while writing she had been able to enter not just Dudley's mind but Mr Killogram's. Was she deluding herself? Was her contribution worthy of them?

She gazed at the screen until she knew only that she didn't know. More than once her fingers strayed towards the Delete key or the Undo command. She mustn't make these judgements on Dudley's behalf. When she realised how late the afternoon had grown, she saved the story and printed it out before shutting down the computer. She hid the typescript under her pillow and hurried to the kitchen. Although she'd forgotten to have lunch she wasn't hungry, but Dudley needed his dinner. She suspected she might be able to eat very little until she learned what he thought of her help.

EIGHTEEN    Dudley wasn't sure how long he had been watching the job centre from the metal bench. The mounting sun in the relentlessly blue sky above the sharp harsh concrete edges of the roofs appeared to be training most of its light on his skull, shrivelling his brain around a very few thoughts. How soon would spying on the office help him write? While he was having plenty of ideas, they were simply wishes, too constricted by anger to grow into a tale. Inspiration might walk by, but how would he recognise it in the midst of so many people, let alone follow it where he could use it? As he peered around in search of it he saw that he was being watched.

A security guard was observing him from the doorway of a household goods store less than a hundred yards away, and another was eyeing him from the entrance to Woolworth's, closer still. Their gazes slipped askance as he found them, which made it even clearer that they were discussing him via their microphones. Did they take him for a criminal? They were the guards who'd failed to intervene when he was assaulted by the brother of yet one more woman who had made life unreasonably difficult for him. Perhaps they were alerting Lionel; he'd stepped out of the job centre to survey the crowd. Before Dudley could think how to react, or more importantly how not to, his mobile rang.

It gave him an excuse to crouch unrecognised away from Lionel. When he said "Yes" it was at least half a hiss.

"Listen, it sounds like you're busy there at the office. The message we picked up just now seemed kind of urgent, though."

"It was. It's more so now." As much to blame Walt as to detain him Dudley said "I'm not in the office. I'm just going to write." This was by no means accusing enough, and so he blurted "The paper says you gave in."

"I can tell you I'm not happy with how I've been quoted."

"It reads like you'll do anything to please her stupid family, this girl that's been dead for years because she was stupid too, and they won't be satisfied till you stop the film being made at all."

"That won't happen. You have my word on that."

"What are you going to do, then?"

"We'd like you to look at the script so far. Can we email it to you?"

"You better had."

"It would be great if the story you're writing could be incorporated in the movie. Can you make that work?"

"I'll see." Dudley's gaze followed a young mother with a push-chair up an alley until the wall of Woolworth's hid her, and at once he understood how he had to approach writing his next story. "Let me get on with it," he said.

"Before you do, there's someone who'd like a word. He's going to write fulltime."

As Dudley gathered that the last remark was about him, his father said "Dud? What's the boss saying, you're joining us wordsmiths?"

This felt as inadequate and beside the point as his father's presence at the launch had. "I've been one for a long time," Dudley objected.

"You're giving up the day job though, aren't you? I hope someone gets it that knows what it's like to live on the dole. Don't take this personal, but you were dealing with plain ordinary types like me, is that fair? I reckon they're entitled to expect whoever's handing out the jobs to be their class. Any rate," Monty said, "now you've got time to fix your image."

"What's wrong with it?" Dudley dodged into the nearest alley in the hope of not being overheard when he made his next call, but two shopgirls were piling it with funereal bags of rubbish. "I don't know what you're getting at," he complained.

"That's sad, lad. Gad, that's bad. Think I'm a cad? I won't get mad. Well, just a tad. I should place an ad if I've been had and I'm not your dad. This could start a fad. Better write it on my pad." Having apparently run out of rhymes, Monty said "I just want to help you get a name."

Dudley emerged into a concrete yard walled in by the backs of shops. "I've got one," he protested.

"That's right, you've got mine. I'm thinking you and me could put on a fair old show."

The unlikeliness of this made Dudley blurt "What kind?"

"Better than your last one. Trust me, your first performance is your worst." Monty paused as if searching for more rhymes and said "The pensioners' union want me to do an evening. How about being the other half of the act? A lot of them love a bit of a thrill still. You could read them a yarn or two that's not too strong. It's for charity. That's got to make you look good."

Dudley failed to see why he should require that, but saving time was more important. "When is it?"

"End of the month. Can I tell them you're in? They'll need to put the posters up."

"Go on," Dudley said, since he could think of no other way to terminate the conversation.

"That's ace. First of many, yes? We'll be the family firm."

Dudley broke the connection and typed a directory enquiries number. The foremost of several Indian voices greeted him with its formula. "Liverpool," he had first to tell it, and then "Eamonn Moore."

"How are you spelling that, please?"

"Eamonn. Eh mon. Aim on." None of this saved him from having to spell it twice, and Moore too. Suppose Eamonn was so anxious to stay aloof that he'd hidden his listing? The overseas babble of voices yielded up Dudley's informant and the information, however. "Would you like me to connect you?" she said.

Might that render his phone less identifiable? He wasn't sure and couldn't take the risk. He cut her off and strained to hold the number in his memory while he keyed the digits to mask his. Eamonn's phone rang several times, followed by as many, so that Dudley had reminded himself not to speak if an answering machine responded by the time a woman did. "Hello?" she said, more breathless than welcoming.

"Is that Mrs Eamonn Moore?"

"It's Julia Moore, yes."

"I do beg your pardon." However unreasonable he found her attitude, it could be useful. "I won't need to speak to your husband if you're one of the householders."

"You couldn't anyway, and yes, I am."

He was starting to see her: the elbow of the arm that held the receiver was propped on her other hand in a stance of angular aggressiveness, her legs were planted wide apart in a man's posture, her nose and chin were defiantly stuck up. All this went with the way she said "Who am I speaking to?"

He was ready for this, and so was his grin. "The name's Killan, Mrs Moore."

"I haven't heard that one before."

"It's real, I promise." He'd once dealt with a client of that name in his previous mundane life. "It's Irish," he said.

"What are you calling about, please?"

He was taking a breath to begin his approach when he heard a noise beyond her: the slowing drone and dying tick of an electric train. "Will you be close to the station?" he hoped aloud.

"We're by it, yes. Don't tell me you're selling double glazing."

"I won't be doing that, Mrs Moore. Do you and your husband have children?" he pretended not to know.

"Two little ones. Why?"

"I can understand you wouldn't want double glazing if it meant you couldn't hear them."

"And if we could, what's the point of having it?"

"Exactly. So what would you say to a revolutionary new soundproofing system that you can switch on when you want it and off when you don't?"

"I've no idea what I would say."

"You won't till you've seen it in action. I guarantee you can't imagine how quiet it will be for you." With sudden concern, which wasn't entirely manufactured, he said "Can you hear your children now?"

"Of course not. They're at school."

"Forgive me, obviously they will be. I shouldn't have thought you're the kind that keeps them off." His absolute conviction that everything would fit into place made him risk asking "Would you prefer to wait till everybody's home? Will Mr Moore be responsible for the final decision?"

"Which is that supposed to be?"

"About the demonstration I'll be delighted to give you."

"I'm entirely capable of dealing with that."

"That's what I like to hear. I'm in the Aigburth area. I can be with you in about an hour."

"No you can't."

"When would be convenient? Unfortunately I'm only in your district till early afternoon."

"I won't delay you, then. Good luck with finding someone else."

Dudley responded before she'd finished, not least because it was clear from her tone that she wasn't wishing him luck. "There's absolutely no obligation on your part, Mrs Moore, but I can personally promise you a truly special experience. You have my word you can't imagine what it's like till you've been through it yourself."

"I shouldn't be surprised when I haven't the least notion what you're supposed to be talking about."

"Then may I show you? It shouldn't take much of your time, and believe me, it'll change the way you live."

"We're perfectly happy with that, thank you. I should have told you sooner that we never invite salesmen into it. Now you'll have to excuse me. I really must—"

"Could we send you some literature at least? It'll tell you what's on offer better than I can over the phone. Throw it in the bin if you'd rather, but it'd prove I'm doing my job."

"We don't bin paper, we recycle it. We get far too much of it from firms like yours. What's the name of it, by the way?"

Dudley had to scrabble in his mind for one. "Dead Quiet," he no sooner thought than said. "It's all recycled, everything we use."

"That's something, anyway. Not a very enticing name, though, is it?" That sounded like her final word until she sighed and added

"All right, send us your brochure. I don't suppose that can do any harm."

"I'll make sure you receive everything that's necessary." Though he relished saying this, it was much more important to ask "May I just take your address? We don't appear to have it in the system."

"Desford Road," she said, and the number and postcode.

"Death in Desford Road." While he didn't utter that, his grin hindered his pronouncing "Thanks very much for all your help."

Perhaps she mistook his comment for sarcasm. She cut him off without another syllable. He closed his aching eyes to raise a grin towards a sky that felt as wide, and then he made for a stubby alley that ended opposite the Bingo building. As he hurried past that and the baths to the station he wondered if he would ever see them again. He had a sense of unfinished business: why hadn't he copied the addresses of clients who had struck him as having potential? He had only ever followed up one address from work, and he'd had to carry on past her shabby house when he'd seen two battered cars in the drive. He needn't feel frustrated now that he had Julia Moore's address. He was certain that she'd turned Eamonn against him, but nobody would make the connection. He didn't realise how broad his grin was until it startled one out of the ticket office clerk.

The lift opened onto the platform as the doors of a train did. In less than ten minutes Dudley was at Liverpool Central. While he was borne up one escalator and down another to the Northern Line he reflected on his title. "Death in Desford Road" gave away too much; even "Assassinated in Aigburth" did. "Slaughtered in the Suburbs" appealed to him, but perhaps he shouldn't settle on a title until he had the material. Though he wasn't yet used to the process of seeking his theme before he could write rather than writing to fix his memories and improve on any unsatisfactory elements, he could make the method work. He was a professional now, after all.

It seemed only right that a train was drawing alongside the platform at the foot of the escalator. He was alone in the carriage and at Aigburth Station, where he climbed steps to the ticket office. He turned his back to the manned window as if he was nodding in agreement at a poster forbidding antisocial behaviour on the railway. Indeed, he did agree. Too many people these days had no idea how to behave in public.

Outside the station parked cars greeted him with the absence of their owners. Beyond the car park there was nobody to observe him either. To his left, across a bridge that a sign described as weak, shouts and leathery thumps echoed in a football field. On his right two pairs of houses warty with pebbles led to a cul-de-sac—Desford Road.

The Moores lived halfway down the side that backed onto the railway, in the left-hand of two houses with a shared frontage like a levelled pinkish pebble beach. Dudley strolled past it and several extra houses before turning back. On the drive next to the glassed-in porch was a solitary car and space for another. Over the low thick wall of the paved sliver of garden he saw a room far too full of mirrors through the single downstairs window. He heard children playing somewhere behind the houses, a detail that suggested to him how innocent he would look if anybody had been watching him. He was crossing the road with absolute certainty that the events of the next few minutes would fall in his favour when he glimpsed activity reflected from mirror to mirror. Before he could react, a woman opened the front door and stepped into the porch. "Are you looking for someone?" she called.

She was shorter and wider than she had sounded on the phone. Between her skin and her abbreviated auburn hair he couldn't tell which had been modified to tone in with the other, especially when her reddish shorts and singlet confused the issue. A tall glass of lemonade or water was fizzing in her hand. He remembered not to recognise her aloud or to speak until he was close enough to avoid raising his voice. "Is Eamonn in?" he amused himself by enquiring as he opened the hot unpainted wooden gate.

"I'm afraid not." She gave Dudley a look with which she might have greeted an unwelcome child. "Should I know you?" she said.

"That'd be up to him, would it? I'm an old friend."

"So old that you've lost touch, you mean."

"We may have for a bit. Why?"

"Otherwise you'd know he's at work. Shouldn't you be?"

"I am," Dudley said, and took equal delight in adding "Just mixing business with pleasure."

By now he had a foot in the porch and was close enough to hear the nervous fizz of her drink. Anyone observing the conversation would see a figure in a grey suit, a visitor so nondescript as to be invisible. "What business?" she said.

"Research."

"None for you here, I'm afraid. I never answer questionnaires."

"Not that kind of research. You won't have to do anything."

That wasn't entirely true, and for a distracted moment he thought her stare had identified the fallacy until she said "You are, aren't you. You're who I thought you were."

It didn't matter what she thought, because she didn't, and very soon would matter even less. "Who's that?" he nevertheless said.

He had to grin for as long as she glanced down the bright fawn hall, a gesture implying that she thought he meant someone who'd crept up behind her. "The writer," she said as she faced him again. "You got back in touch with him the other week and now you're in the paper. Dudley Swift, isn't it?"

"That's me." Holding her gaze with his made Dudley even more conscious of the doorstep against which her ankles weren't quite resting. One good shove and she would sprawl on the mushroom carpet while he slammed the door after them both, but he couldn't forego asking "What's Eamonn told you about me?"

"I haven't time to go into it," Eamonn's wife said. "Ask the girl you sent to interview him. He said all he had to say to her."

"I didn't send her," Dudley objected.

"Your people did, didn't they? The ones that are publishing you and putting money into your film," she said and gave a frowning blink. "I hope you aren't researching that round here. I don't want my children thinking your sort of thing happens where they live."

The sounds of children were more distant. The car next to the porch emitted a single metallic tick like the final stroke of a pendulum. "It can anywhere," he said.

"Not in my street. Nowhere near here if you don't want trouble from a lot of people who know how to make themselves heard. Now I'm afraid you must excuse me," she said and turned to step into the house.

He could still hear the hiss of her drink, a brittle sound like a promise that the glass would break. The edge and, he hoped, some additional fragments would cut her throat open when she fell on the glass. He'd lost count of the number of throats he'd seen slashed or mangled in films, but he was sure that the real thing would be different and worth witnessing—worth at least a paragraph, possibly more. "Can I leave Eamonn a message?" he said and advanced into the porch.

"I suppose so," she said, barely in his direction. "What is it, then?"

It was about to be her, and a pity that it would go unrecognised as such. "Have you got something I can scribble it down on?" he said.

"Haven't you? I thought you were meant to be a writer."

She succeeded in conveying both impatience and reluctance as she stumped to a bow-legged table next to the thickly padded stairs and picked up a note-pad from beside a modern antique phone. "I'll close this, shall I?" said Dudley and shut himself into the house.

At the muted thud of the door she swung around, but whatever she did now was too late. She still had the note-pad in her hand. As Dudley strode at her he glimpsed his decisive progress in a mirror to his right and, more importantly, how there was nobody in the street to notice him. In a moment he was out of range of any mirror and within arms' length of Eamonn's wife. "Here's your writing material," she said, apparently as her notion of a joke.

Indeed she was. Dudley was beguiled by the insight and by realising that he was acting out the character Vincent thought he'd created for him. He was less inclined to resent the presumption this involved since the character had helped him slip into Eamonn's house. He had only to sidle by her as though he intended to rest the pad on the table, and then he would be at her back. His stomach felt exquisitely tight, his mouth was deliciously dry. He held out his left hand and took a pace past the end of the stairs just as she stood her glass on the table so as to offer him a pencil.

He almost clutched the glass and thrust it into her hand. Barely in time he remembered not to touch it with his fingertips. He reached for it with the pad in his hand and took hold of the glass through the paper. "Here you are," he said and felt as if he was proposing an ironic final toast to her.

As she accepted the glass a blink seemed to spread down her small pouchy face, twitching her snub nose at the same time as her permanently pouting mouth. She had noticed how he was keeping his prints off the glass, which simply made her fate still more inevitable. In less than a breath he was past her and dropping the pad on the table. She turned her head towards the sound, and his left hand sailed up beyond her vision to grab the back of her neck. He hadn't caught her when the door at the far end of the hall sprang open like a trap, releasing the no longer muffled sound of children in a garden and revealing a woman at least as squat as Eamonn's wife in a dress that resembled a cartoon of a flower-bed. "Julia, would you like me to—" she called before lowering her voice. "Oh, I didn't realise you had company."

"I won't have in a minute. Don't go away, Sue. Mr Swift is almost on his way."

"Don't be on my account," the woman said with a smile that appeared ready to be secretive. "What were you doing just then?"

"Finding Mr Swift the tools of his trade."

"Not you, your friend. He looked as if he was going to give you a massage if you want me to leave you to that."

"I most emphatically don't," Eamonn's wife said and swung to confront Dudley. "What's she talking about, may I ask?"

He thought of making them his first double act, but the newcomer was carrying no glass, and what would he have to do about the children? Dealing with them would take longer than was safe, especially since he was running out of ideas. The situation had grown so intensely frustrating that he was scarcely able to manufacture an answer or pronounce it. "I was just after the pencil," he mumbled.

"Is that what you call it?" the flowered woman said as a version of innocence widened her eyes. "I'd have said he was after you, Julia."

"Was it more of your research, Mr Swift? Trying to find out if a woman would spot someone like you skulking behind her. Well, I did."

"Heavens, why would he be interested in that?"

"Mr Swift fancies himself as a bit of a storyteller. Not our kind, though. Nasty stories from what Eamonn says."

"Should I have heard of you, Mr Swift? Have you had anything published?"

"It isn't Swift, it's Smith. Smith. Smith. Smith. Smith." Each parched repetition, emphasised by the fists he shook, sent him farther backwards, away from the women and the children's laughter. "Dudley Smith," he said louder still. "Some people don't want me to be known, but I am."

"He's certainly got the temperament, hasn't he, Julia? Let's hope he has the talent to go with it."

"I've no intention of finding out. Won't you be writing after all?"

Even when he grasped that she was asking him Dudley was inclined to continue his retreat, but suppose she told Eamonn that he'd tricked his way into the house? His life was more than complicated enough just now. He marched to the table and scribbled *Sorry missed you. Be in touch.* He was signing the note when Eamonn's wife craned to read it. "Hardly worth the paper, was it?" she said. "Why, they aren't even sentences."

She would never know how much the presence of her friend was protecting her. "You ought to save it," he said. "You might be able to sell it for a lot of money someday not too far off."

The women covered their mouths as if they thought not quite hiding their mirth was civil. They might as well have been practising ventriloquism, for the unseen children immediately burst out laughing. "I thought—" Dudley was provoked to blurt before he succeeded in controlling himself. "Aren't those children meant to be at school?"

"Only in the morning," Sue told him. "They're too little yet for all day."

Eamonn's wife hadn't finished staring hard at Dudley by the time she spoke. "Did you phone me this morning?"

"Me?" Dudley said and, too late, simply "No."

Her stare wasn't prepared to relent. "You didn't pretend to be a salesman."

"Why would I want to do that?"

"That's what I'm wondering. Did you? Why?"

The gap between the questions was so tiny that he couldn't be bothered to dissemble any further. "See if you can figure it out for yourself," he said.

"Research." In case the contempt with which she filled the word was insufficient she added "Playing at being a criminal, in other words, like the way you held that glass. I think Eamonn's right, you're really rather sick."

With an effort Dudley managed to restrict his answer to words and a grin that stung almost as much as his eyes did. "You bet I am, and if this is how you have to live if you aren't, I'm glad."

"Well, I won't be reading any of his books," he heard Sue promise as he slammed the door behind him.

Emerging into open sunlight felt like a lucky escape. Suppose Eamonn had somehow connected his wife's fate with Dudley—with the way she must have made Eamonn ashamed to own up to friendship? Dudley had to find someone who could never be suspected of giving him a motive to use them for research, and soon. Surely circumstance would bring him someone. It always had.

The problem was that he couldn't wait for a subject to present herself. He hurried to the station, no longer troubling to hide his face from the clerk in the ticket office. While he paced the deserted platform he heard childish laughter above the opposite side of the cutting, and had to keep telling himself that neither the children nor the sky nor any god it concealed could be mocking him. Eventually a train arrived, neglecting to position any of its doors in front of him. As he stamped on board, his mobile rang. "Dudley Smith," he said, less a greeting than a challenge.

"Dudley. Don't let me interrupt if you're busy," Walt said, but also "Where are you?"

"Trying to research."

"I'll leave you to get on with it. We just wanted you to know that Vincent has emailed you his script so far."

"All right," Dudley said with no sense of how ironic he was being.

"And Patricia would like to sit in on your casting session. We thought we could run a journal of the whole production."

"Patricia."

"Patricia Martingale. Our journalist who wants to do her best for you."

"Think so?" said Dudley. "That's good. I'm going underground now."

"We'll be in touch, but I can tell Patricia she's okay, yes?"

"She definitely is. Thanks for calling." Dudley clasped the mobile between his hot palms while he shook hands with himself. "Patricia," he mouthed, and almost experienced a pang of regret as the train sped into the secretive dark.

NINETEEN     Less than half an hour before Dudley was due home from work, Kathy began to dread his arrival. How could she have invaded his room when she knew there was nothing he valued more than his privacy? Suppose he never trusted her or spoke to her again? Suppose he moved out of the house? The idea brought others with it that made her unhappy with herself. Wasn't she indulging his untidiness to ensure he had no reason to leave? Did she secretly yearn for him not to grow up, or was she using him as her excuse not to find another partner? Perhaps she was as private as he liked to be, in which case her example was to blame. He wouldn't always have her to look after him, and what would happen to him once he was alone? Should she invite Patricia Martingale for dinner again? She wouldn't mind knowing the girl better or encouraging Dudley's friendship with her, but she mustn't let that distract her now. She had to decide what to do about the story she'd finished for him.

She was in the kitchen, and emptily surrounded by evidence that she hadn't yet thought about dinner. Shouldn't she tell him as soon as she saw him how she'd helped? The prospect turned her mouth dry. She could postpone his discovery until she found the best moment to prepare him, she thought suddenly: she had only to rename the file that contained her additions and restore his work untouched under the original name. She hurried out of the kitchen and was almost at the stairs when she heard the clank of the latch of the garden gate.

She dashed to the stairs and halted halfway up as footsteps that she did her best not to recognise arrived at the front door. If they were Dudley's, could she sprint to his room and somehow keep him downstairs while she used his computer? If she claimed to be naked, might that deter him? She'd seized the banister to impel herself upwards when a key scraped at the lock. Before she could reach the landing, Dudley strode into the house.

Kathy strove to tone down her surprised expression as she turned to him. "You're early," she no more than remarked.

"There's work I need to be doing," he said and came fast up the stairs.

She didn't quite block his path, but her hand began to, though only so that she could blurt "How was your day?"

He stared at the hand until it withdrew enough to let him sidle quickly by. "Same as usual. What do you expect?" he said, already with his back to her. "Wasn't yours?"

"Pretty much the kind of day I'd like." There was her chance, but she flinched from taking it, not least because he was staring at her comment as if he couldn't be bothered to grimace. "Except I haven't made any dinner," she said.

That stopped him with one foot on the landing. "It doesn't matter," he grumbled and made for his room.

"We don't want you ill. Shall we get a Chinese?"

"I haven't time to go for it."

"I can go." All at once she was anxious to be out of the house, but lingered to ask "Is there anything you'd particularly like?"

"Yes," he said and poked his head out of his room. "Being left alone."

"I'll get your favourites, shall I," she promised and hastened to put the front door between her and her son.

She mustn't feel demeaned by his brusqueness. Nothing was more important than his success. She hurried downhill to the Chinese takeaway on the main road. By now he must be reading the completion of his tale about Mish Mash. As Kathy ordered the dishes he liked—prawn crackers, chicken with water chestnuts, sweet and sour king prawns, chicken curry—she grew so dry-mouthed at the thought of learning his verdict that she hardly recognised her own voice. Might he be deleting all her work at that very moment? Surely he liked her writing too much to do that, unless he was enraged by her interference. She would have to bear whatever decision he made, but the extra heat of the tiled room didn't help her prepare for it, nor did the incessant incomprehensible chatter in the open kitchen. Far too eventually, after several other customers had carried off fish and chips, her order arrived. She grabbed the plastic bag of metal containers, which bumped and scraped against her no matter how she held the flimsy handles, and sent herself uphill.

Silence met her as she opened the front door. She was tempted to ease it shut, but dealt it a moderate slam. When this didn't earn any audible reaction she called "I'm back."

The sound Dudley made was less than a word and certainly less than welcoming. Kathy retreated to the kitchen, where she entrusted the containers of food to the oven and set the table for two. The prawn crackers came in a bag, which she emptied into a dish. She tried eating one, but it squeaked like polystyrene between her teeth and left her mouth still drier. Having done her utmost not to mind being left alone with her imagination, she ventured to the foot of the stairs and cleared her desiccated throat. "Is there anything you'd like me to be doing?" she called.

"Haven't you done enough?" She heard him say that even though he hadn't spoken. He must surely have heard her, which meant he would rather not speak to her, and that was worse than any retort he could make. She was drawing an effortful breath that might have turned into a plea when he said just audibly "I'm nearly finished."

She took refuge in the kitchen, where she used an oven glove to transfer the containers to laminated table-mats printed with various sizes of rainbow. As she deposited the last container and snatched her hands clear of the heat that was cutting through the padded glove she heard Dudley emerge from his room. Each of his unhurried if not deliberately ominous paces down the stairs seemed to add weight to a bar that was stiffening her shoulders and pressing on her inflamed neck. She had to turn her entire body to discover that he was withholding all expression from his face. "How hungry have you ended up?" she almost couldn't ask.

"I don't know yet. Why don't you stop going on about it?"

"I will," she said with the barest hint of rebuke. "I'll let you serve yourself for a change."

She watched him load his plate with rice and dump table-spoonful of the various courses on carefully separated quadrants of it. She had to derive some comfort from his taking so much. Once he'd swallowed a forkful of prawns she said "How is it?"

"Same as last time."

"That can't be bad, can it?" When he just about shook his preoccupied head she took a few spoonfuls. "I'd say that was fine," she said, having lingered over tasting each item, and then she seemed to have no option but to ask "How's anything else?"

"I can fix it."

"That's the main thing, isn't it? I'm glad."

"So you're glad."

"Seriously, I am. Whatever you have to do is fine as far as I'm concerned."

"I'll remember you said that," Dudley said, but looked not quite sure of her.

"You should whenever you need to. This isn't about me, it's about you."

"I never thought it wasn't."

She would have appreciated any praise he cared to dole out, but he must be too preoccupied with his own work. "You'll have more time to get on with whatever you're planning, won't you?" she said.

Lines like the marks of wires dug into his forehead and made her wince. "Who says?" he demanded, dropping his knife and fork on his plate with a single shrill clank. "Who've you been talking to?"

"Only you, Dudley. Don't finish yet."

"Somebody from work, was it? Did one of them call?"

"Why would—" Kathy began and then saw he needn't be referring to the job centre. "They haven't put off publishing you again, have they? They wouldn't dare."

"That's right, they wouldn't. They better hadn't."

"I haven't made it harder for you to write." When he merely stared at her she had to ask "Have I?"

"You will if you keep going on. I'm trying to think. I've only just read the bloody thing."

"Is it so awful?"

"Probably not awful. I can't tell yet. I don't know how much of me is in it."

"As much as you want there to be. I promise I won't be upset."

"Why should you be?" His eyes had narrowed as though to trap whatever he was feeling. "What's it got to do with you?"

"I thought it might have a little. No more than you think it deserves to have."

"Look, Vincent is enough to deal with without you. It's meant to be our script. Mine and his."

By no means for the first time that day Kathy felt as if an assumption had been wrenched from beneath her. "You're talking about the film."

"He emailed me what he's written and I've just read it. He says it may change once we've got our cast."

"Are they allowed to change things? They're your characters, after all."

"They aren't all mine at the moment. Mr Killogram will be, that's for sure." Dudley seemed as impatient with her as with the situation. "He wants me at the casting sessions," he said. "He won't be using anyone I don't believe in."

Kathy opened her mouth and considered hushing it with a random forkful, but couldn't even feign an appetite until she learned "What's happening about the story you were trying to write this morning?"

"I'm not any more."

Despite the risk of aggravating his impatience she said "What's going to become of it, then?"

"Nothing. It's no good for publishing or putting in the film. It was just in the way. I've figured out how to write what I've got to write."

Kathy saw that all the emotions she'd suffered since leaving his room had both exhausted her and wasted her time. "Am I allowed to ask how?" she said.

"By being a writer. I thought you thought that's what I am."

"You know I do. You know you are." Being emptied of her accumulated feelings had left room for hunger, but as she lifted her fork she said "And you're going to be filmed. It's exciting, isn't it?"

"Not as much as some things."

"Who'd have thought you'd be meeting film stars? And they'll be meeting a star as well," she was quick to add. "If it's a workday I can always call the office and tell them you're sick."

"You won't have to. Mrs Wimbourne is giving me time off. I've let her know what's most important."

"That's better still. We don't need people thinking you're un-healthy when you aren't." Deep down she felt she might almost have wished sickness on him that morning by proposing the ex-cuse. At least he was making up for it now, and she was happy to regain her appetite in sympathy with his. She wondered if the reason behind it could be that he'd met a girl he cared for, but she mustn't risk putting him off by questioning him. She had to let him tell her in his own time, however frustrating that might become—indeed, already was. "We're two of the healthiest people I know," she declared and stopped herself from saying more with a forkful so tasty it did away with any need to think.

# TWENTY

Trying to plan was useless, Dudley told himself. It simply made the inside of his skull feel scraped bare of thoughts. Life would come to him as always, and he only had to lie in wait for it. Once he'd met the man who would play him in the film, he would be able to think of dialogue that was worthy of his character. He had to let working with Vincent ease some of the pressure on him. If Vincent thought of any tricks sufficiently clever for Mr Killogram to perform, Dudley mustn't resent it just because they wouldn't be his. Nevertheless waiting frustrated him so much that he couldn't stop pacing the station platform as if he was bearing the empty relentlessly sunlit receptacle of his skull up and down in the hope that inspiration might stray into it. He hadn't caught a solitary notion by the time the train from West Kirby pulled into Birkenhead North.

It was crowded with pensioners travelling on passes. With his back to the engine he had the impression that a scrap of the world was being paraded past him for his approval. He imagined rolling someone down the grassy banks into the path of a train, but who? His gaze ranged over pallid pouchy faces, some of which appeared to be in the process of leaving their gender behind—he had to look twice to be certain that one balding figure was female—and then his attention was drawn to the far end of the carriage as if the banks racing by on both sides had snatched it with them. Watching him from the farthest seat was Patricia Martingale.

As their eyes met she replaced with a smile whatever expression she'd worn. The train was slowing in anticipation of Birkenhead Park. When an unsteady couple in the middle of the carriage rose to their feet, she pointed to the vacated seats. Lurching down the train to join her felt like one of those scenes in films his mother liked where characters ran into each other's arms, except that this made him grin even wider. He regained control of his mouth as he sat opposite her and objected "You never said you lived over here."

"Maybe we should exchange a few secrets if I can write about yours."

She wouldn't be writing once she learned his. He felt a little wistful at the possibility of never reading how she would have rounded off her appreciation of him. He was silent while the train approached Conway Park, where Mrs Wimbourne could no longer make him appear to be reduced to her level. Patricia leaned forward into the spotlight of the sun to ask "Any sign of a story yet?"

He tried not to grin at the way the sight answered the question. "Working on one," he said.

"Any chance of tomorrow or earlier? If we don't have it by then we'll need to save it for the next issue."

"This is the next issue."

"The one after that, I mean. Maybe the longer we keep people waiting the more excited they'll get about you."

The light receded behind her as the tunnel drew over him. His mind was feeling scraped again, and his question came out harsh. "Have you finished writing about me yet?"

"Pretty much."

"When am I going to see it?"

A copy of her tribute would prove that he was the last person who could have wanted to harm her, and he stared at her until she said "I'll do a last little bit of work on it and then perhaps I can give you a peek."

The roar of the tunnel through the open window silenced her. She glanced at him only occasionally as the train sped to Hamilton Square and under the river to Liverpool. He didn't mind how closely she observed him; all she would be seeing was the famous writer. She left the train ahead of him at James Street and preceded him into an uninspiring lift, no more than a grey metal cell so cramped that it almost pressed her against him. It raised them to a corridor too short to be useful, out of sight of the ticket collector but not of the escalator from the platform. A second lift was several times the size of the first but offered even less, given the proximity of the staff. In any case, the station setting would bring him too close to repeating himself.

At the bottom of James Street three lanes of traffic raced along either side of the dock road. It occurred to him that if you were holding a girl's hand you could fling her in front of a car or better still a lorry, but it would have to be late at night with limited visibility, and she would need to be more at ease with him. The Albert Dock was useless—cars, tourists, shoppers, guards on patrol—but beyond the glass doors to which Patricia had the combination, the stony corridor and walled-in stairs lit by luminous white bricks seemed promising: suppose somebody unknown followed her in? Then he noticed the dead eye of a security lens up in a corner, and only just refrained from grimacing at it as he followed her to the office of the *Mersey Mouth*.

Six men of about his age were seated on chubby leather sofas in the reception area, between a table low enough to kneel at and a brick wall full of Tom Burke's misty views of Merseyside. If they were the actors, none of them much resembled Dudley. He attempted to decide whether that was to the good as the scientifically tanned girl behind the desk gave him a generalised smile. Patricia led him through the solitary right-hand door of an inner corridor, into a long room occupied only by Vincent. A line of chairs huddled against the conference table that had been pushed to the side of the room overlooking the river, leaving three chairs with their backs to the wall at the far end. "Did you check the hopefuls?" Vincent said in not too low a voice. "Any first impressions?"

"They don't look like Mr Killogram. They don't look like anyone."

"He's meant to be somebody nobody notices."

"I thought they were meant to be stars. I've never seen any of them. What have they been in?"

"Plays more than film work, some of them. Commercials, some have, or local soaps. They're all good, that's the main thing." When Dudley met that with a blank stare, Vincent shook his head vigorously enough to set his round face quivering and almost to dislodge his glasses. "We'd have to spend our entire budget and then some on a major star," he said. "This is Merseyside, not Hollywood."

"I thought Walt only hired the best."

"We're all proof of that, aren't we?" Patricia intervened. "Look at it this way. If whoever you choose had a familiar face, people would see that and not your character."

Dudley grudged acknowledging this when she'd presumed to class him with herself and Vincent. "Let's get on with choosing," he told Vincent.

"I'll start them off," Patricia said.

He resented how she was trying to involve herself, returning with the first of the actors. He saw little reason why she should feel entitled to sit next to him and Vincent, and might have said so except for concentrating on the hopeful. "Bob Nolan," the bony sharp-faced actor said.

"Whenever you're ready," said Vincent.

"You don't know me, but you will. I'm a writer. Murder stories, they're my meat. Want to hear something funny? They're all real. How do I know? Because I did them . . ."

His voice was too high and his face too eager to please. He looked ready to break into a grin, but the wrong sort—not the way a predator might bare his teeth when he saw his kill. By the time the actor completed the opening voice-over Dudley was almost sure that he'd been poking fun at the character. He could hardly wait for Nolan to leave so that he could turn on Vincent. "Do you think it's funny?" he demanded.

"Wouldn't Mr Killogram think so?"

"I'd say witty."

"Try and make him if you like."

Dudley strove to think of ways while he observed the procession of men who wanted to be him. One had too booming a voice to be unobtrusive, or could the point be that he was so noticeable that nobody would ever suspect him? Another crouched as if he didn't think he was already small enough to go unnoticed, but he was so nondescript that Dudley felt insulted. The next actor watched his audience sidelong throughout his speech as if he was ashamed to admit to being Mr Killogram. By contrast, the fourth man entered the room with an imperfectly restrained swagger. "Colin Holmes," he announced.

For once Dudley managed to head Vincent off from speaking. "In your own time."

As the actor stepped forward he seemed to increase more in stature than his approach quite accounted for. He halted halfway up the room and held Patricia with his gaze. "You don't know me, but you will . . ."

His originally somewhat harsh voice had grown soft and penetrating. If he or Mr Killogram was concealing any amusement, there was no question that it was deepest black. As soon as he'd finished speaking he swung around and stalked from the room. Patricia shivered or returned to herself. "That was convincing," she murmured. "I'd say he wanted the job."

Her assumption that she was entitled to comment would have angered Dudley more if he hadn't shared her view. He contained his impatience as he watched the final candidate, who rested his hands on his stomach as though praying or to cover up its prominence. The gesture was enough without his uneasily fluctuating voice to put Dudley against him. He didn't bother to let the man out of earshot before saying "I know who I want."

"Let me guess," Patricia said, but only that until they and Vincent were alone. "The one I spoke up for."

Just in time not to betray his indignation Dudley saw that by siding with her he would be demonstrating one more reason why he could never have harmed her. "Shall we have him back in and send the rest off?" Vincent said.

Patricia was on his way before Dudley had time to dispatch her. "Thank you all for coming," he heard her say, and "We'd like you to rejoin us." A sudden snigger overtook him, to be disguised as a cough. If she was so anxious to present herself as important to his work, she was bound to get her wish. He had to grin at her, and perhaps Colin Holmes thought the renewed greeting was aimed at him as well, because he widened his eyes and mouth. "We think you're it," Vincent informed him.

The actor's face was as strong as Dudley's reflection, as sharply defined and angular, with an expressively mobile mouth and nostrils that seemed to flare with eagerness. "I must say I'm flattered," he said in his softened voice.

"Colin, this is Dudley Smith. The man behind Mr Killogram."

"Then he's the man I was hoping to meet," Colin Holmes said.

Dudley stood up and stuck his hand out. "Call me Dudley," he offered.

The actor strode forward to grip his hand fiercely enough to hurt. Dudley clasped his throbbing fist with his other hand and lifted them to signal victory. "And I'll call you Mr Killogram. What else have you been in?"

"Soaps mostly. I shouldn't think you watch that kind of thing. Too ordinary for you."

Was there a hint of pique in his wide blue eyes? "They are but you aren't," Dudley said.

"I won't be," Mr Killogram said as the receptionist leaned into the room to announce "The rest of the actors are here."

"We don't need any," Dudley called. "We've got him. Meet Mr Killogram."

She responded with a frown so small he assumed it was meant to be charming, though it wasn't directed especially at him. "Who?"

"The hero. He's the only man we need just now, isn't he, Vincent?"

"I wasn't talking about men," the receptionist said.

Neither Patricia nor Vincent seemed disposed to contradict her. Only Mr Killogram allowed him to glimpse some amusement, enough to convince him that they had more in common than the others might have guessed. When the first victim—a tall slim creature named Jane Bancroft—applied for his and Mr Killogram's approval, he felt as if he spoke for both of them by remarking "That's a good name for an actress."

"Can we try some of the train scene?" Vincent directed her. "It's just to see how you and Colin work together. It won't be in the film."

Mr Killogram gazed into Dudley's face. "Will that be a problem?"

"It's just some family's making a stink. They keep saying it's like how some girl died years and years ago."

Before Dudley finished sensing that Mr Killogram felt as outraged as he did, the actor took his script to the end of the room and waited for Jane Bancroft to join him. "Are you sure you're all right?" he said.

She straightened herself a last inch until she was almost as tall as the actor, and Dudley imagined Patricia straining to be taller than his own shoulder. "Why shouldn't I be?" Jane Bancroft said.

His voice grew even softer yet no less audible. "I don't mean you. That's where I'm starting from."

"Sorry. Sorry," she told the audience as well.

"Whenever you're ready. Go again? Are you sure you're all right?"

She peered at him as if to determine who he thought he was. "I told you once."

That was Dudley's line, and he felt as if he was throwing his voice. "I'm guessing you haven't got a boyfriend," Mr Killogram said.

While Vincent had cut some of the dialogue, Dudley relished the urgency this lent to Mr Killogram. "Maybe," Jane Bancroft said with a wariness that sounded coy to him.

"Are you looking for one?"

"I don't need to look."

"How about one that's shown he can take care of you?"

"I can take care of myself."

"Two can twice as well."

Mr Killogram was pacing her, boxing her in as she followed the wall back and forth. "This isn't the way," she said abruptly. "I've gone wrong."

"You can't with me."

Was that Vincent's line? No, it was Mr Killogram's own. It and the way he was trapping the girl with his deft manoeuvres made

Dudley's stomach deliciously tight with anticipation, and so did her struggle not to appear nervous as she tried to dodge. "What's the matter with you?" she gasped.

"We shouldn't part like this after all we've been through. At least let me give you my number."

"No thank you."

"Or give me yours."

"Thanks even less," Jane Bancroft said and trotted a few side-long steps that she seemed to want to be comical. "Look, I was pretending I was lost before."

It might have been a mating dance if Mr Killogram had gone in for that sort of nonsense. Warmth and tightness spread down from Dudley's stomach as Mr Killogram said "I'll escort you just the same."

Throughout the dialogue Mr Killogram had kept his back to the audience, a stance that helped Dudley feel the other was performing his secret thoughts. He didn't see what expression Mr Killogram turned on her to make her stiffen in order, he was certain, not to flinch. "Sorry. Sorry," she said, more to Vincent than to him. "I didn't realise it was meant to be this serious."

"What did you think it was meant to be?" Dudley asked through some kind of a grin.

"More fun. A nice acting job. I hope I didn't waste too much of your time. I don't suppose you'll keep me in mind for your next film," she said entirely to Vincent, and had barely finished when she fled.

Vincent threw up his hands and then snatched off his glasses to embellish a second take of the gesticulation. "Let's try not to scare anyone else away," he said.

As the pleasurable ache faded from his middle Dudley said "Who are you saying did?"

"You might want to stop suggesting you don't think they're actors," Patricia said.

He mustn't draw attention to their disagreement. "You can tell me if I am."

"Who's next?" Mr Killogram was eager to know. "Don't say they've all bolted."

"Better tone it down a notch or they might," Vincent said, "and can we see your face this time?"

Mr Killogram swung around to display a grin Dudley would have been proud to sport. "Here it is," he said as his next victim ventured into the room.

Did she think he was referring to her? Mr Killogram might have. "Lorna Major," she announced, frowning at him.

"That's Mr Killogram," Dudley said.

"He means Colin's playing him," Vincent quite unnecessarily explained. "He'll take you through the train scene."

Mr Killogram faced her at once, presenting his profile to the audience. "Are you sure you're all right?"

"I told you once."

The swiftness of her retort came close to throwing Dudley, but not Mr Killogram. As they enacted the scene he prowled back and forth, hemming the girl in while he showed her and the watchers an expression of wide-eyed rationality that he kept appearing to strengthen by lifting his upturned outstretched hands. The girl refused to look away, and her determination to confront him prevented her escape. Dudley was so sure he could invent a suitable fate for her that when Vincent asked him for his thoughts he had to restrain them. "She'll be good," he said. "I'd have her."

"We'll definitely be in touch."

Lorna Major seemed slightly less delighted to be chosen than Dudley had every right to expect, another reason why he would enjoy her lingering demise. The same was the case with the other applicants, one of whom kept trying to dart past Mr Killogram only to retreat almost to the wall, while the last had the habit of adding various forms of the same short word—adjective, adverb, directive—in a thick Scouse accent to her dialogue, a trait that failed to rescue her from Mr Killogram. By the end of the auditions Dudley was crouching forward, inflamed by the spectacle of Mr Killogram and his parade of victims, and had some difficulty in sitting up straight until he'd subsided. "You're pleased, then," Vincent said.

For a moment Dudley wondered guiltily how visible that was. "I wouldn't have been without Mr Killogram."

Mr Killogram widened his eyes with eagerness or pleasure. "You won't be."

"Shall we let you go away and think what you want to do with them?" said Vincent.

Dudley had to grasp that the question was addressed to him, not Mr Killogram. "I'd better," he said to Patricia, and wondered why he sounded apologetic. He had nothing to apologise for. However tempting the girls were, they had to be preserved for the film. She was the girl who was going to stir his imagination back into life, and he wasn't about to betray her with them. She was still his choice.

# TWENTY–ONE

Patricia did her best to put up with Dudley's silence, but by the time they reached the road past the Albert Dock she found it too uncomfortable. "Can I ask what you were thinking?" she said over the rumble of traffic.

Dudley extended a hand to the button at the crossing and belatedly pushed it. As the red man lit up like a brand he said "I'll let you know later."

"I was just wondering what you made of our performers."

"I haven't made anything of them yet."

"I meant how you thought they shaped up," Patricia said, not quite concealing some impatience.

"He's perfect and they ought to be."

The stampede of traffic trundled to a reluctant halt as the red man's companion intensified his innocent colour. Patricia crossed the road that smelled of petrol and hot metal so fast that Dudley didn't catch up with her until she was climbing the street to the station. "Are you heading for home?" she said.

"I'm going your way, that's right."

He was assuming too much for her liking, which was why she said "Not now you aren't, Dudley. I'm off into town."

"I'll walk along with you if you want. I'll let you ask me some more questions."

Far from winning her over, this disconcerted her with its childishness. He might almost have been trying to resemble the earliest description of him in Kathy's tale: "a cherub's golden curls that were heavenly in their untidiness, blue eyes that were twin mirrors of the world, a face that would disown its chubbiness too soon". Patricia halted outside the station, next to a news-stand piled with headlines about the reconstruction of a girl's death, to tell him "Don't worry, there's no urgency."

"You can't say how urgent it is. I've got to get on with my writing."

"I'm sure there'll be time for both."

"Maybe I won't be able to write till I've got you out of the way."

"Not literally, I hope." Since his mouth seemed unsure what expression this deserved, she said "Please don't feel under any pressure from me. I'm certain you've told me enough."

"You haven't seen me at work yet."

"Don't you think that might make it harder for you? Has anybody ever been there while you're working?"

He hadn't answered that—his mouth was still considering what shape to adopt—when his mobile struck up its October theme. As he dragged it out of his pocket he bared his teeth at it rather than, Patricia hoped, at her for edging away. "I'll leave you to it," she said.

"You don't need to." His voice grew sharper while he lifted the phone. "Yes?" he said, and not much more gently "Oh, Vincent. I'm working."

Presumably this was a lie designed to end the call. "There's a what?" he said. "Can't it wait? All right, I know I'll have to. I've said I will." As he pocketed the mobile he informed Patricia "Another actress has turned up. You'll have to watch me with this one as well."

"I won't, thanks. I've got plenty already." She saw his hand stray towards his mobile and wondered if he could be thinking of calling Vincent back. "I won't delay you any longer," she said and started uphill.

At the corner she looked over her shoulder. Of course he wasn't just behind her; he was beyond the station, almost at the dock road. He glanced towards her, and she had to dodge around the corner. She might have lurked in Castle Street and then returned to the station, but that would be ridiculous. She'd catch her train at Moorfields, which was ridiculous enough.

Beyond Castle Street, behind the town hall, a skeleton lay in wait for four chained prisoners, but nobody in the offices that boxed in the quadrangle seemed aware of the monument. Patricia crossed the square to Moorfields and ascended an escalator so as to descend twice as many to the platform. She wasn't really following the route of Dudley's story, and felt especially annoyed to have to glance back when footsteps clattered rapidly after her. They belonged to a red-faced man carrying two briefcases as if to prove he was doubly in business. If Dudley had started to betray more of an obsession with her than she welcomed, perhaps she should admit to being too obsessed with him.

As her train emerged from its lair she remembered the one in front of which Greta had been flung, and then she felt ashamed of having thought of a fictitious victim when a real one had been killed. The train bore her around the loop under Liverpool and back to James Street, where she resisted an impulse to duck out of sight in case Dudley was on the platform. The train sped beneath the river and onward, and she wondered if she was retracing the dead girl's journey as well as Greta's invented one. She was glad of the brief respite from the tunnel at Conway Park; she closed her eyes and raised her face to be aware of nothing but the interlude of sunlight. Then her eyes sprang open, and the world appeared to pale. Hadn't Greta passed through this newest station on her final journey? Had Conway Park existed then?

The white-tiled walls slipped away as if to demonstrate she couldn't grasp them either. Dudley had told Walt that he'd written "Night Trains Don't Take You Home" at least seven years ago. She removed her mobile from her handbag and poised it to dial the enquiry number on a poster in the carriage as soon as the train left the tunnel. Daylight had scarcely returned with a vengeance when the number was answered so swiftly that Patricia had to take a breath. "Could you tell me when Conway Park Station was opened?"

"Well, that's a bit out of the common. Let me check." The girl or, despite her voice, more probably the woman had a short muffled conversation offstage. "Over six years," she came back to tell Patricia.

"About seven, would that be?"

"Nearly seven, is that?" A second consultation in the wings allowed Patricia's informant to say "Not nearly. Just over six."

"Thank you," Patricia said, by no means sure that grateful summed up how she felt, and bagged the phone. So Dudley had lied about the date of writing his story. She supposed that was understandable, given the controversy it had stirred up. Was she just bothered by the lateness of her realisation? She was still trying to decide as the train progressed from Birkenhead Park to Birkenhead North, two stations where she might have waited to confront him. She was considering the possibility when her mobile rang.

Was it Dudley? She felt as if he'd tracked her to his station—

as though he'd tapped her thoughts. Her feelings were absurd, but she hoped he was the caller. "Patricia Martingale," she challenged him.

"I'm sorry, Patricia. It's only me."

"I'm the one who should be sorry, Kathy. I wasn't shouting at you."

"I won't pry. Have you finished casting? I keep thinking it sounds like casting about," Kathy said with nervous humour.

"It'll be over for today, I should think."

"You're on the train, are you? By yourself? How did it go?"

"The casting, you mean."

"What else? How were the girls he was having to consider?"

"He seemed pleased. I believe he's working on another."

"And how was the most important one?"

For a moment, perhaps unfairly, Patricia thought she could only mean Dudley. "Mr Killogram? I think he convinced everyone. He's definitely hired."

"So Dudley's happy."

"I'd say so. I imagine you can ask him, can't you?"

"I can now. I didn't want to risk bringing up a subject that might annoy him when he has to crack on with his writing."

The train was approaching Bidston. Patricia remembered walking from the station the first time she'd visited the Smiths' house, and made a swift decision. "Kathy, are you at home?"

"I'm on my lunch. Sitting outside the office in this glorious sun."

"I should have known you'd be at work. I was going to ask you a favour."

"Why, you still can."

"It could be quite a big one. I'd like to have a proper look at Dudley's other stories before I finish my piece about him, but you know him. He wouldn't want me to."

"I know how you must feel. I've felt the same."

Patricia doubted it, especially since she felt guilty for having predicted Kathy's reaction in order to take advantage of it. "Do you suppose there might be a chance I could read them?"

"Would it really make a difference?"

"It might well."

"I know he's out on Saturday. He's reading with his father. We'd have to miss that if you wanted to slip round then."

"If you could bear it," Patricia said, feeling guiltier still.

"I expect I'll be able to if it's for him. I'll ring you when I know exactly when he's leaving."

"That'll be good," Patricia said, though she had no idea for whom. "While we're talking about them, when did you read his stories?"

"Different times over the years. I used to look for a new one whenever I knew he'd been writing."

"You can tell me when they were written, then."

"I should be able to when we're sitting down with them."

"I'll wait to hear from you," Patricia said to end the conversation, though not the rumpus of her thoughts. Now that she'd persuaded Kathy to go against her son's wishes she was unsure what it could achieve. Did she genuinely recall incidents reminiscent of his other tales? If she did, how bad was that? He'd refused to let them be published, after all. The train hesitated at Bidston before moving off, and had barely cleared the platform when her mobile rang as if to warn her she hadn't escaped.

If Kathy had changed her mind, Patricia doubted that she would be capable of trying to delude her further. "Hello," she said to get it over with.

"Patricia? Vincent. Colin's come up with a great idea."

"Oh." She'd been so far from expecting him that she could think of nothing to add other than "Well, fine."

"I think he's the best thing to happen to me since Dudley." Vincent sounded as if he was searching for words to convey the enthusiasm in his voice, and then he seemed to find them. "It's going to be real," he said.

# TWENTY-TWO

"Has your son managed to get himself published yet, Kathy?"

"He will be any day now, Mavis."

"We hope so, don't we, Cheryl? Otherwise we'll be starting to think Kathy made it up."

"I suppose I may have made a few things up about him, the way mothers do. I expect you can understand that even with no children of your own."

"You're admitting you've been fibbing."

"No, Mavis, I'm hoping I helped make him what he is."

"So long as he isn't the writer that was in the paper. He's not, is he?"

"How am I meant to know which you mean, Cheryl?"

"They're ten a penny, sure enough, now anyone can publish

themselves with a computer. Maybe your son ought to do that, seeing it's taking so long. Surely you read about this writer who turned some poor girl's death into a murder. If he can't do better than that he shouldn't write at all, whoever he is."

"You won't be seeing anything like that from him," Kathy had assured her colleagues, but she'd felt her face grow hot with shame and rage. Even if it had been the end of an exhausting afternoon—an unemployed woman who addressed every other comment to the toddler on her lap as though it was a ventriloquist's doll, a man who analysed aloud everything Kathy said, a fiftyish fellow who refused to tell her his exact age, which he appeared to resent as much as not being instantly matched with a job—how could she have avoided trouble by failing to defend her own son? She could only pray to anyone who was hearing her thoughts that the pressures of his office job wouldn't reduce him as she'd allowed hers to lessen her. Perhaps soon he would be able to give in his notice now that his film was under way. He was bound to be more in demand once it helped establish his name.

As the train out of West Kirby veered away from the river the memory faded. Should she have agreed to Patricia Martingale's request? So long as Patricia understood that she must never let Dudley know, he would have to assume she'd obtained any information about his tales on her first visit. Surely anything that brought him and Patricia closer was worth a risk, and in this case Kathy could see none.

She let Bidston Station go and left the train at Birkenhead North. Footballers were jangling their wire cage opposite the supermarket, beyond which the church in the middle of the five-way junction looked unstable with the fumes of impatient waiting traffic. A steaming van was leading vehicles out of the car wash as she crossed the road. She turned the corner to walk uphill and saw Dudley ahead.

As he trudged left into their road he glanced back and saw her. A smile tugged at her lips until he continued only staring. "What are you trying to do?" he said.

Once she was close enough to murmur she said "Not to disturb you, that's all."

"Creeping up behind me isn't supposed to? You wouldn't do it to Mr Killogram."

"People might if they didn't know who he was."

"They'd find out soon enough." In some way this mollified Dudley. "He wants to do a bit of research. There's a police reconstruction of some murder we're going to have a look at."

Was he still annoyed with her? He was jabbing the key into the lock like a knife into a wound. She didn't grasp that he must be eager to work until he headed upstairs. "What do you fancy for dinner?" she risked wondering aloud.

"Don't know. I need to get in the mood to write."

"We'll have chops then, shall we?" As he disappeared into his room she called "We'll have chops."

There were plenty in the refrigerator. Indeed, they outnumbered any other item. She took out six and, having sawn their bones off with a carving-knife, spent a minute in arranging the remains into an attractive pattern on the grill. She found a bag of mixed vegetables that set her fingertips tingling with chill, then grabbed two handfuls of potatoes from the plastic rack. She was fetching the potato peeler from the drawer beside the sink when she heard Dudley make a sound upstairs.

Was it a cry of outraged disbelief? Had the computer crashed? Kathy found she was in no hurry to learn more. She began to scrape the first potato, although the sensation and the dry shrill noise made her feel as if she was peeling her nerves. She dropped it in the saucepan with a hollow clunk, and raised her eyes to glimpse a vague silent movement in the garden. No, it hadn't been a flock of butterflies descending on the tall weeds; it was reflected by the window. She swung around, almost losing hold of the stubby knife, to see Dudley gazing at her from the hall. He was so expressionless that she could have imagined he had ceased to be himself. "Do you want me to think I've gone mad?" he said.

"How could I ever want that?" Kathy attempted to laugh, but there was worse to be discovered. "Why on earth would you think you are?" she managed to ask.

"It can't be you if you're saying you don't know, can it? It isn't you that wants to get inside my head."

Her fear for him felt capable of shrivelling her brain to a cinder. Had the drugs with which she'd tainted his genes overcome him at last? "Nobody does. Nobody's trying," she pleaded, "except maybe Patricia Martingale."

His lack of an expression didn't quite give way to one. "What's she got to do with this?"

"She's been doing her best to find out all about you, hasn't she? I just wondered if she'd gone too far."

"She won't be doing that. Never mind her now. She's not the meddler."

"So what are we—" Kathy set out to enquire, and then she knew.

"If you've no more idea than you want me to believe, maybe you're the one that's mad."

"Call me that if it makes you feel better."

"Maybe you are anyway, doing what you did."

"I know I'll never write anywhere near as well as you, but you couldn't have published that story, could you? I only wanted to finish it for you so you could move on."

"So it was you."

For a moment Kathy felt as if she'd strayed into a trap, but another possibility struck her as even more distressing: that her intervention might have disturbed him so much that he'd imagined someone else had trespassed in his room. "Who else could it have been?" she said, producing a diffident laugh.

"More like who did you think you were being."

"Not you, Dudley. I couldn't ever be you." Since this fell short of placating him, she said "I was agreeing with you, though, I hope you saw. It was terrible what happened to the girl from your magazine, but I couldn't forgive her for joking like that about you. Let's keep what I wrote between ourselves, shall we?"

"I won't be keeping it at all."

Her pang of inner agony felt sharper than the edge of the knife, which she became aware of holding and planted on the working surface with a muted clank. "I don't care so long as it helped," she told him.

"Oh, it did. It showed me what I have to do to write."

"I'm glad, then. I know I was presumptuous. I wouldn't have dared to be if you hadn't seemed so desperate to write, but can I be a little bit proud of myself, do you think?"

He made a show of waiting to be absolutely sure she'd finished before he revealed the expression he had been withholding: slack-lipped disbelief. "You can be what you like when I'm gone," he said.

"Gone." The word felt so massive that she could barely dislodge it from her mouth. "Gone where?" she said more effortfully still.

"Anywhere my writing's safe."

"It is here. I promise I won't go near it ever again unless you say."

"No point in promising. I don't trust you any more," he said and turned his back to stalk along the hall.

"May I drop dead if I ever go in your room again without permission. May Mr Killogram come for me if I do."

Perhaps she oughtn't to have made a joke, or perhaps Dudley

resented her borrowing his character. He halted at the foot of the stairs, but only to establish "It doesn't matter what you say. You promised before and then you went and did that."

"Not like I'm promising now. Don't you know I couldn't bear to lose you?"

"Well, now you have," he said and started upstairs.

As Kathy ran after him the hall seemed to blacken and shrink. It might have been the inside of her head that did, since it felt walled in by loneliness—felt like being left alone for ever in the dark. "Be sensible," she said, although she wasn't sure to whom. "You can't go carrying your computer about with all your stories on it. They're delicate things, computers, and your stories are as well. Suppose you drop it or bang it and lose them?"

"Then it'll be your fault for driving me out of the house."

"I wouldn't, Dudley. I know you've an imagination, but how can you imagine I'd ever do anything that would?" When he didn't falter in his climbing she seized the banister, though only for support. "You know you have to stay really," she said. "There's nowhere for you to go."

"That's all you know. There's plenty of people that would want to have me." Perhaps his protest sounded childish even to him, because he twisted to glare down at her. Then a grin began to reveal his teeth as he said "I know who'll want me."

"You're looking at her. Nobody could more."

"You've had your chance." The grin stayed on his lips, but his eyes grew blank. "Now it's dad's turn," he said.

"You don't honestly believe he'd let you work the way you want to."

Dudley's stare hardened, but it was directed at her. "Why wouldn't he?"

"He'll interfere. I know I did, and you have my promise that I never will again in any way at all, but he wants to change what you write. You remember. He said."

"He won't, though," Dudley assured her or himself, and showed Kathy his back.

"He'll try. He'll stop you working with all his criticism. I know him better than you do. At the very least he'll make it harder for you to work, and just when you can least afford it."

"Then it'll be your fault," Dudley said and wrenched his mobile out of his hip pocket.

He was going to call his father, which made Kathy so desperate she said the worst she could bring to mind. "He doesn't like your writing."

Dudley swung to face her. His eyes had grown inflamed with hatred. As she stretched her hands out and hurried up the stairs in the hope of capturing some part of him, he raised the phone like a weapon. "Let's see what we can come up with instead," she pleaded. "Let me see what I can. I'll do anything to make up for what I did. I'll do anything to help you write."

# TWENTY-THREE

As Dudley emerged from Lime Street Station he wouldn't have minded seeing a girl on her own. Pensioners were crowding out of the Empire Theatre, and St George's Hall offered him nobody among its pillars on the far side of the road. Eventually the rush-hour traffic let him cross into William Brown Street, but he saw nobody alone outside the Walker Art Gallery or the library. Further down the hill a solitary figure in denim was trotting past the museum. It turned the corner at the bottom of the hill, presenting the profile of its chest to him, and even hundreds of yards away he saw it was a girl.

She was following the route he had to take. He should never turn a situation down if it was arranging itself on his behalf. He sprinted downhill to the corner. Alongside the museum, three lanes of traffic raced towards him beneath a concrete flyover and a further one underlined by a catwalk, below which the girl was heading for a six-way intersection overlooked by John Moores University. Some of the roads bore no pedestrian crossings, and the pavements narrowed to little more than ledges. Traffic was every-where, faster than it should be, deafening and self-absorbed. He would be invisible; how could he not take advantage of that? His footfalls weren't audible to him as he ran after the girl and came up behind her on the meagre concrete border at the foot of a three-lane slope. His shadow was even more eager to reach for her than he was; he saw the imprints of his hands appear on her shoulders as he stretched out his arms. He hadn't touched her when the shadows of his hands began to ride the speeding traffic and she looked over her shoulder. "Why, hello, Dudley," she said. "Careful."

She was Patricia Martingale. It seemed a perfect opportunity, but would its story be worth writing? He had to think of that too now. He didn't know what shape his mouth adopted to make her say "Don't worry, I won't fall."

She imagined he'd been hurrying to support her. A lorry taller than a house and as long as several rushed past at arm's length, flapping her denim jacket and raising her hair. "Don't walk in front of the traffic," he said. That would be premature and unsatisfactory; he might even be blamed, which would be grotesquely unfair. "I wouldn't like that," he said.

"I'm sure I wouldn't either." She faced the road as three cars raced one another through a red light, and then she ran to the opposite pavement, where she dodged around a barrier to an of-ficial crossing. By the time she gained the pavement opposite the university he'd caught up with her. "Did you go to uni?" she was prompted to ask.

He thought she was flaunting the nickname, boasting of how casually she took her education and implying that she was supe-rior to him. "Maybe the cleverest don't," he retorted.

This silenced her, which hardly seemed enough. Between the pavement and the university, an elongated eight-storey many-windowed piebald concrete building, witnesses were loitering on a ramp. Beyond the university a grassy slope spiked with a token plantation reduced the width of the pavement until he could feel and smell the breath of the traffic. Frustration clawed at the interior of his skull. Patricia was keeping to the inside of the pavement, but it would be the work of a moment to step back a pace and grab her shoulders and fling her into the road. The uproar was crushing his thoughts, and he had to struggle to remember to save her for later. Worse still, he almost overlooked the need to show ignorance. "Which side are we meant to be on?" he yelled.

"I can't hear you," Patricia shouted through the megaphone of her hands.

"Where are we meant to be going?" Dudley practically shrieked and had to answer his own question, so harshly that his throat stung. "That must be them."

Where the grassy slope ended, past a block of unoccupied houses, a lay-by began. Three police cars were parked in it, and uniformed officers were flagging vehicles down. Further along the lay-by a girl leaned against the waist-high railing above the approach road to the newer of the Mersey Tunnels. At the far end of the lay-by he saw Vincent and Mr Killogram, but he barely glanced at them. He was too disconcerted by almost recognising the girl.

She wore a white embroidered blouse and a short flared bright blue skirt. Her legs were bare, her feet sandalled. Her glossy black hair was spread carelessly over her shoulders as it had been. Her fragile gilded spectacles displayed blank ovals in place of eyes when she turned her head as if she knew him. Of course she couldn't, and he was able to breathe as freely as he deserved once he noticed that her face was a little too round. He stared hard at her to establish that neither of them recognised the other, and was passing a billboard that appealed for witnesses to a fatality on a date he had no need to scrutinise when Mr Killogram called to him over the relatively subdued noise of traffic. "We were wondering if you'd decided not to come."

Dudley joined him and Vincent before demanding "Why would we have done that?"

"I just meant you. I didn't realise you two were together."

His tone was so neutral it seemed clear that he wanted to know whether Patricia was free. It could be worse than inconvenient if anyone took her away from Dudley now. "I'm working on it," he said. "Don't say anything."

"Your secret's safe with us," Vincent assured him as Patricia reached them.

"Only with you?" said Patricia.

Mr Killogram waved a lackadaisical hand as though to gesture her away. "Just for men."

While Dudley appreciated his support, he could do without her taking umbrage. He stared past her at the girl who had begun to pace back and forth. "What's she supposed to be up to?"

"They're reconstructing the movements of the victim," Vincent said.

"Who says she was a victim? It said in the paper she was on drugs and she must have fallen over the wall."

"Her parents always said she wasn't drugged enough to fall," Mr Killogram informed him. "Someone in the police must agree with them."

"So what do you think happened?"

"Her parents say she never would have killed herself. Had no reason and wasn't that sort of person. Maybe someone threw her over."

Dudley understood that he couldn't display too much relish in front of the others, but it was frustrating to have to watch Mr Killogram taking no pleasure in his nature, even secretly. The movements the girl was performing were unsatisfactory too, since they bore no resemblance to the reality—especially not to the spasm, hardly more than a twitch at that distance, that had passed through her on the road below the lay-by in the protracted seconds before an immense lorry had driven all the wheels on its left side over her with a huge belated gasp of brakes. He'd never been sure whether the insect she'd become had retained enough consciousness to attempt to crawl out of the road. She'd seemed to have little enough when he'd approached her and asked her the time, never mind when he'd pointed out that her sandal was coming unbuckled and stooped to dart his arm behind her knees and tip her over the railing. The one regret he'd felt had been for her small delicate gold watch, a good deal more expensive than the unfeminine timepiece her understudy was wearing. He couldn't help being distracted by that, and the girl's mechanical disinterested behaviour was more irksome than his encounter with Patricia had been. "What does she think she looks like?" he was provoked to wonder aloud.

"What are you saying she does?" said Patricia.

"A prostitute."

"I suspect you don't know too much about that."

Was she defending the girl or accusing him of inexperience? "She wouldn't be selling herself with so many people about," he objected. "It isn't even dark."

He stopped short of saying that it had been—that a summer storm had cleared the streets, but the girl had taken refuge in a bus shelter opposite the one he'd used across the road. As he recalled the thrill of stealing up behind her across all six lanes, Vincent said "Are you getting ideas?"

Dudley found the girl's performance more confusing than inspiring; he'd already written about the escapade, and wasn't about to waste time rethinking it. "How about you?" he asked Mr Killogram.

"I'm here to learn from you."

"I expect if you saw her there all by herself with no cars about you'd go and speak to her. If she didn't move away from there when she saw you coming it'd be her fault, wouldn't it?"

Mr Killogram grinned, presumably at that. "You think people get themselves killed and we shouldn't blame the killers."

"Not this one. I wouldn't want to speak for any others."

"You haven't told me why he'd do it yet."

Dudley gazed at him to draw the insight out of him. When Mr Killogram only looked equally questioning, Dudley let a trace of impatience enter his voice. "Why not?"

"He'll pounce whenever he sees an opportunity, you mean. That's all he cares about."

It wasn't quite as simple in this instance; Dudley had needed to patrol the area for weeks after deciding that the equivalent location across the river was too close to home. "He doesn't have to create situations usually," he said. "They're there for him."

Vincent pushed his spectacles higher and opened his mouth, then peered past Dudley instead of speaking. Dudley hadn't turned when a female made herself heard at his back. "Excuse me, why are you waiting here?"

What right had the actress to speak to him or Mr Killogram like that? Even Vincent and Patricia deserved better as long as they were with him. "Maybe we should be asking you," he said and winked at Vincent. "If you're looking for a director, here's one to tell you how to play your scene."

"Dudley . . ." Vincent murmured with a slight but vigorous shake of the head.

"That's me. Mr Smith to strangers," Dudley said as he swivelled to confront the uniformed policewoman who was scrutinising him.

She couldn't have recognised him except as the creator of Mr Killogram, which let him rid his lips of their sudden twitchy stiffness. "Whoops," he said and took time to laugh. "I thought you were the actress."

She plainly didn't know whether to be flattered. "Which actress?"

"The one behind you that's waiting for someone to shove her over the rail," Dudley said and realised he should add "It looks like."

"She's police too."

Dudley jabbed a finger at the understudy. "What's she meant to be up to?"

"Jogging people's memories. Has she jogged yours?"

If she thought that would catch him, she could have no idea who she was dealing with. "Why would she?" Dudley said. "I've never seen her before."

The policewoman's face grew more officially stern. "I asked what you're all doing here."

"Research," said Mr Killogram.

"For what?"

"A film. As he said, he's Dudley Smith, our writer. You're going to be basing your script on real murders, aren't you, Dudley? It'll just be the man who commits them that's out of your head."

Dudley was starting to regret Mr Killogram's enthusiasm. "It's not like that. The murders will be too."

"That's not how I understood it. Sorry if I'm talking out of turn."

Had Dudley disappointed him in some way? The policewoman gave Dudley no chance to ponder. "If it's fiction you've no reason to be here," she said.

"We want to make it as real as we can," said Vincent.

She treated him to an unimpressed stare that she then dared to transfer to Dudley. "How real are you kidding yourselves that can be?"

"You'd be surprised."

"If you ever saw the real thing you wouldn't want to make your kind of film about it. We've heard about you and this film. I'm going to have to ask all of you to move on."

"You can't do that. Tell us what we've done that's against the law."

"Obstructing the police if you carry on. We need this area to pull cars over."

Though he was sure the policewoman had concocted the excuse to oust him, he had no reason to linger; the reconstruction had simply put the original girl back in his head. "I'm going, but only because it's my choice to."

He would have liked to watch the policewoman try to make that into an offence, but Vincent was calling him. "Let's have a word."

He was strolling away from the police and the mechanically pacing actress. As Dudley and the others caught up with him, the scene began to replay itself in Dudley's mind: the girl flailing the air with her legs as she vanished over the rail, the frustrating moment as he'd straightened up too late to watch her fall, the soft flat thud that had made him expect to see her body spread wide and enormous. "I'd be working if I wasn't here," he protested.

"Sorry if you feel you didn't have to come." Vincent reached to push his glasses high but instead gazed over them as if this might render his comments more amiable. "I'd like to start filming next week," he said.

"I don't know if I'll have enough for you by then."

"Let's be honest, I'm pretty happy with my script."

"You need me to get it right. You said so."

"I wouldn't have put it like that." Vincent seemed in danger of forgetting how important Dudley was. "Walt's anxious for us to get started as well," he said. "He doesn't want any more people trying to stop the film. Better keep the controversy for after it's released, he says."

"Can't you stand being misunderstood?"

"You've given us nothing to understand yet." Rather more gently Vincent said "Walt did point out your contract doesn't give you a say in the film, but I'd at least like you to tag along so I can ask your advice if I need to."

"I'd like you there as well," Mr Killogram said.

The repetitions of the girl's fall reverberated like drumbeats in Dudley's skull, pounding his thoughts into less than words. "I've got the weekend to come up with something," he managed not quite to plead.

"If you have any ideas you can always email them." Vincent seemed more at ease with saying "My car's five minutes along here if anybody wants a lift."

"Mine's up there too," said Mr Killogram.

Dudley would have liked to spend time with him, but just now it was crucial to stay with his source of inspiration. "Don't get yourselves tangled up in the rush hour," she said. "I don't mind walking."

"I don't either," Dudley said at once.

He was just as quick to turn his back on the men. If they thought he intended to do whatever they would have done with Patricia, that was another reason why they could never imagine the truth, but he didn't want her glimpsing any winks they sent him. In a few seconds they were out of earshot, and the police-woman had rejoined her colleagues. Not even the actress was watching him. "Patricia?" he said.

"Are you upset?" She halted by the police cars and blinked at him. "You're upset," she said.

"Don't you think I should be? He's mine. I thought of every-thing about him."

"Nobody's trying to steal him from you. You heard Vincent, he'd still like you to be involved."

Dudley had to risk seeming inadequate; nobody else would know he had. "I've got no ideas for him."

"He's given you the weekend. Maybe you'll have some by then."

"I will if you help."

Patricia raised the eyebrow that was closer to him. "What are you asking?"

Below the rail behind her a car sounded its horn like a warning or a fanfare. She was almost close enough to the wall to be thrown over it if the police hadn't been there, but in any case he wasn't about to repeat himself—quite the opposite. "I want you to help me research," he said.

# TWENTY-FOUR

"Research," Patricia repeated and saw a frown twitch Dudley's eyes to indicate the police behind him. He mustn't want to antagonise them further. "Let's talk about it," she said and started past the marked cars.

He overtook her at once. She had to hurry to keep up with him alongside the slope planted with saplings and littered grass. He didn't slow until they were beside the university and well out of sight of the police. "What did you have in mind?" she said.

"Explore a bit and then we could have dinner if you like."

"Explore where?"

"Just walk and see if anywhere gives us ideas." Somewhat less impatiently he said "I want you to say if you get any. You don't know how helpful you could be."

"I don't think I'm very likely to have your kind of idea."

"You never know what'll happen. You could inspire me." Before she had time to demur he said "I wouldn't be having so much trouble thinking of ideas now if you'd published the story you said you would."

That was scarcely her fault, but by aiding him she would be helping the magazine. "Why don't we walk along to James Street and then we'll see," she said.

They had reached the six-way racetrack of an intersection. Several hundred yards away, traffic lights were releasing the competitors for the nearest lanes. Patricia made to outstrip them, but Dudley caught her arm. "Not yet," he blurted and let go at once.

She dealt with the intersection when it was safer and used the crossing by the museum. Above the Kingsway Tunnel, which was swallowing cars with the left side of its mouth and regurgitating as many with the other, Dale Street led towards the river. The sandwich shops on the ground floors of office buildings tall as houses piled on houses were shut now, and the traffic in the one-way street was slackening. Since the setting appeared not to enliven Dudley, she said "Can I talk?"

"Don't let me stop you if you've anything to say."

"I wondered why you took a dislike to that girl back there."

"Didn't you? She was trying to make it harder for us."

"Not the policewoman, the girl in the reconstruction."

"She wasn't in much."

"What more would you have expected her to do? Or are you criticising how she was dressed?"

"It's no wonder someone threw her over when she looked like that, is it?"

"I'm sorry, no, actually I'm not, but I find that offensive." This earned Patricia such a blank stare that she had to ask "Am I missing the point? Are you trying to be your character?"

"I don't need to try." He stared up one of the alleys that squeezed between or, in this case, through the buildings. Five secretaries were chattering and clattering along it to a pub that had grown drunken with age. "No use," he said.

"I won't talk if it stops you concentrating."

"Don't worry. It'll help."

"You go into your role when you work on a story, is that it?"

"That's me." As though to demonstrate he said "You saw that girl. That's not how they described her in the paper."

"So what are you objecting to?"

"They always make out like whoever gets killed is a terrible loss to the world, this person that's so good and so important they're better than anyone could ever be, well, almost anyone. It isn't fair."

Patricia thought he was trying rather too hard to convince her as his character. "People want to think as well of them as they can when they're the victims. Or do you think the killers are somehow?"

"I don't know any killer that's a victim."

They had reached the Town Hall on the brow of a hill, beyond which the rest of the business district sloped down to the dock road and the Pier Head. She was turning towards James Street when the sight of the river set off a thought. "Have you ever used the ferry?"

"Not since my dad took me on it," he said, and then his eyes glinted. "I see what you mean. That could work, couldn't it? Only if you come on it with me."

She could catch the train on the far side of the river. "All right, let's try and make sure you've got a story," she said and started downhill.

All six lanes of the dock road were still racing. The sketch of a man as red as a wound healed at last, and she dashed across into a huge distorted shadow, the silhouette of one of the metal birds on top of the Liver Building. She didn't know what kind of bird the shadow reminded her of. She could almost have imagined

Dudley's were its footfalls as she hurried past the lengthy grey eight-storey façade and across the flagstoned open space to the ticket office above the river.

A boxed-in ramp flattened their footsteps thin while a ferry bumped the tyres at the edge of the landing-stage and a man in a luminous orange tunic tossed a rope to another. A further member of the gang rode a gangplank on its chains until it struck the deck to let the passengers board: Patricia, Dudley, a helmeted cyclist who lingered on the lowest deck. An enclosed staircase climbed to a section of open deck beside a deserted saloon. Patricia was making for one of the pairs of wooden benches that occupied the deck, their backs pinched together, when Dudley said "There's a diagram."

He was gazing at a picture inside the saloon. It showed the workings of the boat, displaying a side view of the innards above an overhead illustration of each of the three decks. It reminded Patricia of the instructions for a boy's model kit, but she suspected it meant something else to Dudley. "What are you thinking?" she said.

"What are you?"

"Someone could fall overboard, I suppose."

"Drowning's not that interesting."

She couldn't help being annoyed by the remark. "You couldn't get caught up in the propellers," she found she was actually disappointed to observe. "They're underneath. If you fell off the stern you'd end up in the wake."

"What about if you fell over the side?"

"I suppose you might be dragged under."

The gangplank rose with a rattle of its chains, and a metal barrier rumbled into place on the bottom deck. "Let's see what we can see," Dudley said.

As they made for the rail beside the stern the ferry swung towards the peninsula. Having lined up parallel with it, the boat began to cruise along the middle of the river past Birkenhead to Seacombe. Patricia gripped the rail and craned over a lifebelt attached to the outside. Fluid tubes of neon streamed past the weathered flank of the boat to merge with the churning wake. "What can you see?" Dudley was anxious to learn.

"Nothing you can't, I should think."

"Can you make out the propeller at all? Anything to do with it, even?"

"Such as what?"

"I don't know. You're better placed than me. It was your idea."

Patricia stood on tiptoe and leaned over. All at once her foothold felt unsteady with the muted throbbing of the engine through the deck. The neon ripples were trying to snag her vision and bear it away. The lifebelt shifted under her fingers as if she was losing her grip on the rail. Perhaps all this was why she fancied Dudley was about to seize her by the shoulders; he was no longer beside her. Why should he expect her to strain like this for him? He was taller than she was—most people were. She lurched backwards and aside before she turned, one hand clutching the rail. "I still can't see anything," she said. "You look if you like."

His fingers were covering his mouth in a shape suggesting prayer. He seemed to be having difficulty in keeping his feet still, as if the sensations of the engine were troubling them. He darted to the rail and leaned over more precariously than she had. Was this meant to demonstrate her lack of daring? Far more quickly than she had, he stepped back. "I can't either. I'll need to bring Vincent, anyway."

"That's a point. Would he be able to film that kind of scene here?"

"He'll have to. It's his job."

As the ferry veered towards Seacombe, Patricia caught sight of a pub half a mile along the promenade. For longer than she was proud of she didn't know why the Egremont Ferry sounded familiar. "Isn't that where Shell . . ."

"Where she what? You can say it. It's not going to bother me."

"All the same, I wish I hadn't gone on about falling overboard just now."

"She only drowned. Your idea's better."

Patricia didn't care much for the praise. She watched the cyclist disembark at Seacombe, where nobody boarded. When the ferry set off for Birkenhead she was unable to stifle a question. "What do you mean, better?"

"More interesting. More spectacular."

"What kind of spectacle are you thinking of? A girl's body being shredded under there? Her bones being ground up and splintered and broken? All her blood?"

"That sounds good."

Her attempt to shock him had merely succeeded in making Patricia feel uneasy about her own depths. At least she'd silenced him. He'd said nothing more by the time they disembarked at Woodside and tramped up the ramp. He hurried past a gathering of dormant buses to Hamilton Square, and she wondered if an idea was driving him.

The chatter of two girls who followed them into the station's capacious lift appeared to distract him. She rather hoped he would recapture his idea, since it seemed to have chased the notion of dining with her out of his mind. He didn't meet her eyes until he'd sat opposite her in an otherwise empty carriage, and he looked so preoccupied that she was inclined to leave him alone wherever he was. Then he stretched his upturned hands towards her as though indicating her to somebody unseen. "Let me know when anything develops if you like," she said. "If my phone's switched off you can always leave a message."

"I thought you'd rather it was while we were together."

"That's imaginative of you." Patricia very nearly said that, but restrained herself to murmuring "That won't be for much longer. If you'll excuse me, I'm off home."

The train gave a lurch that extinguished all its lights. After a moment of utter darkness they flared up to show him crouching at her. "What about dinner?" he said.

Patricia didn't flinch. "Gosh, I've never heard a meal sound so much like a threat."

He peered into her face before sitting back. "Depends who you think you'll be with."

"Nobody tonight. I'm sorry if you thought I said I'd join you. I'm a bit exhausted." Her upbringing prompted her to add more politely than sincerely "Maybe another time."

"You don't mind disappointing Kathy, then."

"It's news to me if I am."

"I told her we were meeting and she said you should come back for dinner. I thought you realised that's what I meant."

Patricia might have relented if he hadn't looked so secretly amused. "You should have told me Kathy had invited me. I hope she hasn't gone to too much trouble. Make my apologies. No, I will."

She was reaching for her mobile when Dudley snatched out his. "I will. It's my fault, isn't it? She's my mother."

He dialled as soon as the tunnel opened to the sky at Conway Park. He hadn't received an answer when the train burrowed once more into the dark. Patricia might have raised the question of when he'd written "Night Trains Don't Take You Home" if he hadn't begun to look nervous. Perhaps explaining to Kathy would be enough of a strain for now.

The carriage had barely emerged into the sunlight when he redialled. Patricia had begun to count the number of rings she was just able to hear by the time he said "She isn't answering."

"Oh dear. I hope she isn't busy on my behalf."

"She wouldn't be this busy." He held the phone away from him to let Patricia hear the small shrill pulse more clearly, then pressed it against himself so hard his cheek reddened beneath his ear. "I don't think she's making dinner," he said.

His eyes were growing watery with more emotion than Patricia had ever seen in them. "What's the matter, Dudley?" she had to ask.

"We had a row."

"People do. Was it bad?" she said, wondering if Kathy had at last not given in to him.

"Some of the things I said might have been. She went on my computer and finished a story I was writing."

"She must have been trying to help, mustn't she?" With rather less conviction Patricia asked "Was it any good?"

"I wouldn't want it to be published."

Patricia tried and failed to imagine a successful collaboration between him and his mother. He ended the call and immediately redialled. "She was really upset," he said. "I thought having you round for dinner might make her feel better."

Had he suggested it, then? Patricia wasn't entirely happy with his using her in this way or assuming that he could. Before she could raise a gentle objection he held the shrill unanswered sound towards her. "She wouldn't have gone out when she thought you were coming. She must be there, but then why can't she answer?"

The train was slowing for Birkenhead North. He switched off the mobile and thrust it into his pocket as he sprang to his feet. "Will you come and see with me? She might have—I don't know."

"What's the worst she could have done? She seemed pretty well in control of herself to me."

"You've never seen her upset. Once she said if she ever thought I didn't love her—I don't want to say. Can't you see I'm scared for her?"

He must be, Patricia decided: otherwise she didn't think he would have exposed his feelings like this. While she wasn't convinced that Kathy would harm herself, she wasn't sure either. "Is there a neighbour you could call?" she said.

"I don't know anybody's number. I don't know the neighbours."

He sounded more desperate than ever. A frown that appeared to be striving to prevent his eyes from widening only made them bulge. "All right, I'll come," she said.

He was off the train before the doors had finished parting. He dashed through the stubby passage of the station and along a terrace of houses that edged the pavement opposite, then halted by an empty playground caged by wire as if a thought had pinioned him. Patricia thought he'd been inspired until she saw that he was staring at the supermarket across the road. "I've got to buy something. Because of her," he explained with very little patience.

"Shall I go on? I remember the way."

"Go on, then. I'll catch up."

Patricia hurried to the intersection that was pinned down by a church. She was halfway up the sloping road opposite a car wash when she heard him running after her. A large supermarket bag thumped his thigh at each step. As he overtook her she glimpsed the contents of the bag. For a dismayed moment she thought it was full of bandages, and then she grasped that they were rolls of heavy parcel tape. "Why do you need those?" she called.

"I said. Because of her," he panted without turning or slackening his speed.

Presumably Kathy had asked him to buy them. Perhaps doing so expressed his hope that she had come to no harm or his reluctance to find out the truth. Patricia sprinted to end up alongside him as he dodged into his road. He glanced at the house next to his, but the curtains—net, which always reminded Patricia of elegant cobwebs—didn't stir. He shoved his key into the lock and twisted it, and shouldered the door wide enough for Patricia to follow him at once.

At first she didn't know why he refrained from speaking even once he'd closed the door behind them, and then she noticed that there wasn't a hint of dinner in the air. She took a breath that seemed flavoured with absence, thinned by it. "Kathy?" she rather more than said.

As if this was his cue or had shattered his trance, Dudley hurried to throw open the kitchen door. "She isn't here," he came close to wailing.

"Do you think she may have left a note?"

Patricia didn't think it was an unreasonable suggestion—not one that deserved to be ignored by him, at any rate. He pushed past her and ran upstairs as she looked into the other downstairs rooms. She heard him fling a bedroom door wide, and then there was silence. She might have found breathing easier once he spoke if it hadn't been for his tone, so hushed as to be uninterpretable. "Patricia."

She took hold of the banister as if that could lend her any necessary strength and began to climb the stairs. She hadn't reached the landing when she saw a crumpled sheet from a notepad lying on the topmost stair. She picked it up and unfolded it, having already seen that it was signed with Kathy's name.

Dudley, I've done as I promised. All your meals are in the top freezer compartment. I've written what they are on them. You won't see me all weekend or know where I'm staying, so please crack on with your writing. If this doesn't help I don't know how I can.

All my love,
Kathy (Mum)
XXXXXXX

How furious ought Patricia to be? At the very least Dudley could have saved her from feeling nervous; it was clear he'd read the note before dropping it or shying it away. He was standing with his back to her in a feminine bedroom that had to be Kathy's. "Dudley," Patricia said and stepped onto the landing.

"I'm here all right." He swung around and thrust out his hand. She thought he was about to snatch the note, but the hand—a fist, to be precise—was directed at her face. "Let's get properly introduced," she heard him say, and the fist struck her chin. It felt like a knuckly club, and then at once like nothing, and so did everything else.

# TWENTY-FIVE

As soon as Patricia regained consciousness she wanted to believe she had done nothing of the kind. Even the last thing she remembered—the fist slamming into her face to knock her into nothingness—was preferable to the state in which she began to find herself. It was so dark that she had to wonder if she was able to see at all. Her blood was throbbing in time with the waves of pain in her jaw, and the way its dull sound was crushed into her head made it apparent that her ears had suffered some damage too. She tried to reach for her jaw to learn how badly it was injured, only to discover that she had no hands. She might have cried out except for her lack of a mouth.

He'd removed it along with her eyes and ears. Her entire body was seized by a convulsion that felt like an attempt to give shape to a scream. Her knees thumped a cold slippery unyielding surface as her spine pressed against the opposite wall of the receptacle in which she was stored. She struggled to stretch out, but the top of her head bumped another wall, and whatever was left at the end of her legs—less than feet, its absence of sensation implied— collided with a fourth. She didn't know if she could bear to find out any more about her situation. Every detail seemed to leave her more helpless. Perhaps she could only withdraw into herself so deep that Dudley couldn't reach.

She remembered fighting Simon off—when words had failed to keep him at a distance, her nails in the backs of his hands and her knee in his groin had—but the memory reminded her that she was robbed of all those defences now. Worst of all was her inability to see or hear. She wouldn't know when Dudley came for her until he set about his research, if he hadn't already finished. All at once she felt as frail as her nerves, an impression that gathered into a mass of prickling on either side of the small of her back.

It was beyond her wrists. While it was growing close to unbearable, it showed she had hands after all. They were recapturing their circulation so as to let her know that they were bound together behind her. She strove to wrench them apart but merely succeeded in digging her knuckles into her back as her fingernails scraped the wall of the container with a squeal that she felt rather than heard. Her ankles were bound too, and as she remembered the parcel tape Dudley had bought she realised why she was unable to move her face. He'd wrapped up her head, leaving just her nostrils exposed. The oppressive darkness in which she was packaged meant that he'd used several thicknesses of tape.

She couldn't open her eyes. When she tried, the adhesive tugged like tweezers at her eyelashes. Attempts to open her mouth simply made the skin of her lips feel in danger of parting from the flesh. She strove to open them with her tongue nonetheless until it retreated from the gluey taste. Her fingernails scrabbled in worse than frustration at the wall behind her, and all at once its hard smoothness let her identify her cramped prison. She was lying on her right side in a bath.

It had to be in the Smiths' bathroom, but that was all she knew. She couldn't even recall where the door was in relation to the bath. Nor did she have the faintest inkling whether the room was light or dark. Just because she felt utterly alone in the blackest hour of the night needn't mean it had to be. All the same, she must have been unconscious for some time—perhaps long enough for Dudley to be asleep despite having captured her. Perhaps satisfaction had put him to sleep.

Or perhaps he was writing about her plight. She had to believe he wasn't watching her if she was ever to move. If she stirred, she fancied he would let her know whether he was there. The prospect paralysed her like the nightmare that it was, and then fury at her panic gave her strength. As the prickling faded from her crossed hands she edged her feet down the bath.

Nothing prevented her. Dudley didn't move or speak—she would surely have heard him, even through the clamour of her pulse—or touch her. However watched she might feel, she had to believe he was elsewhere. By pressing her toes against the far end of the oversized bath and her scalp against the near one she was able to twist into her back. At least she was fully dressed, although that meant a trace of moisture was dampening her T-shirt and jeans. She couldn't take the weight on her hands for long, but neither did she want to rear up and catch her head on the tap. She raised the awkward lump of her bound feet to determine if the tap was at that end. They had just found a thin loose object that she understood to be a chain when they dislodged the plug, which fell into the bath.

She didn't hear it fall, but she felt its impact, and the chain that trailed over her insteps on the way to sagging across her ankles.

She had no idea how many minutes crawled by while she stayed immobile, wishing she could hold even the shaky breaths in her nostrils still. Her tongue bruised itself against her clenched teeth. When the ache in her trapped hands began to turn to agony as her knuckles seemed to grow embedded in her back, she managed to grasp that however long she waited, her sense of being observed mightn't lessen. Surely Dudley would have intervened by now if he'd heard any noise. As gingerly as her blindness and deafness would allow, she eased her feet from under the chain. Once she was certain she was free of it, she set about inching up the bath.

How much noise might she be making that she was unable to hear? Perhaps her heels were squeaking against the surface on which they kept losing their hold. Surely nobody outside the room would hear that. There was no point in being afraid to make a sound. She ought to climb out of the bath as fast as she was able. She would have enough problems once she had.

She thrust herself backwards, clawing at the surface underneath her back for extra purchase. In seconds her spine was propped against the end of the bath. She bent her knees again and levered her shoulders over the edge. Another shove with her feet jerked her bound hands up to it. She clutched at it with her fingertips and felt her nails start to bend away from the flesh. Before she could raise her torso the inch that would let her take a firmer grip, her feet lost their hold and the base of her spine thumped the bath.

Her eyes and mouth struggled to widen inside the tape, which plastered tears against her eyelids. Even when the pain dulled and faded she sat still. She didn't know how audible the impact might have been. Counting slowly to one hundred, and then to another, failed to dissipate the impression of being eyed like a specimen. If nothing would rid her of it, she mustn't let it weigh on her. She lifted her torso as high as she could despite the renewed ache at the bottom of her spine, pressing her feet against the floor of the bath and heaving with all her strength. In a moment her fingers were clamped to the edge.

They started trembling at once. She couldn't hold on for long. She gripped so hard that every finger throbbed, and so did the thumbs at the small of her back as she attempted to swing her legs over the side. The task was even harder than she'd feared. If she had been able to support herself on one leg while the other made its bid for freedom she was certain she would have succeeded, but both legs bound together were more than twice as cumbersome. As she strained to hook them over the side of the bath she was suddenly afraid they would be blocked by the wall of the room. They fell short of the edge, and her left foot slid down the inside of the bath.

She managed to set it down with almost no impact. She took a breath that dragged smells of glue and plastic into her head. With a final effort that bruised her fingers she grasped the edge at her back and supported her entire body on them while she hauled it up. She was shaking from head to foot by the time her left ankle scraped over the side of the bath, but at least she'd encountered no wall. She was going to have to let herself down gradually onto the bathroom floor, otherwise there was far too much risk of alerting her captor. As soon as both feet were over the side she rested her ankles on it, though it dug into them, and settled most of her weight on her trapped hands. She had to bear the posture while she regained some strength, but she couldn't stay like that for long. She was grasping the edge so that she didn't topple helplessly onto the floor, and her hands were growing painfully numb, when she heard Dudley's voice.

She redoubled her grip so as not to fall and strained her ears. He'd sounded so distant that she had been unable to distinguish his few words. Had his mother come home? The possibility felt so much like hope that Patricia almost let her feet drop to the floor to make her presence known. Instead she set about swinging her legs over the edge. She might not have shifted even an inch when an object settled on top of her head.

It was hard and rough. It was the sole of a shoe. It was Dudley's, and as he pushed her down, the thought that he'd been viewing all her efforts was almost worse. Her position cramped her stomach into an aching lump until he kicked her legs into the bath. "Clumsy," he said in her ear.

Did he expect a response? She thought his face was continuing to hover over hers. "Better try and get comfortable," he said. "You won't be going anywhere."

His voice was both louder and somewhat more distant. Patricia emitted a mumble, mostly through her nose. Its inarticulacy didn't matter; indeed, it might lure him close enough for her to butt him. Surely if she did so hard enough he might be knocked out until she somehow escaped. But when he said "Don't understand you" his voice was still more remote.

Patricia struggled into a sitting position and tried again with even less of an attempt at speech. "Sounds like you're buried alive," Dudley said. "That's a help. That could go in a story."

This time she made all the vocal noise she could. It was high and protesting but not, she wanted to believe, as uncontrolled as a scream. When her breath gave out at last he said "I can put that in too."

She repeated the protest and began to swing her feet back and forth, thumping the sides of the bath. However muffled the sounds were to her, mightn't the neighbours hear them? Her hopes seemed to be confirmed at the same time as dashed when he trod on her ankles. "Can't have you breaking anything," he said. "Looks as if you aren't as well brought up as you try and make everyone think. You're like the others after all."

As she felt him undoing her trainers she squeezed her feet together and threw her upper body forward in case she could injure him. It was no use; her legs were too outstretched. She couldn't even prevent Dudley from pulling off her shoes. She heard a faint thud as he dropped them or flung them away, and then he finished treading on her ankles. "Thump all you want now," he said. "Thump like a rabbit if you like and I'll write it. Nobody's going to hear you but me, however much noise you make."

Patricia grew quiet and motionless, though very far from calm. If she gave him absolutely nothing to observe, might he be unable to work? Could that mean he would have to let her go, or would he torment her until she inspired him? The notion made her body clench around her stomach, and it was almost a relief to hear him speak until she understood what she was saying. "Don't worry, you won't ever be alone. I'm sleeping in here."

Did he resent it? Just now the worst of being blind and virtually deaf was her inability to be sure of his tone or see his expression. It was pretty nearly as bad to have no idea of the time of day. Surely it was night if he was talking about sleeping, and so it couldn't be long before her parents wondered where she was. If they rang her, might Dudley be careless enough to answer? She no longer had her mobile, and so he must have it. In any case, Vincent and Colin knew she had gone off with him and would be bound to tell the police when questioned. It couldn't be long before the police came to the house. She did her best to believe this with such force that it fended off his voice. "I'll never be far away," he said. "I'll be thinking up plenty this weekend."

# TWENTY-SIX

At last Kathy slept, but never for long. Far too many thoughts were jostling for space in her head. *Watch Out For The Wife* hadn't proved to be the kind of comedy she was expecting. A young Liverpool woman drowned her violent drunken husband while they were on holiday in Tenerife, only to decide once she returned home that some of her friends' husbands deserved putting down, and eventually husbands of strangers too. Although she was arrested in the end, she looked more than ready for a sequel. Quite a few of the women in the auditorium cheered her actions, and several of the couples around Kathy came out arguing. She supposed that might be the point, in which case it didn't concern her. She was too worried that the film might make life harder for Mr Killogram.

Surely there was room for two films about Liverpudlian serial killers. The woman hadn't convinced her half as much as he did.

Kathy wished she knew how Dudley's research was helping him. Visiting the scene of a death ought to have given him ideas, but would he be able to use them? Mightn't he encounter the same problem he'd had with the girl at Moorfields? Kathy had switched on her phone as soon as she'd left the cinema, but there was no message—nothing from him.

She lay in the narrow bed under the hotel window that admitted shouts and the smashing of bottles and the labouring of taxis up the hill. She oughtn't to keep feeling she was the only person Dudley could turn to. She mustn't be jealous if he found a girlfriend. She was sure that he was more interested in Patricia Martingale than he thought his mother realised—and all at once she was wide awake and staring up at the mocking twinkle of a star. So much had happened since Dudley had found her work on his computer that she'd forgotten she had invited Patricia to the house.

They'd agreed that Patricia would wait for her call, but Kathy's address book with the number in it was at home. Surely Patricia wouldn't try to contact her until at least mid-morning if at all. Kathy had to head that off in case the girl phoned her house. She dragged her legs out of the hot tight bed and consigned some of the effects of her nervousness to the toilet before calling the first enquiry line that came to mind. The number for Martingale in Hoylake was ex-directory, a woman in India informed her.

They should know it at the *Mersey Mouth*. Would anybody be at the office yet? When she obtained the number, Patricia answered at it. She was only a machine, apparently too replete with messages to accept one. Kathy took refuge in the shower, but the cramped cubicle made her feel more imprisoned than refreshed. She dressed and tried the magazine again without success, then knelt on the bed as if to pray, in fact to watch the empty street extinguish its lights beneath long thin gilded clouds. Once the sun began to hurt her eyes she stood up.

In the basement a sullen waitress brought her tea and faintly tinted bread to represent toast, and more tardily a plate scattered with a sausage and a pinkish rasher, not to mention a fried egg with a burst yolk beside a partially flayed tomato. Kathy's calls kept tasting of all this as she climbed the stairs and lingered in her room. She'd lost count of her attempts, and was wondering if she should walk across town to the office, by the time a live voice answered, though not one she had anticipated or was likely to welcome. "North and south, it's *Mersey Mouth*. East and west, we're the best."

"May I speak to Patricia Martingale?"

"I reckon she's having a lie-in this morning. Are we expecting Pat?" Monty shouted, and translated an inaudible response into "We don't think we'll be seeing her today."

"Then may I have her number, please?"

"Don't know if we give them out. I'm not the receptionist, you may have noticed. I'm just the poet that picked up the phone. Do we tell anybody anybody's number, Walt?" he asked in order to transmit "Who wants to know?"

Kathy saw that she ought to have foreseen this, and felt trapped and stupid. "Dudley's mother."

"It's never Kath."

"I should say it has to be. I'm the only one who went through having him."

"I had a bit to do with it, didn't I? As I remember I already said sorry for not wanting to let them down at the gig I was doing the night he came."

"I'm sure you must have. Are you able to tell me the number? It could be quite urgent."

"What are you after her for? Is it something to do with Dud?"

"It's an arrangement I have to break."

"Girly stuff, is it? Didn't Pat want you having her number?"

"It isn't to hand where I am."

"All right, Kath, no need for your office voice." Somewhat less to her he said "It's Dud's mam."

"I guess it should be fine. Go ahead."

After almost enough of a pause to goad Kathy into demanding the reason Monty said "We've got her home and a mobile, Kath."

"If it isn't too much trouble I'd like both."

"Got some scribbling material?"

"Certainly."

"You'll be a writer yet." As she finished copying the digits onto the pad for which the shelf barely had space, Monty said "You'll be seeing her tonight, won't you?"

"Not unless you know something I don't."

"You're not coming to see Smith and Son at their first gig?"

Kathy had forgotten the event in the midst of so much else. "If Dudley's there of course I will be."

"You reckon he mightn't? I'd better talk to him."

"Please don't do anything of the kind. He's having to work to a very important deadline. You'll be taking him away from it tonight in any case."

"It won't hurt him to buck up his image. Maybe you shouldn't encourage the stuff he's been writing so much."

"I rather think your employer's pleased with it."

"Buggeration, that was low," Monty said, and she imagined him clutching his groin.

"I'm just asking you not to disturb him at his work when he's already under so much pressure. That's why I wanted Patricia's number, to put her off coming round today."

"Round where? I thought you weren't at home."

Kathy supposed she had implied that, and cursed herself for carelessness. "I will be soon."

"You're going to remind him about tonight, are you?"

"Of course, if it's necessary."

It wouldn't be, she knew. However fiercely she wished that Dudley wouldn't interrupt his writing, she was sure he would never let his father down. "Where are you on?" she said.

"The Political Picket Club in Everton. By the old washhouse, if you know where that is."

When Kathy tried Patricia's mobile it answered with silence not even enlivened by static. This yielded to an imitation of a bell, and after six twinned rings she heard "Hi, it's Patricia." The voice was so lifelike that she almost greeted it before it added "I can't talk now. If you want me, don't be shy. Leave a message."

"Patricia, it's Kathy Smith. I'm afraid we'll have to cancel this weekend. We'll see if we can do it next week if that's not too late for you," Kathy said and called the Martingales' number.

It had hardly started ringing when the phone was snatched up with a clatter. "Patricia?"

"Is that Mrs Martingale? It's Kathy Smith, Dudley's mother."

With an audible effort at politeness or professionalism Patricia's mother said "Is it to do with the magazine?"

"It is. Could I speak to Patricia?"

"She isn't involved any longer. If you still want her you could try her mobile."

"I have, but I couldn't raise her."

"Then that makes three of us. Gordon? It's Dudley Smith's mother. The writer."

In rather more than a couple of seconds a man's voice said "Mrs Smith? I'm Patricia's father."

"Do call me Kathy. Forgive me, did I just upset your wife somehow?"

"I'm sure you didn't. The problem's closer to home, or more accurately the opposite."

"I think you've lost me."

"Not only you," Gordon Martingale said and cleared his throat. "Has Patricia let you or your son down as well?"

Kathy heard a muted protest in the background as she said "I'm not clear what the situation is."

"She's left her mother's magazine and gone to London."

"Good Lord, that's sudden, isn't it?"

"So sudden she couldn't be bothered to mention it. The first we knew was when she texted her mother last night."

His resentment was beginning to infect Kathy. Had Patricia left without telling Dudley she was quitting the magazine and him? "Has she got another job?" she restrained herself to asking.

"She apparently thinks she's found a better one. Supposedly if she weren't there today it would go to someone else. Now you know as much as she's troubled to tell us. I rather think she was ashamed to say any more to her mother, or at any rate she ought to be."

As the phone conveyed another muffled objection Kathy said "I hope you'll wish her luck from me and Dudley anyway when you're back in touch."

"No doubt she'll put in an appearance when she needs some clothes. For the record, why did you want her?"

"I was going to tell her it's turned out we don't. Dudley's too busy this weekend. Do say to your wife not to be sad. We all have to let our children be themselves," Kathy said and received an unpersuaded mumble for her effort. Nevertheless she didn't feel too piqued as she ended the call. The main thing was that Dudley would be in no danger from Patricia. Now Kathy had to occupy the day in making certain that she wasn't tempted to disturb him.

# TWENTY–SEVEN

A dull thud wakened Patricia. She felt it more than heard it, but it was her head. It had jerked up and bumped the end of the bath. She did her best to gasp through just her nose, and then she tried not to breathe or move. The ache in the back of her head faded as she listened. With her eyes still buried in the dark she felt as if she wasn't quite awake. It was even harder to work her brain when she hadn't believed she could fall asleep.

It was as quiet around her as sleeping without dreams. She might have thought she was dreaming if the tape hadn't been so tight and hot and sticky on her face. Was she alone in the room? If he was working next door she would have heard the clatter of the keyboard, even through the wall and the tape. If he was sleeping next to the bath she mightn't hear his breathing, but she would never be unaware of his presence. Perhaps his work had taken him out of the house for some reason. She had to take the chance. She mightn't have another.

She began to push herself up the bath with just her feet to make less noise, and then she thought she heard a sound that wasn't her. It made her feel examined like an insect under a microscope. She couldn't tell what it had been or even whether it was outside her head. When it wasn't repeated she went back to worming her way up the bath. Even if she had only heard bones creaking in her skull, it forced her to move as slowly as a snail, and she felt as soft and vulnerable as one. She couldn't tell if she was damp from the bath or with her own sweat. When the back of her neck slithered over the edge of the bath she raised her head and turned it, searching for the slightest sound.

The room was on her left. She poked at the bath with her fingers behind her to lift her top half forward and leaned over that side. She was convinced he wasn't down there. She straightened up and swivelled her trapped face towards the room, searching blindly as a mole dug up and unable to see its captor for all the light around him. "So you can hear me after all," he said.

His voice came from where she was facing. She must have sensed him without realising. Perhaps she'd been aware of the scent of aftershave that meant he had recently had his hands on a razor. She thought of pretending she hadn't heard and continuing to move her head, but it had already betrayed her by wavering to a stop. "Can you talk?" he said. "Can you tell me how you feel?"

He must still value her as a collaborator. Mustn't he let her go if she satisfied him? She strained to force words out, but she wasn't sure if she was hearing them except in the hollow of her head. "Not like this," she tried to say.

"Don't bother if that's the best you can do. You don't even sound like a person."

She lifted her face towards him and attempted to plead without using words. "Mmm," she said. "Mmm."

"Are you singing? You must be happy working with me."

Did he want her to be? She was afraid of the opposite. She had to persuade him to unwrap her head, however uncomfortable that might be. "Mm*mm*," she begged. "Mm*mm*."

"Now you sound like a whining bitch. No use to me."

As soon as her mouth was free she would scream for help with all the voice that had been gagged. If he made to cover her mouth she would bite through his hand. If he tried to knock her out again she would be too quick and wriggly for him. "Mmm," she insisted. "Mmm."

"Do you want me to unwrap my present?"

"Mmm."

"I wouldn't like it then, would I? It'd start making a fuss and getting me a bad name with the neighbours."

Was he reading her thoughts? Was she so predictable? "Mmm," she lied, shaking her head as hard as the tape around her throat would let her.

"Why else do you want unwrapping? It wouldn't be to help me, would it?"

She put all her effort into nodding. "Mmm."

"I don't need to hear from you, I've decided. You won't be feeling anything I can't imagine. In fact I'm sure I can imagine better."

She slumped against the bath as if he'd robbed her of any reason to exist, and then she managed to raise her head. "Mmm," she struggled to tell him.

"Are you hungry? Is that what's wrong with you now?"

He was reading her thoughts again, or that was what she wanted him to think. "Mmm," she agreed.

"Had I better go and buy us both some dinner?"

She nodded so hard that the back of her head thumped the bath again, but she didn't care. "Mmm."

"I'd have a job to go shopping in the middle of the night."

Was it really that time? "Mmm," she said in case it mightn't be.

"You want me to go out anyway, do you?"

She wasn't sure how to answer that. "Mmm," she said as appeasingly as she could.

"And then you'll get out of there and do all the damage you can and make a row till someone comes to see."

She felt as if he wasn't just reading her thoughts but inventing them before she had them. "Mmm," she contradicted him. "Mmm."

"I'm getting bored now. I don't think there's anything else you can do for me. I think I've learned all there is to learn."

She could hear in his voice what that might mean for her. She began to thrash about in the bath. "Mmm," she protested so shrilly that the tape buzzed against her lips.

"I like that, though. You can do that for a bit. Nobody's going to hear but me."

Could she carry on inspiring him? Sooner or later she would run out of ways, if she hadn't already exhausted her energy. All at once she stopped moving. At least that would show him that he couldn't order her about. "Have you finished?" he said. "That wasn't any use. Keep it up till it gives me an idea."

She didn't mean to give him another sound. She wished she didn't have to let him hear her breathe. She stayed as still as a dummy in a window, even when he said, "That's useless as well. Better try harder if you don't want me to make you."

What could he really do? He would have to let her go eventually, because people had seen her with him. In any case her parents must have called the police by now. She wondered what he thought he could offer her to persuade her not to betray him. Of course she would pretend to accept till she was out of his reach. She was trying to feel as still as her body when he said, "I know what I can do."

It couldn't be much, she told herself. He wasn't Mr Killogram, he was just a writer who'd made up the character. He wrote about things that had already happened. He didn't do them. All the same, she was anxious to hear what he was planning, and so it was almost a relief when he spoke at last. "This should be fun," he said. "You get a choice which way to go."

Now that it was too late she realised the long silence could have meant he'd been out of the room. What might she have been able to do while he wasn't watching? She wouldn't have had time to manoeuvre herself out of the bath. She didn't understand the choice he was offering her—not till she heard an electrical drone and felt water flooding under her.

She would either drown or be electrocuted. "Mmm!" she tried to scream. "Mmm!" She flung herself about inside her slippery prison. She couldn't even snag the chain to unplug the bath; she would have had to lie flat and helpless in the water that was already spilling hotly over her legs. She was stiffening in dread of the electricity that would surge through it the moment he dropped the appliance in the bath when the drone was pressed against her ear. She recognised it as much from the heat as the sound. It was a hairdryer.

The tape around her face was no protection. She felt as if a red-hot needle was being thrust deeper and deeper into her head. She writhed desperately, but however she tried to escape, the heat followed her. All the same, she didn't duck under the water that had risen higher than her outstretched legs. She only banged her blazing ear against the side of the bath. "That's what dogs do," he said and pressed the dryer against her left eye. When she felt her eyeball shrivel she buried her head underwater. It was the only choice she could make, and he helped her stick to it by planting a foot on her throat.

# TWENTY-EIGHT

The Political Picket was a tall broad Victorian house on the brow of the ridge of Everton. Steps that led between spiked railings down to the pavement had been replaced by a concrete ramp. Kathy offered to help an old man in a wheelchair to mount it but was met with a grunt of refusal. As she waited for him to complete his task she gazed across downtown Liverpool to the river. Beyond it the sun was sinking towards the peninsula, perched on which she saw the observatory above her house. She let herself imagine that the sun was rising over Dudley and whatever effort he was making this weekend—even better, that it was the light of his creativity that was brightening the world. She turned to the ramp in the hope that he was inside the club, having finished his task.

The front door was wedged open. It was painted the same bright red as the large uncurtained windows to its left. Most of the building was to that side of the expansive staircase, where all the ground-floor doors led into a single room that had once been several. As Kathy followed the man in the wheelchair through the nearest doorway he was greeted with a cheer that trailed off at her appearance. The room was close to full, largely of men past pension age. Those that weren't clustered along the bar that occupied the rear wall were seated around tables that looked borrowed from more than one pub and a shabby café or two. The walls were draped with banners bearing legends such as **STOP THE WAR** and **MARCH FOR JOBS**, and further decorated with framed photographs of demonstrations, some dating from her childhood or earlier. She couldn't locate Dudley, though that might be blamed to some extent on all the smoke. The group the man in the wheelchair had joined were making such a performance of welcoming him while they dragged their heavy padded stools over the bare boards to clear him a space that she didn't notice Monty until he spoke in her ear. "You've not brought him, then."

She could tell that he'd been drinking from his breath and the mottling that left only his shaved pate grey. "I wasn't aware that I was expected to do so," she said.

"You shouldn't talk like that round here, Kath. You'll have them thinking you're a foreigner." He waggled his eyebrows, which widened his eyes but still left them too small for his squashed nose and mouth. Once he'd done joking he said "Have you talked to him since you rang me?"

She might have pointed out that she hadn't intended to phone him, especially since he seemed to mean the conversation to impress his cronies, several of whom were puffing in the background, either tobacco or just from shortness of breath. "I take it you've done as I asked," she said. "You haven't been troubling him."

"I didn't reckon he thought his old dad was much trouble. If you're asking have I rang him, not yet."

"Oh, Monty, don't pretend you can't speak properly." Instead of this she murmured "Then kindly don't. I'm sure you know he does what he says he'll do."

"I've not had much chance to find out for a while, have I?"

"You seem to think you can make up for lost time." Kathy regretted having said this even before his eyes winced smaller. "Shall we try to get on with each other when everybody's come to see him?" she suggested. "We don't want to spoil his evening, do we?"

"Anybody's going to perform tonight that wants to. Didn't you read that?"

He was indicating a poster she'd assumed to be historic. **VARICOSE VERSES FROM PASSIONATE PENSIONERS. GUEST PRESENTER MONTY SMITH AND SON WILL READ TOO.** "It doesn't sound like much to interrupt his work for," she objected.

"He'll be hearing what real people think of him and his writing."

"When will he be reading?"

"Second half."

In that case it was even less urgent for Dudley to abandon whatever he was busy with at home. Rather than arouse another disagreement she said "I expect I should arm myself with a drink."

"Nothing brings them back like being bought their booze, eh?" Monty said to nobody in particular and produced his wallet to hand her a fiver. "Keep that and treat him when he shows his face. Time I got the show started."

She hadn't expected to be bought the drink. She crumpled the note in her fist on the way to the bar. As she ordered a gin and tonic from the barman, who sported a grey pony-tail and whose arms looked lagged with tattoos, Monty took up a position at the far end of the room, pint in hand. "Settle down now, all youse, or youse'll get no pomes," he yelled, and before there was anything like silence, began to bellow louder. "I can see lots of fellers that look like they've got pomes in them, and some judies too. Here's your chance to show the establishment you're still alive and they'd better take notice. What are you? Can't hear you. What are you?"

While the room resounded with the answer Kathy found a seat. "Here you are, lovey," a woman called, giving her a less than wholly toothy grin. Kathy took the other place at the small round rusty table as Monty announced "Here's Pat McManus of Anfield to kick us off."

"It's one of me odious odes," the wiry singleted pensioner said from an arthritic crouch. His poem proved to be addressed to a colostomy bag, and Kathy's companion laughed so much that one of her front teeth shook. Kathy did her best at least to smile at the performers Monty introduced, oldsters who read verses about supplying urinary samples, or a ditty on losing the instructions to an old erector set, or a lay whose author had to spell the title aloud: "The National Hellth." For contrast a musician played a harmonica for several more minutes than the number of notes he repeated while accompanying them with great ferocity on a drum strapped around his neck. At last Monty brought the first half of the proceedings to an end by declaiming a piece about taxes with the refrain "Give us back our bloody money then" and sidled over to Kathy through the crowd bound for the bar. "What's he think he's up to?" he demanded. "Keeping us in suspense?"

"Well, that is rather what he's about."

"He should be about doing what he promised his dad." Monty flipped his mobile open. "What's his number?"

"What are you intending to say to him?"

"Find out where he's got to for starters. Maybe he needs directions."

"And if he's so involved in his work he hasn't left the house?"

"He can still make it if he grabs a hackney. What's his number?"

"If someone has to speak to him I will."

Monty stared at her outstretched hand and then at her before planting the mobile in it. "See you tell him what I said."

She meant her words to be all hers. She typed Dudley's mobile number and pressed the scrawny receiver against her ear to exclude some of the uproar of the club. Six rings brought her Dudley's voice, but on a tape. "I'm a machine. Leave a message."

"Dudley, it's Kathy. Sorry to bother you if I am. Don't answer this if you're hard at work, only I—"

Monty looked inclined to snatch the phone, but it was Dudley who cut her short. "What do you want?"

"We were just wondering where you might be."

He was silent, and she strained to hear the tapping of the keyboard. Instead she heard "Who's with you?"

"Your father and, well, your audience if you want it."

"Christ," Dudley said so viciously that it felt aimed at her. "I was supposed to be on with him, wasn't I?"

"Are you busy?"

Monty thrust a hand at her, but she turned her head away, taking the mobile further out of his reach, as Dudley said "I can't leave now. I'm at an important part."

"We'll make your apologies. Most of the people here seem to want to write. I'm sure they'll understand." Though she was anxious to leave him to work, she couldn't help blurting "What was that?"

"It'll be where you are. There's so much noise I can hardly hear you."

"I don't think it was here." In a moment she heard the high muffled sound again through the phone. "It sounds like somebody trying to scream," she said.

"I was watching television to relax," he said with a good deal of resentment. "Then I got an idea and came to write it and it's still switched on."

"Hadn't you better turn it off? I don't know about you, but it would distract me." She was relieved to hear him slam a door, shutting out the noise. "I'll leave you to be creative," she said. "Do you think you'll have finished tomorrow?"

"Should have. I've still got a few ideas I want to try."

"Take all the time you need. I was hoping I could come home after work on Monday."

"I expect you can. I should have done it all by then."

"Good luck and be inventive," Kathy said and released him. She was about to turn to Monty when she thought of a ruse. She thumbed the redial button so as to delete Dudley's number digit by digit before handing back the phone. "He says he's sorry but he absolutely can't get away from what he's working on."

Monty's face grew patchily even redder. "You mean he doesn't reckon this is worth as much."

"You'll have to ask him, but not now."

"Don't feel you've got to hang around without him," Monty said and shut the mobile like a trap. "I don't reckon this is your sort of thing. A bit beneath her," he told the woman at the table, who displayed her lack of teeth.

"I don't want to put you off your work either," Kathy felt able to say before turning her back on him. Once she was out of the building she relished the evening air while she gazed across the river. The sun was disappearing behind the ridge like a circular saw luminous with blood, and she was happy to take it as an omen. Perhaps it was the colour of Dudley's latest inspiration.

# TWENTY-NINE

"Good luck and be inventive," Dudley's mother said and then, to his surprise, rang off. He was expecting her to ask how he was coping on his own. He would have been frustrated to waste energy on repelling questions when he was enjoying himself so much. The idea reminded him that he was hungrier than usual, and he hurried down to the kitchen. No doubt she wouldn't approve of his menu; he had never been comfortable with operating the microwave, let alone the larger oven, and he hadn't been about to try when his mind was so bound up with the package in the bathroom. Last night he'd dined on bread and cheese, and there was plenty left despite their having done for lunch as well, since breakfast had consisted of two bowls of Sticky Rotters. Why, there was another loaf in the freezer. He laid it on the draining-board to thaw and was slicing a couple of hunks off its less frigid relative when a thought made him jab the point of the knife into the breadboard. Could Kathy have neglected to interrogate him about his meals because she didn't need to ask?

It surely wasn't possible. That kind of surveillance belonged in a story, though not one Dudley would have written; Mr Killogram was far too wily to let himself be watched in his own home or anywhere else. Dudley resented having to peer out of the kitchen window, beyond which the garden wasn't quite unkempt enough to conceal even a midget observer. He was angrier yet to feel impelled to skulk behind the front-room curtains as if understudying Brenda Staples. Beneath the crimson light that spilled through the trees the road was deserted, and he wasn't going to imagine that anyone was lurking in the undergrowth opposite; they would never be able to spy into the back of the house. He had practically forgotten the source of all this unnecessary nervousness when he realised he'd only needed to check where Kathy had phoned from. As he strolled along the hall he called the number back, and then he stumbled to a halt. The banisters penned in the edge of his vision with bars while he stared at the number on the screen. It was a mobile, but not his mother's.

Of course there was no reason to assume that it related to the police. She must have borrowed someone else's phone, that was all. He poked the key to dial it and gripped an upright of the banisters, which was creaking in its sockets by the time the ringing was replaced by a message. "It's Monty the metre reader. That's the metre you don't need a uniform to read. Pomes produced and performed for the people . . ."

Dudley silenced the voice before it required him to answer. Hadn't his father considered him worth speaking to? If he was angry with Dudley for letting him down, he couldn't appreciate how crucial Dudley's weekend was. Dudley was grateful to his mother for saving him from having to explain this, but a good deal less so to the package in the bathroom for distracting him until he'd grown confused. He wasn't now. He pocketed the mobile and carved a lump of cheddar off the yellowish block. Dropping it and the bread on a plate, he carried them upstairs.

He set the plate beside his computer and switched on. At least Kathy's interference had shown him he needed a password. He typed "package" and waited for the stories to emerge from hiding. He didn't mind feeling a little indebted to his trophy in the bath, even though he'd done all the work. He'd had so many ideas in the last nearly sleepless twenty-four hours that he'd only been able to sketch some of them. In one the girl was blind, in another a deaf mute, in a third confined to a wheelchair and almost unable to move any of her limbs . . . He displayed the last story and read it again. That was the one he relished most, but couldn't it go further? "It was the only choice she could make, and he helped her stick to it by planting a foot on her throat"— the ending came too soon and fell short of satisfying him. Couldn't he act out at least a few of the events of the story? Surely the only requirement was that nobody except him and his helper should ever know. He was going to have to dispose of the package in any case, and it made sense to use it as fully as possible beforehand. He reread the tale while he gobbled the contents of the plate, and was so anxious to put his inspiration into practice that he almost failed to realise he could take his script with him. It would prove that he was more than capable of writing the film. He printed the story and shuffled the pages together as he made for the bathroom.

Was the package asleep? The faceless head with its nose protruding through the narrow gap in the tape like a toe out of a hole in a sock didn't rise to greet him. He was hoping it would jerk up nervously and twist back and forth in search of its fate. With its hands out of sight and its legs compressed into a single mass, the package seemed as limbless as a worm and even more lacking in personality. For as long as he took to pace to the bath he was amused by the lack of awareness of him, and then it started to frustrate him. He fell stealthily to his knees on the mattress and leaned over the edge of the bath until his mouth was inches from the blurred brown lump of an ear. "Were you missing me? I was here all the time."

To his annoyance, the package didn't flinch away. It merely stiffened its sitting position against the end of the bath. He hoped he had at least undermined one more of its senses—the sense of time. It couldn't know how recently it had kicked up a rumpus in an attempt to be heard through the mobile. "Do you want to know who was on the phone?" he said.

He was meant to think the package didn't care, but he saw the head lift a fraction as though scenting his aftershave. "Kathy. That's my mother, if you remember," he said. "And you know what she was saying about you? Nothing. Not a word."

Though the head tried not to sink it didn't quite succeed, but the spectacle wasn't enough to compensate for the bother it had done its best to cause him when Kathy rang. "Want to know who else doesn't care what's happening to you?" he said and leaned closer. "Your mother, and it'll be your dad as well. I texted on your phone to say you've gone to London for a job."

The package did its best to look as hard as rock, but he imagined how soft it must have grown inside, like a snail in its shell. The notion disgusted him. "We don't want you making a row if my phone goes again, do we?" he said and saw his spit glisten on the tape over the ear. "Maybe we'd better make sure you can't hear it, parcel you up a bit more."

The bulb above the wrapped throat ducked away from him as if it fancied that it could somehow escape. He couldn't carry out his threat just now; he wanted to be heard. He settled into a crouch and found his opening line. "So you can hear me after all. Can you talk? Can you tell me how you feel?"

He wasn't expecting the response. The head tipped back, rubbing its tuft of unimprisoned hair against the tiled wall, and emitted a snort through its nose. Though it put him in mind of a horse, he saw that it intended to express something far too close to mirth, however bitter, for his taste. "Don't bother if that's the best you can do," he said. "You don't even sound like a person."

She didn't look much like one either—only just enough to hold his interest. Should he add that to his dialogue? He didn't enjoy feeling that he'd overlooked a possibility or that he ought to change something he'd written; he never had. It was too reminiscent of the way the other girl's family had spoiled the launch of his career by interfering with his story. "Are you singing?" he said.

The faceless bulb stayed tilted against the wall. He wasn't sure if it had lost its motivation or was pointing its exposed nostrils at him as the best it could do for defiance. "You must be happy working with me," he said louder, but that brought no reaction either. She had to make some noise or the dialogue would be senseless. Suppose he inserted some object in her nostrils—a lighted match or the points of a pair of scissors? For the scene to work in the film he had to establish how it played, not how it read on the page. He was gripping one knee to thrust himself to his feet when the package emitted a sound that might have been a mirthless giggle or a high-pitched sob. "Now you sound like a whining bitch," he was able to respond. "No use to me."

Was she determined not to be? The head was leaning against the tiles as if it had lost even the energy for sounds. "Do you want me to unwrap my present?" he suggested.

That seemed to enliven the package. The head swung blindly towards him and performed a single vigorous nod. Its curtness was altogether too peremptory, and gave him more reason to say "I wouldn't like it then, would I? It'd start making a fuss and getting me a bad name with the neighbours."

The head jerked from side to side twice. He thought it might be entering into the spirit of the script to placate him until he said "Why else do you want unwrapping? It wouldn't be to help me, would it?" It obviously wasn't, because the head kept its blankness still, confronting him with it. He hoped she could sense his grin at her insolence, but she would soon experience something worse. He was aware of the pinkish interior of the nostrils, which put him in mind of skinned wincing flesh. Which item should he apply first? There was no reason not to test both. He stood up, leaving the script on the mattress, and was making for the bathroom cabinet when his mobile rang.

He watched the package do its utmost to persuade him by not moving that it couldn't hear and wasn't poised to create the only thing it was capable of creating—a row—and then he shut the door. As an extra precaution he closed his bedroom door behind him. He was glad the package couldn't see him, because there was no excuse for the way the call had taken him aback; it hadn't caught him. He didn't bother trying to keep the resentment out of his voice. "Dudley Smith."

"Sounds like you're getting ready to hurt someone, Dud. Are you talking to me now, then?"

Monty's voice felt like a threat of interference. "I always did when you let me," Dudley said.

"Don't go twisting me pouches, son. I've had enough of that from your mam. You weren't so keen to speak to me before."

"She had your phone."

"Too shy to tell her to give me it, were you?"

"I'm not shy. I'm not scared of anyone, especially not women." Dudley almost wished his father could see the package trying to pretend it wasn't scared of him. "Why didn't you?" he countered. "It's your phone."

"That's right, it's the one you rang and didn't say boo to. I'd call that being scared, son."

Dudley would have sprawled on the bed to demonstrate his carelessness except for the absence of the mattress. As he lounged in the seat by his desk he grinned at saying "I rang it back because I thought it was my mother's. When it wasn't I rang off."

"You'd rather talk to her than your dad, would you?"

"She's the one who started my career."

"And I'm the one that got you the gig you never bothered showing up at."

While Dudley was having fun with his dialogue, there was more to be had in the bathroom, where a dogged dull thumping had begun. "How did it go?" he assumed he was expected to ask.

"How do you reckon? You made me look like the family couldn't be trusted. I had to tell them you couldn't be arsed to spare them any of your precious time because you were too busy scribbling."

"Kathy said they'd understand."

"What the shite does she know about it? She's not a writer. Tell you one thing you'd better learn and quick if you want to carry on in this game, son—your writing's never more important than your audience."

"Perhaps we'll have to disagree about that."

"And maybe not. I know more about it than you do. I've been at it longer, and I'm your dad if you forgot as well. Maybe I ought to drive over there right now and talk to you like a dad's supposed to. I reckon I'd be failing in my duty if I didn't."

The thumping beyond the wall seemed to lodge in Dudley's head. "You don't know where I am," he blurted. "Kathy won't tell you."

"She's not here. I can get your address out of the directory quick as the shits."

Dudley couldn't judge if the thumping grew louder or the resonance in his aching skull did. "You can't come here," he said through his teeth. "I've got to be left alone."

"Except for your mam, eh? You don't mind having her around. She thinks you're so perfect there's nothing for you to learn from your dad."

"I made her leave too. She's moved out till I've finished what I'm doing."

"You've got too big a notion of yourself and no mistake. Me and Kath may have had our differences, but I don't like you chucking her out of her house while you ponce about being an artist. Right, I'm coming there. I want to do this face to face."

The violent thumping was indistinguishable from Dudley's pulse now. He couldn't tell whether the raw red was in the sky or his eyes or both. "It's the only way I can write," he loathed himself for having to plead. "You're stopping me."

"Try writing a few of the places I've written and putting up with some of the stuff I had to while I did and then maybe you'll have an excuse to whinge. Christ, son, you're making me ashamed of you. I wouldn't mind if you'd got your mam out of the way so you could have a judy in."

Dudley's lips worked, and he felt as if the thumping had forced out his response before he was sure of it. "I have."

His father was silent for so many thumps that Dudley had started to regret the admission by the time Monty spoke. "You sly twat. You've got Kath thinking she's got to stay clear of you writing and you're really just like the rest of us."

"That's me. I'm your son."

"Well, good on you, Dud. I was starting to think you didn't like girls and it was my fault for leaving you all to your mam." Monty laughed before adding "You still let me and dozens of old buggers down."

"I'm sorry," Dudley said and risked saying "You understand, though."

"Why didn't you bring her? Doesn't she like what you're doing?"

"She's learning."

"Just so you don't expect me to. Still got me doubts about your kind of thing. Find your roots and maybe you'll surprise yourself. I reckon I've got to be one of them."

"Can we discuss it another time?"

"Itching to get back to her, are you? Let's hope she sees to your itch. What's her name?"

The thumping had left Dudley's skull, but returned while he struggled to think. "Patsy," he said as soon as it occurred to him.

"I'm eager to meet her. When's that going to be?"

"Not now. Promise you won't come now."

"I will if you promise not to show me up again, and that means no way at all."

"If you promise not to tell my mother Patsy's here."

"Fair enough, that's the stuff men do for each other, except you've not promised yet."

Monty had to be impressed with the eventual products of the weekend. "I swear I won't let you down," Dudley said.

"Then your secret's safe with me. Have a good night and don't do anything I wouldn't do, like you could."

"Tomorrow as well."

"Randy sod. Making up for lost time, eh? I won't waste any more of it for you. I'll call you when we've got another gig."

"I'll make sure I'm free," Dudley said and meant it. He mustn't double-book himself like this again; it drew too much attention to him. He thrust the mobile into his trousers pocket as he strode into the bathroom. "You can stop now," he shouted, "he's gone," but Patsy the package persisted in clapping her bound feet against the sides of the bath. He would find a better noise for her to make—one he would relish more than she would. He was running to the kitchen for a box of matches when the phone started to vibrate against his hip.

Had Monty changed his mind? Dudley was tempted to let the

phone ring until his father left a message for him to overhear, but his nerves couldn't wait. He dodged into the front room to be farther from the thumping and poked the button. "Yes," he snapped.

"It's Vincent. Is this a bad time?"

"No, it's quite a good one."

"Does that mean you're working or you aren't?"

"I will be in a minute."

"Well, great. I won't keep you away from it. I just wanted to let you know I want to start shooting with Lorna and Colin tomorrow."

Dudley felt belittled and excluded. "Where?"

"I thought we'd start with the most famous location. I've got them on the ferry on the way to Birkenhead."

For an instant Dudley felt as if Vincent was stealing both Mr Killogram and his ideas, and then he saw how to reclaim them. "That's my scene. I thought of that."

"Well, that's ace. We've got the same mind. I must be finding your wavelength."

"You better had."

"How was that again? I didn't catch it. The only thing is, if you've written the scene I haven't had it."

"I'm about to."

"Great, then you can email it to me."

"I'll do more than email it."

"Terrific. If it turns out the dialogue needs work when the actors get to it you'll be there to make the changes."

Dudley saw no reason why this should be necessary. On the contrary, he would be there to ensure no changes were made. "When's everyone meeting?"

"Ten sharp at the Pier Head. How soon can I look for the scene?"

"The moment I've finished it. I'm starting now," Dudley vowed and rang off. Thumps resounded faintly through the house. He thought of the matches and the scissors, but he couldn't spend time on that now. He dashed upstairs, shouting "You'll have to wait" before hurrying into his room. When the racket eventually faded and died he was typing **FERRY** at the top of the screen. He was grateful for the impetus to write, and delighted that he'd regained control of Mr Killogram from Vincent, but frustrated as well. He seemed to have robbed himself of the chance to experiment with the package; once he'd delivered the script he would need to catch up on his sleep if he was to keep an eye on the filming. Then he bared his teeth as he typed **MR KILLOGRAM**. Even if they filmed all day, he would have all Sunday night. It would be something to look forward to when he came home.

THIRTY Patricia lurched awake and at once was furious with having fallen asleep. It felt like giving in to Dudley—like being robbed of the last vestige of her sense of self. She was about to drum her bruised feet against the bath in sheer enraged frustration when she managed to regain enough calm to think. She ought to keep still while she discovered whether that was any use. Perhaps if she stayed on her side and facing towards the room, she could tell what he was doing. Perhaps if she didn't strain at it she would be able to hear.

She had no idea how long she'd spent in attempting to distract him by thumping the sides of her prison. It had begun to feel like her only means of proving her own existence. Whenever she'd had to rest because her legs and feet were aching so much, she'd tried to think that she was lulling him to believe she had finished vexing him. More than once he'd dashed into the room to snarl or yell at her. His reaction daunted her, but what else could she do? If she stayed quiescent, might that persuade him that he could risk letting her go? Surely he had no other option in real life—surely he didn't imagine they were in one of his stories. She tried to slow her breathing and relax her entire body so that all she would do was hear.

The last time she'd heard him yelling at her to shut up, his voice had been beside her, yet lower. He must indeed be sleeping on the floor to block her escape, but she had increasingly less sense that he was anywhere near. She couldn't smell his aftershave. Did she dare to trust that and her instincts? Tentatively to start with, and then with mounting confidence, she thumped her heels against the side of the bath.

Suppose he was watching her across the room? Suppose he was grinning at her blindness and awaiting her efforts to climb out of her prison? Her eyes stung with fury and their inability to penetrate the taped blackness. If her intuition had betrayed her and he hadn't left the house, she would make it impossible for him to pretend. She squirmed onto her back, flattening her hands underneath her, and pounded the sides of the bath with her feet until they throbbed. The racket came so close to hurting her deafened ears that she didn't think anyone else in the building would be able to put up with it. She had to believe that he'd left her alone at last—of course, because of the film.

She began to inch into a sitting position. Why was she being so cautious? She thrust hard with her feet, and the back of her neck slid up the end of the bath. She had an image of poking her head out like a soldier revealing her position in a trench. But her head hadn't risen above the edge when she was dealt a vicious blow on the scalp.

Her eyes streamed, her mouth struggled to gape and to produce more than a clogged groan. She fell into a crouch, loathing its defensiveness, and tried vainly to judge where the next blow might come from, though nothing she could do would avoid it. Her fingers writhed, unable to reach up and rub the injury. She could only wait for the pain to fade. Very gradually it dulled and shrank to leave her skull feeling softened and exposed. Her head began to tingle with a wincing anticipation of the next attack. She wasn't going to keep it held low like a victim when she had no reason to believe that would save her. She straightened up in furious defiance, but at the same time she couldn't help ducking. Only the gesture prevented her from banging her scalp as hard as the first time on the object overhead.

She wanted to believe it was the sink. She needed to discover how she could have collided with it twice. She kept her head down while the aggravated pain retreated into tenderness, and then she raised it inch by slow inch. When she encountered the object once more she distinguished how flat and horizontal it was, not curved and slanting like the underside of the sink. In any case, it was too low. It was no higher than the edge of the bath.

It wouldn't let her sit up. She twisted on her side and shuffled effortfully down the bath and strove to raise herself with only her body for leverage. As her upper half wavered erect, the barrier was waiting to press her head down. She fell back, bruising her knuckles, and strained her feet up. The barrier was above them too. By dragging them along the edge and then performing the same exploration with her head at the opposite end she ascertained that the lid covered virtually the entire bath.

There was a gap over the taps, but it was hardly wide enough to push her bound feet through. The lid was as thick as the length of her feet. Surely that had to be an exaggeration, and she mustn't let it daunt her. She lay on her side again and crawled awkwardly up her prison, then used its end to help her rise into a crouch. Once her shoulders and the back of her head were wedged against the lid she heaved with all her strength.

It didn't stir. Though her spine was straining practically up-right, and all the muscles that were left available to her were throbbing with the effort, she felt tethered by her useless arms, unable to apply the purchase that might have made all the differ-ence. At last she subsided, and when her body finished trembling she tried again. She tried until she grew sick and dizzy with striv-ing, and then she switched to lying on her back and planting her feet against the barrier. They were just as ineffectual. She thought she could have been labouring for hours to shift the lid before she finally lay inert, panting through her nose, her blindness flaring dull red in time with her pulse. The lid was utterly immovable, at any rate by anyone in her condition. She might as well be buried in a coffin under six feet of earth.

THIRTY-ONE    Dudley stepped into the sunlight and immediately wondered if he should rush down to the next train home. He had to remind himself yet again that the package was safe. It might have been able to dislodge both of the wardrobe doors he'd laid over the bath, but even he had struggled to wrestle the armchair up the stairs, never mind to heave it on top of the doors to sit with its back to the wall. Nor was there any reason for his mother to sneak home after she'd promised to stay away. Just because he couldn't bolt the front and back doors as he had while he was in the house, that wasn't an invitation to her or any other intruder. He was sure that at the very least she would phone him before daring to invade, and she wasn't going to risk phoning when that might interrupt his work. He turned his back on the station and strode past the massive empty office buildings towards the Pier Head.

There was no sign of Vincent or the cast on the wide paved space. If they were late, couldn't he phone Vincent and persuade him to delay filming until after the weekend? As he hurried down the concrete ramp he was hoping their absence would give him the excuse. He hadn't reached the landing-stage when he was greeted by a shout of "Here's the author."

At least the enthusiast was Mr Killogram. Vincent was there as well, adjusting his glasses with the hand that held the script, and so was Lorna Major, looking as determined as she had when Mr Killogram had hemmed her in at her audition. As they crossed the grubby planks to Dudley he wondered what was wrong, and then he knew. "Where's the camera?"

"The crew's joining us at Birkenhead." As Vincent found a bunch of pages to give him he said "We nearly had someone else with us."

Dudley would have examined the pages more closely if the vagueness of the remark hadn't made him unnecessarily nervous. "Who?"

"Just some reporter." Vincent sent him a glassed-in blink and said "I didn't think you'd want her along."

"Why not?"

"Because of Patricia, I thought."

Dudley's tongue grew as dry as his armpits had turned marshy, and he had to force it to work. "What about her?"

"She'll be here, won't she? We don't want too many press about when we're all getting used to working together. I did tell this reporter she'll be welcome later on." Vincent dealt him another blink that tugged a small frown low on his forehead. "Will Patricia be here?"

Dudley's question was too urgent for him to take time to consider. "Why are you asking me?"

"Me and Colin got the idea you two were palling up. My fault for taking things for granted. I'll call and see if she can join us."

As Vincent took out his mobile Dudley seemed to feel Patricia's stir like an insect in his pocket with eagerness to answer. "Don't bother," he blurted.

Lorna Major's smile was more wry than sympathetic. "Have you been jilted by your publicity person?"

Dudley almost rounded on her and said too much. "I said don't bother," he told Vincent. "She's gone."

A ferry wallowed towards them, rubbing its flank against the tyres that buffered the landing-stage. Vincent turned to it but didn't close his mobile. "Gone where?"

"She got an offer of a job in London. She had to catch the next train or she'd have lost it. She didn't even have time to tell her parents she was going."

The gangplank thumped the landing-stage, and Dudley hurried to be first on the upper deck. He sat on an aggressively hot bench and read the script while Vincent left Walt a message. Mr Killogram had kept all the lines Dudley had emailed, including "Ever heard of Mr Killogram? . . . You don't know me but you will . . . How would you like to help me do my research?" Dudley was beginning to regret not having made the girl know who he was—after all, he was a famous creation—but perhaps the audience needed to be introduced to him. Vincent had given the girl nearly as much to say as Mr Killogram, and Dudley might have protested on his behalf, except that Mr Killogram was more than capable of dominating the scene and her. That was enough reason for Dudley not to care about the sight of Bidston and its observatory sailing towards him, nor their crouching out of view beyond the ferry terminal at Birkenhead. "We're up here," Vincent shouted as the gangplank struck wood.

He was calling to far fewer people than Dudley was expecting. One bore a camera upstairs on her shoulder while her companion brought the recording equipment. "Joan and Red," Vincent introduced.

The brawny sound engineer's short pelt of red hair covered little more than her scalp. Dudley wasn't going to let her turning out to be a girl on close acquaintance throw him. "Are you going to be able to make a proper film like this?"

"It's how we do it," Joan said, widening her eyes until a bead of moisture squeezed between two wrinkles on her high pale forehead. "We shoot fast and light. We're independents."

"We're as good as your script for sure," Red told him.

He didn't like her tone, nor Vincent for saying "We'll show him, won't we? Let's rehearse that single take."

Dudley had an unsatisfactory sense that everyone knew more about this than he did. He watched the camera prowl towards Lorna at the rail and swing to discover Mr Killogram behind her. "Out for a blow?" Mr Killogram said.

The ferry was cruising towards Seacombe and the mouth of the river. "Out for anything that does me good," Lorna said.

"Like talking to strange men on ferries?" said Mr Killogram.

"You don't look that strange to me."

"Maybe the strangest don't."

"Go on then, tell me how you're strange."

"Ever heard of Mr Killogram?"

Dudley almost clapped, not just at hearing his line but at how Mr Killogram spiced it with a hint of secret amusement and eagerness. "Can't say I have," Lorna said.

"Then you'll be on your own soon," Mr Killogram said and, to Dudley's delight, addressed his next observation to the camera. "I'm going to be famous."

"Says who?"

"You don't know me but you will. I'm a writer."

Dudley found Lorna's smile almost insufferably patronising, and had to tell himself that it couldn't be aimed at him. "Have I heard of you?" she said.

"Just call me Mr K."

"Just think, I'll be able to tell my friends I met a writer."

She wasn't meant to say the line with such an undertone of irony, but of course she would never tell anyone. "How'd you like to help me research?" Mr Killogram said.

Though they weren't Dudley's precise words, Mr Killogram had given them more bite. "Depends what you're asking," Lorna said.

"Can you see where the propeller is?"

Dudley was reminded of Patricia—of how she had excited him by seeming to wish for her flesh to be minced—until Lorna said "At the back, I should think."

"Can you look for me?"

"I wouldn't know where. I don't build boats, I'm a student."

"What are you studying?"

"Law. There are too many criminals. I want to be on the right side."

"You think you'll win."

"The good people have to try."

Dudley couldn't stand Vincent's additions now that he heard them, and was on the edge of saying so when Mr Killogram said "Won't you help me? I've hurt my back."

"How did you do that?" Lorna said with little sympathy.

"Just sitting at my desk."

"Maybe you should get out more," Lorna said, then relented as Mr Killogram winced. "Does it really hurt?"

"Too much to bend."

"All right, you can be my good deed for today," she said and craned over the rail. "I can't see."

"You need to lean a little further. I've got you. That's it. A little more. Not much further now. There."

"And zoom in on Colin's face. That's great, Colin. Just a touch of a smirk," Vincent said, and told Dudley "We'll cut in flashbacks later, when Lorna's been made up. Only a few frames at a time but they'll get to the audience. What do you think so far?"

"Can I say I want to help protect people?" Lorna said. "That way the audience will care more. Maybe I could say I want my parents to be safe."

"You've said enough," Dudley retorted without looking away from Vincent. "I think she says too much. I got bored."

"You want to get rid of the woman as fast as you can, do you?" Lorna said.

A mutter of female agreement made Dudley stare harder at Vincent. "We wouldn't dream of getting rid of you," the director said. "We couldn't make the film without any of you. How did it feel to you, Colin?"

"I'll be happy when everyone else is."

This was so unlike anything that Mr Killogram would say that Dudley had to reassure himself it was a ruse. "Maybe we can pace it up a bit," Vincent said. "How about if Lorna says 'Law. There are too many criminals' and then Colin goes straight to asking her to help?"

"That's more like what would happen," Dudley said.

He would have expected more appreciation of his willingness to compromise. Only Mr Killogram sent him a complicit grin as Vincent said "Let's go for a take while we've got the Pier Head behind us."

Dudley watched the film crew perform Vincent's bidding without needing to be told—either that or Vincent agreed with them. He'd expected the director to do his job more as a man should. Perhaps Vincent was trying to prove himself by telling Mr Killogram that he'd begun the take too early. Dudley thought the urgency felt like commitment, and he had to restrain his impatience as Mr Killogram waited for the camera to retreat to its starting point. It had only just swerved to find him when he said "Out for a blow?"

302 ‡ RAMSEY CAMPBELL

"Still too early," Vincent interrupted. "Wait till Joan's framed both of you and then give it a beat. Don't worry, we've got all day."

Dudley reminded himself that he'd known about the possibility and that the package was securely shut up to await his return. He couldn't judge how much of the impatience he was experiencing belonged to Mr Killogram. "Take your time. Enjoy it," he said.

"Believe me, I am." His other self said nothing more until "Out for a blow?"

This repetition went so well that Dudley hardly noticed that his house was creeping closer at his back. Mr Killogram had almost reached his final line when he gave Lorna a quizzical grin. "Am I losing it? You don't look too convinced."

Before Dudley could warn her that she had better be, Lorna said "Is she meant to be stupid?"

"No more so than any of his other victims, would you say, Dudley?"

"Then that must be pretty stupid," Lorna said. "There's a diagram behind you that shows where the propeller is. She wouldn't need to lean over here."

"We won't be filming it," Vincent said. "The audience won't know it's there."

"People that use the ferry may, and I will."

Dudley saw the propeller separating her stubborn expression from the bone, and did his best to be content with the prospect of the diversions awaiting him at home. "Whatever she's called doesn't," he said.

"That's another point. Why don't we know her name? It's like telling the audience she's so much of a victim she doesn't deserve one, like she isn't even human."

Dudley agreed, but might have suggested calling her Lorna if Vincent hadn't pointed out "She gets to say she's a student and what kind. There isn't really anywhere in the script for her to introduce herself. We can give her a name on the end credits. Maybe Dudley won't mind if you choose one."

"I'll let her," Dudley said, since there would be more of Lorna in the victim.

The ferry was too close to Liverpool for the crew to film another take. At least everyone had all-day tickets. As the vessel left the Pier Head behind again, Dudley watched Bidston begin to creep closer and then concentrated on the more immediately important situation. When the camera found Mr Killogram once more, he hesitated. "Doesn't a blow mean something different in America? That's if we're expecting the film to travel that far."

Red emitted such a snort that the microphone with which she'd been fishing for dialogue wobbled. "It means that here too. I thought it was meant to show what a prat he is."

How much of Dudley's confidence did she and her crony intend to try to undermine? He was imagining her being dragged through the propeller—raw Red—when Mr Killogram suggested "How would it be if I say 'Enjoying your cruise'?"

All three girls burst out laughing. "That's even worse," Lorna spluttered.

By now the propeller was clogged with flesh and the wake of the ferry was crimson. Dudley had no idea what might have escaped his mouth if Vincent hadn't said "Out for the day."

Dudley watched the camera back off so as to venture up to Mr Killogram yet again. "Out for the day?" Mr Killogram said.

They seemed to be. First Lorna was overcome by mirth, apparently remembering one of the lines they'd done without, and at the start of the next take Joan and Red were. Next it was Mr Killogram's performance that began to lose control. He smirked too widely at the end of the scene, or he was too openly ironic or amused, and then too menacing as if to compensate. Vincent tried to offer him any enforced breaks in filming as opportunities to regain his skill, but couldn't the director see that it was all the girls' fault? Perhaps Mr Killogram was too busy imagining how he would like to deal with them to focus on his performance. By the dozenth repeat of the scene Dudley's entire head felt parched with frustration, not just at the increasingly unsatisfactory spectacle but because he wondered if he was missing a more diverting one at home: the awakening of the package, its muffled cries and useless struggles. He was further distracted by having to keep passengers out of shot. "It's a film of a story of mine," he kept saying, and some of the voyagers stayed to watch; some even hushed their children before he would have had to. At least there wasn't enough noise to spoil any takes that might have been worth preserving—not until the ferry swung like a minute hand yet again back to Liverpool. As the ferry nuzzled the landing-stage and pivoted to rest against it, Dudley heard a girl yell "On the boat." It was a signal for her and three more to dash down the ramp.

Their racket would be no asset to the film. He loitered at the top of the stairway to warn them, but they grew quiet as they climbed the stairs. "We're filming up here," he said all the same. "You can watch if you like but you mustn't make any noise."

The foremost girl made her eyes big and enthusiastic. "What are you filming?" she whispered.

"It's a story of mine. Mr Killogram."

"It's a story of his," she informed her friends.

If she thought it worth repeating, Dudley wouldn't disagree. The girls lingered on the stairs, giving him a display of four sets of eager eyes and parted lips. "You don't need to wait there," he said. "We aren't filming yet."

"We'll hang on till you start," the foremost girl said.

Dudley thought of introducing them to Mr Killogram, but he could do that later. As the film crew took up their positions he moved away from the stairs to let the girls onto the deck. Vincent called for the camera and then the action, and Mr Killogram said "Out for the day?" precisely when and how he should. The film was happening at last, Dudley thought. He even smiled at Lorna's "Out for anything that does me good." Mr Killogram was responding with surely not too pronounced a grin when the four girls began to stamp and chant. "An-ge-la. An-ge-la. Stop the film. Stop the film."

Mr Killogram peered at them over his shoulder as Dudley confronted them. Their chant subsided into a mutter that gave way to silence. Dudley licked his lips to dislodge a question that felt like a dry hot gag. "What did you say?"

"Angela," said the girl who did most of the talking, and took a defiant step towards him. "Angela Manning. The girl whose death you're making money out of."

He almost spat in her face with asking "What business is it of yours?"

She stared at him as if she meant to equal the contempt he felt for her. "She was my friend."

"So give her a rest. It's people like you that keep digging her up." He was letting his fury distract him when she hadn't answered his first question. "I asked you what you said," he hissed and wiped his mouth.

"I told you."

"You're a liar. You said something about Colin. You said it was Colin."

The girl enlarged her eyes as she had on the stairs. "Is that his name?"

"You know it is," Dudley said with almost more frustration than he could contain in words. "No, it's Mr Killogram."

"If you're so sure of yourself," a second girl said, "why are you asking?"

"I'm sure of everything. It'll take more than a few bitches to stop me." Dudley was about to back up his declaration however he could when a voice behind him said "Leave them alone."

It was Mr Killogram. He must want to deal with them himself. Dudley swivelled to meet him, only to find Mr Killogram staring not at the girls but at him. "They were saying things about you," Dudley felt he should make clear. "They don't care how they mess up our film."

"Pity."

"It's worse than that," Dudley said and found a threat he could allow everyone to hear. "Maybe Walt can sue them for losing us money."

As the girls did their best to sound incredulously amused Mr Killogram said "It's a pity I couldn't carry on."

"You still can if we get rid of them. Vincent, doesn't the captain have to chuck them off for causing trouble?"

"We'd love him to try it," the foremost girl said with an even more spurious laugh.

Vincent jabbed his glasses against the bridge of his nose to scrutinise her. "Don't I know you? Did you phone me?"

"That's me. The girl you told you'd be filming round the river when you thought I was the press."

"How stupid are you?" said Mr Killogram.

Though he was looking at Dudley, he could hardly be addressing him. "Who's that meant for?" Dudley said.

"Christ, you are." Mr Killogram let his grin sag. "You're as stupid as that stupid bloody name of yours."

"What's wrong with my name?"

"The one you keep calling me."

"Mr Killogram."

"No, the name's Colin Holmes. They know it is even if you've forgotten."

"I expect that shows you're famous, but you can't say what your character's called. I wrote him. You're the actor."

"I'll go on acting, shall I?"

Dudley struggled to master his emotions. Just because he and Mr Killogram had disagreed, that needn't mean they had to part. After all, at times he had arguments inside his own head. "You can when there's nobody trying to interfere," he said. "You were getting good before."

"I mustn't have been bad enough, must I."

Dudley felt the deck lurch underfoot as if the world had. Mr Killogram's remark was addressed to the girls. Presumably Vincent was too thrown to notice, since he said "I don't get this at all. Why would you want to be bad in a film?"

"It's these bitches," Dudley said through a grin like a skull's. "They made him sneak into our film to spoil it."

"Wrong as usual," said the false Mr Killogram. "It was all my idea and I'm proud of it."

"Don't tell us you're another of what's her name, Angela's friends."

"She had plenty. I shouldn't think you'd know what that's like." The man who had pretended to be Mr Killogram widened his pitying smile. "I was in plays with her at school," he said. "Quite a few of us carried on acting. Maybe you'll hire some more of us and not know."

"You aren't telling us she was an actress. She couldn't put on much of a performance."

Dudley was remembering how the best she could produce was to throw out her hands as if they could ward off the train. He didn't grasp that he'd said too much until Vincent intervened. "You can't say that, can you? You never saw her. Don't lose it, Dudley."

"It's their fault if I have," Dudley complained, surely not too late. "They've got me so I don't know what I'm thinking."

"Try thinking you shouldn't be making this film," said the man who'd tried to steal Mr Killogram's identity. "That goes for all of you, the ladies in particular. I can't believe you want to be mixed up with a film about killing women for pleasure."

At the end of an awkward silence Joan said "We knew what it was when we signed up. We're professionals even if we're independents."

Dudley was overcome by a rush of appreciation he wouldn't have expected to feel. "You're my kind of people," he told the film crew.

It was Red who answered, and only following a pause. "We need the work."

As Dudley strove to be content with that, the actor said "How about you, Lorna? Surely you've got more ambition than being killed off in the first scene."

"You have to start somewhere," Lorna said, then turned to Dudley and Vincent. "As long as I'm staying with your film, maybe you could give me a bit more to do."

"I should think we can work something out, can't we, Dudley?"

Dudley meant his mutter to commit them to no more than would rid them of the betrayer. The actor left Lorna a disparaging glance and led his admirers downstairs, telling them "Pity you showed up so soon. I'd have had them going for days." Dudley glared after him until Vincent murmured "I'll make some calls when I get home and we'll have another casting session. Is there anyone you'd like to see again that we saw?"

"I wanted him." Dudley knew he sounded childish, which enraged him all the more. "Get someone that can be trusted this time," he said and began to pace the deck like a beast in a zoo as the ferry crawled towards Liverpool. He was so impatient to be home that he had to keep clenching his teeth to prevent his thoughts from shaping his mouth. Patricia had encouraged him to choose the actor, which was one more reason he was glad to have packaged her. At least the time it took to reach her would let him invent more for her to deserve.

# THIRTY-TWO

"Oh, Patricia, how on earth have you managed to end up in this state?"

"I'll tell you when we're outside, mummy. How did you know where I was?"

"We had our doubts about that text that was supposed to be from you and so we had it traced. They can locate where the last message came from, you know."

"Did you bring the police?"

"Just your father. For a bank manager he makes quite a house-breaker. It must be all that working with safes."

"Get me out of here, then, before Dudley comes back."

"I'd like to see him. I'd like more than a word with him."

"So long as you don't find yourself in trouble with the law, Gordon. Patricia, it may hurt while I'm taking this off you. It won't last long, I promise."

How could Patricia have been talking if her head was taped up? Being jerked out of her drowse by the realisation brought her close to tears. She felt moisture prickling the corners of her bound blind eyes until she succeeded in biting her flattened lip. Apart from the lapse in continuity, couldn't she be rescued that way? If Dudley was home, surely her parents would insist on being let in, however plausible he tried to sound. The thought helped her fend off the other scene her mind kept producing, of Dudley pressing his unseen face against hers, smearing the tape with his tongue as he bruised fistfuls of her and scrabbled at her clothes. She was still capable of kicking, however awkwardly, which let her regain some sense of her unviolated self. If her parents didn't save her, perhaps Dudley's mother would. She had started to feel as she used to as a child with her head under the bedclothes, drifting into sleep and dreams, when she understood what that might imply. Was she being starved of air?

She twisted onto her back, stubbing half her fingertips against the bath, and tried to sit up. She'd raised her upper body only a few inches when a wave of dizziness broke in her head, leaving her throat harsh with nausea. Giving it time to subside felt like sinking helplessly into the dark. She reared up, unable to judge how badly she was wobbling, and barely remembered to duck so that just her shoulders and the nape of her neck thumped the lid of her prison. As the impact shook her she thought she felt the merest hint of shifting overhead.

Or was it her dizziness? She did her best to relax before pressing her shoulders against the barrier with all the strength she could find. This time all the unsteadiness seemed to be hers. The weight of her thoughts and the blackness dragged her head low. She no longer had the energy to budge the lid, she realised miserably, if indeed she ever could have—and then she wondered how much Dudley had. Could he really have planted such a heavy object on top of her without wakening her? Mightn't she be trapped by a heap of objects that she could unbalance?

She was afraid to yield to this last hope in case it was dashed, but the alternative was to let the life be crushed out of her by her plight. She was unbending from her crouch when she grasped that she ought to plan. What did she want to happen? If the obstruction ended up on the floor it might leave her way clear, but equally it might create a further obstacle. She needed it to fall into the bath on the side away from the room.

Her mind seemed to be swimming in giddiness. Where would she have to apply the remains of her strength? If she was under the side that fell it might pin her down. She inched away from the unseen wall to prop her shoulders and the back of her head against the lid. Then, with a series of movements so cramped they felt as though she was trying to take it off guard, she attempted to jerk it away from the wall.

Even these efforts revived her nausea. She had an impression of rubbing her head soft, which she suspected had to mean that she was close to fainting. The thought enraged her but lent her no strength. Nor did the notion that Dudley was in the room and relishing her struggles. She had to believe that he wouldn't have covered the bath unless he was leaving the house, but how much longer might he stay away? The idea of wasting precious time drove her to thrust her clumsy body upwards in a last attempt to dislodge the lid. The action set the darkness reeling around her and inside her, but was that the only movement? She levered at the barrier with a residue of energy she wouldn't have believed she had. She couldn't be sure that she was experiencing more than vertigo until she felt and heard the lid crash into the bath.

Had it trapped her afresh? Her effort had robbed her of sensation except for a limpness so generalised she hardly knew which parts of her were which. She was afraid to move, to discover how much she was able to, if at all. Once her exhausted body finished quivering she made herself extend her legs, which felt like rediscovering the single awkward mass they'd become. By stretching out her toes she was able to determine that one corner of the lid had tipped into the farther right-hand corner of the bath. The space above the upper end was clear. There was at least enough room for her to lift her head as high as sitting up would let her. She turned giddy with renewed hope before she recognised that she was back in exactly the same situation as when she had tried to clamber out of the bath.

No, not exactly. Dudley wasn't there. She mustn't imagine that he was watching her. She was resting her spine against the end of the bath before she made the effort to hoist her hands over the edge when she wondered if she had a chance to free them. Could she saw through the tape with the edge of the lid?

She struggled around to prop her left shoulder against the end of the bath and strained to find an edge with her wrists. It was too high. She had to squirm towards the taps and lie on her side in order to drag the tape between her wrists along the edge. Her cramped posture lent her unwieldy movements some force, but not enough; the edge was far too dull. Perhaps she could split the tape with the uppermost corner of the lid. When she managed to grip the edge with one hand and pull herself along the lid, she found that the corner was well out of reach.

She mustn't let that rob her of determination. She still had the chance to escape. She fell on her side, bruising her shoulder, and did her utmost to transform her frustrated rage into vigour. She laboured into her sitting position and rested while she took several of the deepest breaths she could. She stiffened her body and heaved it as high as she was able with what felt like every reserve of her strength. Her nails scraped over the end of the bath, and her hands were just capable of gripping the edge.

If she gave in to the aching temptation to rest for even a moment they might lose their hold. She clutched the edge and performed a desperate shackled kick to lift her feet. As they wavered up she swung her body on the throbbing pivot of her wrists towards the side of the bath. Her feet swung over it, her ankles grazed the edge, and then most of her weight was beyond it. The burden was too painful for her wrists to support. Her hands opened and she sprawled out of the bath.

She had time to worry that the sink would crack her head. Only the floor thumped all the breath out of her. It was the shock as much as the impact; either the floor had grown soft or she had. By fingering the surface underneath her she identified it as a mattress. So Dudley had indeed been her unseen sleeping companion, but that didn't mean he was anywhere near. She mustn't think he'd strewn the floor with obstacles to hinder her escape; surely he believed he'd left her helpless. He was going to be sorry for underestimating her. As soon as she recovered her breath she set out to reach the door.

It was beyond her feet, and not nearly as distant as her blindness and her restricted movements made it seem. She struggled up on her left shoulder and her elbow and squirmed away from the bath. Her elbow bumped off the mattress onto the floor, and in a few inches it was rubbed raw. She could still hitch herself along with her shoulder, and bending her knees helped. Before long her bare soles encountered the outside of the bath. She pressed them against the yielding plastic and skewed herself further, then shoved with her legs. A second thrust carried her off the mattress, and a third slammed her right shoulder into whatever was blocking her path.

It was made of wood. She was sure her muffled ears had heard that. It must be the door. She leaned her spine against it and sat up, and an object dug into her scalp—not a weapon, the doorknob. She ducked as if that might leave the pain behind, and once it faded she decided she'd rested enough. She had no idea how much more time she might have. She needed to stand up and open the door.

She flattened her hands against it and took a breath that made her yearn to use her mouth too. She raised her knees and brought her feet under her and shoved with everything she had. Her dizziness reared up as she did. Had she spent the energy that would have lifted her all the way? Her legs wavered, her knees shook, and she leaned on her aching wrists to find a last trace of strength. Her hands gave her a shove, and she was on her feet but staggering sightlessly forward. She threw herself back, and the door bruised her shoulders. She mustn't care about the pain. Once the darkness finished pitching and tossing she sidled to grasp the doorknob. But it was inches higher than her hands.

She could reach it—just. By balancing awkwardly on tiptoe she was able to capture it between her fingertips. Before she succeeded in twisting it her feet gave way, and she stumbled a pace into the darkness. She'd nearly turned it, she promised herself as she executed a clumsy hop to back up to the door. She strained high on her toes again and pressed her fingertips against the knob so fiercely that they stung. By leaning to her right she was able to move it. The door lurched towards her, tugged by her unhandy grasp, and struck the backs of her legs. She hopped forward an inch, clinging to the knob to bring the door with her. She was about to repeat the process when all the vigour seemed to drain out of her legs through her feet. Her balance collapsed, flinging her backwards, slamming the door.

It was only her first try. She could do it again. Indeed she could, but just the same repetitive performance time after time, slam after mocking slam. When she tried leaving the door open an inch and edging along it to widen the gap, it fell shut of itself even if she didn't overbalance against it. She began to weep, cold sticky trails that zigzagged between the tape and her cheeks. What else could she do except rehearse her grotesque jig with the door until her audience came home? Nothing else in the unseen room was even so close to giving her hope. Her actions had become virtually mindless—wrestle with the doorknob, stagger an inch or two, lose balance, stagger back—when she thought she heard another sound besides her own. However distant it seemed to her crippled ears, was the front doorbell ringing?

It was only when it rang a second time that she realised the chance she was missing. She began to slam the door as fast and as loud as she could. The bell rang again, and she prayed that whoever was outside was impatient with the racket Patricia was making—impatient enough to do something about it. Just the sense of being heard by someone was an agonising relief, so long as it led somewhere. "I'm up here," Patricia tried to call out but couldn't even mouth. "Let me out or get someone who can."

# THIRTY-THREE

Dudley was thinking of the most entertaining way to let the package realise he was home when he saw Brenda Staples outside his front door. She must be looking for his mother, unless she had understood at last that he was worth knowing. She couldn't suspect anything, but he made to dodge between the houses while he thought of a suitably innocent greeting. Before he could, she noticed him. "Dudley," she called like a teacher.

However insufferably she might behave, the package could pay extra on her behalf. Apparently she felt entitled to stand at his gate with her arms folded and require to be told "Where were you about to dash off to?"

"I forgot something."

"It looked as if you didn't want to face me."

"I've got plenty to do, that's all." She was aggravating the rage that the thought of the false Mr Killogram inflamed in him. "What do you want?" he said.

"No need to speak to me like that. I'm sure your mother wouldn't like you to." Having settled that on him, she said "Is someone working in your house?"

"I do. You know that. I'm a writer."

"I mean real work. The kind a workman does."

It didn't matter what he said so long as it cleared the woman out of his path and sent her into her house. "There's none of them. We don't need anything."

"Well, I'm sure somebody's in there."

"There isn't," Dudley said, and had the awful notion that Kathy had sneaked home. "Why are you saying there is?"

Brenda Staples lifted her head, and he thought her flat stare was all the answer she was prepared to dole out to him until he saw that the movement was indicating his house. "Perhaps you can explain that," she said.

It was the package. It must be kicking the sides of the bath. As he willed the muffled thuds to give up so that he could persuade the woman that the noise had been somewhere other than his house, she took his silence for confusion. "Has someone broken in?" she said with at least a simulation of concern. "Shall I call the police?"

"No," Dudley blurted and managed to laugh. "Why would we want them? You'd just be wasting their time."

"Don't try so hard to impress me with your manliness. It might be someone you can't deal with. Half of them are on drugs."

"I can." The thudding was in his head now, which made him feel that it had escaped from the house. "It's only something I left on."

"Left on," Brenda Staples said and gazed at him with incredulity not far short of contempt. "You'll be telling me next you listen to that sort of thing when you write."

"Why shouldn't I?" He was unable to gauge whether the noise was growing louder or just pounding his perceptions raw. "Whatever helps me write is fine," he came close to shouting.

"Well, it certainly won't do for the rest of us. I'm sure your mother wouldn't stand for it if she were here."

"How do you she isn't?" Dudley said in case that could help.

"I hope she would have answered the doorbell. I rang it for long enough. I presume she isn't quite so shut into her own mind as some." Brenda Staples weighed this down with her gaze before adding "Besides which she told me she would be away for the weekend. I take it that's why you've been making such a din."

He was barely able to pretend to be polite. "Why did she tell you?"

"Presumably so that I could keep an eye on the situation."

"What?" His grin was almost too tight to let his words out. "Which?"

"Your house." With a frown and a shake or at least a twitch of her head she commented "I'm amazed you call that sort of racket music at your age. I know some people who haven't been brought up to know better drive around with it in their cars and inflict it on the rest of us, but it doesn't belong in this neighbourhood."

With an effort he produced a laugh to accompany the grin. "I don't call it music."

"Then what on earth is it supposed to be?"

He was about to blame the television when he realised she might have spied through the front window that it was switched off. "The computer," he said the moment that the idea darted into his head.

"You're saying it makes that noise when you're using it? No wonder you write the sort of thing you do."

"Of course it doesn't," he retorted, only to find that the noise was picking his thoughts apart. "It's, it's a, you know what I mean, an alarm. An alarm programme. It's to tell me when I forget to switch off the computer."

"I suggest you do as you're told, then. I'll wait here till you have."

She moved just enough to let him onto the path and turned to watch his progress. "You don't need to do that," he said through the gap he forced between his teeth.

"I mean to, though. And I'll be listening out for any further disturbance."

Surely the banging had grown louder only because he was closer to the house. He snatched out his keys and almost dropped them for realising what the noise was: the slamming of a door. He would have liked to believe a wind was responsible, but the evening was otherwise so calm that it might have been designed to draw attention to the sound. He fumbled the key into the lock and twisted it, and then being watched paralysed him. Hesitating would only aggravate the situation. He threw the door open and fled into the house.

The hall was deserted. The noise was upstairs, and he swung to confront Brenda Staples, who had taken at least one step after him. "Good night," he said and slammed the door.

The sound was echoed from above. As he dashed upstairs the banging of the bathroom door seemed to become entangled with his footsteps. He seized the doorknob, which writhed like a dying insect. He flung the door away from him and stormed into the room.

The package staggered backwards, he hoped with fear as well as lack of balance. The backs of its legs struck the edge of the bath, and it sprawled into the clutter it had made. It finished up with its head and shoulders in the armchair, which was leaning in the corner by the taps and resting on the askew wardrobe doors. At least nothing appeared to be broken. The feeble struggles of the package to right itself filled him with an excited disgust that he was eager to intensify. He was determined to exact some pleasure from the day, to compensate for the rest of it. The package hadn't experienced real helplessness yet, and it would struggle a good deal more enthusiastically before he'd finished—and then, with a rush of frustration that peeled his lips back from his clenched teeth, he saw he had a problem. He couldn't render the package too helpless. He couldn't carry it where he meant to dispose of it, not now that Brenda Staples might be watching. It was going to have to walk.

At the moment it seemed incapable of standing up. Its disabled attempts enraged him. "Get away from there, you useless bitch," he snarled. "Look at the mess you've made." He grabbed it by the shoulders and hauled it across the room to the corner where the mirror ended. He propped the lump of a head against its own reflection and left the package there like a handcuffed suspect while he wrestled the armchair onto the landing and leaned the wardrobe doors against the banisters above the stairwell.

The package was straining to butt itself away from the wall. It didn't know that it was resting against its reflection, and that made it seem as good as mindless. Whatever it had once been, he thought it was barely human now. Soon it wouldn't be at all, but he had to fill the intervening hours somehow. "Back in your trough," he said and took hold of the shoulders to return it to the bath.

It could hardly walk. Its shuffling didn't match his speed as he propelled it across the room. That would be no use when he had to take it outside. "Get where you're told," he growled as he shoved the backs of the legs against the bath. As the package began to topple he let go, and it fell in with a thud.

He would have hoped that might have knocked more than the breath out of it for a while. It appeared to stun the package into keeping still, but not for long. The brown lump of a head rose towards him as the body wormed to sit against the end of the bath. The lump retained just enough of its features to seem to be presenting him with an expression of blind defiance. Did the package imagine that by sitting up it could prevent him from covering it with the lid? That simply demonstrated how senseless it was. "Never mind looking like that. Remember what happened to her in the stories," he warned it, only to realise that the package hadn't read the ones about itself. At once he knew how they could spend the time until dark.

He wanted something to eat first. He would have liked some sleep as well. It was worse than unfair if the package had caught up on its sleep after he'd lain awake to ensure it stayed put. At least it wasn't going to be eating ever again, and he grinned as he left the room stealthily enough for the package to believe he was still watching. He ran downstairs and hacked a chunk off a loaf from the refrigerator, then heaped a plate with it and a hunk of cheddar and a carton of the butter Kathy had given up trying to persuade him to change for margarine. He snatched a knife from the draining-board to butter with and almost forgot to bolt the front door against intruders in his haste to return to the bathroom.

As far as he could judge, the package hadn't moved. He hoped it was afraid to. He stooped to bring his head close to the object it called one, and was pleased to see it jerk at his shout. "I'm back. You never knew I'd gone." By the time he finished it had grown frustratingly calm or at any rate stiff. It wouldn't be able to stay peaceful inside its wrappings once he'd had his snack. He sat on the lidded toilet and stood the carton of butter in the sink while he coated his bread thick. He took a bite followed by a mouthful of cheese. "Bet you don't know what I'm doing now," he said once swallowing let him.

Suppose it thought he was masturbating? He didn't know whether to be amused by its mistake or angered by its presumption that it could cause him to do so. He turned on the cold tap and flung a handful of water at the package. As a stain darkened on its bulging breasts it executed a satisfactory jump before it could control itself. "Wondering what that was?" he called. "I'll bet you've had some of it spilled over you in your life."

The notion put him off his food. He had to breathe hard and swallow harder to regain his appetite. The effort of keeping a mouthful down stoked his loathing and inflamed his thoughts. "Was that why you wanted me to hire that Mr Killogram?" he demanded. "Were you hoping he'd do it to you?"

The idea of her ruining the film for that reason made him wish the knife he was holding were sharper. He could use it to dig out an eye or both, but he would have to unwrap the package ahead of time. He needed to remember not to do anything that would hinder his getting rid of the package unnoticed, but he wanted an answer. "Do you know what I'm talking about? If you don't you'd better show me."

The package didn't stir. Was it daring to defy him? "Move while you can," he shouted. "Did you know that actor meant to spoil my film?"

The lump of a head tilted up. If it nodded, he'd draw some expression from it. In a moment it shook from side to side, just vigorously enough to convey its response. "I didn't think so," Dudley felt generous for saying. "Did you only want to help me? Don't worry. You have."

That deserved a reaction, but the lump betrayed none. The erased face could have been presenting him with mute indifference or even mocking him. Its secretiveness provoked him to say in a voice that made his teeth ache as much as his eyes "We know there's only one real Mr Killogram, don't we? Do you want to hear what he's been doing over the weekend?"

The lump faced him without much of a face. Soon it would look like that even with no wrappings—a brownish object divested of its features. He must remember to put that in a story. "All right, you can," he said. "Just let me finish my dinner."

By the time he had, the lump was resting against the tiled wall. He was going to liven it up. He dumped his knife and plate and the carton of butter on the landing as he hurried to print out his latest tales. The paper smelled as if the heat of the day was concentrated in them. "You ought to be proud," he said as he returned to his audience. "These are about you."

It didn't seem especially proud, even though the name in all the stories was Patricia. Perhaps it was forgetting the name it used to have. At first it held its head up as though eager for its story, but before he'd finished reading about Patricia in the bath the lump sank back. He found its attitude insulting: it had had more chance to rest today than he had. Admittedly it had heard part of the story earlier, when it had failed to put on much of a show in its role, but he didn't see why he should accept that as an excuse. Besides, it was quite as unresponsive to the fates of the limbless girl and the blind one and the deaf. He tried shouting at random and lurching close to an embryonic ear. Even these methods didn't always earn a response, and in any case the effects weren't being achieved by the stories themselves, which he thought unfair to him and to his work. He managed to contain his anger by remembering that he was using the stories to while away the hours. Soon it was sufficiently dark for him to need the bathroom light, but not nearly black enough outside that he could risk taking the package out of the house. He was about to start rereading all the stories when he saw the alternative. "You can have the rest as well," he said and fetched them from his room.

He read the story of Greta at Moorfields first, though it reminded him of one more hindrance to his career. He changed the girl's name to Patricia, except when surges of rage at his audience and at being robbed of publication goaded him to call the character Package. He used that name more in the other tales as the window blackened above the sink. Long before he'd used up the stories the insides of his eyes felt as if they were growing black as well, but he didn't yield to the temptation to be hasty, despite resenting his audience's indolence while he did all the work. He slowed his voice down until it reminded him of a failing audio-cassette, and shouted or ducked close to the package or eventually both whenever he wanted to be certain it wasn't asleep. Finally the last Patricia was done away with, and he gathered the pages from the floor around the toilet. He piled them on his bed on the way to craning out of the window.

A few lamps illuminated the deserted street. Above the glowing green sample of hillside, the sky was as solid as coal except for the stars. The Staples' house and all the others he could see were unlit. It was almost two in the morning, and he grinned at the thought of the mass of his neighbours slumbering like animals in pens, dreaming dull dreams if they had any whatsoever, utterly unaware of him and his adventures. He eased the window shut and made for the bathroom. "All right, we've finished waiting," he said.

He thought the lump of a head was unsure whether to rise or to cower. Of course it didn't know what he was proposing. "It's time to let you out," he said. "You need your shoes on."

The package crouched and swung its wrists towards him. As its hands wriggled eagerly he saw what it imagined or hoped. "You won't be doing it," he said with a grin at the attempt to trick him. "We'll leave them."

The package didn't sit up at once. He was about to use one of its shoes to prod a breast when, reluctantly or burdened with exhaustion, it fell back. He worked the trainers over the hot unappealing feet and tied the laces in bows as tight as Kathy used to make for him until he'd gone to secondary school. "Lift up your legs," he said. "Let's get them apart. I expect you've forgotten how that feels."

For no reason that he could comprehend, the package was

unwilling. "Don't you want to walk out of here?" he had to shout, and even then it only lifted its legs an inch. He grabbed a heel and jerked them high while he found the end of the tape. He dug a fingernail under the sticky edge and peeled it away, all six turns of it. There were as many around the wrists and the head. He managed to unstick the tangled length from his fingers without losing too much of his temper and dropped it in the bin under the sink, and then he thrust his face close to the wrapped one. "You can stand up now," he said.

Perhaps the package couldn't without help. It didn't take long to infuriate him with its attempts, however entertaining they might have been if it hadn't lost him so much sleep. He gripped one shoulder by the bone and hauled the package to its feet. "Step out," he urged impatiently. "Step out of the bath."

It appeared to need to recall the use of its legs, unless it was deliberately trying to frustrate him. Eventually its left foot groped up the side of the bath and wavered over. He held onto the shoulder while the other foot followed. As soon as both feet were planted on the mattress he let go. "You aren't going to fall, are you?" he said. "Not yet," he only mouthed.

He poised a hand above the shoulder, which was working as if it ached, in case the package overbalanced when it stepped off the mattress. Though it wobbled as its foot touched the floor, it didn't topple over. He pulled the door wide and steered the package by its other shoulder out of the room. It accepted his guidance as far as the stairs, but when its foot stepped on air it recoiled so violently that he had to flinch back to prevent its body from touching his. "Don't worry, I won't let you fall downstairs," he said. "We don't want you cluttering the place up."

The package took its time and far more importantly his over descending the stairs. More than once he was tempted to give it a shove instead of simply gripping its shoulder, but he mustn't risk injuring it yet. Once it was safely in the hall he inched the front door open and peered both ways along the street. A treacly breeze came to find him, having lent the trees on the hillside such a sluggish movement that he could have imagined the sky was black water, but otherwise there was no sign of life outside the house. He propelled his burden onto the path and closed the door, then hustled the package across the road and up the grassy track. He didn't slow down until they were screened from the houses by the trees, although he had to encourage the package by speaking with his lips almost touching an ear. "I'll be letting you go," he said, which was true enough—from the unfenced edge above the road that cut through the highest section of the ridge. "You won't be seeing me again," he said.

# THIRTY-FOUR

When Patricia felt the breeze she knew she was outside the house. That was the only way she could tell. Her legs seemed hardly to belong to her, and her feet were unable to identify where they were standing. It had to be the Smiths' front path, but the effort of walking gave her legs no chance to experience anything more specific, and the thick soles of her trainers didn't help. It must surely be late at night for Dudley to risk taking her outside. In that case the street would be as quiet as it sounded to her, and any noise she made would wake the neighbours. She could only stamp, and how long would he let her keep that up? She would never know unless she tried—but she'd barely started flexing the muscles of her legs when Dudley gripped her less bruised shoulder between a finger and thumb as if holding some unpleasant item and shoved her forward into the dark.

She did her best to tramp, but he was urging her so fast that the little strength the act of walking left her was used up by keeping her balance. By the time she found the energy to resist she was being pushed uphill. When something clawed at her jeans and tore free, she deduced that she was climbing the path to the top of the ridge. She felt as if most of her vitality had been crushed out of her along with her sight and hearing. Nevertheless her debilitated efforts to be cumbersome brought Dudley's voice against her ear. "I'll be letting you go. You won't be seeing me again."

Did he mean to release her and go into hiding? However much she yearned to be free, she couldn't let him escape too, not when he might find other victims and treat them worse than her. She had to assume that she was going to survive because she'd formed some kind of relationship with him, however much his mind had warped it. Perhaps he still thought of her as his publicist or some even more unlikely appendage of his writing. The possibility made her want to wrench herself out of his hateful grasp. The path underfoot grew less uneven, or her legs regained some of their steadiness, and she sensed that she'd emerged into the open; there was space for a breeze. It tousled the little of her hair that wasn't bound under the tape, and fondled the stretch of her throat below the sticky wrapping. She shrugged out of Dudley's grip and jerked the fingers of one hand, gesturing him to unbind her wrists. "Not yet," he said. "We can't have anyone hearing or seeing."

She would have assured him that she wouldn't make a sound if she'd had any way to communicate this. It might even have been true for a while. She stayed as she was in case that could change his mind, but when he pinched her shoulder she pulled free. "Don't you want me touching you?" his muffled voice said. "You don't think I like it, do you? Do as you're told and I won't. Walk straight ahead. There's a path."

Either the ground underfoot turned soft or that was her perception of her tread. She'd taken several increasingly less tentative paces and was becoming confident of her ability to remain upright when Dudley uttered a version of a laugh. "Not that straight. Go right or you'll be in a bush."

Did the spectacle of her playing his puppet amuse him? She could bear it if it saved her from worse. She veered in the direction he'd given, only to be told with rather less mirth "Not that right either. Bit left or I'll get hold of you again. Bit more. Are you trying to be funny? That's it, as if you didn't know. Go on."

Apparently her performance satisfied him at last. He was silent for a while as far as she could judge. While she plodded warily forward she strained to gather some impression of her surroundings, but all she was able to sense outside her enclosed darkness was a smell of charred wood and the scent of a night bloom she couldn't identify. "Not so fast," Dudley said.

Was he missing his control of her? All at once it and her bonds and the confinement of her perceptions were almost if not wholly unbearable, and she could only march forward as though she might outdistance them. "Go on then, fall," Dudley said.

She didn't know if he meant to warn her or express a wish. She took a hesitant pace that yearned to be defiant, and her foot collided with an obstruction. "Just in time," he said. "Step up. Big step."

Patricia scraped the toe of her shoe over the hindrance, and her foot wavered into space. As it hovered in nothingness she felt as if she was about to lose more than her balance. She threw her weight forward, and her foot struck a flat surface. The impact jarred her leg and sent pain deep into her knee. She thought the joint was going to give way until her other foot supported her on the rock. "Go left now," Dudley said. "You're on the top."

The rock was more uneven than the path had been. Perhaps the depressions were shallow, but they were deep enough to rob her of any sense whether her paces would take her up or down. The steps she had to execute from one eroded slab to the next were at least as disconcerting, especially since she was being directed by her increasingly impatient captor. She thought he'd lost all patience when he said barely audibly "Stop."

Her left foot came down and found just enough rock for its heel to stand on. She snatched it back and almost toppled into the dark. As she struggled to restore her balance while her bound hands clutched at the air behind her she heard Dudley say "Who's that in the observatory? Is he watching us?"

Patricia twisted around, only to realise that she had no idea which way to face in order to display her plight. She was tilting her head back and forth in the hope of making its state more apparent when Dudley said "It's all right. It's the moon."

Could he actually believe that he was reassuring her as well as himself? Perhaps the interlude had been a joke at the expense of her hopes. It made her yet more conscious of her blindness—of the moon that she was unable to see, and the sky, and everything below it. She felt as if the blindness had gained weight, holding her where she was until Dudley shouted "I said it's all right. Go ahead. Big step down."

The step wasn't as deep as she feared, which undermined her confidence. Before she was sure of her footing again she had to step up, and then down, and then up. As she wondered if Dudley was guiding her along the most difficult route for his amusement he said "What's that, a dog?"

It could be with its owner. Patricia had no idea how distant they might be, but she halted on the skewed rock and turned her head from side to side. Even if she couldn't see, perhaps she could be seen. She held her breath until she heard a laugh. "Don't know how, but you're right. It wasn't a dog," Dudley said as if she should be pleased. "Just a fox."

Had it been either? Had it ever been there at all? She thought he might be growing bored with her progress and so taunting her with jokes. He'd directed her transit over two more slabs of rock when he said "There's a helicopter."

She was unable to hear it if it existed. She considered jumping up and down to attract the attention of the police, if it was theirs. He hadn't told her to stand still; he didn't as she tried to locate a foothold sufficiently level for her to risk prancing blindly about. Wouldn't she look like a reveller? Surely she ought to take the chance, except that Dudley said "There it goes, over the sea."

That was miles distant. She would be no more detailed than a matchstick figure, if she was visible at all, if there was anyone to see her. She thought he would have been more concerned for himself if there had been, unless he'd decided that nobody would hinder his plan. That was how he sounded as he reverted to telling where and how to move. She was almost growing used to his curt phrases—at least they implied that he'd abandoned playing jokes—when he said "It's all black and white. It's like being in a film."

Did he imagine she was in his? It seemed crucial to think of some way to remind him she was real. Failing to comply with his directions might do the trick. She advanced a step and felt her footing level out. As if she'd given him a cue he said "Not there. Go right."

She planted her other foot on the surface, which was absolutely level. It felt more reassuring than anything else had since she'd strayed into his clutches. Could his attempt to steer her away be another cruel joke? As she hesitated he said "Hurry up. Go right and we can say goodbye."

That mustn't be a joke. He surely couldn't imagine that she would continue to obey him if it proved to be one. "More right," he said once she moved in that direction. "Now straight. Bit left. Stop there. Stop."

The last word sounded like the threat of his grip on her shoulder, and she halted on what felt like the top of a slope. She could only think he meant to send her downhill and then make his escape unseen. She braced herself in case he pushed her, and willed him just to speak. When he did, his words confirmed her expectations. "You'll be going down in a moment. This shouldn't hurt," he said.

THIRTY—FIVE "This shouldn't hurt." He meant pulling off the tape, but he didn't think that falling forty feet would either, nor hitting the road. There was no need for him to imagine that she would experience any more pain than her predecessors just because he knew her better. Ought he to wait for a car to make sure the job was finished? He could free her wrists while he was waiting, but how close would the car have to be when he unwrapped her head and gave her a last push? He was peering down at the deserted road that curved away to vanish between the jagged rocky slopes towards the thin sharp white horizon of the black sea when the package wavered forward. "Careful," he shouted. "Step back a step."

Perhaps his choice of words confused the package, or else it lost its footing. Its toes were an inch from the edge, and it seemed content to teeter. The sight was all the more frustrating because he would have enjoyed it and the result if it hadn't been premature. He couldn't let the package fall while it was wrapped up, or whoever found it would know its end hadn't been an accident. With an effort he abandoned his excitement at the spectacle and pinched a shoulder to drag the package away from the brink. "I said get back," he whispered through his teeth and let go as soon as the package was safe.

He wouldn't waste time awaiting a car. He could trust the fall to finish his task. Rather than shove the package over the edge, he would trip it up so that it fell head first. How large and soft was the impact going to be? He grinned with anticipation as he stooped to find the end of the tape around the wrists—and then he straightened up so fast that the blackness overhead seemed to fill his aching skull.

His lack of sleep must be hindering his ability to think, and the other distractions wouldn't have helped: the illusion of a watcher in the observatory, the fox, the police helicopter. He couldn't let the package be discovered so close to his house, especially when it was supposed to have gone to London. The fact that it would have been useful to him alive mightn't prove his innocence. Even if he walked all night with it, would that take it far enough away that nobody could associate it with him? There was also the problem that it might retain traces of its wrappings. Hadn't he ignored faint marks on its ankles as if they were too insignificant to betray him? By far the best solution would be that it was never found at all.

He glared at it and then around him. The entire landscape looked paralysed by moonlight, inert as the windmill beside the bridge. The stillness felt like a refusal to help him. To his left, beyond the river that perspective had engulfed, the sky above Liverpool glowed the amber of a warning. To his right the distant sea bared its rim, the whiteness of which reminded him of the top of a blank page in a typewriter. Behind him the ridge led past the windmill to the defunct observatory, both of whose buildings were locked and no use to him. The sea and the river were too far to walk to. The trains had stopped running, and it sounded as though he couldn't even trust the motorway to offer traffic that would leave the package unrecognisable or at least wipe out any evidence of wrapping. Over the bridge the hill sloped down to Birkenhead, where the streets would be just as unhelpful. He turned to aggravate the stinging of his eyes by staring along the ridge, which the darkness softened so much that he could imagine burying the package in it. He mustn't let his imagination stray, he'd wasted enough of the night—but then he remembered the view from the train.

Beneath the motorway was a field where people walked dogs. He was sure that it was muddy even now, at the height of summer. Facing the railway across the field, below the far end of the ridge, were allotments. Some of the sheds must contain tools—a spade. Reality was on his side again. He opened his mouth to give the package some sense of the good news and saw that it was inching towards the brink. "Not yet," he declared, digging a finger and thumb into its shoulder to haul it clear.

It writhed in his grasp. As he wiped his hand on his trousers, the package planted its feet apart on the rock, a gesture suggesting defiance even before it waggled its fingers in his general direction to show it expected its hands to be freed. "I said not yet," he told it. "We're still too close to people."

While the fingers and the lump of a head drooped, it maintained its stance. Was it trying mutely to argue with him? "Turn around. More. I didn't say stop. Stop. Straight ahead," he instructed and watched it trudge back the way it had come. "It's just as tiring for me, you know. Soon you'll be able to lie down."

So would he once it was safely tucked away where nobody would ever find it. He thought he might sleep for days. No doubt the package didn't understand or care how much the chore of directing it took out of him. By now single syllables sufficed— "Up," he kept saying, and "Down"—but the sense of power this gave him was starting to pall, especially since the package seemed to be in no hurry to reach the end of its trek. He had to use his imagination so as to remain interested. "You're walking on a dinosaur. Those are its scales. Careful you don't wake it up," he said, and later "That's a lip you're stepping off. There's mouths all round you. Watch out or they'll have your feet." He felt as though he was dreaming aloud, but his audience showed not the least appreciation of his creativity. He clenched his teeth on his temper as he passed the observatory and came in sight of the downhill slope.

A lane separated the foot of the hill from the allotments. The rectangular plots put him in mind of graves with sheds for markers. As he followed the package down a narrow grassy track the plots appeared to expand as if they were greedy for a burial. No doubt they would be a pleasure to dig, but mightn't the owner notice if Dudley found an extra use for one? He'd better be content with borrowing a spade. Even then he might have to act like a criminal and break into a shed. "Look what you're going to make me do," he muttered as the package hesitated irritatingly at the bottom of the slope. "No danger. Straight on."

This sent it to a gate in the hedge that bordered the allotments. The gate was fastened only with a latch, but the lever was stiff with rust, and Dudley had to lean on it. The latch gave with a click as loud as the fall of the bar of a mousetrap, and the gate emitted a shrill creak on swinging inwards. All this might have been designed as an alarm, because it roused a muffled shout. "What's that? Who's there?"

The speaker sounded newly awakened, and Dudley felt as if he had been as well. As the door of a shed a hundred yards away burst open he clamped his hands over the ears and forced the lump of a head out of sight behind the hedge. A man almost as broad as the shed blundered out of it and shaded his eyes to peer towards the gate. "What's the game?" he shouted. "After somewhere else to vandalise?"

Dudley took a firmer grip. He could have fancied he was covering a child's ears to prevent it from hearing anything unsuitable, particularly since the package was so small. "Do I look like someone who'd break the law?" he retorted.

"I can't see what you look like, matey. Maybe I should come and see."

The hulking silhouette detached itself from the equal blackness of the shed, and Dudley saw that it was brandishing some kind of club. He almost threw the package face down on the gravel and trod on its neck to keep it unobtrusive. "I don't mind," he said, willing the man not to take him at his word. "I just wanted somewhere private."

"Going to leave us a bit of manure, were you? You think we've put in all this work so you've got a toilet. Sounds like a vandal to me."

"I couldn't see where I was." Though Dudley wasn't forcing the head unduly low, the package had begun to struggle as best it could; it almost dealt him a backward kick before he sidled aside, still holding on. "I only saw the hedge," he was enraged to have to plead.

"Shy type, are you? Bit too shy for your own good." The man dropped the end of his weapon with a clunk on the dim path and leaned on it so as to shade his eyes again. "Who's that with you? What are they up to?"

"Nothing. They're why I needed the hedge," Dudley said, cursing its thinness.

"Can't they speak for themselves? Let's be hearing from them."

"They can't at the moment." As the man advanced a step, dragging his club with a thick rumble over the path, Dudley felt as if the dark was squeezing his brain to a crumb of blackness. "They're, they're a bit ill," he stammered.

"Drugs, is it? Or don't they want me knowing who they are?"

"That's it," Dudley said and flattened his hands on the lump of a head as a kick narrowly missed him. "You don't need to when we didn't do anything, do you?"

"Depends what you were going to." The man leaned over the club, and his voice became something like quizzical. "Are you sure you weren't both off behind the hedge?"

Dudley swallowed nausea. "All right, we were," he said, though it tasted like sickness.

"Dirty little buggers. Couldn't you wait till you got home?"

"I'm not one of those," Dudley objected, because the notion felt still worse. "She's a girl."

"You want to be more romantic then, son. Buy her some flowers. Take her to a decent restaurant. Take her dancing. Show her you care and then you'll both want it. That's how it was with me and my wife."

The voice had grown nostalgic, which aggravated Dudley's revulsion. He had to refrain from trying to crush the sticky head between his hands. He was dodging another kick when the man called "Get going, then. I'll be watching."

Dudley almost couldn't speak for disgust. "What are you asking me to do?"

"I'm telling you both to make yourselves scarce while I'm feeling sentimental. Don't bank on it lasting. This'd nearly be our anniversary, that's all."

Dudley saw the silhouette bow its head. He let go of the ears and gripped the package by its shoulder to urge it alongside the hedge. "Go on," he said low but sharp enough to penetrate the tape. "Faster. Keep on straight. No rest yet. Soon."

When they reached the corner of the hedge he glanced back.

Though the silhouette had raised its head, he thought it could distinguish as little about him and the package as he could of the man. Now that he was barred from the allotments, the plots reminded him even more enticingly of graves. A scent of recently dug earth teased his nostrils, and he had to wipe his mouth. He turned away in a rage, only to notice that the route he seemed to be proposing would lead him home. Then he realised it could take him further—to the old graveyard at the end of his road.

So his mind was functioning, however sleepily. Perhaps it had needed the hint of the allotments, though he was more inclined to believe that the thankless business of guiding the package had distracted him. How many hours did he have until dawn? Where was he to find a spade? He would have to improvise, and surely life would side with Mr Killogram. All the slates were missing from the roof of the church in the graveyard; he could use one to dig. "Keep going," he ordered, and eventually "Right. Not stop. Go right, you brainless dummy."

The lane had met the road that led to his. The road climbed between walls of exposed rock, which gave way to houses that were quite as lifeless. He urged his plodding burden past them, and barely resisted the impulse to kick it along. It might take umbrage at that, perhaps even turn defiant, and he had no time to waste on its antics. All that mattered was to speed it to its grave. At least he wouldn't have to kill it. Burial would solve that problem.

He dodged ahead of it to the crossing that sloped down to the main road. He'd heard a car. It passed without appearing and left behind a stillness that the murmur of the city emphasised. He directed the package to step off the pavement and onto the next one, which led past his house. "Not much further," he said and had to grin, because the undertaking seemed to have enlivened the package; it increased its pace, at any rate. He was in sight of his house when he heard a car behind him.

As he twisted to look it poked its nose around the intersection. He was able to imagine that it was borrowing its whiteness from the moonlight until it swung into his road. It was a police car.

He had only an instant to think as he hid his face from it so swiftly that pain flared up his neck and clutched his skull. An instant was enough for Mr Killogram. As the vehicle caught up with him he overtook the package and made to hide it with his body while he shoved it down the nearest front path. There wasn't time; the gate was yards away. Instead he had to clasp the package in his arms and apply his mouth to the bulge in the tape that contained the lips.

The bound hands squirmed as if they were trying to express his disgust. Even the taped lips attempted to wriggle, and he could have thought they were struggling to reach his. From the corner of one stinging eye he managed to gather that the police car had sped past him and his house. When the brake lights brightened outside the graveyard he let go of the package and rubbed his mouth savagely with the back of a hand. "Don't worry, that's all you're getting," he said through his teeth.

The police car had halted by the graveyard. As the doors sprang open, several figures dashed out of the gates and fled up a path onto the hill. "That's right, chase them out," a woman's voice exulted from a bedroom window next to the churchyard. "Let them stick their needles in themselves somewhere else." The police from the car ran after the fugitives, and Dudley glimpsed flashlights in the graveyard. He couldn't take the package there or back onto the ridge.

He had to hide it where he could while he had the chance. He kept his mouth close to one blurred ear to make sure the police didn't hear him, although the notion of touching the package again with his lips sickened him. He talked it to his gate and through, and sidled around it to the front door. He fumbled his keys out of his pocket and nearly dropped them from exhaustion.

As he scraped the key into the lock, he heard a rumble like a thunderclap above him, and Brenda Staples leaned out of her bedroom window.

She was craning towards the graveyard. He turned the key and pushed the door open in a single movement, then gripped the package by a shoulder. "Up," he said in its ear as its toes nudged the front steps. He propelled it into the hall and glanced up. Brenda Staples was still intent on the chase. He bared his teeth at her and nearly slammed the door to make her jump. He eased it shut and bolted it as he turned to the package, which was loitering near the foot of the stairs. "Keep on," he said. "Step up. Step up."

It obeyed him until it was halfway upstairs, at which point doubts appeared to set in. It inched its feet forward on two adjacent treads to identify the location or take a firmer stance. "Don't stop or you'll fall," Dudley was amused to improvise. "There's nothing either side of you to stop you falling." Perhaps the situation he'd described was too vivid to be helpful. The package wavered and toppled towards him until he planted a foot in the small of its back. "You'll be all right if you do as you're told," he said. "Step up. Step up."

This took it as far as the landing, where it almost fell over with the unexpectedness of no more climbing. He enjoyed the idea that it was terrified of straying over some unseen edge. "Straight ahead," he directed while he grinned. "Stop there." It was in the bathroom now, and unaware of standing in front of the bath. "Turn round," he said as he retrieved the last roll of tape from beneath the sink. "Keep turning. Stop."

Although he liked the sound of unsticking the tape, that might alert the package, and so he took a minute to pick a stretch loose with his nails. He crept up on the package as the sightless lump of a head began to pivot back and forth, and sank to his knees, holding the section of tape behind the package at arms' length. "Don't think I'm kneeling to you," he muttered. "I'm not praying for you either." He bound the tape around the ankles, pulling it tight, and as the package commenced struggling for balance he wrapped the ankles a second time, and a third and a fourth. He was able to bind them yet again as the package toppled over the side of the bath, where only its sudden forward crouch saved it from thumping its head rather than its shoulders against the wall. As it writhed in search of a less awkward position, he had no trouble in pulling off its shoes before hoisting its legs with his foot into the bath.

He'd done enough for one night. Tomorrow he would call his mother at work and tell her that he needed to be left alone until Tuesday. He could buy a spade for tomorrow night's job in the graveyard. As the package started thumping its feet against the sides of the bath he shut the door to keep the noise in and lay down on the mattress. The package would tire of its racket eventually, and he wouldn't be surprised if by that time he was asleep. "That was research. That was the rehearsal," he called and made his head more comfortable on the pillow. "Don't worry, next time it'll be real."

# THIRTY-SIX

As Kathy wheeled her suitcase away from the hotel Dudley's mobile rang six times, and then he gave in. "Dudley Smith, writer and scriptwriter," he said. "Me and Mr Killogram must be busy. Leave us a message."

When had he changed the response? She had never heard that before. "I just wanted to check how things are going," she told him. "I'll try again in a bit." Perhaps his train to work was in a tunnel. She pocketed the mobile and hurried through the mainline station, where the sunlight through the glass roof was uttering pronouncements like a god. She bumped her suitcase down the escalator and bought her ticket on the way to riding more stairs to the underground platform.

It was hot with commuters and with her inability to use her mobile. She begrudged every one of the five minutes the West

Kirby train took to arrive. She sat at the front of the first carriage, where her luggage could take some of the space left for wheelchairs. She felt like a child pretending to drive the train—urging it not to loiter underground, at any rate. As soon as it emerged into the open beyond Conway Park she tried Dudley's number again, but he was still only a message.

Might he be stuck in the tunnel? Her train had passed another in there, but she was as certain as she could be that Dudley hadn't been aboard. She phoned a third time as the train swung away from Birkenhead North towards Bidston, offering her a view of allotments across a field and reminding her how close to home she was. Could he have switched off the phone so that he wouldn't be disturbed, only to oversleep? She had to smile wryly at wondering how much of a mess she would find. At the very least Dudley was going to help her clear up.

Perhaps Monty was right, and she indulged Dudley too much. Even if his writing was the most important aspect of his life and so of hers as well, that needn't mean he had to be deficient in any other way. She would be less of a mother if she let him. It wasn't too late for them to change. The train halted at Bidston and admitted a hint of a breeze, and Kathy was tempted to make for her house. She imagined dragging her suitcase for miles under the sun, and resumed her seat. Surely if he'd been writing all weekend he deserved a day off from his other job.

She couldn't spend nine hours wondering where he was. She didn't want to spend any. She managed to wait until the carriage rose level with the ample houses of Hoylake before she called again. Only the recording answered. "I'll keep trying," she said as she had to stand up.

Mr Stark was unlocking the office on the main road around the corner from the station. Kathy's colleagues turned as they heard the rumble of her luggage. "Been on your hols?" Mavis suggested.

"Something like that."

"Don't say you've had a wicked weekend," Cheryl cried.

Kathy didn't, nor anything else, though she produced a fleeting smile as she hurried her case to the staffroom. The office would be open in five minutes, which meant that Dudley's workplace would be, and someone must be there by now. She found the number on the list behind the counter and snatched out her mobile. "I'll just be a minute," she told Mr Stark.

She was longer. The phone in the Birkenhead office rang for at least two minutes before it was picked up. Kathy opened her mouth and left it open, because whoever had answered immediately hung up. "I'm phoning Birkenhead," she informed Mr Stark with some vehemence and tried again. In rather more than another minute the ringing ceased. "Don't cut me off," she said at once.

"We aren't open yet," a girl's voice objected.

"You very nearly are. Did you cut me off before?"

"We weren't open."

"I'd call that extremely unprofessional behaviour, and I know what I'm talking about. I'm in the same job. This is your Hoylake branch. May I speak to Dudley, please?"

"He isn't here."

"Of course, I should have realised. I've been away but I know he's had a particularly demanding weekend. I should say I'm his mother."

"It's Dudley's mother."

"I'd like a word with her." This was an older woman, who arrived with a rattle of the plastic of the receiver. "That's Mrs Smith, is it?" she enquired.

"I suppose Ms might be more like it. Dudley's father has been out of the way for really quite a few years."

"That's no excuse."

Kathy felt as if the conversation had tilted, robbing her of the balance she'd achieved. "Sorry, excuse for what?"

"Don't you know what he's like when you're not there?"

"I'm sure I do. I'm sure he's just the same as when I am."

"Then I don't think either of you have got much to be proud of."

Mr Stark was raising his thin greyish eyebrows to enlarge his ostentatiously patient gaze. Kathy met it with a stare that might contain some of her growing anger. "Am I meant to ask why?" she said. "I don't even know who I'm speaking to."

"I'm Vera Brewer. Another of the people your son insulted. Told us he was better than all of us. What do you say to that?"

"I'm not sure," Kathy said, too busy trying to cope with the woman's tone to be other than honest. "I haven't met you, after all."

"So you've brought him up to think he's superior to everyone else in the world."

"He's already done more with his life than I have with mine. I'm sorry if you thought he was rude. He's been under quite a bit of pressure lately, you may not know. Anyway," Kathy said as Mr Stark took hold of the latch of the entrance door while straining his left eyebrow and the same side of his mouth high at her, "has he called in?"

"Not that I've heard."

"I just wanted to let you know that with the weekend he's had he's unlikely to be in today. You can put him down as sick."

After more of a silence than Kathy thought was called for, Vera said "You'd better speak to Mrs Wimbourne."

"Can't you—" When a thump made it clear that Kathy would be addressing a deserted receiver, she wondered with as little patience as Mr Stark was exhibiting how much she would have to repeat. She was trying to consolidate her thoughts when a further voice said "How can I help you, please? We've just opened for the day."

"So have we," Kathy said and looked away from Mr Stark's compressed face that a frown was cramping even smaller.

"I understand you're Dudley's mother." This sounded no more favourable than "Did you have something to tell me?"

"Just that I want him to take the day off. Nervous exhaustion. I hope that counts as sickness."

"I'm afraid I don't understand. Off from what?"

"From you." The conversation seemed to be tilting again, and Kathy tried to regain control. "From work, I mean," she said. "From his day job."

"Can I stop you for a moment? Are you under the impression that your son still works here?"

The room grew charred—hot and dark—and Kathy had to find the breath to speak. "Doesn't he?"

"Not since the middle of last week."

Kathy heard her words becoming stupid with panic. "Do you think there could be some misunderstanding? I'm certain he's been going to work."

"Not here, I'm afraid."

"Then where?" Kathy barely managed not to ask that, and had to force herself to substitute "What happened?"

"He was insubordinate, and on top of that he was abusive to his colleagues and myself, and then he flounced out before I could deal with him."

"I do apologise. I apologise on his behalf. He's had a few difficult weeks, I should say, because I don't think he would tell people." Yet more painfully she continued "If he comes and says he's sorry, would you—"

"I'm afraid matters have progressed too far for that. I can't operate this establishment with two empty positions. I've taken on a replacement for him. An official letter is on its way to him."

"Did he really do anything so bad? I thought we had to behave a lot worse than that to be thrown out of this kind of job."

"Perhaps you should spring to his defence a little less and learn a little more about him. Now you really must excuse me. I have an office to run," Mrs Wimbourne said, and was gone.

Kathy closed her eyes as she switched off the mobile. At least inside her eyelids it was supposed to be this dark. The phone in her hand felt both hollow and burdensome, very much like her thoughts. She was beginning to wonder what else she mightn't know about Dudley when Mr Stark spoke, closer than she had realised he was—virtually in her ear. "Ready for work now?" he said.

# THIRTY-SEVEN

"I'm not answering," Dudley mumbled. "I'm busy. I'm asleep. Don't wake that either." Before he'd finished the ringing fell silent, and he settled back into the comfort of the mattress. At least the ringing hadn't roused the package. Perhaps it was indeed asleep or simply couldn't hear. He knew it was safe in the bath; if it had tried to escape again it would have tripped over him. He didn't need to check, and he was sinking towards the vision of the premiere of *Meet Mr Killogram*—of his own regal walk along the red carpet as autograph hunters held out copies of his book like petitions to him—when the bell shrilled afresh. Its identity was underlined by a hammering of metal on metal. It wasn't the phone downstairs. It was the front doorbell.

He could still lie low. The door was bolted, and only the police would be able to batter it down. They had no reason to be there:

he wasn't one of the addicts they were chasing, nor was he hiding any in his house. Suppose the insistent caller was the postman with an important delivery? Not knowing nagged at Dudley, and so did the thought that the clamour might waken the package. Presumably it was tired from walking, as if he hadn't walked just as far. He floundered off the mattress, blinking his sticky eyes, and had to sprawl on his hands and knees to hoist himself above the surface of the insubstantial yet clinging medium of sleep. The doorbell continued to shrill as he wobbled to his feet and shut the bathroom door on the way to blundering into his room.

He could hardly see for daylight. As he collided with the end of his depleted bed, the bell and the clanking of the knocker hushed at last. He rubbed his bruised shins and then his eyes, and stumbled to the window. Leaning over his desk, he saw Brenda Staples at the gate.

How dare it be her? She had nothing to complain about—no excuse whatsoever to have disturbed his sleep. He unlatched the window and flung the sash as high as it would rattle so as to thrust his upper half over the sill. He was naked from the waist up, and hoping to embarrass her. He took a hot breath to demand why she'd made so much noise, and then the breath turned dusty in his mouth. The person at the door had moved into view below him. She was his mother.

His instinct was to dodge out of sight even though she'd seen him. He tried to believe she was raising her gaze in admiration, but her face was too guarded for his liking. She held out her hands and curled the fingertips up. He was close to imagining that she expected him to jump into her arms until she said "Don't stand there. Come and let me in."

Panic made him blurt some of the truth. "I'm in the bathroom."

"Then hurry up and put something on and come down."

"She can't come in," he said in case the protest gave him time to plan. "She can't see me when I'm not dressed."

"Brenda only came to see why I couldn't get in my own house. You're satisfied now, aren't you, Brenda? Stop wasting time, Dudley, and open the door. I'm tired and I want to talk."

He was unable to grasp how the two were meant to fit together. If she was anxious to sit down, why couldn't she in Brenda Staples' house? He was almost desperate enough to suggest this, but it might make her suspicious. He withdrew into his room and leaned on the sash to slam the window, and wished he could feel safer now that his mother wasn't watching. Mightn't she leave him alone if he refused to unbolt the door? She might be so concerned for him that she would have someone break in—someone else who would learn about the package. It was going to be bad enough if Kathy did, but how was he to prevent her? The only way she could fail to notice it would be if it was making no noise—and at once he saw that he still had a chance. He simply had to silence the package.

Everything was ready. Reality was on Mr Killogram's side as usual. Perhaps he'd been preparing this solution without knowing. Once the package was dealt with he could store it in his room until he had an opportunity to smuggle it out to the graveyard. He strode into the bathroom and grabbed his towelling robe from the hook on the door. The package was lying on its side as if to hinder its own escape. Dudley leaned over it and pressed the plug into the hole, and then he turned the taps on full.

The package didn't react at once. He watched the tape and its clothes darken as the water inched higher. He was wondering if the package had expired without his intervention when it lurched awake. He was able to observe how it tried for several seconds to understand its situation before it commenced thrashing about. Presumably having realised that this wouldn't save it, the package struggled onto its back. It attempted to kick and claw itself into a sitting position as the water sloshed around it and spilled into its nostrils. For the moment the lump of a head was winning the race with the rising flood. Dudley was poised to trample on the scalp if it succeeded in clearing the edge of the bath when the doorbell rang curtly twice.

Couldn't his mother even wait until he'd finished? Another ring told him the opposite. The longer he kept her waiting, the more distrustful she would be. He only had to bluff her into staying downstairs until he completed his task. The package would take minutes to lever itself out of the bath, if it could at all. Though he was frustrated to miss any of its antics, he dashed downstairs and threw the bolts out of their sockets. "It's open," he shouted and ran for the stairs.

He was hoping to be in the bathroom by the time his mother reached the hall. He wasn't even halfway up when she unlocked the door and stepped into the house. Without bothering to close the door she said "No need for you to run away, or is there?"

She couldn't know there was. She was only talking the way women talked. "I told you," Dudley said with all the impatience he had in him. "I'm having a bath."

"Have it later. You aren't even wet. You haven't been in yet. We're overdue for a talk."

"I want to relax. I've been working all weekend."

"So do I, Dudley." He thought he'd won her over until she said "Let's talk first and then maybe we both can." She turned from retrieving the keys from the lock and gasped as if she'd been punched in the stomach. "What's that?" she cried.

He felt shrivelled by panic for as long as it took him to recognise that there was no sign of the package. Kathy might have heard its struggles, even if he'd thought the sounds were unidentifiable. They were; that was why she'd asked the question. "Just the water running," he said.

"Then turn it off." Before he could move she said "I don't mean that. What on earth have you been doing?"

"I said," he said and managed to do so again. "Writing."

"You've decided that's all the work you've time for now, have you?"

That sounded so disparaging that he twisted to face her. "I thought you wanted it to be."

"Don't try and blame it all on me, Dudley. Perhaps your father's right, though, and I've encouraged you a little too much. I talked to your boss this morning. She says you've left your job and didn't even give in your notice."

How many people had his mother discussed him with? His resentment almost overcame his dismay at having been found out, which only aggravated his fear that she might discover the rest. "There's no room for it in my life any more," he gabbled, desperate to learn what was happening upstairs and to complete his task. "I've got my writing and my film."

"There are proper ways to do things, Dudley. I'll support you if I can, you know that, but you could have discussed it with me first," Kathy said, and then her gaze veered past him once more. "You still haven't explained that. Are you seriously telling me it has to do with your work? You aren't taking drugs, are you? Say you aren't taking drugs."

All at once he realised that she was looking at the armchair and the wardrobe doors. "I needed them for research," he said and grinned. "The furniture, I mean, not drugs."

She looked so relieved he found it pitiful. "Did you think up a good story?"

"Obviously. All mine are."

"Just the same, I hope nothing got damaged."

"Nothing we need to be bothered about."

"I'll trust you and not ask." Her gaze was still beyond him when she said "Well, see to it for heaven's sake."

She wasn't referring to the package, he had to remember. She must have tidying away the furniture in mind. "I want to have my bath first," he said.

"That's what I'm talking about. Turn off the water or you'll have it through the floor."

"You shouldn't have kept me so long, then," he objected, suddenly afraid that if the water overflowed she would use that as an excuse to invade the bathroom. All the same, she'd offered him a reason to sprint upstairs, and he did, to see that the package had almost succeeded in tricking him.

It had hooked its bound hands over the end of the bath and was straining to lever itself to its feet. He supposed he should admire its effort, which deserved to be put in a story. He slammed the door and strode to the bath. As the lump of a head swung blindly to acknowledge the slam he used a foot to shove the package away from the end of the bath until the hands lost their purchase. It slithered into the water, and he could have taken it for some amphibious creature returning to its chosen medium. He planted his heel on its forehead to keep it on the bottom, and saw that he ought to tread on its ankles as well to prevent the legs from sloshing water out of the bath. He should also turn the taps off before the water spilled over the edge, but first he needed to bolt the door. He was reluctantly lifting his foot as the nostrils of the wrapped head gave vent to a gurgling bubble when he heard his mother call "I'll put these doors back. Before you lock yourself in there I just want to say—"

Her voice was too close. He jerked his foot out of the bath, splashing the mattress, and raced for the door. His hand was nearly on the bolt when the door opened an inch, and then another. "If you'd like me to—" Kathy said, and was silent for a moment that felt to Dudley like the beginnings of suffocation. "Who's that?" she said in a voice that sounded unconvinced of its own existence, and shoved the door wide.

"Nobody."

For as long as it took him to say it he was able to believe that enough of a denial might convince his mother. Then the water heaved up, drenching the mattress, and two bare feet reared above the surface. "Just someone that's helping me with my research," he said and stared so hard at his mother that his eyes stung.

When he saw her falter he was sure that he had a chance. "Leave us alone or they'll be embarrassed," he said.

Kathy was still on the landing. He took hold of the bolt and moved the door steadily towards her. "If you want to help," he said, "go out for a while or I'll lose my inspiration. I won't have a story any more."

Her eyes winced, and he saw that she would do as he asked if he could think of one more reason. He hadn't managed when she moved. She retreated a step, and then she took it back, and her face stiffened with a clarity he had never seen before. "They can't be embarrassed," she said. "They're dressed."

Dudley glanced at the package. It had raised its denimed legs beside the taps, either trying to find them and shut off the flow or in a confused attempt to shove itself into a less fatal position. The distraction was all Kathy needed. She pushed the door aside and marched past him. "For the third time," she said, "this wants turning off."

She grasped the taps, but seemed capable of forgetting to wield them as she gazed into the bath. He was thinking that she might collaborate with him again, however inadvertently, when she twisted the taps shut and hauled on the chain to unplug the hole. Part of his mind urged him to flee, but she was still his mother. If she wouldn't trust him, who would? She gazed at him with worse than disappointment, as if she hardly recognised him. "What on earth have you been up to while I've been away?" she said.

"I keep telling you, research and lots of writing. There's the research."

He heard the water draining and the package floundering about in it, and had to remember that the package couldn't speak.

Of the many questions his mother visibly had in mind, she chose "Who is she?"

"She wouldn't want me to tell anyone. That's why she'd be embarrassed. Don't worry, she agreed to do this. She'll be fine." He ventured to the bath and grinned at the package, which was stranded on its back. "She'd tell you herself if she could," he said.

It writhed onto its side, displaying its bound hands as it snorted water out of its nostrils. "See, it'll be all right," he said. "She will."

His mother stared at him, and something left her eyes. "She'll have to," she said and stooped to the package.

"What? What are you doing?"

"Tell me herself," Kathy said and took hold of the shoulders to lift the package into a sitting position. "Can you hear me? Can you talk?"

The lump of a head swayed from side to side, and Dudley seized the opportunity. He could still be as convincing as Mr Killogram. "I told you," he said. "She doesn't want to."

The lump wavered and then wobbled up and down. "See, she's agreeing with me," he said.

The lump hardly seemed to have the energy to change direction once again, but it did. "Look, you're just confusing her," he objected. "Let her rest where she is and I'll stay with her."

"Yes, you stay. Don't think of going anywhere," his mother said and leaned closer to the package. "Do you want to talk?" she said in its ear.

He was hoping that it had expended the last of its strength when the lump bobbed up and down twice. "All right, I'm going to take this off for you," Kathy said. "I'll try not to hurt you. I don't know what you two thought you were doing."

She would believe him and not the package, Dudley vowed. She was his mother, and he was Mr Killogram. Perhaps the package mightn't even be able to disagree with him; his mother was having difficulty in locating the end of the soaked tape and in peeling it loose. He watched, hands on hips, as she unwrapped the reddened throat, and the chin, and the mouth. It didn't speak, and he thought it was waiting to cry out when the tape was unstuck from its eyes. That was another detail he needed to write down. The nose came into view, and he saw the teeth sink into the bottom lip as the tape plucked off several eyelashes. Either water or tears ran down the cheeks, and then the face was fully exposed and blinking with what Dudley hoped was sightlessness. "Patricia," Kathy said and seemed scarcely to know how to continue. "I thought it was you," she said.

# THIRTY—EIGHT

When Patricia felt the water sink away from her she knew she wasn't going to drown, unless this had been merely a rehearsal. She might have fancied that she was being reborn. She'd taken the deepest breath she could as her head was shoved underwater, but she had been coming to the end of it. As she drew another one, water trickled into her nostrils, and she was suddenly afraid that he was playing with her, that he'd been inspired to drown her with the shower instead. Turning her head failed to clear her nose of water, and she had to struggle onto her side. At least the water level was still falling. The thudding of her pulse subsided, and she heard voices. One belonged to Dudley's mother.

She mustn't leave Patricia alone with him. Patricia was trying frantically to think how to communicate this when hands closed around her shoulders and lifted her. They were too gentle for Dudley's. Her mind felt softened, difficult to wield, but she managed to realise that Kathy was unlikely to abandon her, since she must be seeing Patricia's condition. Then she wondered if that was assuming too much, because Kathy asked "Can you hear me? Can you talk?"

Once Patricia was certain that the questions must be meant for her, she had to recall which way to move her head in a negative response. She was regaining the technique when Dudley said "I told you, she doesn't want to."

How was she going to deny that? She didn't know how long it took her to grasp that she had to nod, and then she thought her confusion had trapped her, because he said she was agreeing with him. He even accused his mother of bewildering her, and indeed Patricia could have blamed them both for aggravating the effects of her plight. Then she heard him offering to stay with her, and she was about to use her entire body to express her aversion when Kathy spoke close to her ear. "Do you want to talk?"

Patricia could have imagined by now that she was being forced to play a game that involved having to decide which movement of her head was most appropriate. She put all the strength of her taped sticky neck into nodding three times, and seemed to have made her point, since she heard Kathy undertaking to unwrap her head. As she braced herself for the ordeal Kathy said "I don't know what you two thought you were doing."

Patricia found this so far in excess of unreasonable that she could hardly wait to speak. For the moment she had to concentrate on bearing the pain as the tape began to yank at her hair. She felt the air on her gluey throat, and her tacky chin, and her mouth and cheeks. She bit her lips and strained to hold her eyelids shut while the tape tugged at them, but it peeled them away from her eyes and didn't let them drop until it had removed several lashes. She saw Kathy's concerned face above her, and Dudley in a towelling robe behind his mother. Patricia didn't know if it was her confusion that made him look not just defiant but sure of himself. She was furious not to be able to keep back the tears that escaped as Kathy uncovered her forehead and the rest of her hair. "Patricia," Kathy said. "I thought it was you."

Patricia could make nothing of that. "Could you untie my hands, please," she said.

"I was just going to. Did you have to be so realistic?"

Patricia gathered this was addressed at least partly to her, and didn't trust herself to speak. She crouched forward while Kathy unbound her, and then she eased her arms in front of her despite the aches that were clamouring in all their joints and set about rubbing her wrists. "Have you anything to change into?" Kathy said.

For a moment the question sounded reasonable, which was why Patricia found it hard to grasp. She knuckled one cheek dry and then the other. More than anything else she wanted to run out of the house as soon as her ankles were free, but she was barely steady enough to reach for them. "No," she said.

"Oh, Patricia."

That sounded almost intolerably close to a rebuke. Patricia wondered how much Dudley's mother was trying to pretend. She felt as though she was having to act in a scenario Kathy was inventing. "You'd better have my bathrobe while we dry your things," Kathy said. "Dudley, take your mattress away before it gets any wetter. I can't imagine what you've been doing with it in here."

Presumably that meant she could. Patricia watched Dudley pick up the mattress and finish staring at her as he dragged it out of the room. Once she succeeded in clawing the tape off her ankles, she had to support herself with a hand on the sink as she hoisted one aching leg over the side of the bath and followed it with its equally painful twin. "Do you need any help?" Kathy said.

"Not just now, thank you."

"I'll be outside, then, and you can hand me your things."

This might mean Kathy would be taking them downstairs, leaving Patricia alone with Dudley on the upper floor. "I'll bring them," Patricia said.

As soon as Kathy was out of the room Patricia staggered after her to bolt the door, almost falling more than once. She couldn't think what to do first: remove her soaked clothes or drink all the water her parched mouth was yearning for? In the end she grabbed a tumbler from the shelf above the sink and gulped water until she felt sick, and continued to drink more warily in between peeling off her clothes. She might have liked a shower in case that washed away the sensations that were clinging to her, mentally as much as physically, but she didn't want anything further to do with the bath. She managed to be content with scrubbing her face and wrists and most painfully her ankles before drying herself with the only towel in the bathroom. Its lurking scent of aftershave made her fling it away while she was still wet. She fumbled the solitary bathrobe off the hook on the door and pushed the sleeves back so as to tie the cord at her waist. The robe must be knee-length on Kathy; it trailed over Patricia's shins. It made her feel childish and vulnerable, not least because she no longer knew who might be waiting outside. She'd heard low voices while she was busy, and a series of slow awkward thumps on the stairs. "Kathy?" she did her best to shout.

"I'm here."

She was no closer than downstairs. "Could you help me after all?" Patricia called.

Suppose Kathy told her son to help? Patricia heard footsteps hurrying to her, and a knock at the door. She didn't unbolt it until Kathy said "Here I am."

The armchair and the wardrobe doors had vanished from the landing, and the house seemed ominously quiet. "Where's Dudley?" Patricia was anxious to learn.

"He's just leaving. He's decided he should sort things out face-to-face where he used to work."

Patricia was certain he intended to do nothing of the kind. If she was too weakened by her ordeal to escape just yet, she was going to ensure he didn't either. She hung onto Kathy's arm and leaned over the banister. He was fully dressed and heading for the front door. "I wouldn't go anywhere if I were you, Dudley," she said as evenly as she could.

"Why shouldn't I?"

"I think you might want to hear what I'm going to say to your mother."

He stared at her so blankly it was almost convincing. "Such as what?"

"Shall we all sit down and be comfortable?" Kathy intervened. "I'm certain Patricia would like to. And I think she's right, you ought to be here. You've plenty of time to go to the office later."

He stood at the foot of the stairs while Kathy helped Patricia descend, and then he stalked into the front room and sat in the armchair he'd used to trap her in the bath. She held onto the lowest post of the banisters until Kathy returned from hanging out her wet clothes, at which point she found the strength to walk to the other chair. "Well, what do I need to know?" Kathy said, perching on the edge of the couch. "Dudley was saying how you did all that for him because you'll be able to write about it as well. I still think it was going too far, but I expect people do worse things for a story these days. Look what they get up to on those reality television shows."

Patricia let her finish, more out of disbelief than from any lack of a response. "You honestly think I chose to do that," she said.

Kathy frowned, but the expression seemed intended to look wry. "What's the alternative?"

"That he knocked me out and tied me up and did a lot more than you saw."

"That would be it, I imagine," Kathy said and actually smiled.

Patricia was steeling herself to destroy Kathy's trustfulness when Dudley said "Are you threatening to write that, Patricia? What are you asking us to do so you won't?"

"You're making her sound like a blackmailer. I'm sure you aren't like that, are you, Patricia?"

Patricia's mouth was dry, and she had to swallow. "You can see how I am. No, I didn't choose to be this way."

"I did say it had gone too far. I wonder if it may have confused you a bit? All sorts of things can affect your mind. I know that from my own experience."

Patricia swallowed again and gave up working on Kathy. "It's your turn, Dudley. I know what you can do."

"What's that?" he said and looked ready to grin.

"Tell your mother what you were afraid of."

"When?" At once he grinned as if to deny that he'd asked. "Nothing," he said.

"Yes, you were. You were afraid of being published."

"That was just him being modest," Kathy said. "I'm afraid his father may be to blame if he wasn't as sure of himself as he deserves."

"It wasn't modesty. That wouldn't have stopped him wanting you to read his stories, would it? Not you of all people when you've been so supportive. He was afraid for anyone to read them, even you. Maybe especially you."

"That's crap," Dudley said and wiped his grin with the back of his hand. "You think you know so much about me and you ended up how you did."

"I don't understand what you're trying to get at, Patricia. Why on earth would he have been afraid?"

Patricia had a sense of stepping over an edge and doing her best to take Kathy with her. "In case you or someone realised where his stories come from."

"And where are you saying they do?"

"Real cases. Real murders that have all happened round here."

Kathy opened her mouth and then closed it while she turned to her son. "I did wonder that. Is it true?"

"Who are you going to believe, me or a hack?"

"I don't think you need to be nasty about her, do you? She's been quite a friend to you, after all. If you got your ideas from life, writers often do. We know you did when you were at school. And you're making up new ones now, aren't you?"

So they weren't at the edge yet, though Patricia felt dizzy enough. "It isn't just where he got the material, it's how he knew so much."

Kathy lowered her head to peer from under her wry brows. "And how is that supposed to be?"

"You tell her, Dudley." In this sunny suburban lounge, in what any observer would have taken as a conversation between a visitor or even a member of the family and a doting mother and her son, Patricia was suddenly uncertain how to proceed. "You've kept it from her long enough," she said.

Kathy gave him a smile so inviting that Patricia grew apprehensive for her and impatient with her, but he met it with the stare he'd trained on Patricia earlier. "Research," he said. "You knew that."

Kathy gazed at him before admitting "I don't think I like how you said that."

"How do you want me to? I only can the way I tell the truth."

"I know that's what you're trying." She transferred her attention to Patricia, whose mouth felt withered by tension as she waited for Kathy to speak. "You've made this up between you, haven't you? It's meant to be like his character, the writer who's a killer. Were you seeing how convincing it was for the film?"

The interior of Patricia's head seemed to sway like water, and she thought she might be sick. "How do you think I could make anything up with him when I couldn't talk?"

As Kathy held out her loose fists as if grasping for an answer, Patricia said "What do you think would have happened to me if you hadn't saved me?"

"Only what did, I'm certain. I realise that's bad enough, but you'd agreed to be part of it, you know."

Patricia was almost sure that Kathy was striving to convince herself. "Don't the others matter because you don't know them?" she blurted.

"Of course they—" Kathy said and attempted to look as if she'd been fooled. "Who?"

At once Patricia saw how to confront her, and it lanced her confusion. She was about to respond when Dudley said "You two carry on talking if you want. I've got to sort out this misunderstanding at work."

Before she could speak he was on his feet, and she was almost overwhelmed by her lack of strength. "You don't want to leave your mother wondering," she said. "I know what you can do first so she won't be worried."

She was suddenly afraid that Kathy might send him on his way, but his retort was too quick. "What?" he said.

Patricia nearly tripped across her eagerness and said too much too soon. "Show her your stories. Show both of us."

"You've seen them," Dudley said with a good deal of pique to his mother. "And you let her read them too."

"Not printed out," Patricia told him. "On the screen."

"Why on there?" Kathy didn't seem certain of wanting to learn.

"Because he could have changed them, couldn't he? The printouts might be just what he could risk letting people read."

Of course that wasn't the point at all, and she was nervous that Kathy might object to its unlikeliness. Indeed, Kathy was beginning to appear skeptical when Dudley said "That's rubbish. That's ridiculous."

"I'm sure it is, but shall we have a look anyway? I wouldn't mind seeing her proved wrong, if you'll forgive me, Patricia."

As Patricia shrugged an aching shoulder Dudley said "I don't want her coming in my room."

"It might be best if she did though, do you think? That way she'll see for herself and there can't be any argument. You wouldn't want her writing that sort of thing about you. I should think once she's had to admit her mistake we won't be seeing her again."

For the moment Patricia had to stand being disparaged, though it or her enervation made her feel unexpectedly weepy. She watched Dudley tramp into the hall only to hesitate, and wondered if he was thinking of fleeing. Before she could find words to head him off, Kathy said "You go up, Dudley. We'll follow."

Suppose he deleted the evidence and pretended the computer had crashed? Patricia dug her nails into the arm of the couch to send herself across the room. She had to grab the doorframe and then the banister for support. At least the banister helped her stumble upstairs, though the treads seemed to quiver underfoot like jelly. Perhaps some of that was the vibration of Kathy's footfalls behind her. "Are you all right?" Kathy asked not too sympathetically as Patricia clutched at the doorframe of Dudley's room.

"I will be." She would, because she'd arrived in time to glimpse Dudley typing his password if she needed it: p, a, letter, letter, a, letter, e. She almost said aloud the word that came to mind as Kathy took her by the elbow. "Thanks," she murmured instead.

"Let Patricia have your seat, Dudley. She's been through quite a lot for you, whoever's idea it was."

Patricia accepted the chair he grudgingly vacated, and stayed well clear of any contact with him as he avoided touching her. "What do you think I've got to show you?" he said with half a grin.

"The first one. 'Night Trains Don't Take You Home'."

"That old thing? I've got a bit sick of it, it's been so much trouble. Or it hasn't, but people tried to make it into some." He opened the document with a flourish of his fingers. "There," he said. "Compare it with the printout and good luck."

"Actually, we don't need to read it. There's just one thing we have to see."

He was silent, perhaps warily, and it was his mother who said "What have we?"

"The date."

Apparently his mother didn't sense his tension. "Which is that?" she said.

"The date the story was finished."

"I don't keep a record," Dudley said a little too forcefully. "It won't be there."

"It will. Let me show you," Kathy said and clicked the mouse to exhibit the properties of the document. "See, there's something your mother knows and you didn't. You can do that for every document. Why you'd want to, Patricia, that's a different matter."

"Do you remember when Angela Manning was killed?"

"Sorry, who?"

"Angela Manning. Dudley can tell you about her."

"She's the girl they made all the fuss about. They still are," he added even more bitterly.

"And when did it happen again?"

"I couldn't tell you. Why should I know that?"

"I thought you might, seeing it's her anniversary round about now. Wasn't that part of the objection?"

"If you say so. You know as much as me," Dudley said and stared red-eyed at Patricia.

"Then let's find out precisely. Go on and search for her."

"Yes, go on," Kathy said as he hesitated. "That can't do any harm."

Dudley scowled at her and concealed the keyboard with his free hand while he typed his Internet password, but Patricia had no difficulty in identifying the cramped bunch of keys. They spelled "secret", which seemed to confirm the lack of imagination that his old schoolmaster had found in him. He called up a search engine and tapped the keys with his fingertips, too playfully to make an impression. "Is she important enough to be on here?" he mused aloud.

Patricia controlled her loathing. "Only one way to find out, isn't there?"

He typed the girl's name without capitals, which Patricia thought was one more form of derogation. In a few seconds the search engine produced a list of references to Angela Manning, all of them irrelevant. Some were in America, some in Scotland or south of London; the only ones in the north of England referred to a hair salon and a portrait painter. Patricia was beginning to think that Dudley had received the answer he wanted when Kathy said "There's another page."

He clicked on the arrow that led to it. Either his swiftness betrayed defiance or he believed the second page offered no threat, unless he knew. Mightn't he already have searched the web for anything that could expose him? Had he simply been feigning reluctance in order to appear even more innocent once he'd demonstrated that there was no evidence? Patricia did her best to swallow and tried to keep her head on an even keel as the page was replaced. An American lecturer, a South African political activist, a reference to manning pumps on a ship, a site devoted to a female falconer . . . "Will that be it?" Kathy said. "Student killed by train."

Dudley hesitated until she reached for the mouse. "I'll do it," he said and clicked on the listing. "See, I was right. She didn't rate much."

"Oh, Dudley, don't say things like that just because your story hasn't been published yet. I'm sure it can be somewhere." Kathy peered at the few inches from the *Liverpool Daily Post* and then at the top of the page. "Well, that is strange," she said. "It's a week today five years ago."

"And you know what's stranger," Patricia said. "The date he wrote his story."

"I can't remember," Kathy said and turned her sudden harshness on him. "Show me again."

Dudley covered the mouse with his hand as if he was about to crush it, then recalled the window that contained the tale. "It's the same day as the paper," Kathy said. "Were you so inspired when you read about it that you wrote your story straight off? I wish I hadn't sent that one in for you. I made the wrong choice, and even if I didn't know I apologise."

Patricia struggled to control the frustration that made her skin feel stretched and raw. "I'll bet there's a story where someone's thrown onto the road into the Mersey Tunnel," she said.

"You must have seen that when I let you see his stories."

Patricia hadn't, but arguing would only waste time. "I expect you remember the title, do you, Kathy?"

"Show us 'Head First into the Rush Hour', Dudley. Go on, there's nothing to be afraid of."

He bared his teeth at the remark or at her eagerness, and opened the document. "And when did you write it?" Kathy said as if he ought to welcome the answer. "Well, that's even stranger, isn't it. Two years ago last Friday."

"Look at the news site," Patricia said with all the restraint she was able to command, "and see what happened then."

"Don't say it was another of his instant inspirations."

Patricia didn't trust herself to face Kathy. She watched Dudley rest his hand on the mouse, and then, as he returned them to the Internet, she saw him grin. He brought the page for the day in question onto the screen, and stepped back. "I don't want anybody thinking I'm hiding anything. Take a good look."

Kathy scrolled through the news reports and repeated the exercise with a sidelong glance that suggested she was humouring Patricia. "Well, unless I'm blind, I don't see anything. Nobody at all local killed that day, and certainly not like the girl in his story. Are you satisfied now, Patricia?"

Patricia closed her eyes and took an arid breath. So she was more confused than she realised, and it had played into Dudley's hands. She couldn't even swallow as she heard him say "Am I allowed to go and sort things out now?"

"You be on your way. I'll wait downstairs with Patricia till her clothes are dry."

"Goodbye, Patricia. Sorry you felt you had to try and turn my mother against me. I suppose Patricia must have thought our story wasn't sensational enough. That must be what journalists are like."

At first Patricia didn't know what was rushing into her mouth, but they proved to be words. "Wait a minute, Dudley."

"What now?"

It was Kathy who said that with worse than impatience, but Patricia wasn't about to be deterred. "Kathy, have a look at the next day's news."

"Oh, that's just silly. You know perfectly well there'll be nothing."

"If that's the case I'll give up," Patricia said, only to fear that she was being too hasty. "If you don't want to look, I will."

"I'm sure Dudley would prefer me to."

Dudley took a backward pace that could have been described as surreptitious. "Do what you like if you can't see what she's up to."

Kathy typed the date in the search box and clicked the mouse as if she was clipping a fingernail. Paragraphs with headlines began to fill the screen. A warning of drought that had been imminent two years ago, a series of arson attacks, a train derailed because a track had buckled in the heat, an old couple who had died of dehydration . . . Then a headline grew blacker and more solid as Patricia's vision fastened on it. **MERSEY TUNNEL DEATH FALL**, the headline said.

Kathy read the paragraph and turned to find her son. "I'm sorry, Dudley, but I'm going to say this in front of Patricia. I really hope you won't write any more about actual murders after all the trouble people gave you over just one. If I'm going to be honest, it makes me feel a bit uncomfortable."

Patricia waited, willing her not to have finished. When Dudley's indifferent grunt made it clear that the admonitions had come to an end, Patricia said "What about how he knew?"

"You must have heard it on the radio, must you, Dudley? They'd have had the news."

"Does he listen to the radio that much?" Patricia said, not too desperately, she hoped. "I didn't know you had one."

"Of course we have," Kathy protested, but kept her eyes on her son. "I don't remember hearing this reported, though. When *did* you find out about it?"

"Are you going on at me like she did now?"

"I'm only trying to show her how wrong she is about you. Don't be offended. Just tell us when."

Dudley fixed his stare on Patricia. "I read it in somebody's paper on the train home."

"But it says it was at night," Kathy said. "It was after you came home from work."

Dudley passed the tip of his tongue around his grin as if to soften it. "I made that up to see what she'd say. Couldn't you tell?"

"Then what's the truth?" Patricia said. "Surely you can't mind if I hear that."

"I've got to agree with her, Dudley. Show her you've nothing to hide."

Was Kathy still convinced of that, or was she pleading to be? It simply earned her and Patricia a stare from the defiant mask of Dudley's face. When they gazed back at him he licked his lips again. "I've had enough," he blustered. "Both of you can get out of my room."

"That won't solve anything, will it?" Kathy said. "Just tell—"

"I'm not telling anybody any more. Believe her if you want, if you think I'd be bothered lying. You wouldn't be upset now if you hadn't let her in my room. This all started when you gave her my stories to read and I never said she could."

"No, it started years before that," Patricia said. "I wonder when exactly? When was the first—"

She hadn't time to dodge as he darted at her. Her exhaustion might have sent her sprawling, and in any case she wasn't going to show fear. Whatever he did to her would betray him to Kathy, and so Patricia braced herself. As he ducked she wondered if he meant to pick her up and fling her at the window, and pressed her knees against the underside of the desk. But he was stooping to snatch the plug of the computer out of the wall socket. "Look what you've made me do," he cried or snarled. "I hope you're happy now. I expect that's deleted all my stories."

"I'm sure it won't have," Kathy begged. "Switch on again and see."

"Not while anybody's here." When his stare didn't move her or Patricia he said "I'm not wasting any more time. Stay in here for all I care. I've got important stuff to do."

She ought to have grabbed him while he was within reach, Patricia realised. His reaction might have been all that Kathy needed to convince her. He was nearly at the door when Kathy said "No, Dudley. You stay too."

She sounded as if she was addressing somebody not even half his age. His mouth and teeth worked to fasten on a grin but couldn't quite. "Who do you think you're talking to?" he demanded.

"My son, I hope. You stay and make your case while you have the chance."

"I don't need you to give me a chance." In seconds he was at the door, where he swung around with a disdainful look. "Nobody tells Mr Killogram what to do," he said, "especially not women."

"Dudley, do as I ask you for once. Dudley. Dudley." His mother ran onto the landing, to be silenced by the slam of the front door. Patricia tried to stand up, but her muscles wavered so much that she had to sink onto the chair. She watched Dudley sprint across the road and up the path that climbed the hill. Kathy returned to stand beside her as he disappeared between the trees. "He'll have to come back," she said.

"You really think so."

"When he calms down. Why wouldn't he? Where else can he go?"

"You don't think anything that's happened would keep him away."

"There has to be an explanation, hasn't there? It's only one story. Maybe the news site got the details wrong. Even the media can be mistaken, you know."

Patricia didn't know how personally she was meant to take the remark. All that mattered was ensuring Dudley didn't go too far before the police heard about him. She could see that Kathy wasn't ready to call them. "We can soon find out," she said and crouched gingerly to plug in the computer. She was afraid that Kathy might try to stop her, or that the information might indeed prove to have been erased. But Kathy allowed the screen to revive, and once the computer had searched itself for errors Patricia was able to type both passwords. Now she only had to be afraid how Kathy might react when the truth became unavoidable. "You still think it's just one story?" Patricia said without pleasure. "Let's look."

# THIRTY-NINE

At last Kathy saw that she had to get rid of Patricia. It wasn't just that once she was alone she might be able to think, although her mind felt as if it was being dragged into a pit whose darkness hovered at the edge of her vision, cancelling the sunlight. She did her best to blame that on Patricia's insistence on showing her date after date and the sympathy she kept letting Kathy sense, perhaps unaware how patronising Kathy found it. None of this was why she would do anything to send Patricia on her way, however. Dudley was up on the hill, watching the house.

She'd glimpsed him minutes ago, and was afraid Patricia would. She'd had to pretend to want to be shown yet another pair of dates in order to keep her tormentor occupied. At least she had a reason to be glad that Patricia was at the desk: Dudley could see it wasn't safe for him to venture back to the house. Kathy feigned interest in the details on the screen until she was certain he was observing the situation from behind a clump of ferns. "All right," she said then, hoping that in some way it could be.

Patricia raised her head so steadily it looked effortful and met Kathy's eyes. With almost more pity than Kathy could bear, and its discreetness only made it worse, she said "You've seen enough, then."

"I definitely have."

"Will you call or do you want me to?"

"I will, of course."

"Sorry if I sounded interfering. Actually, I don't know where my mobile is. He used it to text my parents that I'd gone to London." Kathy was thinking she had no use for the belated explanation when Patricia said "I hope he's still got it. They'll be able to trace where he is."

"I hadn't thought of that. Do you want to see if your clothes are ready while I phone?"

Patricia gazed at her not quite long enough to be openly suspicious. "I may as well," she said.

While Patricia made carefully for the landing Kathy switched off the computer. She couldn't locate Dudley now, but it didn't matter if he had retreated; once they were rid of Patricia she would be able to call him home. As she followed Patricia downstairs and watched her retrieve her clothes from the line she felt almost protective of the girl. Perhaps it was the sense of domesticity she was anxious to preserve—the notion that as long as life depended on this kind of detail it would remain solid and familiar or at any rate be capable of reverting to that condition. "All right?" she asked Patricia like an echo of herself.

"I'm going to be. You haven't phoned yet, have you?"

"I was seeing how you were first."

"I'm dealing with it," Patricia said and renewed her gaze.

"Get changed down here if you don't want to be bothered going up."

As Kathy expected, this sent Patricia in search of privacy, but she left the bathroom door open. Kathy had to crouch over the phone and keep her voice almost too low to be heard on it. Patricia emerged from the bathroom, looking dishevelled but resolute, as Kathy finished the call. Kathy saw there was another question on the way and headed it off. "Would you like to phone your parents? I should think they must be wondering about you."

"I might," Patricia said, then seemed to remember the demands of politeness. "Thank you. I would."

"Do you think you could just let them know you're safe and tell them the rest when you're home?"

She wasn't sure what the postponement would achieve, but anything that might protect her son had to be worth trying. She was wondering if she'd asked too much when Patricia said "I just want this to be over."

Kathy didn't know whether to take that as a threat to her son. It became apparent that Patricia wasn't sure which number to call. Eventually she settled on one that had to belong to a mobile, and Kathy was belatedly afraid that Patricia was trying to track down her own. She held her breath, and before Patricia spoke it had begun to feel like an exaggerated heartbeat. "Mummy, it's me," Patricia said.

Kathy wished her son would speak to her like that. She let the breath go, but found the next one quite as difficult; she was still nervous of how much Patricia might communicate. "I'm not there" sounded potentially dangerous, as did "I didn't" and "There wasn't one." Not until Patricia said "Can I tell you when I see you?" did Kathy start to any extent to relax. "Where are you?" Patricia said. "Can you get away? Could you meet me at home? I'd like to be at home. I'll see you there."

She parked the receiver and faced Kathy. "May I ring for a taxi?"

"I already have."

"Thank you." After a pause so curt it hardly deserved the name Patricia said "Have you called anyone else?"

"Not yet, no."

"Someone has to, Kathy."

"Then please leave it to me. I'll handle it. I'm his mother."

Kathy was struggling to look earnest without letting the effort show when she heard a car draw up outside. It couldn't be the police, she had to remind herself. "I think that's your cab."

Patricia held her gaze until the driver honked the horn, and then she said "Where's my bag? Has Dudley taken that as well?"

"He isn't a thief, Patricia." If he'd kept the girl's mobile, it was surely out of forgetfulness. "I brought it downstairs," Kathy said and fetched it from the kitchen. "You'd left it on the landing."

Patricia seemed ready to argue even once she'd checked the contents of the handbag, but a second honk intervened. "You'd better go before the neighbours start complaining," Kathy said.

Indeed, Brenda Staples was glowering through her front window. Kathy accompanied Patricia to the taxi, both in case she needed support and to shut her in the vehicle. "Drive carefully. She's a little fragile just now," she advised the driver.

Perhaps she oughtn't to have said that, since the look Patricia left her was by no means wholly grateful. Kathy watched the taxi disappear around the corner, and then she turned to confront the neighbouring window. "Only a visitor," she informed Brenda Staples and retreated into the house.

She had to speak to Dudley. Beyond that she couldn't think. Trying to do so made her feel surrounded by darkness that the sunlight was unable to dispel. She grabbed the phone in the hall and prodded the digits of Dudley's number as she ran upstairs to sit at his window. She thought of opening it, but suppose Brenda

Staples overheard Kathy's side of the call? As she peered through the glass, Dudley's voice brought the ringing to an end. "Dudley Smith, writer and scriptwriter. Me and Mr Killogram must be busy. Leave us a message."

"I don't want to leave a message, I want to speak to you," Kathy said, trying to fend off too many thoughts. "You aren't busy. You aren't so busy you can't talk to your own mother. Are you there? Are you there, Dudley? I know you're there."

None of this brought her a response, not even movement on the hill. However much more she had to say, she couldn't address it to a recording. As she broke the connection she realised that she needed to establish Patricia didn't have her mobile. Suppose she had pretended that it wasn't in her handbag? She could be calling the police—she could have while Kathy was attempting to reach her son. Kathy typed Patricia's number and squeezed her eyes closed, but had to open them to lessen the darkness. It was still lurking at the edge of her vision when the mobile ceased to ring. Silence was its only message. "Hello?" Kathy said.

She strained her ears as she heard a sound. It was a whisper, but not a voice. It was the rustling of leaves. They were ferns on the hill, she thought so fiercely that she could almost smell them. "I know it's you, Dudley," she said. "You can talk now."

At once she was terrified that she'd made a mistake—that the whisper was a breeze through the window of a taxi and that she'd addressed the remark to Patricia. The darkness was rushing in to render the sunshine irrelevant when Dudley said "Why?"

Kathy had to sigh before she could speak. "Patricia's gone."

"Where?" he said, and even more harshly "Did she make you think she had to go to hospital?"

"Home. Never mind her. We need to talk, but not like this."

"Why, do you think it's bugged? They can't catch Mr Killogram that way."

The possibility hadn't occurred to her. It felt like another layer of darkness, but surely there hadn't been time for the line to be tapped. "I want to see your face," she said.

"You expect me to come back after you agreed with that bitch."

"How do you know I agreed with her? You weren't here. You ran off and never gave me an explanation."

"I didn't run. If you need an explanation that's as bad as agreeing with her."

This was exactly the kind of confrontation she didn't want to have while she couldn't see him. "I don't think you'd better come home," she said.

"You're throwing me out because of what that bitch said."

"Of course I'm not, Dudley. I'm saying you ought to stay clear because I think she may contact the police."

The phone spat with at least a simulation of mirth. "What's she going to tell them? She's got nothing to show them. It's her word against mine, and she's the one that's got a reason to make up a story."

Kathy found she was able, however feebly, to hope. "What reason, Dudley?"

"She's a journalist, isn't she? That's what they do when they decide they don't like someone."

"And what about your stories?" Kathy stared at the blank screen and saw her own dismay gazing back. "What are we going to say about all those dates?" she almost couldn't add.

"You've been looking while I was out of the way, have you? You're as bad as her."

"I'm your mother. I need to know." Kathy was struggling not to believe that his retort was an admission, and pleaded "What would you have said if you'd been here?"

"Try and think. See if you can imagine something for a change."

"I'm imagining too much. I don't want to. I'm asking you."

"You think it's all evidence, do you?"

"Dudley, what am I supposed to think?"

"Then you'd better destroy it if you want to protect me," he said and immediately rang off.

"I can't," Kathy told the phone in her hand. She stretched out a finger to recall him and establish where they could meet, and then she wondered if Patricia had already contacted the police. Suppose she'd stopped at a phone box or asked the driver to get in touch for her? Suppose the police were on their way to impound the computer? Dudley would never have urged her to do away with his work unless he had a copy somewhere else. "I've got to," she said, no longer to the phone, and jumped up.

She pulled out the leads from the monitor and cradled the computer in her arms. It felt as vulnerable as baby Dudley had—as she thought he might still be under the personality he'd constructed. The notion of injuring it brought darkness crowding around her vision and her mind, but how could she leave it to harm her son? Dropping it might corrupt the documents, but she couldn't be sure that would erase them. She was almost unaware of sobbing as she carried it into the bathroom and placed it with lingering gentleness in the bath. "I've got to," she repeated and thrust the plug into the hole and turned on the taps.

A few bubbles emerged from the computer as the water closed over it, but it was unable to raise itself. She let the water run until the bath was nearly brimming, because she was unable to see for tears. She knuckled her eyes fiercely and bruised her fingers in twisting the taps shut. Couldn't she at least keep the printouts of his stories? She didn't know how accurately the police might be able to date them, the way technology was developing. If Dudley had meant her to spare them he would surely have said so. Nevertheless she found it hard to see once more as she collected the stories from his room and took them into the back garden, where she laid them on top of a handful of parched weeds. She was halfway through reading the uppermost page, as if she might commit every word of them to memory—it was the opening of "Night Trains Don't Take You Home"—when she remembered that she had to be quick. She set light to the weeds and the corner of the pages with a kitchen match, and straightened up as the flames raced to erase the lines of print. She turned to see Brenda Staples frowning over the fence at her, and had to dab her eyes vigorously. "Smoke in them," she explained.

"What are you burning?" her neighbour asked without slackening her frown. "Are they stories of your son's?"

"Why, Brenda, you do have an imagination. What an idea, really." Kathy hurried indoors to retrieve the phone and call her son. "Dudley," she kept saying as his voice recited its message, and as soon as it finished "I've done it. You can come back."

The sole response was an electronic noise somewhere between a sigh and a hiss. Kathy ran upstairs to watch from his window, although she could hardly bear to stay so close to the orphaned computer monitor. Might he answer Patricia's mobile? Only Patricia's voice replied. Kathy left her message again and gazed at the overgrown slope, which was as devoid of any activity as the deserted road. She was almost sure that he would still be observing the house to check whether it was indeed safe, but had he picked up her advice? Perhaps he wasn't answering either phone for fear that would be traceable. In that case he might have stolen away, though surely he couldn't have gone far since she'd last spoken to him. He mightn't even have left the hill yet— and at once she realised how she ought to be able to locate him. She couldn't endure staying in his room when it felt so emptied of him and his stories. She pushed herself away from the desk and ran to grab her handbag from on top of her suitcase in the hall.

She hadn't time to see if Brenda Staples was watching her

dash down the path. As she sprinted across the road and up the path narrowed by unkempt vegetation, she had a sense of leaving behind far more than her house and the street. If she had to for Dudley's sake, she would. By the time she reached an open space at the top of the path she was typing his number.

It didn't matter if he refused to answer. So long as he hadn't switched the phone off she would be able to hear it if it rang anywhere nearby. She was so anxious for the sound that when the ringing began she had to remember to take the mobile away from her ear. She clasped it between her hands as though it was helping her pray and was convinced that she was hearing his ringtone, however distant or muffled it was. "Dudley?" she called. "I can hear you. Come where I can see you. Didn't you get my messages?"

Of course other mobiles could play the same tune, and she was suddenly afraid that she'd betrayed his presence on the hill to someone else. Suppose the police were already surrounding her and her son? The possibility felt like a cordon of blackness that was capable of encompassing the blue sky and the white sun. Then the theme from *Halloween* was switched off like an alarm, and Dudley trudged out from behind a clump of bushes to her left. "You've done what?" he demanded.

Kathy turned her mobile off and shut it in her bag so as to extend a hand to him. "What you said I should."

"I didn't tell you to do anything. Christ, what do you think I said?"

She could have imagined her lips were shrivelling under his gaze; she had to lick them before she was able to operate them. "Your stories."

That gave him problems with his own mouth, which seemed uncertain which shape to adopt. "What have you done with them," he said, not even a question.

"You saw what Patricia thought. What do you think the police would?" Like far too much, she was afraid to put it into words. "You'll have kept copies of your stories somewhere, won't you?"

"Yes, the ones I printed out. The ones you gave her to read."

Kathy's mouth felt smaller than ever and almost immovably stiff. She had managed to say nothing else by the time he said "You've destroyed those as well, have you?"

"Dudley, I was trying to protect you. This can't just be about your stories any more."

"It can't, can it? They're gone. Lost forever. Nobody's ever going to read them now." He stared at her until she had to dab her eyes, and then he said "You haven't protected anything. You've destroyed everything I ever was."

"Don't say that. You're still my son, whatever you've done."

"God, are you trying to sound like my dad? You rhyme worse than him. You can both tell people what you think I was like. Thank Christ I won't be around to hear it," Dudley said and stalked onto the path up to the ridge.

"Where can you go?" Kathy pleaded. "Who's going to look after you?"

"Where you won't be able to follow me. I've nothing to live for now my stories are destroyed."

She could barely see him for the darkness in her head. The sunlight only made it feel more charred, a condition she fancied she could smell. She stumbled after him across the parched slabs of rock. "You can write them again," she tried to coax him. "You can write more and they'll be even better."

"My inspiration's dead. You've killed it."

This seemed worse than unfair, but she wasn't anxious to examine it in detail. "You don't just stop being a writer," she cried.

"Why not? You did."

"I didn't really, did I? I finished that story for you."

Before she could tell him what she'd realised—that it was still under her pillow—he strode onto the ridge and twisted to stare down at her. "Call that writing? I wouldn't have even when I was at school."

He was only doing his best to lose her, Kathy strove to think. She watched him swing away from the disused observatory and march along the ridge towards the inert windmill. The route would take him into Birkenhead—and then she remembered the road that cleft the hill, and the unfenced edge from which she'd had to save him when he was nine years old. "Don't go that way," she begged, sprinting to catch up with him. "There'll be people. Do you want to be seen?"

"I won't be going that far."

She wouldn't have been sure that he had the drop to the road in mind if his gaze hadn't strayed in that direction and immediately veered aside. She made a grab for his arm, but he was already out of reach. She skidded on a patch of lichen and fell to her knees on the rock. "Stop, Dudley, listen," she cried, but could think of nothing to add. Then he halted like a runner awaiting the start of a race, because his mobile was ringing.

Kathy scrambled to her feet and overtook him again. "Are you sure you ought to answer that?" she chattered as he snatched out the phone. "You don't know who may be trying to find you."

"I don't care. They'll be too late." He continued staring at her as he said "Dudley Smith. Mr Killogram."

She saw the response bring regret into his eyes. "Hello, Vincent," he said. "No, I'm not writing now . . . More actors? That's men, is it? How many? . . . You know who we ought to have got to play Mr Killogram?"

Kathy knew at once but was beyond grasping what difference it would ultimately have made. "Me," Dudley said, and she was dismayed not to know if she ought to agree. "Don't worry, I can't now," he told Vincent. "Start without me if I'm not there. I can still trust you, can't I? Choose whoever you think is most like Mr Killogram."

He slipped the phone into his pocket and hurried towards the bridge over the road. "There you are, you'll have something to remember me by," he said without looking back. "*Meet Mr Killogram.*"

"I don't want to remember you. I want you with me." That was too vague, but she could scarcely bear to add "I want you alive."

"You should have thought of that before," he said and picked up speed as he passed the windmill.

Kathy peered across the bridge in the hope of seeing somebody out for a walk. She'd warned him away from people, but surely their presence would inhibit him now. Everything was as immobile and useless as the vanes of the windmill. She willed him to be heading for the bridge, even if that meant he was continuing to flee her. He had almost reached it when he swerved towards the unprotected drop to the road. "Don't," she nearly screamed, then tried to laugh. "You're just acting like someone in one of your stories."

"Why shouldn't I? I always was."

Whether by accident or from bravado, he kicked a stone. It rattled across the slab ahead of him and vanished over the brink. After a silence like a lack of breath it hit the road. Though the impact was barely audible, it made Kathy's head ring like a rusty bell. It failed to daunt her son, who strode after the pebble as if eager to follow it down. "Dudley, listen," she cried.

He hadn't waited to do so last time, and he didn't now. "I'll tell them it was my fault," she promised as she dashed past the bridge. "Not just the way I brought you up by myself. I used to take drugs before you were born. That has to have something to do with it. I'll make them listen. They'll have to understand, and then . . ."

She didn't know how to go on, but she must. He'd halted at the edge of the drop and was gazing at her with some kind of invitation in his eyes. Her next words might be the most important act in the whole of her life. "We both need help," she pleaded. His expression flickered as if he couldn't even make the effort to look contemptuous. "I don't," he said and stepped over the edge.

Kathy felt the darkness flood her skull. She could hardly see as she lunged to snatch him back. The blackness seemed to delay her sight, so that she scarcely knew whether she was imagining that Dudley hadn't fallen after all—had saved himself by stepping on a ledge immediately below the brink. The image might have been projected on her dark—the spectacle of her son dodging aside and thrusting out a leg to trip her up. She heard him speak as if he no longer cared what she overheard. "I should have got Patricia first," he muttered.

There was nothing she could clutch for support except him. Her arm hooked his waist as she toppled over the edge. She saw him gape down at her as he tried to wriggle free and to maintain his footing. He managed neither. Though she was gazing up at him, her tall son, he looked like a child outraged and terrified by the unfairness of the world. She couldn't bear that, and she made a final bid to protect him, though she was barely able to suck in enough of the air that was rushing past them to speak. "There was a boy and his mother who could fly," she began.

# EPILOGUE

When all the party had visited the buffet at the Year of the Liver Bird restaurant more than twice, and an Oriental rock band called Hung Like Sammo had finished its first set, Walt stood up at the head of the long table. "Well, was that the greatest Chinese meal you ever had in Liverpool?"

The general murmur could have been taken for at least qualified agreement, although Tony Chan kept his peace on behalf of the Chinese community, and as the restaurant reviewer Denise Curran murmured "This week."

"There's that Scouse humour. Nothing like it in the world. Don't forget it isn't just all you can eat, it's all you can drink on me. Has anyone not had enough?"

He was gazing at Patricia, perhaps only because she was seated at the far end. "I'm fine," she said and really didn't need Valerie to pat her hand.

"Okay, so long as nobody has an empty glass, why don't we raise them to the magazine. Here's to *Mersey Mouth*."

Patricia felt as if the jumbled responses were blurring her words. "*Mersey Mouth*."

"We went for three great issues. I'm just sorry there wasn't more of a public for us, but absolutely nobody should feel they're to blame. I guess the controversy didn't help after all, and people saying we couldn't make up our minds what we were going to publish. And maybe there's something to the notion that some Brits don't like enterprise and want to see it fail, but let me tell you it was as fine a magazine as I've ever been a part of. So here's to everybody that was involved, even if they aren't here tonight. Raise a glass to yourselves."

When the enthusiastic clinking at the edges and along the middle of the table died down, Walt said "I could name everyone, but I don't want to monopolise your evening, so let me single out just a couple. Let's hear it for our more than talented editor Valerie Martingale."

Patricia met her mother's eyes and lifted her glass high. "Valerie," she agreed loudest of anyone, and was sipping her Chardonnay as Walt said "And Patricia, for doing so much more than anyone has a right to be expected to do."

She could tell that he'd worked on his phrasing, but she sensed that it made her fellow diners almost as uncomfortable as she felt. She spoke before it could revive the nightmares that she didn't have every night now—wakening to find her head wrapped in tape when it had only strayed under the bedclothes, or feeling water close with infinite slowness over her bound body, or opening her eyes to see Dudley grinning down at her. "I should never have got myself into that situation. I wouldn't make much of a detective."

"But you were there as a journalist. I don't know any reporters that would have put themselves through that."

"She didn't have a choice," Valerie said. "She was there as a victim."

Patricia laid one hand on her mother's and gazed along the table. "No, I was there as an idiot."

"Sounds like you've come out of it feisty at any rate," Walt said. "I'd say anything positive we can salvage from that whole sad business is worth having. Do you all know about Vincent's new project?"

"Nobody's mentioned it to me," David Kwazela said with enough hauteur for his entire African community.

"He's found a way of dealing with the issues his other film would have brought up."

Vincent pushed his spectacles closer to his eyes. "I'll be questioning them, anyway."

"Tell him about it, Vincent," Walt said and sat down.

"I'll be investigating how Dudley Smith is becoming a cultural icon. Somebody's set up a web site about him, the Scouse Slayer. People think he killed more people than the police are letting on. The new thing at school is kids saying they'll send each other a killogram. The council's trying to stop a stall in Church Street selling mugs with his face on them that say Dud the Lad . . ."

"How are you going to investigate all that?" David Kwazela interrupted.

"And other things as well, like how fiction and reality depend on each other. I think maybe it'll be a new kind of film. I'll be filming parts of the script we had and intercutting them with reconstructions of the actual events and interviews with the relatives if I can get them. They ought to agree when they hear what my approach is."

"Don't you think it could still be controversial?"

"I hope."

As David Kwazela stuck out his bottom lip and took his gaze elsewhere, Vincent said across three intervening diners "I definitely need to film you, Patricia. It won't be complete without the survivor. I thought I could show how that last weekend might have seemed to him and how it really was for you. I'd use an actress if you didn't want to go through it all again. So long as you can talk about it."

Patricia sat up straighter, because everyone was either watching her or avoiding it. "I don't know what I could say that would be any use."

"Try saying you encouraged Dud."

Walt stood up again as the speaker advanced. "Monty, we thought you weren't coming."

"I've been drinking with some of me mates that write pomes. That's why you reckoned you could say anything you like about Dud, was it?"

"I don't believe we've been doing that."

"That's a rhyme. Watch out or you'll end up a poet."

"Excuse me," Valerie said before Monty had quite finished. "May I ask how you think Patricia encouraged your son?"

"You did and all. And you, Vince. I'm surprised at you. You started out like a true Scouser and then you wanted to make a film about one that's a criminal, like people don't reckon we all are."

"I wouldn't have without Dudley, you know."

"That's what I'm saying. You could have tried to get him to write something healthy but you made him worse."

"I don't see how anybody here can be said to have done that," Valerie objected.

"Forgot Shell Garridge already? I thought she was one of your mates."

"I wouldn't have said she was responsible for, if you'll forgive me, what he was."

"Me neither. Never did. They're making out now he may have killed her too. Killing anybody's out of order, but how could he have done it to someone like her if he'd known what he was doing? If he did it shows he was totally warped in the head."

Patricia was thinking that her experience did, and trying not to let the memories spring up at her, when Monty said "Still, I don't reckon anyone's to blame so much as his mother."

"You don't," Valerie said and kept her eyes on him.

"She killed him, didn't she? Killed both of them. If you ask me that's because she couldn't stand the guilt. Used to take drugs, maybe that's why. Pity about her, I'm not saying it's not, but I wish she'd left him so he could have got some help."

"Unless it was Dudley who killed them," Patricia felt bound to propose.

Monty let her feel his stare before he said "I'm not that convinced he killed anyone."

"Are you suggesting she made up what he did to her?" Valerie demanded. "Or are you trying to blame her for that as well?"

"I'm sure he can't be," Patricia said. "Anyway, the police are certain about Dudley. They managed to retrieve the dates on his computer."

This was addressed to Monty, who redoubled his stare. "I don't need you to tell me. Doesn't prove that much. He never wrote that crap about Shell Garridge, that's for sure. That was his mam. She hid it from everyone, even him."

She was wondering if there was anything truthful to be said that might leave him feeling less robbed of his son when Monty turned on Vincent. "I'm betting you'll believe whatever makes you the most money. Thank shite I haven't got to work with you any more."

Vincent gave the cluttered table his attention, widening his eyes so vigorously that his spectacles slid down his nose. "I'm off back to drink with some real people," Monty announced. "If any of youse want to join me, come ahead."

When he'd finished observing the general discomfort he

made his way with studied dignity to the exit and stalked away along the dock. By then Walt had cleared his throat. "I guess we can understand how he feels even if we don't agree with everything he said. But you carry on doing what you do best, Vincent, and Patricia, I hope you will too."

"What are you thinking that is?"

"I'll tell you what I think it could be. I was talking over some ideas with a publisher in London, and the one she liked best was a book by you."

"What about?" Patricia said and immediately knew.

"All your encounters with Dudley Smith. We agreed nobody living could have more insight into him. You could interview people if you like, but it's your story. The only thing is she'd want the book as soon as possible, while he's hot."

Patricia was quiet long enough to suggest she was considering the proposal. "Thanks, Walt, but it isn't for me. I don't want to write, I want to survive."

"Can't you do both? Mightn't one help the other? If it isn't for you it isn't for anybody."

"You wouldn't have time, would you, Patricia?" Valerie intervened. "You'll be too busy with your other work. She's just been made the Merseyside correspondent for *Northern Girl*," she informed the diners with some pride.

"Isn't that the magazine you're working for now?" Vincent enquired.

"That's *Northwest*. Patricia's being independent."

"Sounds that way," Walt said.

Patricia didn't know how censured she was meant to feel. "I'll talk to you for your film, Vincent, but that's going to have to be all."

His was by no means the only face that grew sympathetic, which seemed almost as burdensome as Walt's disappointment. "Thanks for everything, Walt, really," she said, easing her chair backwards. "Good night, everyone. I think I'd better walk this off."

"Would you like me to come with you?" Valerie said.

"I don't mind."

She didn't, but her mother took it as an appeal. She caught up with Patricia in the colonnade outside the restaurant, alongside which the water in the Albert Dock appeared to have borrowed a heavy sluggishness from the overcast September night. "Do you want to talk?" Valerie said.

"Not particularly. I'm just thinking."

Her mind was busy, at any rate. She was remembering how Dudley had dogged her along this route after the casting session. Might he have been intending her some harm if Vincent hadn't called him back? It needn't trouble her: she had eluded him. Around her the night was no darker than it ought to be. Beyond the Albert Dock she waited for the green man to seize illumination from his red counterpart, and then she crossed the six deserted lanes of the road, only to hesitate outside James Street Station. "Shall we walk to the next one?"

"Whatever's best for you, Patricia."

She'd followed that course to leave Dudley behind, but that wasn't the memory she was determined to outstrip. She strode along Castle Street and past the town hall, hardly glancing at the skeleton that peered out of the shadows of a metal robe. Echoes of their footsteps kept her and her mother company across the quadrangle and the roads beyond it, and the escalator that climbed to the unstaffed ticket barriers, and both escalators that led deeper than the street. She wasn't in a story about Moorfields, Patricia told herself when she heard feet running down the metal stairs at her back. "Don't look," she murmured. "Don't bother looking."

She wasn't speaking only to her mother, who retreated from

beside her to the next step up. She was making way for the runner, of course; she didn't need to protect Patricia. The youth clattered past them, his ears hissing and pounding with headphones, before Patricia could be sure of the legend on his T-shirt. She had to glance around at him when she reached the platform, because he was loitering in the tiled white passage. His scrawny chest did indeed say **BRING BACK MR KILLOGRAM.**

Why was he lurking behind her and her mother after having run past them? Because his train hadn't arrived yet, she supposed—certainly not because he had ambitions to shove them under it—but she couldn't shake off the notion that he might be imagining some such deed in memory of his apparent hero. She felt the first cool breeze of the day on her face as a train approached. She rested her gaze on the slogan before searching his eyes. "Why would you want to?" she said.

The headphones hissed so loudly that he must be deaf to any other sound. For a moment it reminded her too vividly of the water that had closed over her ears and the rest of her face, and she couldn't breathe. Even if the youth didn't understand her, she had clearly antagonised him. He glanced from her to Valerie, two women alone on an underground platform with nobody else in earshot, and she glimpsed someone altogether too reminiscent of Dudley Smith spying from deep in his eyes. Then the New Brighton train drew alongside the platform, and he swaggered onto it to plant his heels on the seat opposite him.

Valerie didn't speak until the rumble had died away along the tunnel like the last trace of a storm. "It's like Walt was implying. Dudley Smith is just the latest fad. He'll be forgotten soon enough."

"I hope so."

Valerie scrutinised her expression and reached out a hand in case Patricia wanted to be touched. "Are you all right?"

"I will be." The exchange reminded Patricia too precisely of another, and she tried to leave it behind. She gazed into the tunnel as the darkness began to rumble again. "Here it comes," she said. "This is our story now."